PRAISE FOR IAN HAMILTON AND THE AVA LEE SERIES

PRAISE FOR *THE WATER RAT OF WANCHAI*
WINNER OF THE ARTHUR ELLIS AWARD FOR BEST FIRST NOVEL

"Ian Hamilton's *The Water Rat of Wanchai* is a smart, action-packed thriller of the first order, and Ava Lee, a gay Asian-Canadian forensics accountant with a razor-sharp mind and highly developed martial arts skills, is a protagonist to be reckoned with. We were impressed by Hamilton's tight plotting; his well-rendered settings, from the glitz of Bangkok to the grit of Guyana; and his ability to portray a wide range of sharply individualized characters in clean but sophisticated prose." — Judges' Citation, Arthur Ellis Award for Best First Novel

"Ava Lee is tough, fearless, quirky, and resourceful, and she has more — well, you know — than a dozen male detectives I can think of… Hamilton has created a true original in Ava Lee." — Linwood Barclay, author of *No Time for Goodbye*

"If the other novels [in the series] are half as good as this debut by Ian Hamilton, then readers are going to celebrate. Hamilton has created a marvellous character in Ava Lee… This is a terrific story that's certain to be on the Arthur Ellis Best First Novel list." — *Globe and Mail*

"[Ava Lee's] lethal knowledge… torques up her sex appeal to the approximate level of a female lead in a Quentin Tarantino film." — *National Post*

"The heroine in *The Water Rat of Wanchai* by Ian Hamilton sounds too good to be true, but the heroics work better that way… formidable… The story breezes along with something close to total clarity… Ava is unbeatable at just about everything. Just wait for her to roll out her bak mei against the bad guys. She's perfect. She's fast." — *Toronto Star*

"Seldom does one get a thriller about white-collar crime, with an intelligent, independent lesbian and Asian protagonist. It's also rare to find a book with such interesting and exotic settings...Readers will find great amusement in Ava's unconventional ways and will certainly enjoy accompanying her on her travels." — *Literaturkurier*

PRAISE FOR *THE DISCIPLE OF LAS VEGAS*
FINALIST, BARRY AWARD FOR BEST ORIGINAL TRADE PAPERBACK

"I started to read *The Disciple of Las Vegas* at around ten at night. And I did something I have only done with two other books (Cormac McCarthy's *The Road* and Douglas Coupland's *Player One*): I read the novel in one sitting. Ava Lee is too cool. She wonderfully straddles two worlds and two identities. She does some dastardly things and still remains our hero thanks to the charm Ian Hamilton has given her on the printed page. It would take a female George Clooney to portray her in a film. The action and plot move quickly and with power. Wow. A punch to the ear, indeed." — J. J. Lee, author of *The Measure of a Man*

"I loved *The Water Rat of Wanchai,* the first novel featuring Ava Lee. Now, Ava and Uncle make a return that's even better...Simply irresistible." — Margaret Cannon, *Globe and Mail*

"This is slick, fast-moving escapism reminiscent of Ian Fleming, with more to come in what shapes up as a high-energy, high-concept series." — *Booklist*

"Fast paced...Enough personal depth to lift this thriller above solely action-oriented fare." — *Publishers Weekly*

"Lee is a hugely original creation, and Hamilton packs his adventure with interesting facts and plenty of action." — *Irish Independent*

"Hamilton makes each page crackle with the kind of energy that could easily jump to the movie screen...This riveting read will keep you up late at night." — *Penthouse*

"Hamilton gives his reader plenty to think about...Entertaining."
— *Kitchener-Waterloo Record*

PRAISE FOR *THE WILD BEASTS OF WUHAN*
LAMBDA LITERARY AWARD FINALIST: LESBIAN MYSTERY

"Smart and savvy Ava Lee returns in this slick mystery set in the rarefied world of high art... [A] great caper tale. Hamilton has great fun chasing villains and tossing clues about. *The Wild Beasts of Wuhan* is the best Ava Lee novel yet, and promises more and better to come."
— Margaret Cannon, *Globe and Mail*

"One of my favourite new mystery series, perfect escapism."
— *National Post*

"As a mystery lover, I'm devouring each book as it comes out... What I love in the novels: The constant travel, the high-stakes negotiation, and Ava's willingness to go into battle against formidable opponents, using only her martial arts skills to defend herself... If you want a great read and an education in high-level business dealings, Ian Hamilton is an author to watch." — *Toronto Star*

"Fast-paced and very entertaining." — *Montreal Gazette*

"Ava Lee is definitely a winner." — *Saskatoon Star Phoenix*

"*The Wild Beasts of Wuhan* is an entertaining dip into potentially fatal worlds of artistic skulduggery." — *Sudbury Star*

"Hamilton uses Ava's investigations as comprehensive and intriguing mechanisms for plot and character development." — *Quill & Quire*

"You haven't seen cold and calculating until you've double-crossed this number cruncher. Another strong entry from Arthur Ellis Award–winner Hamilton." — *Booklist*

"An intelligent kick-ass heroine anchors Canadian author Hamilton's excellent third novel featuring forensic accountant Ava Lee...Clearly conversant with the art world, Hamilton makes the intricacies of forgery as interesting as a Ponzi scheme." — *Publishers Weekly*, *Starred Review*

"A lively series about Ava Lee, a sexy forensic financial investigator." — *Tampa Bay Times*

"This book is miles from the ordinary. The main character, Ava Lee is 'the whole package.'" — *Minneapolis Star Tribune*

"A strong heroine is challenged to discover the details of an intercontinental art scheme. Although Hamilton's star Ava Lee is technically a forensic accountant, she's more badass private investigator than desk jockey." — *Kirkus Reviews*

PRAISE FOR *THE RED POLE OF MACAU*

"Ava Lee returns as one of crime fiction's most intriguing characters. *The Red Pole of Macau* is the best page-turner of the season from the hottest writer in the business!" — John Lawrence Reynolds, author of *Beach Strip*

"Ava Lee, that wily, wonderful hunter of nasty business brutes, is back in her best adventure ever...If you haven't yet discovered Ava Lee, start here." — *Globe and Mail*

"The best in the series so far." — *London Free Press*

"Ava [Lee] is a character we all could use at one time or another. Failing that, we follow her in her best adventure yet." — *Hamilton Spectator*

"A romp of a story with a terrific heroine." — *Saskatoon Star Phoenix*

PRAISE FOR *THE TWO SISTERS OF BORNEO*
NATIONAL BESTSELLER

"There are plenty of surprises waiting for Ava, and for the reader, all uncovered with great satisfaction." — *National Post*

"Ian Hamilton's great new Ava Lee mystery has the same wow factor as its five predecessors. The plot is complex and fast-paced, the writing tight, and its protagonist is one of the most interesting female avengers to come along in a while." — *NOW Magazine* (NNNN)

"The appeal of the Ava Lee series owes much to her brand name lifestyle; it stirs pleasantly giddy emotions to encounter such a devotedly elegant heroine. But, better still, the detailing of financial shenanigans is done in such clear language that even readers who have trouble balancing their bank books can appreciate the way conmen set out to fleece unsuspecting victims." — *Toronto Star*

"Hamilton has a unique gift for concocting sizzling thrillers." — *Edmonton Journal*

"Hamilton has this formula down to an art, but he manages to avoid cliché and his ability to evoke a place keeps the series fresh." — *Globe and Mail*

"From her introduction in *The Water Rat of Wanchai*, Ava Lee has stood as a stylish, street-smart leading lady whose resourcefulness and creativity have helped her to uncover criminal activity in everything from illegal online gambling rings to international art heists. In Hamilton's newest installment to the series, readers accompany Ava on great adventures and to interesting locales, roaming from Hong Kong to the Netherlands to Borneo. The pulse-pounding, fast-paced narrative is chocked full of divergent plot twists and intriguing personalities that make it a popular escapist summer read. The captivating female sleuth does not disappoint as she circles the globe on a quest to uncover an unusually intriguing investment fiasco involving fraud, deception and violence." — *ExpressMilwaukee.com*

"Ava may be the most chic figure in crime fiction." — *Hamilton Spectator*

"The series as a whole is as good as the modern thriller genre gets." — *The Cord*

PRAISE FOR *THE KING OF SHANGHAI*

"The only thing scarier than being ripped off for a few million bucks is being the guy who took it and having Ava Lee on your tail. If Hamilton's kick-ass forensic accountant has your number, it's up." — Linwood Barclay

"One of Ian Hamilton's best." — *Globe and Mail*

"Brilliant, sexy, and formidably martial arts-trained forensic accountant Ava Lee is back in her seventh adventure (after *The Two Sisters of Borneo*)...Ever since his dazzling surprise debut with *The Water Rat of Wanchai*, Hamilton has propelled Ava along through the series with expanded storytelling and nuanced character development: there's always something new to discover about Ava. Fast-paced suspense, exotic locales, and a rich cast of characters (some, like Ava's driver, Sonny, are both dangerous and lovable) make for yet another hugely entertaining hit." — *Publishers Weekly*, *Starred review*

"A luxurious sense of place...Hamilton's knack for creating fascinating detail will keep readers hooked...Good fun for those who like to combine crime fiction with armchair travelling." — *Booklist*

"Ava would be a sure thing to whip everybody, Putin included, at the negotiating table." — *Toronto Star*

"After six novels starring Chinese-Canadian Ava Lee and her perilously thrilling exploits, best-selling Canadian author Ian Hamilton has jolted his creation out of what wasn't even yet a rut and hurled her abruptly into a new circumstance, with fresh ambitions." — *London Free Press*

"As usual with a Hamilton-Lee novel, matters take a decided twist as the plot unrolls." — *Owen Sound Times*

"One of those grip-tight novels that makes one read 'just one more chapter' and you discover it's 3 a.m. The novel is built on complicated webs artfully woven into clear, magnetic storytelling. Author Ian Hamilton delivers the intrigue within complex and relentless webs in high style and once again proves that everyone, once in their lives, needs an Ava Lee at their backs." — *Canadian Mystery Reviews*

"The best of the Ava Lee series to date…*Princeling* features several chapters of pure, unadulterated financial sleuthing, which both gave me some nerdy feels and tickled my puzzle-loving mind." — *Literary Treats*

"*The Princeling of Nanjing* was another addition to the Ava Lee series that did not disappoint." — *Words of Mystery*

PRAISE FOR *THE COUTURIER OF MILAN*
CANADIAN BESTSELLER

"The latest in the excellent series starring Ava Lee, businesswoman extraordinaire, *The Couturier of Milan* is another winner for Ian Hamilton…The novel is a hoot. At a point where most crime series start to run out of steam, Ava Lee just keeps rolling on." — *Globe and Mail*

"In Ava Lee, Ian Hamilton has created a crime fighter who breaks the mould with every new book (and, frankly, with every new chapter)." — *CBC Books*

"The pleasure in following Ava's clever plans for countering the bad guys remains as ever a persuasive attraction." — *Toronto Star*

"Fashionably fierce forensics…But Hamilton has built around Ava Lee an award-winning series that absorbs intriguing aspects of both Asian and Canadian cultures." — *London Free Press*

PRAISE FOR *THE IMAM OF TAWI-TAWI*

"The best of the series so far." — *Globe and Mail*

"One of his best…Tightly plotted and quick-moving, this is a spare yet terrifically suspenseful novel." — *Publishers Weekly*

"Combines lots of action with Ava's acute intelligence and ability to solve even the most complex problems." — *Literary Hub*

"Fast-paced, smoothly written, and fun." — *London Free Press*

"An engrossing novel." — *Reviewing the Evidence*

"Hamilton's rapid-fire storytelling moves the tale along at breakneck speed, as Ava globe-trots to put clues together. Hamilton has always had a knack for combing Fleming-style descriptors with modern storytelling devices and character beats, and this book is no different." — *The Mind Reels*

"An engaging and compelling mystery." — *Literary Treats*

THE
GODDESS
OF
YANTAI

Also in the Ava Lee Series

The Dragon Head of Hong Kong: The Ava Lee Prequel
(e-book)

The Water Rat of Wanchai

The Disciple of Las Vegas

The Wild Beasts of Wuhan

The Red Pole of Macau

The Scottish Banker of Surabaya

The Two Sisters of Borneo

The King of Shanghai

The Princeling of Nanjing

The Couturier of Milan

The Imam of Tawi-Tawi

THE GODDESS OF YANTAI

AN AVA LEE NOVEL
THE TRIAD YEARS

IAN HAMILTON

SPIDERLINE

Published in Canada in 2018 and the USA in 2018 by House of Anansi Press Inc.
www.houseofanansi.com

22 21 20 19 18   1 2 3 4 5

Library and Archives Canada Cataloguing in Publication

Hamilton, Ian, 1946–, author
The goddess of Yantai / Ian Hamilton.

(An Ava Lee novel: the triad years)
Issued also in electronic formats.
ISBN 978-1-77089-950-6 (softcover). —ISBN 978-1-77089-951-3 (EPUB).
—ISBN 978-1-77089-952-0 (Kindle)

I. Title. II. Series : Hamilton, Ian, 1946- . Ava Lee novel

PS8615.A4423G63 2018   C813'.6   C2018-901837-2
                              C2018-901838-0

Library of Congress Control Number: 2018940096

Book design: Alysia Shewchuk

We acknowledge for their financial support of our publishing program
the Canada Council for the Arts, the Ontario Arts Council, and the
Government of Canada
through the Canada Book Fund.

Printed and bound in Canada

MIX
Paper from
responsible sources
FSC® C004071

For my wonderful and diversely talented
nieces and nephews.

In Toronto: Graeme, Alasdair, and Kate Hamilton.

In Ottawa: Charlotte Field.

In Vancouver: Amber Devlin and Chris Hamilton.

And in Edmonton: Allen, Christopher, and Phillip Zuk.

AVA LEE SAT NEAR THE REAR OF THE PACKED BEIJING cinema. She was there to watch the premiere of *Mao's Daughter*. The film was set in Yunnan province in 1959 — a year after the launch of the Great Leap Forward, Mao Zedong's disastrous attempt to impose industrialization and collectivization on Chinese agrarian society. Many farms stopped producing crops, and more than twenty million people died in the famine that resulted from Mao's misguided effort.

A fictional drama, the film followed a young woman named Yu Yan who would defy Chairman Mao. Yu Yan was the mother of one child, the wife of a rice farmer, and the caregiver for her aging parents. The land had been in her husband's family for generations before Mao's Great Leap Forward prohibited the private ownership of farms. When her husband resisted turning the land over to a collective, he was prosecuted, labelled as a counter-revolutionary, and sent away to do forced labour. His wife was allowed to stay in their modest home, but any means she had to support her child and her parents was stripped away.

As the family's situation steadily deteriorated, the young woman's reaction morphed from submissiveness to fear, then to anger, and finally to an unbending determination to fight against the government. She confronted local Communist officials and they turned her away. Undeterred, she walked several hundred kilometres to the provincial capital of Kunming to petition senior officials for return of the farm, only to be turned away again. Those rejections strengthened her resolve, and she decided to take her case all the way to Beijing. She walked the entire distance, nearly 2,700 kilometres. To make her cause known, she hung a piece of cardboard around her neck that read: I AM A DAUGHTER OF MAO. THIS IS MY LONG MARCH FOR JUSTICE.

As the film ended, a heavy silence filled the theatre. Ava took a deep breath, overcome by emotion. Pang Fai — her friend, her lover, and the actress who portrayed "Mao's daughter" — had been luminescent. Her body language, her facial expressions, and her penetrating eyes had strikingly conveyed the woman's emotional and physical journey.

Fai was regarded as the finest actress in Chinese cinema and was building an international audience. Ava's involvement with her had started as a business venture — Fai was the public face of the PÖ fashion line, which Ava owned with her partners in Three Sisters Investments — and then had evolved into a full-blown romance.

"Pang Fai!" a man shouted as he rose to his feet several rows ahead. His voice seemed to liberate the rest of the crowd, and more than a thousand people stood as one, clapping and calling her name.

A man in a tuxedo walked onto the stage in front of the screen. He held up an arm in an attempt to quiet the crowd, but the cheering didn't die down. Finally he shrugged and spoke into a microphone. He was almost yelling, but Ava could still barely hear him. He looked into the wings and motioned for some people to come forward. Two men joined him; the only one Ava recognized was Tsang Min, the film's director.

When Tsang took the microphone, the crowd quieted. He introduced the other person on stage as the film's producer. Then he spoke for a few minutes about how difficult it had been to shoot in so many parts of China, and how they'd felt at times like a travelling circus, putting up their tents in a different town or city every night. "But the truth is, even if we had been rooted in one place or had even been limited to just one room, as long as our cameras were capturing Fai's performance, the story could still have been told," he said.

He looked off to the right and nodded. Pang Fai stepped into view and glided towards him. She was wearing a pale blue cheongsam with a high slit that exposed her long legs. She was tall, about five foot ten, and in three-inch heels she towered over everyone else on stage. The audience erupted. She kissed Tsang and the others on each cheek and then turned to face the audience. She placed her palms together, raised them to just below her chin, lowered her head, and bowed. She held that position for at least a minute as the cheering continued.

Tsang handed her the microphone. She held it against her chest and said, "I want to thank you all for coming, for your support, and your generosity. Without you, films like this could not be made." The audience exploded. Pang Fai bowed one more time and then left the stage. The others followed and the house lights came on.

Ava stood up, feeling something approaching awe. It was the first premiere she'd ever attended, and she'd had no idea what to expect. She saw Chen Jie, Fai's agent, standing in the aisle about twenty rows ahead. He was about sixty and had the rotund physique of a man who'd enjoyed a lifetime of good food and liquor. He had been Fai's agent since her early days in the business. He knew her intimately, including her true sexual orientation, which he had managed to keep a secret. Public knowledge of it would severely damage, if not destroy, Fai's film career in China.

Her affair with Ava was the first real relationship that Fai had had with a woman, and Ava knew Fai had shared that information with Chen. He hadn't taken it well, and whenever Ava met him at lunch or dinner, he made his dislike of her and the reason for it quite plain. Now, as she made her way down the aisle towards him, she wondered what kind of reception she would get. She thought he had seen her when she was ten metres away, but he either didn't recognize her or chose to ignore her. He was speaking to another man when she finally reached his side. He acknowledged her with a quick glance and then resumed his conversation.

Ava waited, her anger at his rudeness slowly building. Finally he turned to her. "You aren't supposed to be here," he said.

"I was invited," Ava said. "Besides, I was with Fai in Kunming the day before she started making this film. I thought it fitting that I see the end product."

"I was told you couldn't make it."

"My plans changed."

"Does Fai know?"

"I thought I'd surprise her."

"She doesn't like surprises. And neither do I, where her career is concerned."

"I'm hardly a factor in her career."

"You are in her life, and the two things are not easily separated."

"Chen, will you take me to her?" Ava said sharply. "Or do I have to find her myself?"

He sighed. "Come with me."

He walked to the front of the theatre and turned right, to a small door that was blocked by two security guards. The guards moved to either side when they saw Chen, and one of them opened it for him. Ava felt the guards eyeing her. "She's with me," Chen said.

The door led into a small corridor. Chen walked briskly towards the far end. Ava trailed, the heels of her shoes making music on the tile floor. The corridor was lined with storage rooms, and Ava wondered where they were going until they reached a door that read "Manager." Chen knocked and then opened it. Ava peered past him and saw Fai sitting in a chair by a desk, surrounded by Tsang, the movie's producer, and three other men she didn't recognize.

"I brought you a visitor." Chen took a step to one side so that Ava could pass.

Fai stared at her with wide eyes. Then her mouth flew open and she leapt to her feet. In three strides she was in front of Ava, throwing her arms around her neck. Ava felt Fai's fingers digging into her shoulders, and she was pressed so hard against her lover's chest that she could hardly breathe. "I'm so happy you're here," Fai said in a rough whisper. Ava thought she could feel her body trembling.

"I wasn't sure I could make it until last night," Ava said. Fai clung to her, and Ava began to sense disquiet among the others in the room.

"Perhaps we should leave you two alone for a moment," Tsang said.

"Please," Fai replied.

Ava didn't move until the men had filed out of the office and the door was closed. She placed her hands on Fai's arms and gently pushed herself free of the embrace. "I didn't mean to shock you," Ava said. "I just thought you would be happy with the surprise — although Chen would probably disagree."

"I'm so happy you're here," Fai repeated.

"The film was wonderful, and you were fantastic," Ava said. "For the first ten minutes or so I felt I was watching you, but then I was drawn completely into the character. By the time the film ended, all I cared about was Mao's daughter."

"It was a good role, and Tsang is a great director," Fai said, her voice catching.

"Are you okay?" Ava asked. "Or are you always this emotional at premieres?"

Fai stepped back until she found the chair and sat down. "I've spent the past two days in hell," she said. "All I could think about was how much I wanted to see you and how much I needed you. I started to call you so many times, but then I always stopped."

"Why? You know I would want to hear from you."

"It was me, not you. I wanted to tell you what's going on, but I couldn't do it over the phone."

"Fai, what's the matter?" Ava asked, moving next to her.

Fai looked up at her, her eyes brimming with tears. For

a second Ava was reminded of a scene from the film she'd just watched, except this time Fai wasn't acting.

"What happened?" she asked.

"You may have just seen the last film I'll ever make."

FAI SAT WITH HER HEAD DOWN, HER FACE GRIM AND
her hands clutched in her lap.

Ava took a chair from against the office wall and placed it
next to Fai. Then she pried her friend's hands apart and held
one between hers. "It can't possibly be that bad," she said.

"You have no idea."

"That's true, and I won't have until you tell me what the
problem is," Ava said, taking a tissue from her bag and wip-
ing a few tears from Fai's cheeks.

"I don't want to talk about it here."

"Then we'll leave. Come back to my hotel."

"I can't right now," Fai said. "There's a reception planned
and I owe it to Tsang to make an appearance. Believe me,
I don't want to go, but it is the right thing to do."

"Do you want me to come with you?"

Fai shook her head. "It would be harder for me to cope," she
said. "I was doing okay until I saw you. Then when I did, I fell
apart because it felt so safe. I'm scared that I'd have the same
kind of spontaneous reaction during the reception. People
are expecting to see Mao's daughter, not Pang Fai in tears."

"But you'll come to the hotel after? I'm at the Éclat."

"Of course."

"And you'll stay the night?"

"Try to stop me," Fai said. "I've missed you so damn much."

"Stopping you from seeing me is the last thing I'd ever do," Ava said, leaning over to kiss Fai lightly on the lips.

There was a knock at the door, and after a slight pause Chen said, "Fai, we should be heading over to the reception."

"I'll be right there."

"Is Ava coming with you?"

"No."

"That's just as well," he said. "I'll wait for you here at the door."

"He's jealous of you," Fai whispered.

"He cares about you," Ava said.

"I know, but that doesn't mean he isn't a pain in the ass."

Ava smiled, but when she did she saw Fai's face contort, and realized that whatever was bothering her ran very deep. "You weren't exaggerating, were you, when you said this might be your last film," she said.

"A little, perhaps, but I'm not just being dramatic. I'm at a crossroads."

"Then skip the reception and let's go to the hotel now and talk."

"I can't. I have to pretend everything is fine. I'll manage. Besides, in addition to Tsang there will be senior officials from the China Movie Syndicate at the reception. I can't risk insulting them by not showing up."

"What's the China Movie Syndicate?"

"That's too complicated to get into right now," Fai said, standing up. "I'll explain it to you later."

"I really don't like leaving you alone," Ava said.

"Chen will be with me. Besides, I'm an actress," Fai said. "I'll go to the reception and act."

AVA AND FAI SAID A RESTRAINED GOODBYE UNDER THE watchful eyes of Chen and the other men.

"Our limo is in the laneway at the rear of the theatre," Chen said to Ava. "You'll have to leave the way you came in."

See you later, Fai mouthed.

Ava waited until they had left before retracing her steps to the theatre's front entrance, where she quickly caught a cab. It had been an eventful evening, she thought as she settled into the back seat — first the raw power and drama of the film, and then Fai's emotional outburst. Ava wondered if her surprise arrival had contributed to the intensity of the feelings Fai had displayed. She hoped it had, and that things weren't quite as dire as Fai had suggested. Either way, Ava was relieved that she was in Beijing and grateful for the business circumstances that had contrived to bring her here.

Ava had travelled to Beijing from Hong Kong, where she had been attending a regularly scheduled planning session for Three Sisters, the investment firm she had started a few years earlier with May Ling Wong, her best friend, Amanda Yee, her sister-in-law, and Xu, a silent partner who also happened to be the head of the Shanghai Triads and Ava's closest male friend. They had barely begun the first day of what was supposed to be three days of meetings when Suki Chan called from Shanghai. Three Sisters had invested in and was continuing to finance Suki's warehouse and distribution company located there. She had owned the business with her husband for many years but he had refused to expand. His death and the infusion of capital from Three Sisters had liberated Suki, and she was determined to make the business grow as large as she could, as fast as she could.

At Suki's urging they had already bought one Beijing-based distribution company. Her phone call was to tell them that an even better one would soon be coming onto the open market, and that they'd been given the opportunity to short-circuit the process by making a pre-emptive bid. The problem was that the timeline was exceedingly tight and they had to move fast. Suki had already spent several days in Beijing doing her due diligence. Now she needed someone from Three Sisters to review things with her and, if everything was as it was supposed to be, help her pull together an offer. That was normally Amanda's job, but she and her husband, Michael, Ava's half-brother, had planned a Japanese holiday immediately after the Hong Kong meetings. Ava volunteered to go in her place, feeling almost guilty at not mentioning her ulterior motive as Amanda thanked her effusively.

Ava had left Hong Kong in the afternoon and landed in Beijing with only a few hours to spare before the premiere. She wasn't overly familiar with the city, which was unusual for her. She had spent considerable time in just about every major city in Asia, the result of ten years as partner in a debt-collection business that had an Asian base.

Her partner in that business had been a man she called simply Uncle. He had been in his seventies when, at the age of twenty-five, Ava had aligned herself with him. Uncle lived in Hong Kong; prior to getting into debt collection, he had been the Mountain Master of a Triad gang in Fanling and had served multiple terms as chairman of the Triad societies in Asia. Many people thought their partnership odd, and more than once it had been the subject of gossip, which Ava and Uncle ignored. They had adored each other. She was the child he'd never had, and he was like a grandfather to her and the most important man in her life. When he died, her grief had brought out depths of emotion she didn't know she possessed.

Uncle's Asian connections had brought a steady stream of business to their door. Most of their clients had been cheated out of substantial amounts of money and had exhausted all their legal options to recover it; Uncle and Ava were their last resort. As important as getting back the money was in financial terms, Uncle also cared about the human costs: ruined lives and reputations and families put at risk. However, that didn't prevent Ava and Uncle from charging their standard fee of thirty percent of the funds they recovered. Over the years they were successful at getting the money back more often than not, and Ava had become a wealthy young woman. That wealth more than doubled when Uncle died and left her almost his entire estate.

The business with Uncle had taken Ava to most of the countries in Asia more times than she could remember. Since China offered particularly fertile ground for thieves, she had visited nearly every one of its numerous provinces and all of its major cities — except for Beijing.

Suki had made the hotel reservation. Ava hadn't heard of the Éclat and expected a hotel that reflected Suki's understated style. The Éclat was the furthest thing from that. It was in the Parkview Green development in the Chaoyang central business district, about ten kilometres from the movie theatre and seven from Tiananmen Square. It was an all-suite luxury boutique hotel, its one hundred suites occupying five floors of a spectacular towering glass pyramid surrounded by a latticed metal framework. It had caught Ava's eye immediately as she approached the area in her airport taxi, and she was delighted when she discovered that the building was her destination. She had checked in, left a voicemail for Suki saying she'd arrived and would be available for meetings the next morning, and then quickly departed for the premiere.

Now Ava was making the return trip from the theatre to the hotel. It was dark and some of the landmarks were spectacularly floodlit. None had more impact than Tiananmen Square. Ava looked at it out of the taxi window. At more than one hundred acres it was one of the largest city squares in the world, containing, among other things, the Great Hall of the People, the National Museum of China, and the mausoleum of Mao Zedong. The name Tiananmen meant "Gate of Heavenly Peace"; the gate was at the north end of the square, separating it from the Forbidden City. Originally built in 1415, the gate had undergone various transformations, mostly as a result of damage caused by war rather than just age. But it hadn't been damaged during the protests of 1989, when hundreds, if not thousands, of protestors had been killed in the square. Ava wondered if the Chinese found the name ironic, given the violence it had seen.

* * *

Twenty minutes later she reached the Éclat. As Ava walked through the lobby she glimpsed a wall lined with paintings that she hadn't noticed earlier. She went over to it and stood surprised, then transfixed. Four of the paintings were attributed to Salvador Dali, another to Andy Warhol, and one to Zeng Fanzhi. They were all identified as originals, and if that was true, their value ran well into the millions. She stayed in the lobby, marvelling at the artwork, for several minutes before making her way to the elevator and up to her suite.

Ava had been in a hurry when she checked in and hadn't unpacked. Now she did, putting her running gear, T-shirts, and underwear into dresser drawers and hanging most of her Brooks Brothers shirts, slacks, and skirts in the closet. Then she took her first good look at the suite. The bedroom and sitting areas had rich brown wooden floors and furnishings that were sleek and modern, in an array of colours from subtly white to tan and other shades of brown. It reminded her of the chic boutique hotels she'd stayed at in Amsterdam and New York. But there was a difference: her Éclat suite had a terrace. Enclosed in glass, it was large enough to accommodate two easy chairs, a coffee table, and side tables, plus a white upholstered couch covered in hot pink, teal, and dark jade-green cushions. She could picture Pang Fai and herself sitting side by side on the couch drinking glasses of Pinot Grigio or Prosecco. Ava paused as she realized that the image wasn't in tune with the Pang Fai she'd seen less than an hour ago.

Ava couldn't begin to imagine what had caused Fai so much distress. Their relationship had started eight months before but their time together had been intermittent. It had no sooner begun when Fai left for a film shoot that was supposed to last ten weeks but was extended to eighteen. They had agreed not to meet while Fai was working, and except for a few wonderful exceptions, they made it work, staying in constant daily touch by phone, Skype, and text. The film shoot was followed by a glorious month in Thailand and then several months of meeting wherever and whenever they could — but, strangely, not at Ava's Toronto home base or in Beijing, where Fai lived. It had been almost a month since they'd seen each other; Fai had been in China fulfilling some contractual obligations, and Ava was heavily involved in preparing for the launch of the PÖ fashion line in North America. Prior to the month-long separation, they had agreed to make it the last of any extended duration. They were tightly bound, Ava thought, in a relationship that was at once intense and joyful.

She checked the time and wondered how long Fai would remain at the reception. She was contemplating taking a shower when her phone rang and she saw a familiar name. "Hi, Suki," she said.

"Welcome to Beijing, and thanks for coming. I'm downstairs in the Sun Ming Yuen restaurant. Do you want to join me for something to eat or drink?"

"No, thanks. I think I'll crash early."

"Then I'll see you in the morning in the lobby. We're being picked up at nine."

"That's great," Ava said. Her phone signalled another incoming call, and she switched lines. "Ava Lee."

"It's me," Fai said.

"Where are you?"

"I've just left the reception. I couldn't handle it anymore. I'm in a limo by myself."

"Do you know where the hotel is?"

"Yes, but I've been thinking that it might be too public."

"What do you suggest?"

"Come to my house," Fai pleaded. "It's only thirty minutes from the Éclat. I'll pick you up."

"That's fine."

"I should have thought of it when we met at the theatre, but I was too emotional."

"Fai, don't worry about it. I'll be happy to see your home," Ava said.

"Bring your things so you can stay," Fai said, and then paused. "Assuming you'll want to stay."

"Of course I will."

"Thanks," Fai said. "One more thing. I'd rather not get out of the limo when I get to the hotel."

"I'll wait outside at the entrance," Ava said.

"I'm in a black Bentley."

Ava ended the call, feeling even more disquieted by Fai's manner. *What the hell is going on*, she thought as she started to pack. Fifteen minutes later she left the room and rode the elevator down to the lobby. She thought about checking out but decided to keep the room for at least another day.

She walked to the entrance and stood outside. A steady stream of Porsches, BMWs, and Mercedes came and went in the fall evening. There was a chill in the air. The only jacket Ava had was in her Shanghai Tang Double Happiness bag; she was thinking about getting it out when a black Bentley stopped in front of her. Its rear window lowered and Fai's face appeared, smiling tentatively. Before Ava could react, the car's front door opened and the driver stepped out and reached for her bag. She gave it to him and slid into the back seat.

Fai leaned towards her. "Sorry to change my mind," she said.

"Was the reception okay?"

"I got through it," Fai said. "Chen wasn't happy that I left early, but I fulfilled my obligations."

Ava slipped her hand into Fai's and found it warm and sweaty. "This isn't how I imagined this evening," she said.

"We can talk about that when we get to the house," Fai whispered. "This is Chen's car and that's his driver."

Ava nodded. "Where are we headed?"

"I live in Xicheng."

"I don't know Beijing very well."

"It's near Beihai, the Northern Sea Lake, in the western part of the city," Fai said.

"That still doesn't help me much."

"Well, it's past Tiananmen and the old Forbidden City and north of where the premiere was held," Fai said. "Just south of us — though it might as well be a million miles away — is Zhongnanhai."

"Which is?"

"A compound where the most senior government officials live. We call it the 'New Forbidden City,' as it's strictly off-limits. My neighbourhood is much more modest. In fact, I live in a hutong. It doesn't get more modest than that."

"That's funny, we've never discussed our actual homes," Ava said. "I almost took it for granted that you lived in some new high-rise luxury condo."

"Lau Lau bought the house after his second film. It didn't cost very much. Then the neighbourhood was occupied mainly by writers, artists, and academics. Many of them are still there, fighting off the developers. I bought it from him when we divorced."

"I've heard of hutongs but I've never seen one."

"When I first came to Beijing, there were a lot of them. Now they're disappearing," Fai said, her voice trailing off in sadness.

Ava suspected that it wasn't the fate of the hutongs that had triggered the emotional reaction. "I'm sorry to rattle on like this," she said, squeezing Fai's hand.

Fai drew nearer, closed her eyes, and rested her head on Ava's shoulder. They rode in silence for what seemed to Ava like an eternity. They passed Tiananmen Square, but after that she lost all sense of location. When the driver stopped at what looked like the end of an alley, she thought he might be lost as well. Then he said, "We've arrived, Ms. Pang."

Fai lifted her head, fumbled in her purse, and tipped him a handful of money. "We have to walk from here," she said. "The lane is too narrow for the car."

The driver retrieved Ava's bag from the trunk while the two women stood shivering in the cool night air. "I have a jacket in my bag if you'd like it," Ava said.

Fai looped her arm through Ava's. "We don't have that far to go," she said.

The alley's grey stone walls, two storeys high and no more than ten metres apart, were crowded with stalls in some sections, while others housed recessed shops. Ava noticed doorways that she assumed led into homes. They walked for several minutes, their heels clicking on cobblestones and their path lit by red hanging lanterns. Fai finally guided her to the right and towards a red double door that had GOOD FORTUNE TO ALL WHO ENTER HERE inscribed in gold above the lintel. Fai pushed open the door and led Ava into a courtyard. It was surrounded by a half-circle of houses from which a myriad of lights shone.

Fai led Ava towards the middle of the stone courtyard, stopped in front of a navy-blue door, inserted a key, and opened the door. She stepped inside the house and flipped a light switch. "It's small, but it's mine," she said.

Ava entered the house and immediately held out her arms. They hugged. Their embrace wasn't as intense as it had been in the manager's office at the theatre, but Ava could still feel tension in Fai's body. They remained entwined for about a minute, and then Ava gently released herself, stepped back, and looked around at the house. The living room couldn't have been more than twenty square metres. It had a worn black leather couch and matching chair, a long wooden coffee table, and a set of end tables flanking the couch. A large high-definition television sat against the wall on the right, and next to it was a wooden bookcase that reached almost to the ceiling. It was the only wall not covered in posters from films Fai had made or Lau Lau had directed. On the left side of the room was an open door that led to a small kitchen, and a closed door to what Ava assumed was the bathroom. A narrow stairway was to the left of the couch. Ava remembered Fai's remark about her home being modest. She hadn't exaggerated.

"Not many people have been here," Fai said. "Lau Lau thought of it as a sanctuary, and I feel the same. Chen came once and was appalled. He said it wasn't a suitable place for a movie star. I told him I couldn't afford anything else. Though that was partially true at the time, it wasn't the real reason I didn't want to move."

"Who are your neighbours?"

"There's an artist, a couple of writers, a government official, an ex-policeman, and two elderly couples whose children look after them. They've all been here for as long as I have, and that's approaching nine years. We respect each other's privacy, but if anyone needs help it's always there," Fai said, and then smiled wanly. "But they can't help me with the problems I have now."

"The ones I still don't know about," Ava said.

Fai pointed at the stairway. "My bedroom is upstairs. Why don't you take your bags up while I prepare some tea. We can talk in the kitchen."

Fai's mood seemed sombre but less panicky. Ava wondered if being back in her home had something to do with that. "Do you want to change clothes?" she asked.

"No, this dress feels right."

For what? Ava thought, but simply said, "Okay."

The stairs were narrow and led Ava into a short hallway with two doors. She opened the first and saw a small bathroom that had a toilet, sink, and shower stall squeezed into it. Fai's bedroom was proportionally not that much larger. It had a double bed with no headboard that was covered with a fluffy snow-white duvet and four pillows. The wall behind the bed was covered in movie posters. Two large wooden dressers stood against the wall at the foot of the bed, and to Ava's right a large window looked out onto the courtyard. On the left, clothes racks ran from the front wall to the back.

Ava put her bags on the floor near the racks and was turning to leave when she saw two framed pictures on top of one of the dressers. One was of an elderly couple sitting side by side on a bench in a park while behind them couples danced. The other photo was of Ava. She was seated at a table in a restaurant, leaning forward to talk to May Ling; she was grinning exuberantly and pointing a finger at May. Ava guessed that it had been taken in London when they were all there for the PÖ launch at Fashion Week. She was surprised by the photo, not because Fai had it but more because Ava had never seen it and couldn't recall herself looking so happy in one.

She made her way back down the stairs and went into the kitchen. Fai sat on a wooden stool at a small round table that had a pot and two cups on it. Ava occupied a second stool and glanced around the kitchen. The traditional water Thermos and rice cooker were sitting on the counter, but next to them was a large microwave oven, and across from the counter stood a modern-looking stainless-steel stove and refrigerator.

Fai poured tea into the cups and then raised hers. "Thank you for being my friend."

"I hope I'm more than that," Ava said.

Fai turned her head. "I've been thinking about us for the past week," she said softly.

Ava felt a knot in the pit of her stomach. "What do you mean?"

"I realized that all the time we've spent together has been completely in the present," Fai said. "We've never really talked about the past."

"I've told you about my family, a bit about Uncle, and some things about my relationships with Xu and May and others."

"Yes, but what I'm trying to say is that I've never talked about me and you've never asked."

"I didn't want to pry."

"I thought maybe you didn't want to dig up memories of me with Lau Lau, Tsai, or other men," Fai said, her voice catching.

Ava took a deep breath. The first time she had met Fai was at a dinner in Shanghai. Ava had been invited by Xu. Fai was there with Tsai Men, son of the governor of Jiangsu province and a wealthy, corrupt, married businessman.

"We've all done things that we'd rather not remember," Ava said. "I have a Triad gang leader as a partner, who I treat like a brother. I've done things to people that were terrible, and for which I may never be forgiven."

"But you were never a whore. You must have thought I was one when we met," Fai said. "I know I spoke and acted like one."

"You made it clear that Tsai was paying for your company. Beyond that I knew and assumed nothing."

"I needed the money," Fai said. "Being an actress in China doesn't pay as well as people assume. Then there's Chen, who takes his cut; an image I have to maintain; the money I have to set aside for the day when I'm no longer in demand as an actress; and the money I send home to Yantai."

"You've never mentioned Yantai," Ava said, hoping to steer the conversation away from Tsai.

"It was my home. My parents and one grandparent still live there."

"You're supporting them?"

"Yes. My father was a fisherman, and that's a job for young men. His body started to give out when he turned fifty. My mother worked on the production line in a scallop plant, until her back became so bad she couldn't stand for more than a few minutes at a time."

"I know that Yantai has a seafood industry, but I didn't realize it was so physically demanding."

"You've been to Yantai?"

"Yes," Ava said. "I was chasing a guy who'd passed off a container of cheap frozen fish as scallops. I had to fly into Qingdao and drive north for a couple of hours from there. I stayed in a new waterfront hotel. I thought Yantai was a pretty place, or at least the waterfront was. We overlooked the Bohai Strait and the Yellow Sea. I also remember a lot of Korean signs there."

"The Korean peninsula is directly across the strait. A lot of the local businesses are operated by Koreans or depend on them as customers."

"When did you leave?"

"I had just turned seventeen when I got accepted into the Central Academy of Drama. That brought me to Beijing."

"How did that happen?"

"I was lucky. I had a schoolteacher who had a cousin who had a senior position at the Academy. The teacher kept telling me she thought I could make a career out of acting. All I'd done to earn that opinion was appear in some school plays and local amateur productions, but she seemed convinced and gave me enough confidence not to discount the possibility. What I didn't know was that she'd been telling her cousin about me, and she finally talked him into coming to Yantai to see me. He auditioned me in the teacher's living room. Somehow I impressed him enough to be given a place at the Academy."

"And that's where you met Lau Lau?"

"You mean that's where he claims he discovered me."

"That is the prevailing opinion."

Fai poured tea into both cups, even though neither woman had come close to emptying hers. "I was in my third year at the Academy. He had graduated six or seven years before and had served his apprenticeship as a director. He thought he was finally ready to break out on his own. He had a script that the China Movie Syndicate had approved and was prepared to finance, and the leading role called for a young woman. He came to the Academy to find one," Fai said. "When he asked who they would recommend, my name was at the top of the list. So you see, he hardly discovered me. My talent had been acknowledged and I was already building a reputation. If it hadn't been Lau Lau casting me in his film, it would have been someone else."

"Why don't you set the record straight?"

"What good would that do? People like the story that he picked me out of a crowd of anonymous, untested actresses and turned me into a star," Fai said, and then paused. "Besides, I've hurt him enough. Discovering me is one of his few remaining claims to fame. Let him keep it — he doesn't have much else to cling to these days."

"How long before he asked you to marry him?"

Fai shivered and slowly shook her head. "That's such a simple question, but what you're really asking is why did I marry him."

"Yes, you're right," Ava said, reaching across the table for Fai's hand.

"The answer is much more complicated. It's a question I couldn't bring myself to answer until I met you."

(4)

THEY SAT QUIETLY FOR A FEW MOMENTS, THEIR ATTEN-tion focused on the tea. Finally Ava said, "I think I'd like something a bit stronger to drink. Do you have any wine?"

"I have a bottle of Chardonnay in the fridge."

"That will do fine."

Fai got the wine and took it to the counter to uncork the bottle. She struggled with it, and that gave Ava some extra moments to think about their conversation. She suspected Fai wanted to unburden herself about her relationships with Tsai, Lau Lau, and who-knew-how-many other men. From her point of view, it wasn't a necessary discussion. She had already thought it through and frankly didn't care what Fai had done with whom. But she was prepared to listen if it helped her friend get rid of whatever guilt or remorse she was carrying around.

Ava watched as Fai finally uncorked the wine and reached into a cupboard for two glasses. Everything she did physically seemed effortless, as if she existed in a vacuum, like an astronaut floating in space. The contrast between that and the electricity she generated in bed thrilled Ava, and that reaction hadn't diminished one iota during the months they'd been together.

"What are you thinking about?" Fai asked when she returned to the table.

"Nothing," Ava lied. "You were talking about why you married Lau Lau. Do you want to continue?"

"I was a virgin when we married," Fai said, and then drank deeply from her glass. "We had tried to consummate our relationship before that, but somehow it never worked. Sometimes it was my fault, but just as often it was his."

"Is he gay?" Ava said.

"Why do you ask that?" Fai said, suddenly uncomfortable.

"I read something in one of my mother's Hong Kong gossip magazines a few years ago about him hanging around with one of the more openly gay Canto-pop performers."

"He would describe himself as bisexual."

"How would you describe him?"

"I'd prefer not to put any label on him," Fai said.

"Sorry."

"No, you don't have to say that. I know I'm going around in circles, and it has to be hard for you to follow," Fai said. "I guess what I'm trying to say is that I was confused about my sexuality, and now that things have become clear, there are ramifications I have to deal with."

"How confused were you?"

"Well, I said 'confused,' but I could have said that I was in denial. When I was younger, in my teens, I fantasized about having sex with girls, but I told myself that was just a phase and that I'd get over it. It didn't occur to me that not fantasizing about men was a sign. I just figured I'd meet a man and he'd show me the ropes and make me happy... Ava, I didn't know any better. Yantai wasn't exactly at the forefront of the sexual revolution, and it certainly wasn't liberal."

"You weren't worried about discrimination?"

"Maybe subconsciously, but my first awareness of that reality came later, when I was in Beijing and the students in the drama class talked about it. Some of them were gay, of course, and they worked hard at hiding it. They knew they wouldn't have any kind of career if it became known. Many of them got married, or at least tried to create a public perception of being involved in an ordinary relationship."

"Like you did."

"No. I was in such a deep state of denial, or ignorance, or whatever you want to call it that I thought all I needed to do was meet the right man."

"When did that change?"

Fai emptied her glass and refilled it. She took two sips, put the glass down, and grasped Ava's hands. "Lau Lau and I had been married for about three years. His first few films had been successful. I'd had my own share of success, but truthfully he was the star in the family; I was getting as much credit for marrying a great director who would cast me as I was for my performances. As his fame grew and he started earning serious money, he began to indulge himself. It started with liquor and then grew into drugs, and I went along for the ride.

"We were never completely out of control, but we were self-absorbed. Lau Lau in particular began to think of himself as being bigger than the system that supported him. So when opportunities came along to indulge in sexual adventures, he persuaded me to go along. The turning point for me came when he talked me into participating in a foursome. It would be boy-girl, boy-boy, girl-girl, girl-boy, he said — except it didn't work out that way. He and the boy locked onto each other, and I had sex with a girl for the first time in my life. I didn't know her and I never saw her again. What I did know was that I enjoyed the sex in a way I couldn't have imagined."

"Did you talk about it with him afterwards?"

"No. I was almost in shock."

"Did you have sex with him again?"

"Of course I did. I told myself I'd had an adventure, and that was all," Fai said. "I didn't really believe it, but I knew it was what I had to believe if I was going to have a career."

"What happened next?"

"We drifted apart. He became more and more out of control and I started to find my own way. When we split, I like to think it was a relief for both of us not to have to live such a big lie."

"What do you mean when you say you found your own way?" Ava asked.

"My career."

"Not your sexuality?"

"No. I had a few one-night stands, usually with other women in the business who knew the importance of discretion, but I was still kidding myself that all I had to do was find the right man."

"So what's happened to cause you so much anxiety?"

Fai lowered her eyes. "You already know that I slept with Tsai for money," she said slowly. "Well, there were others, although it wasn't always for money. Sometimes I needed other kinds of favours and I used sex to get them."

"What kind of favours?"

"I mentioned the China Movie Syndicate earlier. Do you know anything about it?"

"No."

"It's a government conglomerate that controls every aspect of filmmaking in China. It develops, finances, and produces most of the films made here. It owns theatres and controls the majority of the distribution system. It's the only group allowed to import foreign films into China and it decides which Chinese films can be exported."

"Is there a problem with them?"

"They won't allow Tsang to release *Mao's Daughter*."

"What?" Ava said, stunned. "We were just at its premiere."

"That could be its only showing."

"Why?"

"They think it's critical of the government. They think it's subversive."

"It's a historical period piece."

"But it doesn't reflect well on the Party or on Mao."

"Didn't they approve the script?"

"Tsang made some changes as we were shooting. They were minor, but it gave the senior functionaries at the Syndicate the excuse they needed to get heavy with him."

"How do you know the film won't be released?"

"Chen told me. He's Tsang's agent as well as mine."

"Then why bother with the premiere?"

"The Syndicate will say they wanted to see the full version, that all they'd viewed before were random scenes."

"What can Tsang or Chen do to make things right with them? I read somewhere that Gong Li faced this kind of opposition to some of her films. She refused to back down and won in the end."

Fai's eyes became teary and Ava saw her hands tremble. "No one in our industry today has the kind of power that Gong Li had," Fai said. "She was a true international superstar, and the times were different then. The Syndicate wasn't quite so politically or morally sensitive. I'm not sure even Gong Li could win today."

"So Tsang or Chen can't do anything?"

"The Syndicate doesn't care what they do. Their interest is in me."

"What do you mean?"

"The chairman of the Syndicate is a man named Mo, and the vice-chairman is Fong. They're going on a golf trip to Thailand in two weeks. They asked Tsang and Chen to invite me to join them," Fai said, the tears now starting to flow. "If I do, and if I entertain them sufficiently, the film will be released — with some minor changes. If I don't, the film is dead."

Ava's face flushed and her hands clenched into fists. "I don't believe that this kind of thing can go on in this day and age."

"It's been going on here for years, and the truth is that I've slept with Mo before to get things I wanted. But I'm finished with that kind of thing. There's no amount of coercion that can get me to change my mind," Fai said. "I didn't say that so directly to Tsang. All I said was that I couldn't do it. Then Chen pressed me and I told him what he already suspected."

"About us?"

"Yes, I told him we were lovers. I said I wasn't going to deny you or let you go, and I wasn't going to do anything that might risk our relationship. That included having any more to do with Mo or Fong or anyone else involved in the Syndicate. I told him those days are over."

"How did he react?"

"He was calm enough but said I was being foolish. He said that at my age I had another five to ten years of filmmaking ahead of me and that throwing those years away would be crazy. He suggested that I see you on the side and he'd find a way to keep things quiet," Fai said, and then paused. "But he also told me that sleeping with Mo has to happen if *Mao's Daughter* is ever going to be seen in public. And then, of course, he said it's the best film I've made in years and that with the right kind of support from the Syndicate it could get widespread international distribution."

"Is not distributing *Mao's Daughter* the only fallout from not doing what he wants?"

"There was also the clear implication that any future film I'm attached to won't get funded, and if it manages to self-finance it won't get distributed in China and they'll make it difficult for it to be shown abroad," Fai said, shaking her head. "Ava, I'm a realist when it comes to the power the Syndicate yields. They can make all those things happen if they choose."

"But you aren't completely sure they'll go to those lengths?"

"Not yet, but we'll know soon enough. There's a meeting scheduled between Chen and Mo tomorrow afternoon. I have to call Chen in the morning with my final answer about going on that trip. He'll then have to deal with Mo. But maybe I'm just anticipating the worst result and things won't be as bad as I think."

"What kind of animals are these people?" Ava muttered. "It's disgusting that you have to be worried about shit like this."

"Until now I just assumed it was normal for the business I'm in," Fai said. "Now my world has changed. What was normal is now abhorrent."

5

THEY LAY NAKED, WRAPPED IN EACH OTHER'S ARMS.
It was three in the morning and they hadn't slept. They'd
finished the bottle of wine, made love, talked, made love
again, and talked some more.

Ava found it difficult to accept that the people running
the China Movie Syndicate could have that much power and
be that venal. She asked question after question until she
understood that Fai's experiences with them had been first-
hand and had not been exaggerated. She knew that prob-
ing like that was probably causing Fai some discomfort, but
she wanted to understand, and she didn't know how else to
proceed. Finally she said, "As I see it, we've got a couple of
options."

Fai's face was only inches away and her eyes stared into
Ava's. They were full of doubt, although Ava liked to think
she saw in them a touch of hope as well. "How can we have
options?" Fai said.

"Who is the ultimate decision maker in the Syndicate?"

"Mo sets the tone and calls the shots. He's been there for
years and years."

"So he's a dedicated and loyal Party member?"

"He wouldn't have survived otherwise."

"We have to find a way to get to him."

"How?"

"I don't know yet."

"And to do what?"

"We need to convince him that it's in his own best interest to leave you alone and to authorize the distribution of *Mao's Daughter*."

"He's stubborn and vindictive. If I don't go to Thailand, he'll make me pay."

"Uncle, my former partner, used to say that people always do the right thing for the wrong reason. All we have to do is find the reason that will motivate Mo."

"You make it sound so simple. It can't be that easy. What do we do if he won't budge?"

Ava put her hand gently under Fai's chin. "Maybe you should leave China for a while. It could be a good thing. I'm sure there are film companies and directors in the U.S. who'd be thrilled to have you in one of their productions."

"I don't speak English well enough for that."

"You could learn."

"I've tried, but I don't seem to have an ear for other languages," Fai said, and then caught herself. "I don't mean to sound negative, but it is something Chen and I talked about before and he made some calls on my behalf. The language issue was a big problem. We even discussed the possibility of me learning the lines in English phonetically, like Gong Li did for some of her non-Chinese films. I gave it a try, but I became so focused on the language that I couldn't act."

"Then we could consider making Chinese-language films somewhere else, like Taiwan or Hong Kong."

"The Syndicate would never allow anyone in China to import or distribute a film I'd made elsewhere, and they'd lean on markets like Hong Kong and Taiwan to boycott me."

"You would still have PÖ," Ava said. "And I'm sure you could find other product endorsements."

"It would feel like charity. And besides, if I'm no longer in films, how long would my value as a spokesperson last?"

"So, back to option one," Ava said.

Fai wrapped herself tighter around Ava. "I hate sounding so negative, and I'm not a quitter, but I've been thinking about this for ages, even before *Mao's Daughter*. It's time I was true to myself, and I know that if I am there's no way out of this mess other than leaving the business. One person can't take on a system like this. It isn't only the Syndicate that you have to beat; it's the powerful people behind it — the Party officials who control ideology and propaganda. They have a vision of how they want China and Chinese people to be represented to the rest of the world. Anyone who doesn't play along is crushed. I could be the best-known Chinese actress in the world, but in their eyes I'm entirely disposable."

"No one is going to dispose of you," Ava said.

"That's nice to hear, even if I have trouble believing it."

Ava kissed Fai casually. She was preoccupied, her mind turning as she thought about what kind of pressure she could bring to bear on Mo. She needed to talk to Xu, she realized, and she needed time.

"Fai, I have meetings today with Suki Chan, one of our partners, and I can't cancel them. There are some people I want to speak to about your situation and there's some more thinking I want to do. Are you prepared to call Chen and tell him that you still haven't made a decision, that you need at least another couple of days?"

"He'll have to contact Mo."

"I know. That's the idea — I want to buy us some time. Tell Chen you're leaning in the direction of going on the trip, if that makes it more palatable for him."

"What if he says no? What if Mo says no? What if he wants an answer right away?"

"The trip is two weeks from now. Why would anyone be that unreasonable?"

"Mo is a sadistic bully. It isn't enough that the answer he wants is yes; it has to be on his terms, and that means he wants Chen and me on our bellies, begging him to be kind."

"If Mo still demands an immediate answer, then tell Chen it's yes," Ava said. "You are never going to Thailand with him, but I need a few days to get things organized. If it takes a lie to get us what we want, then so be it."

"Get what organized?"

"I have to talk to some people. After I have, I'll tell you what's possible," Ava said. "Do you have a problem lying to Chen?"

"Not at all, and he wouldn't think twice about lying to Mo."

"Is that also a characteristic of the business you're in?"

"Yes, it's one of the more predictable ones."

6

AVA LEFT HER BAGS AT FAI'S WHEN SHE CAUGHT A TAXI the next morning at eight to take her back to the Éclat. She'd slept for about two hours but was full of energy, fuelled by adrenalin. This had been her normal state when she worked with Uncle, and there had been many occasions since when circumstances caused it to kick in. The most recent had coincided with Fai's first day of filming *Mao's Daughter,* taking Ava to the outermost regions of the Philippines as she looked into an Islamic college as a favour for Chang Wang, an old friend of Uncle's who lived in Manila. That investigation had ended more dramatically than anyone could have envisioned, and the repercussions were still being felt in the Philippines, and elsewhere.

Fai had made coffee while Ava showered, brushed her teeth and hair, and put on black slacks and a light blue button-down shirt. For business meetings she usually wore lipstick and mascara, Annick Goutal perfume, and her Cartier Tank Française watch, but Suki was the plainest dresser imaginable and Ava felt she should match her simplicity. The one exception was the ivory chignon pin she used to hold her hair in place.

"I don't know how long my meetings will last," Ava said as she drank her coffee in the kitchen. "Suki is normally quite aggressive, so I'm guessing she'll already have collected most of the information we need and will have started to confirm it. I'm sort of her second set of eyes. With any luck we'll soon know if there's a deal to be done. And I don't have to be there when the offer is made."

"When do you think you'll be able to make those calls you talked about?" Fai said.

"I can't do it while I'm with Suki or in the meeting, but I'll find the time."

"I'll phone Chen at ten. He's never up until then."

"Are you still comfortable with doing what we discussed?"

"I'm going to see this through to the end," Fai said. "When I woke this morning, my heart was the lightest I can remember. Maybe it's because I've made a decision that I know is right, but I also feel as if my life is finally under my control and going in the proper direction. I was even thinking I could make another try at learning English. Who knows, it might stick this time."

"It would be nice if it did, but let's not make it a necessity," Ava said.

Fai went with Ava to the end of the hutong to flag a cab. She certainly didn't live there anonymously: virtually every vendor and passerby nodded, waved, or spoke to her. Fai held Ava's hand as they walked. Two women holding hands in public was a common enough sight in Asia. It signified friendship and usually nothing more than that, but Ava's North American sensibility was more open to other interpretations. In her mind, Fai's hand in hers represented the first step in Fai's coming out. The thought made her smile.

They kissed before Ava got into the cab, and then Fai waited until the taxi drove out of sight.

Ava took out her phone and called Shanghai. She got Xu's voicemail. He was usually up by this time, sitting outside by his fish pond with his cigarettes and a cup of coffee. She left a message.

They were in the middle of morning rush hour, and after half an hour of inching forward, Ava thought she might be late getting to the hotel. The volume of traffic surprised her. She associated gridlock of this kind with Manila, Jakarta, or Bangkok; she hadn't factored in that Beijing could be as bad. She mentioned it to the driver.

He shrugged. "The only time it isn't like this is when the air quality is so poor that half the cars in the city are forced to stay off the roads. Depending on your licence plate number, some get to drive on Monday, Wednesday, and Friday, and the others on Tuesday, Thursday, and Saturday."

"What about Sunday?"

"Back to a free-for-all."

"How often does the air quality get that bad?"

"It used to be once a month or so, depending on the weather. Rain usually clears the air. But now it's more frequent, maybe three or four times a month, and sometimes even the rain can't help."

Ava checked the time and saw that she was definitely going to be late. She phoned Suki. "I'm in a taxi trying to get to the hotel, but I won't get there by nine," she said.

"I thought you were staying here," Suki said.

"I decided to visit a friend in Xicheng. I'm going to be staying there and not at the hotel."

"Well, there's no problem with your being late. The people

picking us up just called to say they're stuck in traffic as well."

"I'll see you when I get there," Ava said. She ended the call just as Xu's Shanghai number appeared on the screen.

"*Mei mei*," he said.

"Sorry to call so early," she said, pleased by his quick response and his use of the endearment "little sister."

"Is there a problem?"

"Yes, there is," she said, and then she saw the cab driver's eyes looking at her in the rear-view mirror. Suddenly she realized she shouldn't be using Fai's name in such a public situation. "But I don't feel comfortable talking about it right this moment. When will be a good time for me to call back?"

"I'll be at the house until one o'clock."

"I'll get to you before then, *ge ge*," Ava said, addressing him as "big brother."

Ava had first met Xu at Uncle's funeral. He was already the head of the Triad gang in Shanghai and was ambitious for more success. Unknown to Ava, Uncle had been mentoring Xu for years, and he was as close to Uncle as Ava had been. With Uncle's passing they had transferred the loyalty, trust, respect, and perhaps even love they'd felt for him to one another. And since that first meeting they had helped each other in both large and small ways, without hesitation or question. They were almost like real brother and sister, Ava thought. All they lacked was common blood.

In the distance Ava saw the pyramid shape of the building that housed the Éclat. "How much longer?" she asked the driver.

"Ten minutes."

It took twenty, and a frustrated Ava finally walked into the hotel lobby to find Suki sitting by herself. She waved at Ava and stood to greet her.

Suki was dressed in black slacks and a gray Mao jacket. She wore no makeup and her silver hair was cut in a bob. Ava guessed she was close to sixty, but her face was unlined, and she had the energy of a much younger woman. "They're still twenty minutes away," she said to Ava.

"Good. That gives me time to make a phone call. If you don't mind, I'll do it from my room. I didn't check out last night, but I'll do it this morning."

"Go ahead. I'll wait here."

Ava hurried to the elevator. She found Xu's number while she was riding to her floor, and pressed it as soon as she exited.

"That didn't take long," Xu said after two rings.

"My meeting has been delayed."

"Where are you?"

"Beijing. I came to assist Suki with due diligence on a logistics business she has her sights on," she said. "It just so happened that I also managed to go to the premiere of Pang Fai's new film, *Mao's Daughter.*"

"How was the film?"

"Fantastic. It's actually the reason I'm calling"

"You don't have to recommend it to me. I love Pang's work."

"Well, we need your help if you want to keep enjoying it."

"What's happened?" Xu said, suddenly serious.

Ava carefully related her conversation with Fai, leaving out any references to Lau Lau and their sexual adventures. Xu listened attentively and didn't ask any questions until Ava finished. Then he said, "Are you sure this China Movie Syndicate has that much power?"

"I'm taking Fai's word for it, but she should know, and you should be able to confirm it quickly enough."

"And these guys — Mo and Fong — are using it like their own private bordello?"

"Yes, but I'm sure sex isn't the only thing they're getting out of it. If we dig deep enough we'll probably find dirty money as well."

"What do you want to do about it?"

"I want Fai left alone for now and the foreseeable future, and I want that film released and heavily distributed and promoted."

"How much do you know about Mo and Fong?"

"Nothing. I was hoping you could help."

"And how will you proceed if you find something you can use against them? Beijing isn't an easy place to get to anyone, let alone a senior functionary and member of the Party."

"I haven't thought about that yet."

Xu was silent for a moment. Ava could hear him inhaling. "Lop is my man with the best Beijing contacts and the most knowledge of how things operate there," he said finally.

Ava knew Lop. He had been a captain in the People's Liberation Army, assigned to Special Forces, but his primary loyalty lay with the Shanghai Triad gang that Xu headed. Lop's father had been a member of the gang, and Xu's father had arranged for Lop to get into the officers' academy. Lop had stayed with the PLA until Xu needed him. As soon as the call came, Lop had answered it, going on to organize Xu's defences in Shanghai and orchestrate offensive attacks elsewhere. One of those attacks had taken place in Wanchai, a district in Hong Kong. It had been successful and Lop was now de facto head of the gang there — a gang that was ultimately controlled by Xu. "I'd be very happy to work with Lop on this," Ava said.

"I'll call him right away."

"He has to move quickly, though. We need to resolve this issue within the next week."

"That's a longer time frame than you usually give me," Xu said with a chuckle.

Ava ignored the gibe. "How will communications work?" she asked.

"I'll talk to him and then get out of the way unless either of you need me to get involved," he said. "Are you comfortable with that?"

"As long as he is."

"You'll have no problem with him. He's one of your many admirers."

"What if I need him to come to Beijing?"

"I'm sure that can be arranged."

"Thank you."

"Ava, you never have to say that to me."

"I want you to know that I'm not taking you for granted. I treasure our friendship and I don't want to abuse it."

"I sense that Pang Fai is very important to you," Xu said carefully.

"She is."

"I mean on a personal level."

"I know."

"Is she the one?"

Ava paused. Xu knew about her sexuality, but she'd never discussed it with him in any detail. "She might be."

"That's all the more reason for me to light a fire under Lop — although normally that isn't necessary."

"I don't think there's any reason to share details with him about my personal life," Ava said softly.

"I'd never do that," Xu said. "All he'll know is that keeping Pang Fai's public profile prominent is important to our business."

"And that's true enough."

"I'll call him now."

"I'm about to go into some meetings and I don't want to be rude, so my phone will be off for a while. But you can leave me a message and let me know how to proceed."

"If you don't hear from me, you'll hear from Lop."

Ava put down the phone, feeling more pleased than she'd let on to Xu. First, he had sensed the true nature of her tie to Fai, and she knew that, if anything, it would make him more determined to help. Second, with Lop assigned to be her point man, she couldn't have a more ferocious advocate.

She had seen Lop in action three times. He was smart, tough, disciplined, and entirely fearless. If you got into a fight with him, he was the kind of opponent you'd have to kill. Unlike Xu's enforcer Suen, who was a mountain of a man, Lop was of medium height, with a slight, wiry build. He didn't appear threatening until you got close enough to see the tension that rippled through his body, and his eyes, which were in a perpetual state of alertness. Ava had once described him as manic. Xu responded by telling her that Lop might appear manic on the surface, but at his core he was cold and controlled. The combination was frightening if you were his enemy, comforting if you were an ally.

Ava looked at the time and realized she should be heading downstairs. A day of going over financial statements didn't hold much appeal, but at least it would be distracting.

When Ava exited the elevator, Suki was standing near the hotel entrance with a man and a woman. She started towards them, remembered that she hadn't checked out, and made a left-hand turn towards the front desk. She handed in her room card and cancelled the remainder of the reservation. When she approached Suki, she could sense the other two people eyeing her. They were both short, round, and plainly dressed — he in a baggy black suit and she in a dark green wool dress that came below the knees.

"Ava, this is Mr. and Mrs. Sun," Suki said.

"Pleased to meet you," Ava said to them, noting Suki's formality.

They nodded at her.

"I have known them for many years," Suki said. "My husband and Mr. Sun used to go on gambling junkets to Las Vegas together, leaving Mrs. Sun and me to run the businesses."

"And the businesses never suffered when they were gone," Mrs. Sun said.

Another Suki, Ava thought. *Except this one's husband didn't die.* "I've heard only wonderful things about the business you built."

"It's time to sell," Mrs. Sun said. "We have two children who have no interest in it, and we don't have Suki's ambition. But I told my husband that I don't want to pass our life's work to a stranger, to someone who might not appreciate how much effort went into it."

"So we thought of Suki," he said.

"All things being equal, we prefer to sell to her," Mrs. Sun said.

"By 'equal,' you mean that we pay the price you want," Ava said.

"It's fair," Mrs. Sun said.

"I will let Suki be the judge of that," Ava said. "But in addition to being Suki's partner in other businesses, I'm an accountant. I'm here to look at your books, your financial statements, and your tax returns. If there are no discrepancies, then Suki can come up with an evaluation based on the standard indices you use in your field."

"We know what we want. We know what we think it's worth," Mrs. Sun said.

"Do you doubt Suki's experience or objectivity?" asked Ava.

"No," Mr. Sun replied.

His wife stepped forward and offered Ava her hand. "Our SUV is outside. It's an hour's drive to our office in this traffic. We've told our accountants to organize all the information we think you need, and they're available to answer any questions you might have. We should get going."

As they walked from the hotel, Ava said quietly to Suki, "Mrs. Sun reminds me a bit of you — less the husband, of course."

"She's tough enough, if that's what you mean, and I take that as a compliment," Suki said. "But when she asked me about you, I told her not to be fooled by your age or your appearance. I told her that you're tougher than her and me put together."

Ava glanced sideways. Suki returned the look.

"I've heard enough stories about you. Why do you think I wanted you and May Ling as my partners?" Suki said.

7

THE DAY PROCEEDED WITH A BOREDOM THAT REMINDED Ava of her earliest jobs. She had graduated from York University in Toronto and then from Babson College in Wellesley, Massachusetts, with degrees in general and forensic accounting. Her first two employers had been large international accounting firms, but the jobs didn't last long. Ava wasn't very good at taking orders, and the firms had no interest in doing things the way she thought they should be done. So they parted ways and for a short time she had her own one-woman firm, catering mainly to friends referred by her mother. One of those contacts, though, had resulted in a debt-collection job that took her to Hong Kong and eventually led to her first encounter with Uncle. Now, as she sat in the Suns' boardroom going through years of consolidated statements, Ava couldn't help feeling grateful for her escape from traditional accounting.

The Suns hadn't understated the information they were making available. There were stacks of it, suitable enough, Ava thought, for a business that they'd spent thirty years developing. She focused on the last five years and directed most of her questions to Suki. When Suki couldn't provide an answer, they called in Mrs. Sun. And when she couldn't answer, they talked to one of the in-house accountants.

After a couple of hours, Ava knew she was looking at a well-run, profitable business, but she also knew that she shouldn't be too quick to say so. If there was still price haggling to be done, some seeds of doubt had to be planted. Besides, by one o'clock she was hungry.

"I can't drink any more tea. I need something to eat. Is there a restaurant nearby?" she asked.

"I think they've organized some food to be brought in," Suki said.

"When?"

"One-thirty."

"Please ask Mrs. Sun to make sure that happens."

Suki left the boardroom and returned a few minutes later. "The food will be here in a few minutes," she said. "They'll join us to eat, and they'll ask what we think about the business."

"They want six hundred million renminbi for it?"

"Yes."

"What do you think it is worth?"

"A bit less, but not by much."

"What will they get if they go into the open market?"

"I expect they'd get that, but I doubt if it would all be in cash. Most of the other operators around here are highly leveraged, and the Suns would get offers that involved installment payments or shares in a company."

"I think six hundred million is high, but let me go over the latest financials again," Ava said.

"Does something trouble you about them?"

"I didn't see any depreciation of their trucks and other equipment in the last statement, and I think the estimated increase in the value of their real estate holdings is very aggressive."

"We need to get an independent assessment of the real estate," Suki said.

"I'd rather get three assessments and average them. There's less chance of either side being short-changed if we do. The Suns can't really argue with that."

"It will slow things down."

"I know, but I have no difficulty with reaching an agreement in principle on a price after the depreciation is put in. In terms of the real estate, for now we can use their evaluation, with the understanding that it will be adjusted after the assessments."

"What do you want to offer?"

"That depends on how badly you want to acquire the business."

"They operate in parts of the north that no one else really serves. It will open up markets for some of our Shanghai customers, and vice versa. It will benefit us in far more ways than just making money from their current business — and that's profitable enough as it is. So I want us to buy it, but I agree that the price has to be right."

"Would you be comfortable, and the Suns not insulted, if we offered five hundred and fifty million?"

"Cash?"

"Yes, we can do that."

"And that amount would be subject to a final real estate evaluation?"

"Yes," Ava said. "I would also need to talk to their bank

to confirm some of the other numbers in their financials."

"That would be expected, and I have one more warehouse to visit. My plan was to finish that later today. Do you want to join me?"

"No, thank you. I can't imagine I'd have anything to contribute. You know your business, Suki. What I know are numbers."

Suki turned her head towards the door as voices were heard outside. "What do you want me to tell them when they join us?"

"That we're impressed and we're prepared to make an offer subject to agreement on finalizing a real estate value, and assuming that no surprises are uncovered this afternoon."

"They'll be happy enough with that," Suki said, and then added as the door opened, "We won't regret doing this deal."

Two young women entered the boardroom carrying trays that were loaded with food. Mr. and Mrs. Sun and their accountant followed them in. As Mrs. Sun supervised organization of the food, plates, cups, and chopsticks, Ava turned on her phone and saw she had two text messages. The first, from Fai, said, Chen managed to convince Mo to wait two days for an answer. Miss you. The other, from Lop, read, Call me.

"Excuse me for a moment. I have to make a quick call," Ava said. She stepped into the hallway, moved away from the boardroom door, and pressed Lop's number.

"Hello. Is this *xaio lao ban* calling me?" he answered.

Ava smiled. *Xaio lao ban* meant "little boss." It was a term that some of Xu's men — and Xu himself when she wasn't present — often used to refer to her. She was surprised and pleased that Lop respected her enough to say it. "Is this the Dragon Head of Wanchai?" she said.

"Not by title — that's still Sammy Wing. And not in the power I have — that still flows from Xu."

Lop said it lightly, but Ava wondered if she'd been insensitive. Xu's Shanghai gang had taken control of Wanchai the year before but had left Wing, its former boss, in place as a figurehead. Lop ran the day-to-day operations, but obviously Xu was directing the broader business. "All I know is what I'm told," Ava said, "which is that you're doing a fantastic job there."

"Thank you for saying that," he said. "When I spoke to Xu this morning, he implied you might need my help."

"I hope he did more than imply."

"I didn't want to be too presumptuous."

"I'm not embarrassed to say that I most definitely need your help, and I'm delighted that you phoned."

"He mentioned the China Movie Syndicate and some guy named Mo."

"Mo seems to be the source of my problem."

Lop paused and Ava heard the sound of traffic in the background. She imagined him walking back and forth while he was talking to her; she'd never seen him be still for more than a minute at a time. "If it is Mo, you're dealing with someone who's really connected. His cousin is Zhang Jinlong; he's number four of seven members of the Politburo Standing Committee. Zhang is responsible for propaganda and ideology. He appointed Mo."

"That explains some things," Ava said.

"Xu said you need to lean on Mo."

"I do."

"Well, I don't think you'll be able to do it through the government, like you did with Tsai. Zhang will protect him, and Zhang is well beyond our reach."

"What does that leave us?"

"We'll have to get personal."

"What does that mean?"

"Xu said that you need Mo to stop harassing Pang Fai and to distribute that new film of hers."

"That's what I want."

"Then we need to find something we can use against him," Lop said. "And something that will intimidate or embarrass him enough that he won't go running to his cousin."

"What are you proposing?"

"I don't have an idea yet. I've just started gathering information about him."

"So when do think you'll have something?"

"It had better be by tomorrow morning, because you and I have a meeting scheduled with Mo at one o'clock tomorrow afternoon at his office in Beijing."

"Are you serious?" Ava said.

"I just assumed that meeting with him face-to-face would be something you'd want to happen," he said. "And Xu said you wanted to move quickly, so I called some friends."

"Military?"

"That's the only type of friends I have in Beijing. They arranged it."

"Do they know the reason we want to meet with Mo?"

"No reason was necessary."

"What did they tell Mo about us?"

"Only that we were friends and that I needed to talk to him."

"And that got us an appointment?"

"The friend who made the call is a prominent general in the PLA. He emphasized my military background and said he would consider it a personal favour if Mo gave me and a friend fifteen minutes of his time."

"That's terrific. When do you arrive in Beijing?"

"Tomorrow morning at ten," he said.

"Where do you want to meet?"

"Their office is in Chaoyang, the business district."

"That's close to the Hotel Éclat. Why don't you go there directly from the airport. I'll meet you in the lobby."

"If my flight is on time, I could be there by eleven. It will give us a chance to talk."

"I hope you'll have some useful information to share by then," she said.

"It isn't actually me who's gathering it," he said. "Some other friends are doing that for us, and they're good."

"Then I look forward to tomorrow morning. Call me if there are any delays. Otherwise, I'll see you at the Éclat."

She ended the conversation feeling more confident than when it had started. If Lop's connections were powerful enough to open Mo's door, it was up to her to make the best use of the time they'd been given. She thought of Lop's remark about intimidating Mo and smiled. There wasn't much in her mind that was off-limits when it came to doing that.

8

IT WAS ALMOST FIVE O'CLOCK WHEN AVA LEFT THE Suns' offices. There hadn't been much discussion while they ate lunch, but as soon as the last chopstick was put down, Mrs. Sun asked Ava, "What do you think you're going to do about our business?"

"I'm going to leave it to Suki to explain our position," Ava replied.

Mrs. Sun frowned, and Ava realized that her choice of words may have sounded negative. "By that I mean Suki will go over our offer with you," she added.

Suki nodded, her face sombre. She shuffled some papers in front of her and then leaned towards the Suns. "We think the business is worth five hundred million," she said. "But that's only if the real estate is worth what you claim."

The Suns exchanged looks that went from shock to disappointment to something approaching anger. "We wanted six hundred and fifty. We were willing to settle for six hundred only because it was you, Suki," Mrs. Sun said.

"The numbers don't justify that kind of price, and we have doubts about the real estate valuation," Suki said.

"You must be looking at different numbers than us," Mrs. Sun said.

And so began more than two hours of haggling between Suki and Ms. Sun, with everyone else in the role of interested bystander. This was the first time Ava had been party to this kind of negotiation with Suki, and she quickly became impressed with how low-key, patient, persistent, and stubborn she was. Mrs. Sun was more emotional, twice storming out of the room. When she did, Suki just sighed and waited for her to return. *It's like watching theatre*, Ava thought.

Mrs. Sun was the first to blink, when after an hour-long stalemate she lowered her asking price by ten million. Suki countered by going up ten million, and then slowly the two sides moved towards the RMB550 million offer she had agreed on with Ava.

"But if I take that price, you'll have to accept the real estate valuation as is," Mrs. Sun said.

Suki looked at Ava.

"Mrs. Sun, we want to be fair, but the real estate is a large component of the purchase. I just want to be certain we're paying market price. We've suggested getting three independent assessments. We're prepared to average them and pay whatever that amount is, even if it is more than what you're currently asking," Ava said.

"I don't see how you can argue against a proposal like that," said Suki.

"Would whatever you pay be entirely in cash?" Mr. Sun asked.

He had been so quiet that Ava had almost forgotten he was there. "Yes."

"And would you send it to any bank that we designate?"

"Certainly."

"Then I'm okay with the offer and the way it's structured," he said to his wife.

Mrs. Sun shot him an annoyed look, but he didn't flinch, staring back at her. She turned to Suki. "I guess we have an agreement in principle."

"That's wonderful," Suki said, a broad smile splitting her face.

Both Suns smiled as well. "But we still have to decide how we choose those independent assessors," Mrs. Sun said.

"What I suggest is that we get a phone book, select three companies, call them together, and give them their instructions," Suki said.

After all the hours she'd spent fighting over every renminbi, Ava couldn't believe that Mrs. Sun would accept such a random solution.

"That sounds good to me," Mrs. Sun said. "Let's do it now."

Ava looked at her watch and saw it was four-thirty. During the negotiations she had been so absorbed that she'd lost track of time. Now Lop popped into her head, and she wondered how he was progressing.

"You'll join us for a celebratory dinner tonight?" Mr. Sun said to her and Suki.

"Yes," Suki said.

Ava began to say no and then caught herself. It would be insulting to the Suns and disappointing for Suki. "Yes, of course. But I have another issue I'm dealing with and I need to make some private phone calls first."

"Is the issue important?" Mr. Sun said.

"It's rather urgent, and truthfully, I don't know how long I'll be tied up."

"Would you prefer to have dinner tomorrow night?" he asked. "We still have some work to do here and we haven't made any reservations. It might be better for everyone."

"That's very considerate of you. Tomorrow would be preferable."

"Do you want to make your calls from here?"

"I'm staying with a friend in Xicheng. I think I'd rather do it from there."

"We'll have our driver take you," Mr. Sun said.

After a round of handshakes, Mr. Sun left the boardroom to get the driver. Ava and Suki followed him, several paces behind.

"You did an amazing job," Ava said to Suki.

"Will you call May Ling and Amanda to let them know we have an agreement?"

"No, I think you should do that. It's your deal."

Suki nodded, a satisfied look on her face.

The driver was already at the warehouse entrance when they arrived. "Where shall I tell him you're going?" Mr. Sun said.

"I don't actually know the exact address," Ava said, feeling instantly silly. "Let me call my friend."

Fai answered immediately. "I've been waiting for you to phone."

"We just finished our meeting and I'm heading back to the house, but I don't know your address. I'll pass my cell to the driver so you can give him instructions. Don't hang up after you do, so we can talk."

A moment later the driver passed Ava's cell back to her and opened the back door of the SUV. She climbed in, with the phone stuck to her ear. "I got your text. Did Chen have any problems with Mo?" she said.

"He was abusive as usual, but Chen was persistent."

"I hope you thanked him."

"For doing his job? I don't think so. Besides, when it comes to choices between me and Mo, I'm quite sure that Chen takes Mo's side most often. I'm not his only client, after all, and he can't do much for any of the others without the support of the Syndicate."

"You know best."

"In this case, I do."

"We'll have to talk about Mo tonight," Ava said.

"Why?"

"I'm meeting him tomorrow at one o'clock. I need to know more about him; I need to understand what motivates him."

"You're meeting with him? How did that happen?"

"Through a friend of a friend."

"Does Mo know we're connected?"

"Of course not, but after tomorrow he will. If we handle it properly, that shouldn't make any difference to your future. But if we misread the situation or botch the meeting, it's possible it could. Are you okay with that?"

"I'm not backing down. Whatever happens, happens."

"Good," Ava said, just as her phone vibrated. She saw the call was from Lop. "Fai, I have a call I have to take. I'll see you in a while."

"Ava, its Lop. How strong are your North American connections?"

His abruptness didn't surprise her. "That depends on what you need done."

"Mo has one child, a son who lives in the U.S. He's taken the English name David and is attending UCLA. I'm told David is the most important thing in Mo's life, that he absolutely dotes on the boy."

"That is a very expensive school, and Los Angeles isn't cheap to live in. The annual bill must come to more than a hundred thousand dollars. How does he pay for something like that?"

"No one in the Party would care about that. There isn't a senior Party member who doesn't have a kid at a university in the U.K. or the U.S. I'm more interested in the fact that Mo loves his son so much."

"Yes, I can understand that."

"Do you have any way of finding out exactly where he lives?"

"For what purpose?"

"Let's find out what we can about him. He might be our leverage."

Ava hesitated and then said, "I have a friend in Canada who's good at locating people. I'll contact him."

"Perfect. See you in the morning."

9

FOR THE SECOND CONSECUTIVE MORNING, FAI WALKED with Ava to the entrance of the hutong, waited until she flagged a taxi, and then kissed her goodbye.

The night before had been quiet. Fai had prepared a meal that they ate in the kitchen. It was northern Chinese cuisine: steamed pork buns, pork and chive bread dumplings, and a large plate of suan cai — pickled cabbage — that had been made by Fai's mother and sent to Beijing.

As they ate, they chatted about Chen and Mo and the meeting the following day. Ava found that Fai's knowledge of Mo was surprisingly meagre. She seemed to know nothing about his personal life, and her assessment of his character, while harsh, wasn't exactly deep. When Ava pressed for more detail, Fai held up a hand.

"Wait a minute," she said. "What you don't understand is that I had no interest in knowing this man, or anything about his life. It was easier for me to deal with him, and others like him, if I thought of him as a non-person."

Ava saw the logic in that statement but still felt a stab of pain at the thought of what had created that mindset. One thing was evident as they sat at the table — Fai was calmer than she'd been the night before, but with a calmness that Ava thought verged on fatalism. Ava didn't believe in fate, because she couldn't believe that life was predetermined. There was always something that could be done, an action to be taken that could change the course of events. It was her experience that people who thought otherwise, those who spoke often about fate, were prone to inaction and more ready to accept defeat. When she mentioned this, Fai smiled.

"You are mistaking my lack of worry for not caring," Fai said. "I care passionately about what's going to happen, but I trust you. And when I'm with you, I feel that I can survive anything. You give me a foundation of support I've never had."

Ava thought about the weight of that responsibility and felt a slight touch of panic. She was used to being more emotionally isolated, and Fai was breaking down those barriers. Then she thought of her mother, and May Ling, Uncle, and Xu. Why should her devotion to Fai be any less than it was to them? "You're right, we will survive," Ava said. "I just want it to be on our terms and not someone else's."

After dinner she phoned Derek Liang in Toronto. Derek was an old friend who was married to Mimi, an even older friend. Mimi and Ava had both attended Havergal College, a private girls' high school, and they had remained close. Ava had met Derek at the dojo of Grandmaster Tang. He and Ava were the only two students deemed worthy by the Grandmaster to learn bak mei. Derek was an only child with wealthy parents and had no reason to work. During her early debt-collection years he had been her reliable sidekick — someone who was loyal and, with his bak mei training, lethal. After he met Mimi and they married and had a daughter, Ava had stopped asking him to accompany her on jobs, but he had computer and investigative skills that she still called on from time to time.

It was early morning in Toronto when she reached him, but he sounded alert. Ava could hear a child's voice in the background and assumed he was looking after his daughter. She told him what she needed to find out and he said he'd get right on it. When Ava then asked to say hello to Mimi, Derek told her she'd already left for the office. Ava smiled as she wondered how his very traditional Chinese parents were handling that kind of role reversal.

She and Fai went to bed early. Neither of them had slept much the night before and now they made up for it. Ava's head hardly touched the pillow before she was asleep.

She woke to the smell of coffee and pale light from a sun shrouded in what looked like fog but was more likely polluted air. She went downstairs to find Fai standing in the kitchen in her underpants, the PÖ T-shirt from London Fashion Week, and nothing else. Ava wrapped her arms around Fai's waist. Fai gently pried herself free, turned, and threw her arms around Ava. They stood like that for several minutes, Ava's breath hot against Fai's neck.

"Do you want to go back to bed?" Fai asked.

"I'm horny enough, but I don't have a lot of time," Ava said. "Besides, being horny gives me an edge. I should take that feeling into the meeting."

They eventually sat down at the table with cups of coffee and a plate of leftover dumplings. "I should leave here around nine-thirty," Ava said. "I'm meeting my friend Lop at the Éclat at eleven."

"You haven't told me what this Lop does that he's so connected," Fai said.

"He was an officer in the PLA, in Special Forces. Now he runs an operation for Xu in Hong Kong."

"Was it Xu or the military connection that secured this meeting?"

"It was the military, but when it comes to our getting what we want from Mo, I imagine that Lop's current job and state of mind will be more important factors."

"Is he a dangerous man?"

"Very."

"Good," Fai said.

After breakfast, Ava showered and dressed. Given who she was meeting, she took some care with her makeup, put on her Cartier watch, and joined her shirt cuffs with an exquisite pair of green jade links. She had debated which clothes to wear before opting for a light pink button-down, a black pencil skirt, and a pair of crocodile-skin stilettos she'd bought at the Brooks Brothers store in Tsim Sha Tsui.

Fai was waiting for her at the bottom of the stairs. She was still wearing the PÖ T-shirt but had added a pair of blue jeans. Her hair hadn't been brushed and it didn't seem that she'd washed, because Ava could see traces of sleep in her eyes. For all that, Ava thought she was the most beautiful woman she'd ever seen.

They walked hand in hand through the hutong, Fai waving at her neighbours. Ava was surprised at how openly Fai was displaying her affection, but then remembered that there she was among friends.

"You'll call me as soon as the meeting is over, won't you," Fai said as Ava got into the taxi.

"You can count on it."

"Good luck."

Ava took her phone from her bag as soon as the hutong disappeared from view. She turned it on and saw what she expected — a message from Derek. She accessed her voice-mail and listened. Then she took a Moleskine notebook from her bag, turned to the back page, and wrote *Fai* across the top. The notebook was a standard part of how she worked. Every job she'd taken with Uncle had its own book where she'd recorded names, numbers, observations, and her prog-ress. When the job was completed, the notebook was put in a safety deposit box at a bank near her Yorkville condo in Toronto. She found that the act of putting pen to paper helped her retain facts and assisted her thought processes, so it was a habit she'd taken with her to Three Sisters. The front page of this particular notebook had the name *Sun* written on it, and the following six pages contained information she'd found relevant as she worked through their files.

As the car made its way into Beijing traffic, Ava re-accessed Derek's voicemail and recorded at the back of the book the information he'd left. As usual, he hadn't let her down.

His wasn't the only message on the phone. She had been copied on various texts and emails going back and forth between May Ling, Amanda, and Suki. They were upbeat, and those from May and Amanda complimented Suki. May had also written directly to Ava asking about her schedule. *That will have to wait*, Ava thought. Suki had left a message saying the three real estate appraisals were expected to be finished within a couple of working days.

* * *

Traffic was better than it had been the day before and Ava found herself at the hotel's front door at ten-thirty. She found a seat in the lobby and sat down to wait for Lop. Despite her outer confidence, she had rarely felt so ill-prepared for a meeting. She knew virtually nothing of substance about Mo except for what Derek had sent her about his son. She also had no idea how Lop was going to behave. Her only direct experiences with him had been decidedly nonverbal, and she had no idea how persuasive he could be. It might fall to her, she thought, to convince Mo to abandon his Pang Fai plans, and right now she didn't have much to work with.

As she contemplated these possibilities a text arrived from Lop. *Just landed and am in a cab.*

Great, she thought as she checked the time. At this rate he wouldn't be at the hotel until maybe twelve. She stood up, intending to go to one of the restaurants, but then she saw some more of the hotel's art collection in a hallway to her left. *Why not see it all?* And for the next forty-five minutes that's what she did.

There were about a hundred pieces in total, she figured, and aside from the Warhol and the Dalis she'd seen previously, there were three Pierre Matters and many works by Chinese artists she'd never heard of. What she found most intriguing was that, while the works done by foreigners were very different, even odd, the Chinese art was mostly pedestrian. It was if the Chinese artists didn't want to be too avant-garde, to take too many risks. From the short biographies that accompanied each piece, she saw that most of the artists were under forty. They had been raised after the Cultural Revolution, in a system that didn't value eccentricity or individualism. She thought their work reflected that.

Ava's phone vibrated as she looked at a sculpture by Liu Ruowang that glorified the peasant class, titled *East Is Red*. It was a text from Lop, saying he was a few minutes away. Ava headed back to the lobby.

Unlike most Triad gang leaders, Xu cared about the image his men presented. He frowned on tattoos, mohawk haircuts, outlandish clothes, and gold teeth. His views reflected his personal taste but were also practical. He didn't want his men drawing unnecessary attention; he wanted them to blend in.

When Ava saw Lop enter the hotel lobby, she thought he could be mistaken for a successful businessman. He was a wiry five feet nine, dressed in brown khakis with a sharp crease down the front and a crisply ironed short-sleeved dark blue cotton shirt. His hair was cropped close to the scalp and his face was freshly shaved. He carried a brown leather overnight bag in one hand and a small brown briefcase in the other. He stopped just inside the door and looked around the lobby.

"Lop, I'm over here," Ava said, stepping into his line of sight.

He walked briskly towards her. When he was a couple of paces away, he stopped, brought his two hands together in front of his chest, and bowed slightly towards her. The show of respect stunned her. It was the last thing she'd expected from him.

"Ava, I'm sorry to be so late. I had forgotten what traffic is like here. Hong Kong has spoiled me." He looked at her as he spoke, but then his eyes darted left and right. Ava could feel the energy behind them.

"I'm just grateful that you organized this meeting and

that you came at all," she said. "We still have time to talk. Do you want to go into one of the restaurants or just sit here in the lobby?"

"I'm staying here tonight. I should check in and get rid of my bag. The lobby is fine for us to talk."

Ava found a sofa and waited for Lop. He was back in less than ten minutes.

"Did you manage to locate Mo's son?" he asked as soon as he'd joined her.

"I have his address, phone number, and the names of some of his friends," she said, not offended by his abruptness.

"Any interesting issues around him?"

"There could be, but it's the kind of information I hope we don't have to use."

"Mo and Zhang are really close, and that gives Mo some serious protection," Lop said, not pursuing her comment. "He's also been in this job for years, and evidently the Politburo's Standing Committee is happy with the way he's handled it."

"Are you saying that his son is the only leverage we have?"

"No. Xu and a couple of my PLA associates have given us permission to use their names and their interests as a way of trying to influence him."

"I don't understand."

"There's no point explaining until you agree that we can mention the PÖ brand and Pang Fai's involvement with it as part of the discussion."

"I need to know how all those things fit together."

Fifteen minutes later she did, and fifteen minutes after that she and Lop left the hotel to walk to the offices of the China Movie Syndicate. The sidewalks were crowded and they were forced to shuffle. Even then they were constantly being jostled, and more than once they were brought to a full stop by a wall of people. This would normally have aggravated Ava, but her mind was elsewhere. She couldn't stop thinking about the risk they were about to take. If the meeting didn't go well, if they didn't get the result they wanted, it wasn't just Pang Fai who could be damaged. The PÖ line could be obliterated.

10

THE SYNDICATE HAD ITS OFFICES IN A FORTY-FIVE-STOREY glass-enclosed building with no particular aesthetic qualities that were discernible from the street. The building's lobby was equally generic, which Ava found odd for an organization that was in the entertainment business. She hadn't expected neon lights, but a few framed movie posters wouldn't have been out of place. She and Lop walked across a marble floor to a large reception desk shaped like a horseshoe, passing the building registry as they went. A quick glance seemed to indicate that the Syndicate was the building's only occupant. Four people sat at the desk. Behind them, in brass letters, the name CHINA MOVIE SYNDICATE was affixed to the wall. There had been two security guards at the main entrance, and the desk was flanked by two more.

"We have an appointment with Mr. Mo," Lop said to a young woman.

"Name?" she asked.

"Lop."

She checked a computer and glanced up at him. "It says here there should be two of you, but there's no second name."

"This is Ms. Lee," Lop said. "She's meeting Mr. Mo with me."

"Fill out these name tags. You have to wear them at all times."

When they'd done so, the woman picked up a phone. "Could you please advise Mr. Mo that his one o'clock appointments are in the lobby," she said, and then listened before looking up at them. "Someone will be here shortly to escort you upstairs. You can wait over there."

Lop and Ava walked over to a line of leather-upholstered metal chairs set against the far wall. She continued to be unimpressed by the image presented by the Syndicate.

A constant stream of people filtered through the lobby, but after ten minutes there was still no sign of their escort. Lop's hands rested on his thighs, his fingers tapping like mad. Ava wondered if he was capable of presenting their case calmly.

"Mr. Lop and Ms. Lee," a woman said. She had appeared unseen from the right side of the lobby. "I work with Mr. Mo. Will you please follow me?"

The woman was middle-aged, of medium height, sturdy, and plainly dressed in a black business suit and flat shoes. They followed her beyond the reception desk to the main bank of elevators. She used an access card to open a side door and stood back to let them pass into a small hallway that had a waiting elevator. They stepped inside and Ava saw it had a button for only one floor, the forty-fifth.

The woman didn't speak as they rode to the top of the building. When the elevator stopped, she said, "Mr. Mo is still in another meeting, but I thought it would be more pleasant for you to wait here."

Stepping off the elevator, they walked into a large, square reception area that was far more luxurious than the downstairs lobby. Straight ahead, a young woman sat at a small wooden desk. Between her and the elevator was about twenty metres of hardwood floor covered in part by an immense, brightly coloured carpet. The walls were wood-panelled and festooned with pictures of Mao, Zhou Enlai, and the current premier, citations and awards from international film festivals, and photos of various movie stars, including Gong Li and Pang Fai. To either side of the desk was a sofa, chair, and coffee table ensemble.

"Can I bring you tea, coffee, or some water?" the woman asked.

"We're okay," Lop said.

"Then have a seat and I'll come for you when Mr. Mo is available."

They watched as the woman disappeared through a door behind the desk. "Doesn't exactly make you feel important, does it," Lop said.

"The meeting was at short notice."

"Xu would never keep anyone waiting like this. He has too much respect for other people."

"Are you working up a bit of a hate for Mo?"

"It's an easy thing to do, but he's hardly unique in Beijing. There are a lot of arrogant bureaucrats in this city."

"You'd know more about that than me," Ava said, and then saw the receptionist eyeing them. Could she hear what they were saying? "I think we should leave this topic alone for the moment."

"Yeah," said Lop.

The wait was less than ten minutes, but Ava felt every

second of it as Lop's agitation became more intense. It was a relief when the middle-aged woman reappeared and said, "Mr. Mo is ready for you now. Follow me."

They went through the door, made a sharp right, and followed her down a carpeted hallway towards a glass-enclosed boardroom that seemed to fill an entire corner of the floor. There were three people in the room. Two of them were young women who stood up when they entered. A man, who Ava assumed was Mo, remained seated.

"Welcome, Mr. Lop," one young woman said. "My name is Hua and my colleague is Chuntao. We're Mr. Mo's personal assistants and we're pleased to meet you and Ms. Lee. Have you been offered something to drink?"

"Yes, but there's nothing that we want right now."

Mo sat in a chair that was different from the others around the table. It was covered in red leather, not black like the rest, and it had a higher back. Mo had several files on the large table in front of him and his focus was on them. He hadn't bothered to look up when they entered the boardroom.

"Please take a seat," said Hua.

They sat next to each other, across from the young women and to the right of Mo. Hua smiled encouragingly at them, but Mo still hadn't acknowledged them.

Ava looked at him and guessed he was about fifty. He was wearing a grey suit, a white silk shirt, and a red Hermès tie. He had broad shoulders, a thick chest, and a head that seemed disproportionately large even for a body of his dimensions.

"I'll be just a minute," he said, finally lifting his head. "I have these papers I have to sign."

His voice was hoarse, and it was a match for a coarse

face that featured full, wet lips, a broad nose, and eyes that pressed close together. Ava had a fleeting image of him with Fai and felt a touch of nausea.

"There, all done," Mo said, and slid the files over to Chuntao.

She stood to leave but Hua remained seated.

"Thank you for agreeing to see us," Lop said.

"General Chik was quite insistent that I do, but he was vague about the specifics," Mo said.

"He's a good friend," Lop said.

"Evidently, and if you're going to have a good friend in Beijing, he's among the best anyone could have."

"He also has a personal interest in the outcome of our meeting."

"Are you saying that the General is getting into movies?"

"Not at all."

"Please don't speak in riddles. I've only allocated fifteen minutes for this meeting," Mo said, showing some impatience.

Lop nodded towards Hua. "What we want is clear enough, but it's something best expressed in private."

Mo leaned back in his chair and stared at them through hooded eyes. He had a presence that Ava thought was rather dark and menacing; it reminded her in some ways of Sammy Wing, the former Triad gang leader in Wanchai. Sammy was given to long silences followed by cryptic comments that were usually veiled threats.

Neither Lop nor Ava averted their eyes. As Mo's flicked between them, she saw that Lop was the one who had clearly captured his interest.

"Ms. Hua, could you please leave us alone," Mo said. "But

let me know when Mr. Lop's fifteen minutes are finished."

She hesitated and then said, "Yes, sir."

Mo waited until she closed the door before he leaned forward and almost snarled, "What the hell is this about?"

"We needed to talk to you and the General volunteered to create the opportunity. I'm sorry if we were less than forthcoming about the reason, but the General thought that was best as well."

"Talk to me about what?"

"Money," Lop said.

"That's a very broad subject."

"Specifically, the General and some associates have invested in several businesses in and around Shanghai," Lop said. "One of them is a fashion line. We are talking about an investment in the tens of millions of U.S. dollars, and we are talking about a return that could be in the hundreds of millions."

"What could that possibly have to do with me?"

"The actress Pang Fai is promoting the line. In fact, she's become its face. Her continuing commitment will be instrumental to its success."

"As I said, what does that have to do with me?"

"How blunt do you want me to be?"

"You're here and we're alone. Speak as freely as you want."

"Our understanding is that you, and perhaps some of your colleagues, have been extracting various favours from Ms. Pang for several years in return for financing and distributing films in which she's appeared. She's made it clear to us that she no longer wants to be so giving, but she's afraid that her refusal to maintain the status quo — such as going on a trip to Thailand with you — will have a negative impact on her career," Lop said, and then paused. "Specifically, she's worried that the Syndicate will withdraw its support for any projects in which she's involved. Among them is the film *Mao's Daughter*. She's asked us to intervene on her and the film's behalf, and that's why we're here."

"What the fuck do you mean by 'favours'?"

"There was a suggestion that some of them were sexual in nature."

Mo's eyes closed for several seconds, and Ava saw his upper body stiffen. *He's going to explode*, she thought. Instead he offered a small smile and said, "You have just displayed an amazing amount of arrogance and ignorance."

"I have been known to possess both," Lop said.

"That doesn't surprise me."

Lop shrugged. "My personality failings don't matter. What does is Pang Fai's continuing involvement in promotion of the fashion line. We have it now, but to keep it she's insisting that we persuade you to drop your demands of her. And to continue to maximize her impact, we obviously need you to keep supporting her career and her films exactly as you've been doing. "

"I have no fucking idea what you mean by 'demands,'" Mo said. "We've financed and distributed her films for years, and I'm not aware of a single thing we've asked in return. That Thailand trip you mentioned, for example, is one of several outings we organize each year for people in the industry. It gives them a chance to network and it's considered a privilege to be asked. She's free to say no."

"Maybe we were misinformed," Lop said. "If we were, you have our apologies."

"I don't want an apology. What I want is for you to leave."

"Of course, and we will momentarily," Lop said. "But first, can we assume that you will release, distribute, and promote *Mao's Daughter*, if for no other reason than as a favour for General Chik?"

Mo glared at him.

"And next, can we assume that Pang Fai's career will continue to be as productive and high-profile as it has been?"

"Those are two very different questions," Mo said slowly.

"You can answer them in any order you wish," Lop said.

"Your attitude isn't helping this conversation," Mo said, and pursed his lips.

"I'm sorry if I seem rude," Lop said quickly. "But you should understand that I'm expected to leave here with clear answers for General Chik and the other shareholders."

Mo stared at Lop as if he was trying to determine his sincerity. Then he nodded and said, "Pang Fai has been one of our greatest actresses. Sadly, she's at an age where her appeal is starting to fade. The days are gone when her participation in a film guarantees that it will automatically be financed and distributed. We won't abandon her, but truthfully, it has to be expected that there will be fewer projects that suit her. That may seem cruel, but it's the nature of this business. So you can tell the General and the other shareholders that if they're counting on her being the face of their brand, they'd be wise not to make it a long-term commitment. I understand they may not be happy to hear that, but the Syndicate has its own mandate. It can't make decisions based on someone else's commercial needs."

Ava leaned forward, but before she could say anything, Lop spoke up. "And what about the release of *Mao's Daughter*?"

"We have been directed by the Politburo Standing Committee to support films that extol patriotism," Mo said. "It is important that people maintain correct views of our history, statehood, and culture. We are expressly forbidden to authorize the distribution of films that cater to vulgar interests and provoke unrest."

"And where does *Mao's Daughter* rank in terms of 'correct views'?"

"It doesn't rate well, and I'm sure that's an opinion General Chik would share if he saw it."

"What you seem to be saying is that he'll never have the opportunity."

"That is a decision that will be made within the Syndicate."

"Has it already been made?"

"Nothing is final, but the prevailing opinion is that the film is unacceptable as it is presently constructed."

"Your positions on Pang Fai and the film could cause us problems," Lop said.

"That isn't my concern. I have responsibilities that extend well beyond your commercialism, the needs of an aging actress, and a troublesome film," he said. "Besides, it seems to me that she's your real problem. If that's the case, then you should just pay her more. I can tell you, if you pay her enough the woman will do just about anything."

"I don't believe that insulting Pang Fai is necessary," Ava said softly.

Mo turned and stared at her. It was his first real acknowledgement that she was in the room. Ava had to give him credit for being smooth enough to turn his feelings about Fai and his reaction to the film into a response that neither admitted nor denied anything. He had been cold and bureaucratic until his very last comment.

"I know why he's here," Mo said, nodding at Lop. "But why are you here?"

"Ms. Lee is a partner and a major shareholder in the fashion business."

"And I have a question —"

Before she could say anything else, the boardroom door opened and the assistant Hua reappeared. "You wanted me to tell you when fifteen minutes had elapsed," she said. "It has."

Mo stood up. He was shorter and even broader than he looked when seated. "Give General Chik my regards. Tell him I wish him good luck with his business interests, and even better luck dealing with that woman," he said, and then walked through the doorway.

The assistant stepped aside for him. After he'd gone, she said, "I'll walk the two of you to the elevator. Please give me your name tags before you leave."

"I'll say this for him," Ava said as she and Lop turned to leave the boardroom after Mo's sudden departure. "He sure knows how to end a meeting."

11

AVA AND LOP DIDN'T SPEAK AGAIN UNTIL THEY WERE on the sidewalk. "What did you think of Mo, aside from the fact that he had us removed from the building so efficiently?" she said.

"He's smart and shrewd."

"Did you believe what he said about Pang Fai, the film, and the way the system operates? He made it all seem so innocuous."

Lop's eyes met hers. "I think he's full of shit when it comes to Pang Fai. For the rest of it, I don't know."

"We need to talk this through."

"I agree. Do you want to do it over lunch?"

"Sure. Shall we go back to the hotel to eat?"

"No — I can't come back to Beijing and not have duck. There's a restaurant near here called Da Dong. It's no more than a ten-minute walk."

Lop's ten minutes was optimistic; it took closer to thirty to get to Da Dong. There was so much noise from the traffic, sidewalk vendors, and pedestrians that they couldn't have had a conversation even if they'd wanted to. Ava thought several times that she should call Fai, but she didn't want to shout, and she also thought it would be wise to hear what else Lop had to say before she did.

They had missed the lunchtime traffic crunch but the restaurant was still almost full, and they were fortunate to be seated right away.

"I'm going to have a beer. What are you drinking?" Lop asked.

"Dry white wine."

"The only thing I ever order here is duck. Are you okay with that?"

"Sure."

It took a few minutes for a server to get to their table, and when he did, Lop ordered the food and drink at once. "What did you think of Mo?" he asked when they were alone again.

"I thought he was slick. He didn't give us one direct answer, but all the implications were clear enough. I'm convinced that he plans to sabotage Pang Fai's career and kill the film, but he never actually said so and left lots of wiggle room in case he's ever challenged. He even made the Thailand trip seem innocent."

"He wouldn't have hustled us out of the building the way he did if he was innocent," Lop said. "And I don't think he'll be letting us back in there for a second round."

"I was certainly hoping for more than we got," Ava said.

"I guess I could have been more forceful."

"I thought you did just fine. We just happened to run into a real pro."

"So now what?"

"We need to talk to him again, and we need to get him alone to do it."

"Any ideas on how to make that possible?"

"Not yet."

"I have Mo's home address, if that helps," Lop said.

"Where does he live?"

"I wrote it down but didn't really look at it," Lop said, taking a piece of paper from his pocket. "Fuck, he lives in Zhangnanhai. Have you heard of it?"

"I've been told it's the new Forbidden City."

"Yes. There's no way we're going to be able to visit him there without his express approval. What does that leave us?"

"Let me think about it. I'll come up with something," Ava said, her tone more confident than she felt.

A server arrived with their drinks. As she poured, another server came to the table carrying platters of food.

"I'm looking forward to this," Lop said. "It's the best duck I've ever had."

"What makes it so special?"

"I don't know."

Ava was accustomed to duck brought to the table whole and then the skin being sliced off as thinly as possible by the server. At Da Dong the skin was brought to the table on one platter and the meat on another. As she watched the server place skin, meat, and accompaniments on the table, she asked, "Can you tell me why your duck has such a good reputation?"

The server looked at her as if Ava had made a joke.

"That is a serious question," Ava said. "I want to know what makes it so different."

"Our cook starts by separating the skin from the fat by pumping air between them," the server said carefully. "Then he marinates the bird in a house-made sauce and air-dries the skin before he roasts it. But where we are most special is that he cooks the duck for at least twenty minutes more than is typical, and he does it over burning fruitwood. This removes extra fat and makes the skin crisper and less oily. Here, try some."

The server took a sliver of skin, dipped it in sugar, and passed it to Ava. She took a bite and almost gasped as the crisp skin dissolved into a stream of flavour.

"I also like what they do with the meat," Lop said, picking up a hollow bun, into which he stuffed duck meat, bean paste, julienned cucumbers, radishes, and the white parts of scallions.

They ate quietly, Lop more focused on the meat, while Ava went back and forth between that and the skin. It was the best duck she'd ever eaten, but her enjoyment was dulled by thoughts about Mo and what he might do to Fai and *Mao's Daughter*. She was about to raise the issue again when her phone rang. She didn't recognize the number and hesitated before hitting the answer button.

"This is Ava Lee," she said.

"What the fuck have you done?" an unfamiliar voice growled.

"Who is this?"

"Chen."

"And what is it that I'm supposed to have done?"

"Mo!" he yelled.

"What about Mo?" she said, her heart sinking.

"Did you go to his office today?"

"I did."

"Why? Why did you do that, you stupid fucking bitch?"

Ava drew a deep breath, trying to stay calm and not

overreact. "Our intention was to stop his exploitation of Fai and to secure some kind of future for her and *Mao's Daughter*, but before we could secure those commitments, he rushed out of the boardroom. We aren't finished with him yet."

"Who authorized you to do that? What kind of qualifications or credibility do you have?"

"I've done things like this before," she said.

"Do you mean you've fucked up like this before? Because, believe me, that's what you've done," Chen shouted. "Those intentions you had — those good intentions — well, you've managed to achieve exactly the opposite result. As far as the Syndicate is concerned, Pang Fai is history, and the movie might as well never have been made."

"Mo told you that?"

"Don't show any more of your ignorance."

"Then how —"

"He's too smart to leave his fingerprints on anything," Chen said. "His assistant Hua called me to say that Fai's invitation to Thailand has been cancelled. Then Deng, the vice-president of creative development, phoned to say that two projects we proposed that had parts for Fai have been rejected. And ten minutes ago I heard from the VP of distribution that *Mao's Daughter* isn't going to be released unless major changes are made. What he didn't say — and didn't have to — was that eliminating every scene that has Fai in it is the only change that is acceptable."

"How did you know that I had been there, that I had anything to do with any of this?"

"Hua told me that you and your friend Lop met with Mo and mentioned Thailand. She said that if Fai didn't want to go, Mo was only too happy to comply," Chen said. "Another thing I don't know is, who the hell is Lop?"

"He's a friend. You don't need to know anything else."

"And actually it doesn't matter if I do. It's enough that you've destroyed Fai's career and put my business at risk."

"It's premature to say that."

"Bullshit. It's already happened."

"So that's it? There's nothing more that can be done?"

"Maybe if I crawl on my hands and knees, kiss Mo's feet, and beg for forgiveness he won't take this out on my other clients. But there's nothing I can do to save Fai."

"He really has that much power?"

"No, he has *all* the power. Without Mo's support, very few films get made, and none of them get distributed."

Ava shook her head slowly, and as she did she noticed that Lop was keenly following her end of the conversation. "Have you told Fai about what happened?" she asked Chen.

"Yeah. That's how I got your phone number."

"How did she react?"

"Far more calmly than I would have expected."

"I'm glad to hear that."

"Don't be. I've known her far longer than you and I know her every little quirk. As the weeks and months pass and there's no work, her calmness will turn into panic, and then hysteria. I can tell you from experience that dealing with her then won't be a picnic."

"Chen, she's tired of prostituting herself. She's a great actress. Her talent should be enough to secure her future."

"Prostituting herself? Consensual sex between two adults is hardly prostitution, and until now I've never heard her complain. I blame you for this. You've poisoned her mind with your lesbian bullshit," he said, his voice rising again. "This is how the system works here. It's how it's always worked. There's no magic fairy dust that produces movies or makes stars. Nothing happens unless the Syndicate says yes, and it's not going to say yes just because someone can act or they like a script. There's a quid pro quo that needs to be respected. It's not so much about the sex as it is about recognizing and acknowledging who exercises power in the Syndicate. It's all about power."

"That's a very perceptive comment," Ava said softly.

"What the hell are you talking about?"

"Never mind, it doesn't matter. Let's move on," Ava said. "Tell me, is there anything we can do — that Fai can do — to soften the Syndicate's attitude?"

"She can crawl with me or she can crawl on her own," Chen said after a slight hesitation. "Mo does like her; he likes her a lot. He might back off if she's conciliatory enough."

"You mean submissive enough?"

"You asked me what she could do and I've told you. I'm not going to repeat it, classify it, or justify it."

Ava hesitated and then said, "I'll talk to her."

That seemed to have caught Chen off guard. He started to say something and then suddenly stopped. When he spoke again, his manner was distinctly more subdued. "It would be good if you could. She obviously listens to you," he said. "If it helps, I don't think going to Thailand would have to be part of any arrangement. Mo might let that go if he's sure she's still part of his team."

Part of his team? Ava thought. *That's a subtle way of describing submission.* But all she said was, "So you're sure he would meet with her?"

"If he's approached in the right way."

"Can you handle that?"

"No. It has to be Fai who makes the request."

"You mean if she begs."

"Fuck. For a moment there I thought you were being sensible."

"Sorry," Ava said quickly. "I just find it distasteful. I know it's necessary, but I can't help feeling the way I do."

"As hard as it may be for you to believe, I have similar feelings," he said. "But business is business and sometimes we have to let things go."

"I'll talk to Fai."

"Just like that?"

"Yes. I'll talk to her this afternoon."

"Good. And now can I give you some advice?"

"It sounds like you're going to whether I want to hear it or not."

"First, stay out of my business. You don't understand it, as your escapade of earlier today clearly proves," he said. "Next, I don't care what you and Fai do behind closed doors, but just keep it there. The only thing that could cause her more damage than pissing off Mo is for her adoring public to find out that she's a *lala*. There's no surviving that in this culture."

Ava didn't reply.

He waited for a moment and then added, "I'm not anti-gay. I just need to make sure you understand what's at stake."

"I understand perfectly well," Ava said.

"And you'll still talk to Fai?"

"I will."

"Ask her to call me when she's decided what to do," Chen said. "I think that strategically it might be better if she talked to Mo first, to get the emotions out of the way. Then I can follow up and rebuild some kind of working relationship."

"I'll pass that message along to her," Ava said, and then ended the call.

Lop tried not to stare at her from across the table, but his focus kept shifting from the buns and meat to her, until it was fully on her. "That didn't sound very good," he said.

"Mo's surrogates from the Syndicate called Fai's agent, Chen, and in a roundabout way told him that Fai and the film are history."

"We did expect that outcome."

"I know. They just moved faster than I imagined. I would have liked the opportunity to tell Fai myself what happened. Instead, Chen did."

"So now what?"

"Chen thinks that if Fai begs Mo for forgiveness there is a chance it will be granted."

"Would you really ask her to do that?"

"As I said, I think we need to meet with Mo again, and we need to meet him in a place where he's not surrounded by security," Ava said.

"You'd use Fai as bait?"

"I prefer the word 'enticement,' but I guess they aren't really that different. One just sounds better than the other."

12

AVA AND FAI SAT AT THE TABLE IN THE KITCHEN. IT WAS becoming a familiar and comfortable locale for Ava, a place for conversation, a place where secrets weren't necessary. In some ways it reminded her of the pond in Xu's courtyard. He had a small table and some folding chairs next to it, and that was where he and Ava most often explored whatever dramas were going on in their lives. Fai's kitchen didn't have quite the same atmosphere, but it still made her feel there was nothing that couldn't be said within its walls. Ava realized that level of trust came more from who she was speaking to than where they were, but still, an almost unconscious link was triggered by the locations.

It was late afternoon when Ava finished describing to Fai her meeting with Mo and her phone conversation with Chen. The only things she'd excluded were Mo's description of her as an aging actress and what Ava thought their plan of action should be. Lop had gone to the hotel to wait for Ava to decide what they were going to do next. They decided he should also call General Chik to give him a heads-up in case Mo tried to make an issue of the General's supposed involvement. Lop was confident that he would find it amusing rather than worrisome, since people of his rank in the PLA were typically immune to the anger of bureaucrats and politicians unless they meddled in politics directly.

"Did Chen really use the word 'crawl'?" Fai asked when Ava finished.

"Yes, but he was quite emotional and might not have meant it literally."

"I wouldn't bet on it. He has so much at stake that I can't think of many things he wouldn't do if Mo insisted on it," Fai said. "Five years ago I represented probably fifty percent of his business income. Now I doubt I'm as much as twenty. He's got Tsang and at least one other good director, plus five or six talented young actors."

"Well, whatever he chooses to do, he can do it alone. You don't have to watch him debase himself."

"But if I don't do anything, where does that leave me?"

"That depends on you, Fai. You need to make a decision about what it is you want most and what you're prepared to do to get it."

"I want to continue my career and have *Mao's Daughter* released, but not at the cost of my dignity or our relationship," she said, and then paused. "The night before last we talked about options."

"We still have some. All we've done is exhaust one, and it would have been naive to think our first effort would be successful. Think of it as a trial run, as a chance for my friend Lop and me to size up Mo."

"What else do you have in mind?"

"Well, we tried a subtle approach by invoking General Chik and his business interests. It was worth the effort, because if nothing else if gave us some insight into what Mo thinks is important," Ava said. "For example, when we dangled the idea that there was a lot of money involved, Mo didn't bite. Lop says he doesn't know many other senior officials who would be so blasé; most of them would have been negotiating some kind of payday the moment money was mentioned. We think that Mo has all the money he needs and is now more turned on by power and control."

"Ava, I have no idea what you're trying to say."

"We need to remove his sense of control from a part of his life that he cares deeply about. We need to make him feel vulnerable."

"How is that possible?"

"He has a son that he worships. He's at university in the U.S., and I'm sure Mo's planning the brightest imaginable future for him. We're going to make that future seem much less certain."

Fai recoiled, her eyes blinking and her lips tightly clenched. She began to rub her forehead. "You'd harm his son?"

"Of course not. But we have to create the illusion that his son's future is at risk in other ways," she said quickly. "Remember what I told you about people doing the right thing for the wrong reason? My friend Derek found out some things about Mo's son that he would hate becoming public. Threatening to disclose that information might give us the leverage we need."

"What kind of things?"

"We're still collecting details. I don't think it's worth discussing any further until we have everything pulled together."

"Ava, how do you even start to come up with ideas like

this? And how do you have the nerve to see them through, to take on people like Mo who scare everyone else around them?"

"I've led a life that's developed incrementally, bit by bit, experience by experience," Ava said, surprised by Fai's question. "I didn't start out being who I am today. The debt-collection business made self-preservation a necessity, and there wasn't much room for doubt or inaction. The bottom line was that I had to make the effort to succeed or there was absolutely no chance of winning. And when I made the effort, I put aside all thoughts about losing."

"Was there violence?"

"Sometimes. I tried to avoid it, but there were times when it was inevitable and necessary."

"One of the models in London, a girl from Hong Kong, said she heard that you'd saved Carrie Song's brother's life. Is that true?"

"Yes, but that makes it sound more dramatic than it was."

"How could it possibly not be dramatic?"

"It was a spur-of-the-moment reaction to a situation that was messy and out of control. There was nothing heroic about it; it was all about survival."

"But you did it, and you've done other stuff like that?"

"I was in the business for more than ten years. You couldn't avoid confrontations if you wanted to be successful."

"How did you get so close to Xu?"

"I think I told you before that we were both mentored by Uncle, but we weren't aware of that or each other until Uncle died. Then we met and we bonded."

"And the things Xu must have done don't bother you?"

"If I wanted to live in the past, they might. I prefer to

take people as I find them. Like I said the other night, we've all done things we're ashamed of, or are at least not proud of — me included. But we're all governed by circumstances, some of which we can't control. We do what we need to do to survive, like me with Carrie Song's brother. Once it's done, there's no point in reliving it. Xu has been honest and supportive since the day I met him, and I trust him completely. Why should I let other people's opinions about actions he may have taken in the past colour my view of the man I see and know now?"

"Is that why you were so accepting of everything I told you about Lau Lau, and about what I did with Mo and the others?"

"Would you prefer me to have a different attitude?"

"Of course not," Fai said quickly. "I just find it hard some days to escape my past. I find myself fixating on things I've done that make me ashamed, or I think about things that have been done to me and I feel such...hate."

"I've never carried grudges," Ava said. "If I have an issue with someone, I've always taken it to them directly. Then, once it's out of my system, I move on."

"And now you want to take my issue directly to Mo?"

"I do, but I can't do it without you."

"What do you need me to do?"

"We need to meet with him alone, and we think that's unlikely to happen unless you can persuade him."

"How do you propose I do that?"

"Chen says that if you call Mo and ask him to meet with you, he might do it," Ava said.

"I'm sure the word 'beg' was used instead of 'ask,'" Fai said.

"It was, but it doesn't have to be like that. You can tell

Mo that you made an offhand remark that the PÖ people misinterpreted, and that they contacted him without your knowledge or approval. Tell him you want to make amends, that you want to restore the relationship you have with him personally and with the Syndicate."

"If he says yes?"

"Then arrange to meet him somewhere private. We don't want him making a fuss in public that might draw attention to us. We want to talk to him alone, and we need his undivided attention."

"Do you actually want me to meet with him?"

"No, that won't be necessary. Lop and I will be there waiting for him. We'll handle it."

Fai's eyes wandered from the table towards the small window that faced the courtyard. "In the past we met at the Kempinski Hotel," she whispered.

"A hotel room is perfect."

"He always had the Syndicate book the room."

"This time tell him you're going to do it as a way of saying sorry."

"What if he says no?"

"To which part of it, meeting you at the hotel or you making the room reservation?"

"Meeting me."

"You have to be as persuasive as you can, but if it doesn't work, we'll figure out something else."

"Like what?"

"I don't know yet, and I actually don't want to go there, because it implies you'll fail. Let's keep things positive."

"Okay, I can do that," she said.

"If he agrees, I'll make the booking in my name," Ava said.

"I'll go to the hotel, check in, and phone you with the room number, and then you can pass it along to Mo."

"What if he calls the hotel and asks for me? What if he has to change plans and needs to contact me?"

"You're jumping ahead again," Ava said quickly, and saw Fai flinch. "I don't mean to sound impatient. If you can get him to agree to come to the hotel, tell him to call or text you if things change. I'm quite sure he can understand why you would want to be discreet."

"You're right, he would. I'm not thinking clearly. When do you want me to call him?"

"As soon as possible."

"I'll do it now, but I don't want you to be here when I talk to him. I don't want you listening to what I'll have to say in order to get him to the hotel."

"And I don't want to hear it," Ava said. "I'm going for a walk."

13

AVA HAD SEEN THE HUTONG ONLY IN THE EARLY MORNING
or late in the day, and given that she had been with Fai or
distracted at those times, she hadn't really paid it much
attention. She'd also only seen the half of the hutong that
ran between the entrance Fai used and the house. Now she
walked in the opposite direction, past small shops selling
food, clothes, and tobacco. She stopped in surprise when
she came across doors with signs that indicated they led
to public bathrooms and toilets. She opened one door and
saw a full bathroom. She could only assume that not all the
homes in the hutong had washroom facilities.

She turned away to see an elderly man staring at her from
the other side of the hutong. He was sitting at a table inside a
place called "The Little Tea Room." The sign didn't lie. Five
tables were squeezed inside a space that could accommodate
only them and a glass case that contained a variety of buns
and tarts.

"Let me buy you tea," the man said.

Ava hesitated, not quite sure if he was talking to her.

"I live in the same courtyard as Pang Fai. I've seen you

coming and going," he said. "If you're going to be a regular visitor, we should get to know each other."

What the hell, Ava thought, and in four strides was across the lane. "I'm Ava Lee," she said.

"My name is Fan. Please sit."

The man was wearing blue jeans and a plain white T-shirt. His grey hair was plaited and tied in the back. His face was heavily lined, and when he smiled at Ava, she saw that his teeth were yellow. He had to be close to eighty. Ava was still wearing the clothes she'd worn to the meeting with Mo and felt distinctly overdressed.

"I'm drinking green tea. It's supposed to be the best for your health," Fan said. "But they have all kinds here, so you can have green, black, white, oolong, or scented."

"Green will do just fine, thank you."

The man stood, went to a shelf off to one side, and took a cup from it. He placed the cup in front of Ava and poured. "Would you like a bun? They don't make them here, but they buy them daily from another hutong only a few hundred metres from here."

"The tea will be enough."

"I saw you looking into the bathroom," he said as he watched her sip.

"A public bathroom isn't something I'm used to seeing in the middle of a major city."

"It's a relic. Nearly all of us have indoor plumbing but none of us want to see it closed. It reminds us of our past. There are enough developers trying to destroy the hutongs that the idea of knocking down any part of one is abhorrent."

"How long have you lived here?"

"More than forty years. I'm a writer, and originally I lived with four colleagues in a house about the same size as Fai's. But as they moved out and one died, I gradually acquired ownership."

"So you know Fai — personally, I mean?"

"I do, but I knew Lau Lau better. We used to drink together. I wrote a couple of scripts for him that never amounted to anything, but I rewrote one and it was made into a film."

"Do you still see him or hear from him?"

"From time to time. But he's a very unhappy man, and at my age I prefer not being surrounded by misery. There's enough of it going around naturally that I don't want to invite more in," Fan said. "Besides, I don't like the way he talks about Fai. She's been a good neighbour and friend to everyone in the hutong, and that's all that matters to me. What went on between them should stay between them. I've tried telling him that but he can't help himself, so I try to stay away from him now."

There was something in Fan's manner that Ava found a little off-putting. It wasn't so much what he was saying as the way he said it. She felt that his remark about what had gone on between Fai and Lau Lau wasn't just a comment; it was an invitation for her to ask questions that would give him a chance to gossip and then pry into her affairs. *This is a sly old man*, she thought, and then said, "This is the first hutong I've ever seen. You seem to know a lot about them. How many still exist in Beijing?"

"There are about a thousand left. When I came to Beijing, there were more than three thousand," he said, not seeming to mind her redirecting the conversation. "This one is three hundred years old, but there are some that go back five and six hundred years. The word 'hutong' is Mongolian and

means 'water well.' In the north it was customary to build
large courtyards around wells and then extend lanes and
alleys out like bicycle spokes from the courtyards. Our lane
is a bit less than ten metres across, which is about average,
but I've seen some as narrow as seven metres, and hardly
any wider than ten. Many of the hutongs are interconnected
through various courtyards, so we're all neighbours."

"Have you banded together to fight off the developers?"

"We try, but our biggest problem is the government. The
developers can't do anything without its approval, and until
a few years ago, approvals could be bought. That's stopped
for now, but we have to keep the pressure on. One good
thing is that the hutongs have become a tourist attraction — although not this one, because we're too ordinary.
But Skewed Tobacco Pouch Street, South Gong and Drum
Lane, and Coloured Glaze Factory Street are all fashionable,
so we use their drawing power to help defend our lane," he
said, and then paused. "A few years ago, when Lau Lau was at
his peak, when he was the most famous filmmaker in China,
he wanted to make a documentary about the destruction of
the hutongs, but nothing came of it. He blames Pang Fai for
that as well. He said she discouraged him by telling him he
would only anger local Party leaders and make it harder to
get financing for his other films."

Ava finished her tea. "If I were to visit one hutong, which
one would you recommend?"

"Nanluoguxiang, South Gong and Drum Lane," he said,
again quite nonplussed by her avoidance of talking about
Lau Lau and Fai. "It dates back to the Yuan Dynasty, so
it's at least seven hundred years old. It still has the traditional board-style residences and is the closest thing you

can see to what was the original texture of the hutong."

"Thank you," Ava said, and then glanced at her phone as it alerted her to an incoming text message. It was from Fai and read simply Done. Ava stood up. "I have to go now. I've really enjoyed your company, and I'm sure we'll see more of each other."

"If you don't mind me asking, what is it that you do?" Fan said.

Ava knew the question he really wanted to ask was *What are you doing with Pang Fai?* "I'm an accountant," she said.

"I'm sure Pang Fai could use a good one. Actors and writers aren't trained when it comes to handling money. If Lau Lau had had better management support, he might still be making movies today."

"You could be right," Ava said, and then turned and walked back along the hutong.

She was almost at the entrance to Fai's compound when her phone rang. "Hey, Suki," she answered.

"I'm calling to confirm dinner with the Suns tonight," Suki said.

"Oh shit, I'd forgotten about that."

"You are still coming, aren't you?"'

"Of course."

"Thank god. It would have been hard to explain if you weren't. The Suns have booked a small room in the Lost Heaven restaurant, near Tiananmen Square. Aside from being one of the best restaurants in the city, it serves Yunnan cuisine, and that's where Mrs. Sun is from originally. She only goes there for very special occasions."

"I was in Yunnan not that long ago, in Kunming, the capital," Ava said.

"Make sure you say nice things about it. She's proud of her heritage."

"What time are we booked for?"

"Eight o'clock."

"Can I bring a guest?"

"You can bring as many guests as you want. This is a celebration, so the more the merrier. Mrs. Sun told me the room seats up to sixteen people. So far there's me, you, the Suns, and six other people from their business."

"Suki, if I bring a guest, it will be Pang Fai — the actress."

"You don't have to tell me who Pang Fai is."

"Sorry."

"No, I'm sorry. I shouldn't have reacted like that. You just caught me off guard," Suki said. "All I can tell you is that if you do bring Pang Fai, it will cause a sensation. Mrs. Sun's only addiction is movies."

"Do you want me to let you know ahead of time if she is coming?"

"No. I won't say anything to Mrs. Sun. Let's make it a surprise if it happens. If it doesn't, no one's going to be disappointed, except for me."

"So I'll see you at eight, then," Ava said, stepping inside the small courtyard. She walked up to Fai's door and paused. She knocked to announce her arrival and then, after a few seconds, opened the door.

Fai sat on the couch, her head resting against the back and her eyes closed.

"Are you okay?" Ava asked.

"I'm trying to make myself feel clean again," Fai said, not opening her eyes.

"Do you want to talk about it, or do you just want to move on?"

"Come and sit next to me," Fai said, patting the couch. "Where did you go?"

"The Little Tea Room. I met your neighbour, Mr. Fan."

"He likes to think he's everyone's friend, and he is, until they get to know him."

"That was the impression I had."

Fai leaned towards Ava until her head found a shoulder. "I was very nervous when I phoned Mo," she said. "The receptionist put me on hold for what seemed like forever, and I thought he wasn't going to take my call. But he did, and the moment I heard his voice I started to cry and ramble. It was like I was on autopilot."

"How quickly did he react?"

"He had to cut me off to do it," Fai said. "He told me he'd suspected that there had been some miscommunication, because he couldn't understand how I could think that he and the Syndicate weren't committed to supporting me."

"How did you leave it?"

"Two o'clock tomorrow afternoon at the Kempinski," Fai said, and drew a deep breath.

"Okay, but like I said, you don't have to be in the room tomorrow when he arrives."

"Never mind the room. I don't want to be anywhere near the hotel," Fai said. "I've watched him intimidate, dominate, and humiliate people for years, but as much as I want to see how he reacts when the tables are turned, I'm not sure I could handle it."

"Then I think our decision is the correct one," Ava said, and looked at her watch. "Now I need to make some phone calls so that we're properly organized for tomorrow, and you need to make another decision about tonight."

"Who are you calling?"

"The hotel to make a reservation, and then Lop and my friend Derek Liang in Toronto."

"Toronto?"

"Derek is the person who's been collecting information on Mo's son. I need him to accelerate the process."

"And what about tonight?"

"I'm invited to a dinner to celebrate a business deal that our partner Suki Chan and I just finalized. There will be about ten other people there, most of them local and attached to the logistics company we've just bought. I have to go, and I'd like you to come with me."

Fai looked hesitant.

"They are lovely people, and I know that at least two of them are big fans," Ava said. "They've booked a private room at a restaurant called Lost Heaven, which is supposed to be one of the best in the city."

"I'd rather be at home alone with you, but if you have to go, I guess I'm going too," Fai said.

"If nothing else, it will be a distraction."

"I don't need a distraction," Fai said. "I'm looking forward to tomorrow, and I don't need anything to take my mind off it."

"Fai, there are no guarantees that tomorrow will go the way we want," Ava warned.

"I'll be okay even if it doesn't work, because I've already stopped feeling like a victim."

AVA CALLED THE KEMPINSKI FIRST TO RESERVE A ROOM in the name of Jennie Kwong. It was an identity she'd used off and on while she was working with Uncle, and she always carried a passport and credit card registered to that name. She knew she was probably being overly cautious, but she had no idea how diligent Mo was, and she didn't want to find out the hard way. There were rooms available, but she had to pay a premium to ensure early check-in. Then she phoned Lop and briefed him on the arrangements. They agreed to meet in the Kempinski lobby at noon to review their story.

She waited until six-thirty to call Derek. She knew the baby was usually up by six but wanted to give him time to feed her and have a coffee. Mimi answered the phone, and the two women had a quick conversation before Ava talked to Derek. Mimi knew a lot about Ava's past life, including her sexuality. In fact it had been Mimi who introduced Ava to her previous girlfriend, Maria Gonzalez. Ava didn't mind sharing bits of her personal life with Mimi, but this wasn't the time to talk about Fai, so they chatted generally about the baby and Mimi's job before the phone was passed to Derek.

Ava went over the information he'd given her the day before and then asked him to expand it as much as possible. "I need the information by eleven p.m. your time, and preferably sooner. I know I'm asking for a lot, but I need absolutely everything you can dig up on the son, including photos," she concluded.

"Do you care how you get it?" he asked.

"What do you mean?"

"Do you want it in one package or should I send it to you as I collect it?"

"Send it as you get it."

"And how do you want it sent? Text? Email? Phone?"

"Whichever way works best for you, but if you get pictures I would prefer them to be attached to an email."

"I'll get started as soon as Mimi leaves for work."

While Ava made her phone calls, Fai showered and got dressed for dinner. Ava was sitting in the kitchen when she came down the stairs wearing flat shoes, black jeans, and a plain long-sleeved white cotton blouse. Her hair was still damp and brushed close to the scalp. She wore no makeup, but her cheeks were bright pink and her face almost glowed.

"This is my going-out-in-Beijing look," Fai said when she saw Ava staring at her. "It may not be effective as a disguise, but it does cause people to question if I'm actually who I appear to be."

Ava looked at her own slacks, shirt, and jewellery. "This is the second time today I've felt overdressed, and I'm not often accused of that," she said and stood up. "I'm going to change."

"Don't. I love the way you look."

"At the very least I should freshen up and put on a clean shirt," said Ava.

She climbed the stairs and went into the bedroom, where she took out a fresh pale pink Brooks Brothers shirt from her Shanghai Tang Double Happiness bag. She carried it to the bathroom, hung it on a hook, and slipped off the shirt she was wearing. She went to the sink and turned on the hot water. As the water gradually warmed, she stared at her reflection in the mirror. The bathroom was brightly lit and the mirror was of very good quality. When she'd looked into it that morning, she'd seen creases made by sleep and a firm pillow. Now she examined her face for lines or any other signs of aging. She was closer to forty than thirty, if only by a year or two, and she understood the inevitability of deterioration. But understanding it and accepting it were two different things, and she was her mother's daughter, after all. What did her mother spend each year on face creams and special ointments? At least four thousand dollars, maybe more. Ava didn't use creams yet, but she wasn't averse to the idea; she was determined to look young as long as possible.

She sighed and stared harder. There were no apparent lines in her face, and as she looked down at her half-naked torso, she saw that it was still lean and taut. She was proud of her body, which she kept toned by running and bak mei workouts. Its only blemishes were scars that were reminders of how dangerous her old job had been. The largest was on her upper right thigh. She'd been shot there, the bullet so deeply embedded in the muscle that a Macao surgeon had to cut his way in to extract it. That scar was long and pink, like a fat worm. The others — on her shoulder and down the side of her left knee — were insignificant by comparison. She had been a little shy about the scars the first time she and Fai had really explored each other's bodies. But Fai had put her at ease quickly, sliding down to kiss her thigh and then running her tongue along the pink worm.

I haven't been working out enough, Ava thought suddenly. *I'm going to get fat if I don't get back into some kind of routine.*

Ten minutes later, Ava, in her pink shirt and with her face freshly scrubbed, joined Fai downstairs. They left the house for the now familiar walk to the end of the hutong to catch a taxi.

Traffic was heavy but moving, and at ten past eight the cab stopped in front of Lost Heaven. The restaurant was in a freestanding one-storey building. The front was completely glass, and the walls and double doors had metal discs the size of dinner plates embedded in them. It was an austere look that was quickly contradicted when they stepped into the walled reception area. The floor was a glistening worn, dark wood. Scrolled wooden chairs and sofas heavily padded in bright red cloth stood along each wall leading from the door to a long mahogany desk. The walls were painted a brilliant red, and the lamps on either side of the desk also glowed red.

"We're here to join the Sun party," Ava said to the host.

He nodded, turned, and spoke to a young woman standing next to him. She came out from behind the desk and said, "Follow me," looking intently at Pang Fai.

They trailed her through the restaurant with its continuing theme of dark wooden floors and red lights. When they reached a closed door near the back of the restaurant, their guide reached for the handle, turned it, and stood to one side. As they moved past, she whispered to Fai, "Are you really who I think you are?"

"Probably," Fai said with a slight smile.

Ava saw Mr. Sun sitting at the far end of a long table, with Suki and Mrs. Sun sitting closest to him on either side. The table was covered with a red cloth. The chairs around it were wooden, had beautifully carved scrolled backs, and were padded in purple cloth. The room was, not surprisingly, lit in red, and it made the rows of masks hanging on the walls look almost demonic.

Mr. Sun stood to greet Ava, and both Suki and Mrs. Sun looked in her direction. When Fai stepped up alongside Ava, their gazes froze. Even though Suki had known that Fai might come with Ava, she still seemed startled. Mrs. Sun didn't appear to know what to do; she sat almost frozen, her mouth agape.

"This is my friend Pang Fai," Ava said. "I was told she is welcome to join us for dinner."

The entire table rose to their feet. There were two empty seats next to Suki and across from Mrs. Sun and her chief accountant. Ava and Fai walked to them, mouthing hellos as they went. When they reached the end of the table, Ava made the introductions and everyone sat.

"I don't know what's more exciting, selling our business or meeting you," Mrs. Sun said to Fai. "I've seen everything you've made, and most of them many times. You are a national treasure."

"Would the national treasure like a drink?" Ava asked, pointing to the bottles of red and white wine on the table.

"If you'd rather have anything else, we'll get it," Mr. Sun said. "Scotch, cognac, beer…whatever you want."

"White wine is perfect," said Fai.

"For me too," Ava said.

"And we pre-ordered dinner," Mrs. Sun said to Fai. "But

if you want, we'll get you a menu and you can choose something of your own liking."

"I'm sure I'll like whatever you've ordered."

"It's Yunnan folk cuisine. I'm from there originally, and it just seemed proper to celebrate our business deal by honouring what was my home, and where I met my husband."

"Actually, Ava and I were there a few months ago," Fai said. "I was on a movie shoot in Kunming."

"I'm from a village that borders Myanmar, but I've been to Kunming," Mrs. Sun said.

"Yunnan borders Laos and Vietnam as well, doesn't it," Ava said.

"Yes, and that's why our cuisine is so diverse. It's all a bit of this and a bit of that."

"I'm anxious to try it," Ava said.

Mr. Sun poured wine for Ava and Fai and then returned to his feet. "A toast," he said dramatically.

Everyone raised their glasses.

"*Ganbei*," Mr. Sun said. Ava blinked in surprise; she'd expected some kind of speech.

As everyone drank, the food began to arrive.

"Wild vegetable cakes and pork ribs in a black rosé sauce to start," said Mrs. Sun. The servers portioned food onto plates, passed them to the guests, and then left the platters in the middle of the table.

Ava put a rib to her mouth and found that the meat was so tender she could separate it from the bone with her lips. "Wow," she exclaimed.

Fai, who had as healthy an appetite as Ava, bit into a vegetable cake and was equally appreciative.

Mrs. Sun smiled proudly. Mr. Sun refilled their

wineglasses, something he would do many times over the course of the evening, and not necessarily because they were empty — he simply wanted to make sure their glasses were always full.

The food began to arrive in earnest, and Mrs. Sun provided an ongoing commentary. They had pan-fried crispy chicken thighs served on a small mountain of scallions and herbs, Tibetan-style stir-fried beef, crunchy prawns with *jizong* mushrooms, a huge steamed cod served with what Mrs. Sun boasted were Yunnan black truffles, and, to end the meal, fresh rice noodles cooked with a variety of mushrooms.

As much as they all ate and drank, the conversation never waned. Fai was the focal point for most of it and gamely answered question after question, although she danced around any that were too personal about her or fellow actors.

When the last of the noodles had been consumed, the table was cleared of platters. The servers, accompanied by the man who'd greeted them at the entrance and another in a black suit, carried in a large mango cake.

"We didn't order that," Mrs. Sun said.

"Compliments of the management," the host said. "And in honour of Ms. Pang eating in our restaurant tonight."

"That's lovely. Thank you," said Fai.

"Ms. Pang, do you think we could inconvenience you for a few photos?"

Fai nodded, and for the next few minutes she was surrounded by an ever-changing assortment of restaurant staff as she smiled for camera phones and other devices.

"Is it always like this when you go out in public?" Suki asked when things had calmed down.

"Yes, and that's why I don't go out much."

"It was very kind of you to come tonight. We appreciate it, and we'll never forget it," Mrs. Sun said.

"Ava is a special friend. I couldn't say no to her."

"Thank goodness for that."

"And now we have to call it a night," Ava interrupted. "We have a business meeting of our own tomorrow and we need to be sharp."

"I'll walk you to the door," Suki said.

It took a while to say goodbye to everyone, but eventually Ava and Fai made it to the door of the private room. Suki said to Ava, "The real estate appraisers start their work tomorrow. We'll have numbers in a day or two."

"That's great."

"And your meeting tomorrow, is it about PÖ?"

"You could say that."

"Good luck."

"We may need it," Ava said.

As Ava and Fai worked their way back through the restaurant, they drew the attention of all the staff and most of the customers. Ava wasn't used to being gawked at and found it uncomfortable. Fai acted as if she were oblivious to it all. The host nodded at them when they reached the front of the restaurant and asked if they wanted a taxi. When Ava said they did, he ran out the front door to hail one.

"I'm not used to being spoiled like this," Ava said.

"I feel smothered rather than spoiled," Fai said as a taxi arrived.

They sat in the back and Ava got out her phone. There were two text messages from Derek that made her smile. She was amazed by the kind of information available to people who really knew how to use a computer. She was reasonably competent, but Derek was outstanding. Then again, why wouldn't he be? He'd never held a regular job, and now, as a stay-at-home dad, he had lots of time to devote to his computer skills. Great start, she texted back. See if you can find some names and more pics to attach to your second message.

As Ava put her phone back in her bag, Fai's rang. In all the time they'd been together, Ava couldn't remember that ever happening.

"*Wei*," Fai said, and then listened intently for about a minute.

Ava turned her head away, not wanting to intrude.

"Yes, I did call him earlier today," Fai said finally. "I'm meeting him tomorrow and we'll get things settled." She listened again and then said, "You'll have to handle that yourself. I have my own issues to resolve."

"Was that Chen?" Ava asked when Fai ended the call.

"Yes."

"What did he want?"

"He talked to Mo and knows that I'm meeting him at a hotel tomorrow. He has his own meeting scheduled later in the day, but he still wants me to make it clear to Mo that he had nothing to do with your visit," she snapped.

"Why does that make you sound so angry?"

"Because although he thinks I'm going to have to debase myself, all he cares about is that I make Mo so happy he'll be able to cover his own ass."

"Why do you keep him around?"

"I need an agent, and from what I've seen, he's no different than the others when it comes to protecting his self-interest."

"From what you've told me, it sounds like he hasn't done that great a job for you financially."

"I think that's mainly because of the market. Chinese actors who are restricted to China can't command the same kind of money as those who break out in Europe or North America," Fai said. "And until PÖ came around, I was unwilling to do a lot of commercial or promotional work. I have colleagues who spend every weekend at the opening of some shopping mall or fast-food outlet. That isn't for me. Maybe it's my ego talking, but I have a brand I want to protect."

"China's best actress?"

"Best film actress, anyway. And one reason I'm thought of that way is the roles I've taken. As you know, I don't do comedy," Fai said with a little laugh as she squeezed Ava's hand. "More seriously, after the first few films with Lau Lau, it was Chen who went over the scripts and made recommendations to me. Despite everything else, he has a wonderful sense of what will make a great movie, and he has a tremendous eye for roles that will enhance my career."

"Then I guess you should keep him."

"After tomorrow he may be the one making the decision about who keeps who."

AVA'S MIND WAS SO FULL OF THE DAY LYING AHEAD that she had trouble sleeping. Three times she got up, went downstairs, and checked her phone for messages from Derek. He didn't disappoint her. He sent a steady stream of information by text, and finally an email that summarized what he'd found, with four photos attached. She couldn't have asked for more. It seemed to her that if Mo really loved his son as much as he was supposed to, they had a lot of leverage to apply. Now it would come down to how well she used it.

She was sitting at the kitchen table with her notebook open in front of her when Fai came downstairs just before eight. Her hair was tousled and her eyes bleary, and she was wearing only underpants and a thin T-shirt that accentuated her breasts rather than covered them. Ava raised her head as Fai leaned down to kiss her.

"You were up and down all night. What was going on?" Fai asked.

"I was getting ready for today's meeting."

"And are you ready?"

"I think so. My friend in Canada was able to provide

information about Mo's son that should get his full attention."

"What kind of information?"

Ava opened her phone, accessed the messages from Derek, and showed a series of photos to Fai. "His son is obviously the young Chinese man."

Fai shook her head. "Are those real?"

"Yes," Ava said, and switched to some different photos.

"Mo would never want anyone to see those."

"That's my hope."

"You aren't certain?"

"I don't like to take anything for granted, and I don't know him well enough to predict his reaction. But if he loves his son as much as we've been told, it's hard to believe he won't co-operate."

"Then why do you seem so anxious?"

"Well, I'm praying that we never have to use this information beyond our meeting with Mo. The idea of its becoming public is repugnant," Ava said. "Anyway, I'm always like this when I'm getting ready for a big meeting. I need to burn off some energy. I'd like to go for a run."

"I wish I had some energy. I keep thinking about Mo and the film. It's exhausting — I didn't get out of bed like you, but I hardly slept."

"It will be over today," Ava said.

"I guess that's true, one way or another," Fai sighed, and then turned towards the window. "I don't know where you could run around here. The streets are crowded, and the only park nearby is hardly big enough for twenty couples to dance in."

"Maybe I'll just do some bak mei exercises in your court-yard. Would that bother the neighbours?"

"They'd probably find it entertaining, and I'd enjoy the distraction."

"Then that's what I'll do," Ava said and stood up. She left the kitchen, went upstairs, and put on her Adidas training pants and a black Giordano T-shirt. When she returned to the kitchen, Fai was standing at the window with her back turned and her shoulders slumped. Ava started to speak and then stopped. There was nothing she could say that wouldn't sound trite. The only thing that would ease Fai's stress was eliminating the Syndicate's power over her.

Ava stepped into the cobblestone courtyard and walked towards the centre. She turned in the direction of Fai's house and saw her face in the kitchen window, staring out at her. She waved, then closed her eyes, took a deep breath, and began to immerse herself in the art of bak mei.

It was an ancient martial art that had originated in southern China. It was conceived as a marriage of Shaolin and Taoist philosophies, a combination of the body's inner mental and outer physical strengths. Its proper application was lethal, and for centuries bak mei was forbidden and only practised in secret, its techniques passed on from father to son or, in Ava's case, from mentor to student.

Specializing in hand strikes and low, powerful kicks at close range, the art was typified by explosiveness. What made it even more effective was that those explosions came from positions that seemed soft and relaxed, until it was too late for the target to react to a finger jab, an elbow strike, or the classic and highly destructive phoenix-eye fist. Ava's favourite practice method was to mimic the tiger, and for half an hour she did that, coiling and recoiling with such sudden ferocity that she knew she must look strange to onlookers. When she finished, she closed her eyes, let her arms dangle loosely by her side, took some deep breaths for several minutes, and then turned and walked back to Fai's blue door.

The door opened before she got to it. "I've made a couple of movies that had kung fu in them, but I've never seen anything like that before," Fai said.

"It's called bak mei. I started to learn it while I was a teenager. It has saved my life more than once."

"No wonder I feel so safe around you," Fai said with a smile.

"What's made you so cheery all of a sudden?" Ava asked.

"Two cups of coffee and watching the woman I love look so terrifyingly silly in front of the entire courtyard."

"I'm glad I could provide everyone with some cheap entertainment."

"I haven't offended you, have I?"

"Of course not." Ava laughed. "And as silly as it might have seemed, that workout cleared my mind and invigorated my body. I'm ready for Mo."

"How invigorated are you?"

"What do you mean?"

"Do you want to share a shower?" Fai said, reaching for Ava's hand.

"Oh yes," Ava said, without hesitation.

AVA WALKED BY HERSELF TO THE END OF THE HUTONG to catch a taxi. It was only eleven, but she was nervous about traffic and wanted to give herself ample time to check into the Kempinski.

She'd left Fai sleeping in her bed, where she'd nodded off after the shower and lovemaking. Ava had thought about waking her to say goodbye, but instead left a note on her dresser saying she'd phone her as soon as the meeting with Mo ended.

She caught a taxi right away, and it took only a few minutes to get to the Kempinski. It was just south and a little east of the hutong, directly across Renda Huitang West Road from the Great Hall of the People. The actual name of the hotel was Kempinski Hotel Beijing Lufthansa Center, and from a distance its plain, primarily beige-tiled exterior looked like something Ava might have seen in Germany. As the taxi neared the entrance, she saw that on either side of the revolving doors the hotel operators had made a concession to something more Asian, with large, brightly lit blue glass walls decorated with cartoonish-looking golden lions.

The hotel lobby was long and narrow, its grey and beige marble floor flanked by recessed concierge and check-in desks. The upper half of the lobby's walls were clad in wood, again suggesting a Germanic or perhaps Scandinavian influence.

Ava checked in, declined an offer from the clerk to accompany her to the room, and then headed for the elevator. She exited on the fifth floor and made her way to the room, which was at the end of the corridor. During the final years of her business partnership with Uncle, and as her wealth had grown, she'd become accustomed to staying in suites at five-star hotels. There wasn't any need for a suite for the meeting with Mo, so she'd booked a single room. As she opened its door, the difference was immediately apparent.

The room was smaller and more cramped than she'd imagined. It was dominated by a king-size bed. Facing it was a desk that ran along almost the entire wall. At the farthest point from the door, a small oval table sat next to the window. There were two small chairs on either side of the table and a high-backed black leather office chair pressed against the desk. She pictured Mo sitting with his back to the window, with her and Lop facing him. Their faces would be well lit and he wouldn't have much else to focus on. Certainly the plainly furnished, monochromatically brown and beige room wouldn't be much of a distraction.

Ava sat at the desk and took out her phone and the Moleskine notebook. She called Fai first.

"*Wei*," Fai said after four rings, her voice heavy with sleep.

"I've checked in. I'm in Room 520."

"I didn't even know you'd left."

"I didn't want to wake you. You looked so peaceful."

"I wish you had."

"I'll remember that for next time," Ava said. "For now, I need you to contact Mo, give him the room number, and confirm that he's still coming here at two."

"I'll text him in a few minutes and I'll get back to you as soon as I get an answer."

"That's perfect."

"I hope it is. I mean, I hope everything goes the way you think it will."

Ava looked at the Moleskine and the notes she'd made in preparation for meeting Mo. "Things never go exactly the way they're expected, but I'm flexible enough to adapt on the fly."

Fai sighed. Ava sensed some hesitation in her manner, but then Fai said, "I'll text him right now."

Ava ended the call and stared at her notes. What if he didn't come? That was the one contingency she hadn't considered. *It's too soon to start worrying about that*, she thought as she called Lop.

"Are we set?" he asked before the first ring concluded. Ava imagined him waiting by the phone all morning.

"Yes, I'm checked in. Head over now and I'll meet you in the lobby," she said. She had considered meeting in the room, but she had things to do downstairs, and there was something off-putting about the idea of sitting with him in what was essentially a bedroom.

"How about your sources in North America? Did they come through?"

"Yes."

"Great. I'll see you in about twenty minutes."

"That was abrupt, even for Lop," she murmured to herself

as he ended the call. Was he having second thoughts? If he was, it was a bit too late for that. She calculated that twenty minutes should give her enough time to download and print Derek's messages and the attachments.

She went downstairs to the business centre, found it crowded, and had to wait for more than fifteen minutes to get access to a computer and a printer. When she returned to the lobby, Lop was already there, sitting in a chair directly in the centre. He looked calm and composed, and any doubts Ava had about his state of mind evaporated.

"Hey, *xiao lao ban*," he said, and stood up as she approached.

"We should find a less public place to talk," she said. "There's a pastry and coffee shop across from the elevators."

"Let's go."

As she led him towards the Kempi Deli, Ava's phone vibrated. She glanced at the screen and saw a message from Fai. He says he'll be there at two, and he's looking forward to it, it read.

"Mo is still on schedule," she said to Lop.

The deli was small but they were the only customers. Taking a table as far as possible from the service counter, they each ordered black coffee and then sat quietly until the cups were in front of them. When the waitress left, Ava opened her notebook, took out a small stack of paper, and slid it over to Lop.

He leafed through the documents, looked up at her with a blank expression, and then went through them again.

"Those are for you. I have my own set, and another one for Mo," she said.

"You're sure these are legitimate?"

"Yes."

"Holy shit. I wasn't sure you'd get anything we could really use, let alone stuff like this."

"This is the age of selfies, and given that these websites are banned or blocked in China, they probably didn't think they had anything to worry about."

"Do you think it's possible the pictures could be a bit too much?" Lop asked carefully.

"What do you mean?"

"They might freak him out. It's one thing to scare Mo, but it's another to make him desperate. We don't want him running to his cousin on the Politburo."

"Are you worried the cousin might go to General Chik or some other authority?"

"Chik would support me, and by extension you, but I can't guarantee there aren't some pressures that could get to him," he said. "As for any others, we'd better make sure Mo understands that if anything negative should happen to us, these photos will be released within hours."

"That will be part of our message, and it isn't idle talk. My friend in North America who unearthed most of this stuff knows what to do if there's suddenly silence from our end, and I'm going to plug in Xu and May Ling Wong as well," Ava said. "But I don't want it to come to that, or even close to that. My hope and expectation is that Mo will be reasonable."

"And if he isn't?"

Ava looked at her set of photos and then slowly slipped them into the notebook. "I don't know for certain, but this is one bluff I hope I never have to call."

17

AT ONE-THIRTY AVA AND LOP WENT UPSTAIRS TO THE room to wait for Mo. Lop walked directly to one of the chairs by the window, sat down, and took out his cell. While he focused on his phone, Ava sat at the desk and began to review the notes she'd made.

She assumed Mo would be, to varying degrees, angry, confused, and irrational when Lop bundled him into the room. She would need to calm him down as quickly as she could so they could have a sensible conversation. An over-wrought Mo wouldn't help himself or her. That he would be emotional was to be expected, but it was up to her to bring him back to reality.

In this kind of meeting, this sort of confrontation, Uncle had always counselled her to lead as strongly as possible. Hit your subject immediately with the worst-case scenario. Let them know how dire and hopeless their situation is, and when that has sunk in, gradually throw them some lifelines, so that by the time you state what it is you want, they feel like you're doing them a favour. Would that work with Mo? She wasn't sure, but given the arrogance she'd seen in his office, she didn't think that tiptoing into the subject was an option.

Lop grunted, and Ava glanced quickly in his direction. "Something wrong?" she said.

"Just some Hong Kong stuff. It's nothing to worry about," he said.

Ava's phone signalled that she had a message. She read it and then said to Lop, "I have a text from Fai. It says Mo is a little early. He's only about five minutes from the hotel."

"He's eager. That can't be a bad thing," Lop said as he stood up.

"Let's hope so," she said, closing her notebook. "We should get prepared."

Lop nodded and then walked past her to take up a position to the left of the door. He closed his eyes, took several deep breaths, and flexed his shoulders. Ava imagined that he was picturing how he would handle Mo when the door opened.

She lowered her head and, without thinking, began to pray to Saint Jude, the patron saint of lost causes. The impulse to do so surprised her. When she worked with Uncle, Saint Jude had been most often invoked when she was facing physical danger. Now there was no such threat, but she could feel her emotions surge all the same, and knew they signalled how important the next half-hour would be for her. Jude was the last vestige of her connection to the Catholic Church. She had been raised in the Church, but its stance on homosexuality had soured her; she no longer wanted any part of an institution that rejected people such as her.

She left the desk, went towards the door, and peered through the eyehole into an empty corridor. "I hope he's co-operative," she said to Lop. "But however he is, we need to be firm without hurting him."

"I can handle him," Lop said.

Ava knew he could, and silently chided herself for speaking the obvious. It was an indication of how nervous she was, and another reminder that she was more emotionally invested than usual. She became quiet and focused on the corridor. After a minute that seemed longer, she said, "He's coming."

"Is he alone?"

"Yes."

She took a couple of steps back from the door and waited. When he knocked, she stepped forward and stared through the eyehole again. He looked shorter and bulkier than he had in his office, and Ava wondered if the glass was distorting his appearance. She pressed down the handle and then moved out of sight as she opened the door.

Mo was two steps inside the room when Lop grabbed his left arm, pushed it up towards the middle of his back, and propelled him forward. Mo stumbled, and for a second Ava thought he was going to fall on his face, but Lop straightened him up. "I want you to sit in the chair in the far corner," he said. "And please don't argue with me."

"What's going on?" Mo shouted.

Ava closed the door. "Keep your voice down, or we'll have to help you do that," she said.

Mo looked at her and Lop as if he was seeing them for the first time. "Whatever it is you think you're doing, you won't get away with this," he said in a voice that was a mixture of anger, apprehension, and fear.

"Get away with what?" Ava said. "All we want to do is finish the conversation that we started in your office."

"You're crazy."

"Sit," Lop said, shoving Mo towards the chair.

"I don't know what you think this will accomplish," Mo said.

"If nothing else it will make our respective positions much clearer," Ava said.

"I already know your position, and unless you're stupid — and I don't think you are — you know mine as well," Mo said. "So unless you intend to abduct me or torture me or kill me, nothing is going to change."

"Our only intention is to finish our conversation," Ava said. "Now why don't you sit so we can do it properly."

Lop was standing between Mo and Ava, and now he moved a step closer to the man. "Sit," he said, indicating the chair.

Mo started to say something but stopped when Lop laid his right hand on his shoulder. He sat, then watched as Lop slowly lowered himself into the second chair, leaving Mo separated from Ava by Lop at his side and the bed directly in front of him.

Ava went to the desk and picked up a manila folder. She sat in the desk chair and rolled it towards Mo. It came to a stop at the bed. She opened the folder, took out a photo, and put it on the bed in front of him. "This is a photo of your son, David, with his boyfriend, Mark Simmons. Like David, Mark is a student at UCLA. His father is a bank executive but, ironically, Mark is in the film studies program. They make a nice couple, don't you think?"

Mo's head was lowered and Ava couldn't see his eyes, but she saw that his mouth was open and there was sweat on his upper lip. Then he turned away from them.

"I have other photos if you'd like to see them, although

some are much coarser and more graphic than the one I showed you."

Mo stiffened, and for a second she thought he was going to stand up and do something stupid like try to leave the room or lunge at them. Instead he closed his eyes and shook his head.

"Not looking at the photos won't make them go away. Besides, this one is kind of sweet."

He leaned forward and reached for the photo.

"I assume you didn't know that David is gay," she said. "In Los Angeles it isn't a big deal, and the fact that Mark is black wouldn't bother most people there. They've been a couple for six months, and their friends tell us they're thinking of getting married."

She passed him another photo. In it, the smaller, wirier David was sitting on his partner's lap with his arms around his neck. Both men were fully clothed, their cheeks pressed together as they grinned at the camera. "In case you're wondering, we've been told that Mark is the dominant partner in the relationship. There are some pictures that demonstrate that, but I'm not sure we have to look at those right now."

"What do you want?" Mo said, the words squeezed from his throat.

"I'll tell you what I don't want," Ava said. "I don't want these photos to fall into the wrong hands. I know how prejudiced and harsh and cruel some people in China can be towards homosexuals, especially to one who is openly committed to a same-sex partner of a different race. I also understand that as someone who is charged by the government to uphold a standard of public morality, David's relationship and the photos could cause you tremendous loss of face. If your cousin Zhang supported you, you might survive it, but at what cost to you and him? And perhaps more important, at what cost to your son?"

"You would do this to David?"

"Please believe me, it's the last thing I want to do."

"But you're prepared to?"

"Yes, but I would prefer that you not make that necessary."

"By agreeing to release that fucking film and by supporting that fucking bitch Pang Fai?"

"I'm pleased to hear that you remember what we were discussing when you left your office yesterday, but I have to say that a hostile attitude won't help us reach a reasonable agreement."

Mo looked at Lop. "Does General Chik know what you're doing here? Did he approve this?"

"General Chik knows absolutely nothing about this, at least not yet. We thought it would be more prudent — for your sake more than ours — to keep it that way for now," Ava said.

"So what's the deal? I authorize release of the film and commit to supporting Pang, and you make these photos disappear?"

"You can have a set of the photos if you want them. I'll be keeping one, and so will Lop. There is another set with a colleague in North America, and two more with friends in China who have agreed to act as our agents in the event that something strange or unexplained happens to either of us or Pang Fai."

"You exaggerate my importance and my influence."

"But not your cousin's."

"What makes you imagine for one second that I'd want my cousin to know about this?"

"I don't know the nature of your relationship, and besides, I'm sure you could come up with many other reasons for him to come after us."

Mo wiped the sweat from his upper lip and brow. "I need to go to the bathroom," he said.

Lop looked at Ava questioningly.

"Search him," she said. "Take his phone and anything else you think might cause us a problem."

"Stand," Lop said to Mo.

Mo struggled to his feet, reaching for the photos on the bed.

"Leave those alone," Ava said.

"What harm can it do —"

"Leave them," Ava said.

"And put your hands in the air," Lop said.

Mo shrugged but did as he was told. Lop quickly patted him down, removing a cellphone from his jacket pocket and tossing it onto the bed.

"Don't let him close the door entirely, and stay close by it until he's finished," she said to Lop.

She stood and moved away from the bed and the desk to give them room to pass. As they did, she saw Mo tense, and she flinched, half expecting him to take a swing at her. Instead he walked straight by, with Lop at his heels. She waited until he'd entered the bathroom before she sat again. The meeting was going well enough, she thought. Mo hadn't overreacted, although she imagined he was still in a state of shock. If he was going to present her with any problems, they would emerge as the shock wore off and his natural character began to reassert itself. Were the photos strong enough to deter him? Did he love his son more than his own sense of himself? She sighed and reached for the folder that held the photos. Had she said enough? The idea of piling on even more details about the private life of David Mo repulsed her, and she hated that she'd had to go there in the first place. But what other leverage did she have?

Her attention was drawn by a noise from the bathroom. Mo emerged and slammed the door shut behind him. As he walked towards her with Lop close behind, she noticed that he held his head higher and his lips were pressed tightly together. Were those signs of resignation or defiance?

Mo took the same chair and waited for Lop to take his before he leaned in Ava's direction and said, "I'm wondering if you haven't manufactured that story about my son."

Ava opened the folder, leafed through the photos, and passed one to Mo. In it a naked David was sitting on a bed next to a naked Mark. Neither man could have been more fully exposed.

"I don't need to see any more," Mo said.

"Good, but you should know that Mark has been very active on several blogs and websites that cater to gay men. His relationship with David has been well documented."

"Okay, I get it."

"Even if you didn't, and even if the photos were false, even if David were actually dating a woman, what difference would it make once what I've shown you is in full-blown circulation? Who would believe anything else? You should know as well as anyone that most people love gossip and dirt and are always inclined to believe the worst. That said, the photos are real, and so is the relationship."

Mo nodded. "So what's the deal?"

"You voiced it earlier. We want you to authorize the release of *Mao's Daughter* and to do nothing to inhibit its distribution and promotion."

"And?"

"Treat Pang Fai — both personally and professionally — with the respect that she deserves as one of this country's finest film actresses."

"By approving every project she or Chen brings our way?"

"No. All we can expect is for you and your organization to be professional and judge each project fairly on its own merits," Ava said. "And, of course, you have to understand that the days of demanding personal favours in return are over."

"And if Chen or Pang believes we're not being fair, what then?" Mo said, sliding around her last comment.

"I'll talk to them and draw my own conclusions."

"That doesn't bring me much closure, much certainty."

"It's the best I can offer."

Mo glanced at Lop, then at Ava, and stared down at the photos in front of him. "I thought it was Lop who was calling the shots, but it's you."

"Lop and I are partners. Think of us as being interchangeable."

"But he's connected to General Chik and, I assume, he's ex-military. But who are you, where are you from, and why do you care what happens to that film and Pang Fai?"

"As you were told in your office, our business has a relationship with Fai and we have investments we need to protect. You're threatening them."

He shook his head. "There has to be more to it than that."

"I happen to think that's enough," she said. "Do you want to question that?"

"Would it do me any good?"

"No, and no more questions. You have a deal on the table. Do you accept it or not?"

"What do you think?"

"I believe your son means more to you than any film or any actress could."

"Then you have your answer."

"I need to hear you say it."

He shook his head. "This doesn't come easily for me...I guarantee the film will be released and promoted. I'll also give Pang Fai every courtesy as far as her career is concerned."

"Thank you," Ava said.

"But what kind of guarantee can you give me that those photos will never be made public?"

"You have my word, just as I have yours."

"Two strangers exchanging promises?"

"We're not strangers anymore."

"Except you know who I am and where I am, and I know nothing about you."

"I'm sure you can correct that soon enough if you choose to," she said. "But I can tell you, the results probably won't be worth the effort."

"Why do I doubt that?"

Ava saw Lop fidget in his chair and knew he thought it was time to end the meeting. She touched the folder. "Do you want a set of these documents and photos?" she said to Mo.

"No," he said, a hint of anger resurfacing in his voice.

"Then I think we've concluded our business. You're free to go."

18

AVA WATCHED LOP WALK MO TO THE DOOR. WHEN THEY reached it, Lop put his hand on Mo's elbow and then spoke to him for almost a minute. Ava couldn't hear what he was saying, but Mo's face tensed and he didn't respond. Finally Lop reached past him, opened the door, and almost shoved him out into the corridor.

"What was that about?" Ava asked when Lop came back into the room.

"I told him not to get any funny ideas."

"Do you really think he would risk having those photos made public?"

"He might have doubted that we already have our backs covered," he said. "He might have been thinking that if he moved quickly — like as soon as he gets outside — he could catch us off guard."

"So what specifically did you tell him?"

"I said you'd told him the truth about other people having the photos, but the photos would be the least of his problems if he tried to play games."

"You threatened him?"

"I said he would end up dead."

"I guess that constitutes a threat," Ava said with a smile.

"I know it was a bit overblown, but I've got to get back to Hong Kong and I don't want any problems at the Beijing airport. And I don't like the idea of leaving you here by yourself until things really settle."

"You don't have to worry about me."

"I know I don't, but other people worry about you, and if something happened then I'd be responsible. I don't want to have to get into the explaining business."

By "other people" Ava knew he meant Xu, and probably Auntie Grace. "You've been wonderful. I couldn't have done this without you, Lop, and I'll make sure everyone knows."

"Thanks. You have no objections to my getting on the first plane out of here for Hong Kong?"

"No, but what's going on there that needs such urgent attention?"

"Probably nothing, but I'm naturally paranoid," Lop said. "Your old acquaintance and my supposed associate Sammy Wing was supposed to meet with two of my men this morning. He didn't show and they can't reach him. I'm sure there's a valid reason for his absence, but I'm not comfortable that it coincides with my first trip out of Hong Kong since we took over Wanchai."

"Did he know you were leaving?"

"I told him myself."

"In that case I'm sure there's nothing going on," she said. "Sammy's not stupid."

"But he has a history of being reckless."

"That's true enough," Ava said. "Trying to kill me and Xu wasn't exactly a brilliant strategy."

Lop looked away from Ava for a second, and she sensed some reluctance in him. "Is there something you're not telling me, something else you want to say?" she asked.

"If Sammy is playing games behind my back, I won't let it go," he said.

"No one would expect you to."

"Xu might. He's anxious to maintain the peace in Hong Kong, and Sammy still has friends in some of the gangs in the New Territories. Xu doesn't want to give them any reason to get pissed off at us."

"I'm sure he has his reasons for doing that."

"Ava, you know I'm completely loyal, right?" Lop said abruptly.

"Yes."

"I follow orders and I do whatever it is the boss wants done," he said, again averting his eyes. "But if Sammy is fucking around, I have to go after him. If I don't, I'll lose all credibility with my men, and Sammy will feel encouraged to keep fucking around."

"I can see that," she said. "But I'm not sure why you're telling me all this."

"The boss confides in you and he trusts your judgment. I would appreciate it if you could support my position if it ever comes down to deciding what to do about Sammy."

Ava began to protest any possible involvement on her part, and then stopped. It was possible, given her history with Sammy Wing, that Xu would talk to her about Sammy if he became a problem. And if he did, she had to admit that Lop's reaction was both practical and justified on many levels. "I don't expect it will ever come to that. You'll probably get back to Hong Kong and find out that Sammy was laid up

with the flu or something," she said. "But if Sammy is causing problems and Xu chooses to discuss it with me, you can
be assured that I'll support you."

"Thank you."

"I've told you before, no more thank-yous. We're on the
same team."

Lop nodded and said nothing.

"Let's get out of here, shall we," Ava said. "You have a
plane to catch and I want to let Pang Fai know that her life
is back on track."

19

AVA SAID HER FINAL GOODBYE TO LOP AT THE HOTEL entrance. She waited until his taxi pulled away before getting out her phone.

"*Wei*," Fai answered before the first ring ended.

"It's Ava."

"Is it over?"

"Yes."

"And were you successful?" Fai asked in a rush.

"I'm confident that we were, but the proof will be when the film is released and when Chen gets approval for whatever project you want to take on next."

"How was he? How was Mo?"

"He didn't rant or threaten. He was smart enough to understand the situation and he acted appropriately. He was suitably co-operative."

"I guess he really loves his son."

"I think he does, but he also likes his position and his power. Releasing that kind of information would threaten both of those."

Fai paused and then said softly. "Ava, when I woke up, I

kept thinking about those photos you showed me. Would you really have made them public?"

"Maybe, but I'm relieved that it's a decision I don't have to make now. I didn't take any pleasure in showing them to Mo."

"I'm glad you feel that way," Fai said. "As much as I detest Mo, I wouldn't wish that kind of harm to come to his son. He's an innocent in all of this. He can't help that his father is the man he is."

"There should be no harm to him unless Mo decides to impose it himself, and there's nothing we can do to prevent that," Ava said. "My priority is you."

"I know, and I can't begin to tell you how grateful I am."

"I just finished telling Lop that there's never any reason for us to thank one another. Helping each other is what friends do, it's what lovers do, and we do it in our own way when it's called for. Hopefully we won't have to do it that often."

"How about never again."

"I share that feeling."

"So now what? Are you coming home?"

"I have some phone calls to make first. One of them is to Suki to get an update on our acquisition of the Suns' business. If she doesn't need me I'll be home in the next hour."

"I'll be waiting."

Suki was actually the third name on Ava's mental list. As soon as she hung up from Fai, she called the first, her partner May Ling Wong in Wuhan. Of all the blessings in her life — and she had many, including money and family — she considered her friends to be paramount. Creating and maintaining relationships was something she'd learned from Uncle. He had no family but he was surrounded by people who would do anything for him, because, as he often told her, they knew he would do anything for them. The only times she'd seen him turn his back on friends was when they were disloyal and broke trust with him. He could understand and accept any other indiscretion or fault, but in his mind there was no way to ever forgive or forget disloyalty. She felt the same way, and among her friends she trusted no one more than May Ling and Xu.

"I was wondering when I'd hear from you," May said when she answered her phone. "Suki has been keeping me up to date, but that isn't quite the same."

"It's Suki's deal. I thought it more appropriate for her to brief Amanda and you."

"That's not what I'm talking about," May said. "Suki told me about the dinner, about the sensation you caused by bringing Pang Fai with you."

"Fai caused the sensation."

"I'm sure she did, but the fact that you brought her didn't hurt your image."

"That won't help us one way or another with closing the deal."

May paused and then said, "What's going on? You don't sound the least bit enthused. I thought things were going well with the Suns, and with Fai."

"Things are going well on both counts," Ava said, noticing once again how quickly May could pick up on her mood. "But I need your help with something that might seem a bit odd on the surface."

"There's nothing unusual about that."

"This is even odder than normal," Ava said. "I'm going to forward you some photos, blog entries, and other information. The Chinese boy in the photos is David Mo. His father is the head of the China Movie Syndicate and his uncle is a member of the Standing Politburo. If anything should happen to me in the next few days, weeks, or even months, I want you to make this information public in any way you can, including getting it into the hands of your political contacts."

"What do you mean by 'should happen to me'?"

Ava smiled, pleased at May's focus on her well-being. "If I should go missing or if I get arrested... or if I turn up dead."

"What the hell —"

"May, I'm sure none of those things will happen, but it's careless not to take precautions. Those photos and the other information are my insurance policy."

"Insurance against what?"

"I don't want to get into it right now. The next time we sit down for a drink, I'll explain it all to you in detail. For the moment, just trust me."

"I assume, since you mentioned the China Movie Syndicate, that this somehow involves Pang Fai?" May said.

"It does, but that's all I'm going to say right now."

"But at least you have to tell me if you're in any immediate danger."

"Not at all, and I'm not anticipating that I will be. Like I said, it's insurance."

"Is there any point in my persisting?"

"No."

"Okay, then send me whatever you have."

"You'll have it this afternoon."

"Speaking of this afternoon, have you heard from Suki?"

"No. My phone has been off for hours and I haven't checked my messages yet."

"She's been trying to reach you. One of the companies you chose to do that real estate assessment called her and offered to lowball."

"For a price, of course."

"Naturally."

"What did she tell them?"

"Only that she had to talk to you."

"Did she tell you what she thought about the offer?"

"She was angry about it but didn't want to dismiss it entirely, because she's concerned that the same company will just turn around and make a highball pitch to the Suns."

"Is this how business is done in Beijing?" Ava said.

"This is how it's done in a lot of places in this country. Nearly everything and everyone is for sale," May said. "And you can't discount the possibility that the other two companies you went to will do the same thing."

"I wasn't expecting this nonsensical crap when I suggested getting the assessments."

"But now you've got it, and you have to decide how to handle it."

"I don't want to play these games. We're buying a business and all I want to do is pay fair market value for it. Maybe we should just give the Suns what they initially asked for."

"I'll leave that for you and Suki to decide. You know I'll be okay with whatever decision you make."

"I'll call back after I talk to her," Ava said, and hung up. She started to call Suki and then stopped. *One thing at a time*, she thought as she hit Xu's number.

"Where are you?" he asked.

"Still at the hotel. I didn't want to make my phone calls from a taxi."

"I just spoke with Lop. He told me it went well."

"Did he give you any idea of what we used to leverage Mo?"

"He did."

"Well, I'm going to send you copies of it all. If anything should happen to Lop or me, I want you to make it public."

"It will never come to that."

"Still…"

"I'd do it of course, but it isn't something I want to think about," Xu said. "Lop felt bad about leaving so soon after your meeting. Did he tell you why he wanted to get back to Hong Kong so quickly?"

"He said he's worried about Sammy Wing."

"I told him he was overreacting," Xu said. "But when Lop gets a thought in his head, he can't let it go until he's one hundred percent convinced he's either right or wrong."

"What could Sammy do?"

"He's not without friends, but I don't know a single one of them who would dare side with Sammy, knowing that it would piss off Lop."

"Then there's nothing to worry about."

"I don't think so. And now, with nothing for you to worry about in Beijing, how much longer do you think you'll be staying there?"

"I'll have to talk to Fai about that. It would be nice to get away from here for a holiday."

"Come to Shanghai. Stay with me."

"You'd be comfortable with the two of us sleeping together?"

"It wouldn't bother me."

"How about Auntie Grace?"

"She's the last person on earth who'd be bothered. You know you can do no wrong in her eyes."

"I feel the same way towards her," Ava said.

"So?"

"I'll mention it to Fai. She might be self-conscious around you, given the way you met before."

"Tell her I never thought poorly of her when she was with Tsai. And now that she's with my *xiao mei*, she's practically family."

"I'm sure that will persuade her," Ava said, laughing. "But I still have business to wrap up here. Let me get that done and then I'll talk to her."

"Keep in touch."

Ava shook her head as the call ended. She had no doubts that Xu's invitation was heartfelt and that he and Auntie Grace would be welcoming, but she also sensed that it would be incredibly awkward. They were accustomed to Ava in a certain way, and whether Xu thought so or not, seeing her in such a different light might be disconcerting. Her mother Jennie, for example, could intellectually handle the idea of her sexuality but had struggled whenever Ava and her former girlfriend Maria displayed affection in her presence; she said it was like being in a room that had no air to breathe. Ava wondered how Jennie would react when and if she met Fai. She knew her mother was a big fan of Fai's, which would cause excitement enough, but god knew how she'd react if she knew Fai and her daughter were a couple. *I'm glad I don't have to worry about that just yet*, Ava thought as she phoned the last person on her list.

"I've been trying to get hold of you," Suki said.

"Sorry. I was in a meeting that needed my full attention," Ava said. "I spoke to May a few minutes ago and she told me what's going on with the real estate people. Did you expect anything this unethical?"

"No, but after it happened I called an old friend in Beijing and asked if it's common here. She said it is."

"I guess I shouldn't be surprised by anything that goes on in this country. It's just that I keep hoping for better."

"We're not all corrupt," Suki said. "Still, I admit there's enough shit going on to make it seem that way sometimes."

"And I shouldn't be tarring everyone with the same brush," Ava said, realizing she might have offended Suki. "I've met enough honest people to know otherwise."

"The Suns among them."

"Yes. What do you suggest we do about the Suns and this predicament?"

"I'd like to tell them about the assessor."

"I agree, and you might add that although it seemed like a good idea at the time, we've lost our appetite for multiple valuations."

"What do you mean by that?"

"Tell them we'll accept the value they put on their properties. Let's do the deal at the price they want — that is, unless you think we're grossly overpaying."

"I think it's fair enough."

"Then go and close it."

"Assuming the Suns agree, it will take a day or two for the lawyers to finalize the paperwork. Do you want to hang around Beijing until that's done?"

"Why not? I've come this far, I might as well see it through to the end."

"Great. I'll call the Suns right now and see if we can wrap this up."

"Suki, I'm going to be tied up for the rest of the day and evening, so unless there's a major problem, don't worry about contacting me. We'll touch base tomorrow."

Suki became quiet, and Ava again wondered if she'd offended her.

"Will you be seeing Pang Fai?" Suki asked finally.

"In all probability."

"If you do, would you please tell her how honoured and thrilled we all were to have her as a dinner guest. After you left the restaurant, the manager came to our dining room and bowed to the Suns. Having her at our table gave them tremendous face. Mrs. Sun was as excited as a schoolgirl."

"If I see Fai, I'll certainly tell her," Ava said, not quite ready to concede the obvious to Suki.

"And Ava, I'm quite sure it will go well with Mrs. Sun. We understand each other."

Ava ended the call, and as she did a gust of wind swept across the hotel entrance. She looked up and saw that the sky was suddenly a different shade of grey from the usual smog. Several raindrops landed on her face and she sensed that a storm was coming. She stepped towards the curb and asked the doorman to get her a taxi.

Fifteen minutes later she was less than a kilometre from the hotel, the taxi barely moving as rain pelted down so hard that Ava had to strain to see out the windows. She sent a text to Fai describing her situation and then began to email the David Mo information to May Ling and Xu. She hesitated before sending some of the more graphic photos of David with his boyfriend, but then, figuring they might ultimately be her best protection, she did so anyway.

The rain eased after another fifteen minutes. As the traffic began to crawl rather than just sit still, Ava sent a text to Fai saying the taxi was finally moving.

She wiped the mist from the window and looked outside, into the heart of Beijing. All she knew about it, she thought, was what she'd read. If Suki was right about how long it would take for the lawyers to finalize the agreement, she had maybe two days to correct that. Was Fai up to doing a little sightseeing with her?

By the time the taxi arrived at the entrance to the hutong, the weather had again taken a turn for the worse. Ava groaned as she contemplated how wet she was going to be by the time she reached Fai's. She paid the driver, opened the door, and started to get out.

"Wait there, I'm coming," a familiar voice said.

Ava looked through the driving rain to see Fai walking towards her, holding an umbrella over her head.

20

THE RAIN DIDN'T LET UP FOR THE ENTIRE EVENING, BUT
Ava and Fai were warm and snug inside the kitchen. The
sound of rain pelting against the windows only heightened
their sense of well-being. They ate what was left of the food
Fai's mother had sent from Yantai, finished a bottle and a
half of red wine, and talked about the day that had been and
the day that lay ahead.

Ava underplayed the meeting with Mo, seeing no benefit
in making it sound anything other than a normal business
transaction. One of the few questions Fai had was about the
possibility of Mo using his connections to exact revenge on
Lop or Ava. Ava explained what she'd done with May and Xu.

"Do they know why all this was necessary?" Fai asked.

"Xu does. May doesn't yet but probably will. I don't have
secrets where they're concerned; they're more like family
than friends. Is that a problem for you?"

"Not at all. I just wish I had friends like that."

Ava's phone was on the entire evening but didn't ring. She
assumed that meant things had gone well between the Suns
and Suki, which made a good day even better.

Fai kept glancing at her phone, looking a bit anxious every time she did.

"Are you expecting a call?" Ava asked.

"Chen promised to call after his meeting with Mo."

"What time was it scheduled for?"

"They were having dinner. At least that was the plan. I don't know if your meeting with Mo caused any changes."

"Have you spoken to Chen about our meeting?"

"I felt I had to, but I lied. I called him after we talked and told him I was able to sort things out without going to the hotel, and that *Mao's Daughter* was going to be released and I'd keep getting support."

"All that is true."

"I didn't mention your involvement."

"He didn't press you for details about how you made it happen?"

"He tried to, but I was evasive."

"Are you worried about what might happen with him?"

"Even if things have worked out for me, I don't want harm to come to him or his business," Fai said. "I may not like him that much, but it isn't that easy to separate myself from what he's done for me in the past."

"He'll call eventually, and when he does, I'm sure it will be to report good news," Ava said. "In the meantime, let's talk about tomorrow. I should have a free day, and if I do, what's the one thing you'd recommend I see?"

"There's the Forbidden City, the Palace Museum, and other places like that near here. But they're always so crowded, and everyone is pushing and shoving."

"Okay, if we don't want to be among crowds, what does that leave?"

"I love the Great Wall. Have you seen it?"

"No."

"I went to parts of it when I was on location for a couple of films. I particularly liked the section at Huanghuacheng. It's built along the sides of mountains, and you look down on a lake from the summit. There's a chestnut orchard at the base of the wall that's supposed to be five hundred years old, and south of Huanghua town there's a mausoleum built by one of the emperors that's now one of the famous Ming tombs."

"How far is it from Beijing?"

"Maybe an hour by taxi."

"And no crowds?"

"Huanghuacheng isn't really one of those touristy parts of the wall. The walkway on top is slanted and really steep in some places. It's hard to walk along. You'd need to wear your running shoes."

"How far could we walk?"

"The wall is six thousand kilometres long."

"I know," Ava said and laughed.

"What I'm saying is that you can go as far as you want."

"It sounds like a perfect way to spend a day, as long as it's not raining," Ava said. Then she yawned so suddenly she didn't have time to cover her mouth.

"I'm ready for bed if you are," Fai said.

"I am tired."

"It's been a long, emotional day."

"One that turned out well."

"I'd feel a bit more confident about that if Chen felt the same way," Fai said.

"Then phone him."

Fai nodded but then hesitated before reaching for the phone.

Ava wondered if her presence in the kitchen was the reason for Fai's reluctance. "Would you prefer it if I left?" she said.

"No, stay."

Ava watched Fai hit speed-dial and then deliberately turned towards the kitchen window, looking out into the wet lamp-lit courtyard.

Fai said, "Chen, it's me. I was wondering how it went with Mo tonight."

Ava's attention flitted between Fai and the window. For several minutes Fai was tense and quiet as she listened to Chen. It seemed longer than that to Ava, but as the conversation continued she saw Fai's tension ease and stopped worrying about what kind of story Chen was spinning.

"Is everything okay?" Ava asked when Fai put down her phone.

"According to Chen it couldn't have gone much better. We're back on track. He said he's rarely found Mo so pleasant and co-operative."

"I'm glad he's doing the right thing."

"Even if it is for the wrong reason."

"You remember me telling you that?"

"Specifically you said people always do the right thing for the wrong reason. It stuck with me."

"I know it sounds cynical, but it is true."

"Do you think I'm cynical?"

"What?"

"Do you think I'm sleeping with you, telling you that I love you, only because I need your help?"

"No," Ava said, taken aback by the question. "It never occurred to me, but maybe that's just my ego at work. And besides, you didn't need my help until I arrived in Beijing."

"How do you know that for certain?"

"I don't."

"So you're putting that much trust in me?"

"I am."

Fai closed her eyes and reached blindly across the table for Ava's hands. "I love my career. I was born to act and I never want to stop doing it. But what that means is that I've spent my entire adult life in an industry where no one trusts anyone, where everything is spun and exaggerated, and where ultimately the only interest that matters is self-interest. Letting go of that mindset isn't going to be easy, but I promise you I'll try."

21

IT WAS DARK BY THE TIME THEIR TAXI FOUND ITS WAY back to the hutong from Huanghuacheng and the Great Wall. It had been an unusual day for Ava. It was the first time she and Fai had spent that much time in public as a couple, and there had been some awkward moments as they tried to figure out how much intimacy could be on display. If they'd been in Canada Ava wouldn't have thought twice about it, but given that Fai might be recognized — even though she was wearing sunglasses and a cap — and the general Chinese tendency towards homophobia, they had been cautious.

What had made the day odder still was that Ava had no access to a cellphone. She had brought hers but had forgotten to charge it the night before, something she didn't notice until she tried to turn it on when they were more than halfway to Huanghuacheng. When she asked Fai if she could borrow hers, she discovered that Fai hadn't bothered to bring it. This left Ava out of touch with her world. She couldn't remember the last time she'd been in that situation, and for the first hour or so at Huanghuacheng she felt anxious. She knew there was no real basis for her anxiety other than the perception that she had somehow lost control. *Control of what?* she asked herself, and began to calm down. After an hour of walking along the top of the Great Wall, the calmness had taken a firm hold.

Her initial reaction to the wall itself was disappointment. At about seven metres it wasn't nearly as high as she'd expected, but after she climbed the stone stairway and reached the top, her appreciation began to grow. The wall was approximately six metres wide at its base and five metres wide at the top. Its sheer mass was formidable, and looking down from the ramparts, it seemed even more imposing. But it wasn't until she gazed in either direction and saw it snaking around mountains for as far as she could see that she realized how forbidding it must have appeared to invaders. There was nowhere to attack that couldn't be defended.

There was a large group of tourists at the entrance point. Ava listened as their guide briefed them in English about the wall's six-hundred-year history and its two-hundred-year construction. The guide made the wall seem like a testament to perseverance rather than to military foresight or architectural brilliance. Ava wondered who had written the script.

"Let's get away from this crowd," Fai said. She pointed to the left, where the wall rose haphazardly towards a mountain and there were fewer walkers in sight. "We can get a terrific view of the town and the lake from up there."

As close as the mountain appeared, they walked for almost an hour along the wall path before reaching its base. The path required concentration to navigate. It was paved in bricks that rose and fell haphazardly, while the path itself veered erratically left and right, but always uphill. As a result,

Ava was mostly watching where she was walking rather than looking at the scenery.

Their walk took them through several sentinels, or watch-towers, where the tourists tended to congregate. But the farther they went, the fewer tourists there were; by the time they stopped in the middle of a long run of wall, they were the only people in the vicinity. Fai leaned against the rampart and stared at the lake and the mountain. "In the summer this entire area is carpeted in yellow flowers," she said. "That's where the town gets its name, Yellow Flower City."

"I like the way older Chinese cultures weren't afraid to state the obvious," Ava said as she slipped her arm around Fai's waist.

Fai pressed close. "Now everything is so coded. Words have no real meaning on their own. I can't tell you how many times the most innocuous phrase in a script is branded as unpatriotic because of some off-the-wall interpretation."

Ava glanced sideways. Fai was looking straight ahead, her face in profile. She wasn't wearing makeup; her lips were pale and her eyes naked, and her skin looked almost translucent. There wasn't a wrinkle or a blemish anywhere on her face. Fai looked almost girlish, and that made Ava feel her own years — years of experience rather than calendar time. She wondered if Fai measured her life in terms of films made in the same way that Ava calculated hers in terms of jobs completed. A job might last for a few days or a few weeks, but every one of them took its toll.

"What are you looking at?" Fai asked suddenly, turning her head.

"You. I've never seen anyone quite so beautiful."

"You aren't half bad yourself, you know," Fai said, laughing.

"Besides, my mother always said that beauty is what beauty does, and that makes you the real princess in our universe."

"Beauty is what beauty does?" Ava said.

"My mother is full of sentiments like that. They're substitutes for her inability to express real emotions or thoughts."

"More code?"

"In a way."

"My mother says things like that as well, but when you really stop to think about it, some of them make real sense."

"That's what I always tell her — whether I think they do or not."

"You're a good daughter."

"Not so much, but I'm better than I was," Fai said.

"I am too," Ava said. "For years I resented my mother for the way she lived her life — you know, being a part-time wife, which made my father part-time as well — and for having no sense about money management. I hated her gambling and the fact that she never planned for the future. Then one day I looked at her and I saw a different woman. She hadn't changed, but I had. I realized I have a mother who would sacrifice everything she has — without a second thought — for her children, and who accepts us and loves us for exactly who we are. It's all so unconditional and so absolute."

"Did she always know you're gay?"

"I never hid it, but it's something we never discussed directly. I think it was enough for both of us that she knew and that I knew she knew — if that makes any sense," Ava said. "All she wants is for me to be happy."

"Has she met any of your girlfriends?"

"Yes. She always got along quite well with them, but again in an arm's-length sort of way," Ava said. "Are you worried about how your parents would react if you told them?"

"I don't think it would make any difference to them in terms of me. But they'd probably be worried about how others would treat me," Fai said. She looked down onto the deep blue lake. "Will you come to Yantai with me?"

Ava was caught off guard by the question, which immediately generated more questions in her head. She put those aside and said, "Of course."

"I don't mean right away," Fai said. "But eventually, when I'm ready to tell them about me, about us. They aren't complicated people and they haven't travelled much. Their world is inside the walls of their house in Yantai. I would find it difficult to explain my feelings to them in the abstract. It would be so much easier if you were with me and I could simply say, 'This is the woman I love.'"

"Let me know when you're ready to go."

"Soon enough, I think," Fai said. She took a deep breath and then shook her head. "I find it hard to believe that we're only an hour from Beijing. The air here is so completely different."

"And look how blue the lake is."

"When I was here for the film shoot, the director told me that the local government pumps blue dye into it."

"Well, they can't pump anything into the air." Ava laughed and looked up into the sky. "But there are rainclouds gathering. Shall we walk some more before they empty themselves on us?"

22

THE RAIN HELD OFF UNTIL LATE IN THE AFTERNOON.
By then Ava figured they'd walked off and on for four hours,
and as fit as she was, the uneven pathway had taken a toll on
her legs. She was pleased to call it a day when the sky turned
from dull grey to almost black and the prospect of rain
became certain. She and Fai were close to Huanghuacheng
by then and scurried into the town to find a taxi. They were
just climbing into one when the downpour began. Sheets
of rain, driven by a suddenly emerging strong wind, lashed
against the windows.

"Perfect timing," Ava said.

"I was going to suggest that we visit the Ming tombs, but
not in this weather," Fai said.

"I've had enough walking for one day anyway. My legs
ache," Ava said. "How come you don't seem the least bit
tired?"

"I've always had the ability to walk for miles and miles. I
have no idea where it comes from. When I first moved to
Beijing, I spent every Sunday walking around the city. It was
a good way to learn about it. I saw my first hutongs then and

fell in love with them, although I never imagined I'd have a chance to live in one."

"Does walking make you as hungry as it makes me?"

"I'm starving, but there aren't many restaurants around here."

"Can you wait until we get back to Beijing?"

"No problem," Fai said, and told the driver to head for the city.

The rain eased as they reached Beijing's outskirts, and it had stopped entirely by the time the taxi pulled up at the entrance to the hutong.

"Where do you want to eat?" Ava asked.

"There's a place called the Hai Wan Canteen a couple of streets from here that I really like," Fai said rather hesitantly. "It isn't fancy, but it may have the best zhajiang noodles in Beijing."

"I don't care if it's fancy as long as the food is good," Ava said. "I have an urge for hot and sour soup. Would they have that?"

"They usually do. The owner hires cooks from all over and the menu is a mixture of this and that."

"Let's go," Ava said.

It had rained heavily in Beijing as well, and they had to step over and around puddles on the way to the restaurant. Ava was so focused on keeping her feet dry that she didn't notice at first when Fai came to a stop in front of a steam-covered window. She saw chairs and tables inside and assumed it was the canteen, although there were no signs anywhere to indicate it.

"Good, it isn't too crowded," Fai said, opening the door.

The restaurant was a square with about ten large, round

tables occupying the centre of the white-tiled floor and another ten smaller tables lining the walls. The tables were covered with plastic sheets. The chairs were of the metal folding variety that Ava's mother pulled out of the closet to set up around the mah-jong table.

Fai waved to one of the female servers. The woman pointed to a table against the wall and a few minutes later came to them with cups and a pot of tea.

"Great to see you again. It's been a while. The boss isn't here. He'll be pissed to hear that he missed you," the woman said. Then she glanced curiously at Ava, as if surprised to see her. "Do you need a menu?"

"I think I'll just let my friend order for both of us," Ava said.

"Do you have hot and sour soup tonight?" Fai asked.

"We do."

"Fine. Then we'll have that and zhajiang noodles and jiaozi —"

"Jiaozi with pork or with scrambled eggs and chives?"

"Eggs and chives. And I think I'm in the mood for gong bao," Fai said. "That should be enough food, yes?"

"I can't see you two finishing it all."

"We've been walking all day and we're starving," Fai said. "Besides, you won't believe how much this woman can eat."

The server nodded. "Do you want something stronger to drink?"

"Do you have wine?" Ava asked.

"Only beer or cognac."

"I'd better stick with tea."

"I'll have a Yanjing," Fai said.

"I didn't know you drink beer," Ava said when the server left.

"Only on special occasions."

"And what makes this so special?"

Fai sat back in her chair and looked around the restaurant. "I've eaten here at least a hundred times. I discovered it by chance when I went for a walk after an argument with Lau Lau. It became my refuge, the place I came to when I needed quiet," she said. "You're the first person I've ever brought here."

"I'm flattered."

"I don't want you to be flattered. I'd much rather you understood how happy you make me, and how content I am when I'm with you," Fai said. "Today was wonderful, just being together, and walking and talking was wonderful."

"I enjoyed it as well after I stopped worrying about not having a phone."

"Speaking of which, I'm sure we can borrow one now if you really need to make a call."

"I can wait until we get home," Ava said as the server returned with a bottle of beer, an empty glass, and a large bowl balanced on a tray.

As Fai poured her beer, the server spooned hot and sour soup into their bowls. It was maroon coloured, a darker red than Ava was used to, and also contained more ingredients than was usual. Ava could see thin slivers of chicken and a brown meat that was either pork or duck; she also noticed wood mushrooms and fungi, small translucent shrimp and scallops, strips of green pepper, red chilis, and a tangle of bean sprouts. Across the soup's surface she could see chili oil shimmering like an oil slick on water. Ava added white pepper, mixed it in, took a spoonful of soup, and sipped carefully several times.

"How is it?" Fai asked.

"It has some heat to it but it isn't overpowering, and it has a delicate vinegar nip that I really like. Too often I find that restaurants go heavy on the heat and completely forget the traditional sour component. It's something I eat all the time, and what I love about it is that no two chefs, let alone restaurants, make it the same way. At the most basic level I'm sure there are similarities, but I think I've had every possible variation of hot and sour and a myriad of different ingredients, and I've seen it range in colour from bright red to dark brown."

"How does this one rate?"

Ava ate another two spoonfuls. "It's very good," she said finally. "Near the top."

Half an hour later she was saying the same thing about the rest of the food they'd ordered. Although she knew she was biased, it reconfirmed her belief that in terms of variety and quality, Chinese cuisine was the best in the world. How else to explain that, in a city as large and sophisticated as Beijing, she could find herself eating dinner in a restaurant that wasn't much larger than a hole in the wall, had the plainest of appearances, and didn't even bother putting its name on a sign (assuming that it actually had a name) and yet still have a meal that any five-star hotel restaurant would have been proud to serve?

The zhajiang noodles, tossed with a rich minced pork sauce and then dotted with fresh greens, and the crescent-shaped jiaozi dumplings were both excellent, but the gong bao really amazed her. It was a dish commonly known in North America as "kung pao" and usually made with chicken, but even the best she could remember was a pale imitation of what the chef in this small unnamed restaurant had conjured in his wok, using chicken thighs, soy sauce, sesame oil, Chinese black vinegar, rice wine, hoisin sauce, cashews, and chili peppers that the server said had come directly from a private source in Sichuan. Wherever they were from, they were tiny morsels of dynamite that Fai quenched with another beer, while Ava drank two large glasses of water.

"That was a terrific meal," Ava said as Fai paid the server for a bill that amounted to less than thirty American dollars. "I'll come back here anytime you want."

"You should make that soon," the server said, and then smiled at Ava. "We love Fai and we've missed her. She's not only our most famous customer, she's also our favourite."

"I'm quite sure those two things go hand in hand," Fai said.

"She can never accept a compliment," the server said to Ava as the women stood to leave.

The restaurant had been warm, its air infused with the aromas of garlic and ginger. It came as a bit of a shock when Ava and Fai walked into the dark, damp night and the smell of gasoline fumes. "It feels like rain again," Ava said, zipping up her jacket.

Fai did the same, then looped her arm through Ava's and pulled her close. "Let's hurry home."

The streets had lots of traffic but the sidewalks were quiet; it took them only a few minutes to reach the hutong. It began to rain as they stepped through the courtyard doors, and they scurried across the yard to Fai's. She fumbled with her key but they got inside the house just in time to avoid a suddenly vicious downpour.

Ava held out her arms and they hugged. The passions

they'd been withholding during the day were turned loose as they pressed every part of their bodies against each other.

"Let's go to bed," Fai said.

"In a minute. I should call Suki first," Ava said. "She'll be wondering what happened to me."

"Then call her. Do you want my phone?"

"I'll use my own. I'll go upstairs and get the charger."

"Hurry. I'll join you in a few minutes."

Ava took the phone from her jacket pocket as she climbed the stairs. The charger was sitting on a table by the bed. She plugged it in, inserted it into the phone, found Suki's number, and pressed.

"My god, Ava, are you all right?" Suki answered. "May and I have been trying to reach you for most of the day."

"I'm so sorry. I went to visit the Great Wall and took a phone that wasn't charged."

"So you're okay?"

"I'm fine."

"Good, but when you're finished talking to me, you have to call May Ling. She's worried sick about you."

"What did she think could have happened to me?"

"That's the point. Given your history, it could have been anything."

"I guess there's some truth in that."

"I wanted to reach you to tell you the Suns have agreed to the deal."

"Did they have any issues with foregoing the property assessments?"

"None. Actually, she told me that she suspected something like that might happen. They didn't say anything because they didn't want us to think they had some other motive for being opposed to it."

"Well then, I guess it's congratulations, Suki. You've done it again," Ava said. "When will the paperwork be finalized?"

"A day or two. I'm going to stay here until it's done."

"I will as well. Call me when you need me."

"Okay, I'll stay in touch, but make sure you phone May tonight."

Ava felt a touch of relief as the conversation ended. She hadn't expected anything negative to happen during the day, but she never discounted bad luck. Just as that thought left her, she heard voices from below. She dropped her phone onto the bed and walked to the top of the stairs.

"What's this?" Fai said.

"It's a package for you."

"I can see it's a package, but why do you have it?"

"What's going on down there?" Ava called out.

"Mr. Fan is here. He has a package for me," Fai said.

"Why does he have your package?" Ava asked, starting down the stairs.

"I was just asking the same question."

"Hello. Nice to see you again," Fan said as Ava reached the hallway.

"Nice to see you too."

"So what's this all about?" Fai said, looking at the large brown padded envelope that he still held in his hands.

"A man left this at your door earlier this afternoon. I didn't mean to interfere, but it began to rain quite heavily and I thought I should keep it dry until you got home."

"How did you know I wasn't at home?"

"I saw you and Ava leave earlier in the day."

"How did you know we'd left?"

"What else do I have to do but watch people come and go?"

Fai hesitated and then said, "Give me the package."

He handed it to her. She looked at the front and then the back. "All it has on it is my name on both sides," she said. "There's no address and no information about a sender."

"I thought that was a bit odd myself."

"This man who brought it, what did he look like?" Ava asked.

"I don't really know. He was wearing what they call a hoodie. I couldn't see his face."

"So he wasn't wearing the uniform of any delivery service?"

"Just jeans and a hoodie."

"That doesn't mean much. There are a lot of freelance delivery companies," Fai said to Ava.

"But why isn't there an address on the envelope?"

"He could have had it on a piece of paper."

"I think you're reading far too much into this," Fan said.

Fai stared at him. "Mr. Fan, thanks for your help delivering my package in a dry condition. I think we can handle it from here on."

"Sure. You two ladies have a nice evening, now," he said. He hesitated for a few seconds and then turned and walked out.

"That was a bit creepy," Ava said as the door closed behind him.

"It's as I told you: he wants to know everyone's business."

Ava looked at the envelope. "And I'm sure he's eager to know what's in there."

Fai nodded and tore open one end. "It's a plain DVD," she said, taking it out. "There's nothing else in here."

"Why would someone send you a disk?"

"It isn't that unusual. I get three or four a year from wannabe actors and directors."

"Still... No note, no name, no address?"

"Also not that unusual. All that information is normally in the introduction," Fai said, then paused. "Have you finished making your phone calls?"

"No. I should call May Ling."

"Then why don't you do that while I take a quick look at what I've got here. Then all our obligations will have been met and we can indulge ourselves in ourselves."

"I like the sound of that," Ava said.

23

AVA TRIED MAY'S MOBILE FIRST, BUT WHEN IT WENT directly to voicemail, she called her Wuhan office.

"Finally," May said after one ring. "We thought we'd lost you."

"I took a day off to tour and then my phone battery died. Sadly, there was nowhere on the Great Wall of China to recharge it. I guess they didn't think of that when they built it."

May Ling laughed. "Were you really on the wall?"

"For about four hours. I'd never seen it before."

"Me neither. What kind of Chinese does that make us?"

"Typical?"

"You're probably right," May said.

"I spoke to Suki, so I know that we have a deal here. I'm sorry I was out of touch, but I'm sure she didn't really need me."

"We all need you in our own way," May said. "And I have to say that, however highly Suki thought of you before — which was considerable — it skyrocketed when you took Pang Fai to dinner with the Suns."

"You told me that already."

"I know, but Suki keeps going on about it. She has heard so many stories about you, and this gives her a personal one to add."

"I was actually worried what she'd assume about Fai and me."

"Fai is a superstar; she lives on another planet. Suki and the others were thrilled just to be in her presence. No one thought twice about why she was there with you."

"Is it that simple?"

"For them it very well might be," May said. "I remember when we were in London for the PÖ launch. It astounded me how overwhelmed people were when they met her."

"And yet the truth is, she's as vulnerable as any of us."

"I don't doubt that," May said. "And I imagine that when you tell me the full story about this China Movie Syndicate guy, Mo, I'll learn more."

"When we have the chance to sit and talk, I'll fill you in," Ava said. Then she flinched as she heard what sounded like a wail. She took the phone from her ear and listened. It was quiet. "May, I'm going to stay here until the acquisition is fully complete. Then I'm going to talk Fai into taking a holiday. She's mentioned going to Yantai to see her parents, and after that I'd like to have her come to Toronto with me. Whatever I decide, I'll let you know."

"Your timing is good. After we're finished in Beijing, there isn't much going on in the business that Amanda can't handle. But it would be nice to see you before you head back to Toronto."

"Maybe I could stop in Hong Kong on the way?"

"I'd like that."

"Then I'll work on it," Ava said. She heard another noise, and this time she was certain it had originated downstairs. "May, I have to go. I'll be in touch."

She left her phone on the table and walked to the top of the stairs. She stopped and listened, wondering if the sounds were coming from the television and the DVD Fai was playing. She started to walk downstairs and was halfway there before she realized that the voice she was hearing was Fai's.

When Ava arrived in the living room, she saw Fai standing in the middle of the room with her back to the stairs and her attention focused on the television. She had a remote control in her right hand and was pointing it at the grainy black-and-white picture on the screen.

The picture quality was terrible, and Ava couldn't make out what it was supposed to represent until she stood alongside Fai. She lightly touched Fai's arm.

Fai recoiled, startled, and then slowly seemed to recognize that it was Ava. The hand that held the remote was shaking. "When will this end?" she said, her voice cracking.

"Is this all there is on the disk?" Ava said.

"No. There's a man who introduces it, and then he asks for money."

"I'd like to see him."

24

THEY LAY ON TOP OF THE BED FULLY CLOTHED, WRAPPED in each other's arms. There had been no attempt at lovemaking and little conversation beyond words of comfort from Ava since they had climbed the stairs an hour before.

"I can't put you through any more shit from my former life," Fai said finally, almost in a whisper. "The mess with Mo was bad enough, and you did more than I ever expected, or probably deserved. But the shit on that video and those demands...I can't ask you to help."

Ava didn't respond immediately. She pulled Fai closer and held on tight until she began to feel her become less tense. "Let's just talk about it," Ava said. "We can't ignore it, and I can't know about it and not want to help any way I can. You can't keep me from caring."

"But I can't keep throwing my problems at you."

"You didn't send that disk. But whoever did, my hope is that it's just a coincidence."

"What do you mean?"

"My hope is that the guy on the DVD is what he says is — a blackmailer — and that if we pay him we can make him go away," Ava said, glad to be talking about something other than Fai's state of mind. "I don't want to think that this is somehow connected to Mo, because if it is, it's either certain to become public or he'll want to trade it for the leverage we now have."

"Even if he isn't connected to Mo, he still wants five million renminbi, and I don't have that kind of money," Fai said. "And if I did, what guarantees do we have that he won't make that film public anyway?"

"Let's not go there just yet. Let's back up," Ava said. "Tell me, do you recognize the girl in the video, and do you know when it was shot?"

"She's an actress. I met her seven or eight years ago, when things were crumbling with Lau Lau. I was out of control and quite unstable. We went to her place after a day's work, had a few drinks, did a few lines, and went to bed. That's all I remember. I never saw her again."

"Do you remember her name?"

"No, but I'm sure I can find out."

"And you had no idea you were being filmed?"

"Of course not, and I wasn't so unstable that I wouldn't have noticed something like that. Besides, the quality is so crummy that it was obviously shot with some cheap hidden camera."

"I think you're right that the quality is poorer than you'd expect from any professional," Ava said. "But what's strange is that if it was a setup, if the plan was to film you in such a compromising act and then blackmail you, why would someone wait this long to do it?"

"It doesn't make sense, does it."

"I don't think it does, unless you're prepared to believe

in incredible coincidences," Ava said. "And Uncle used to say that believing in coincidences was a way of hiding from unpleasant truths."

"God, I don't want that video to become public," Fai said in a rush. "And it's not because I'm having sex with a woman. I know that, sooner rather than later, I'm going to have to come out. I'm getting emotionally and mentally prepared to do that and I believe I can live with the consequences. But when I do come out, I want it to be under my terms, and I want it to be as dignified, as classy, and as graceful as possible. I want to do it with pride, not with apologies. That video cries out for apologies, because the woman in it looks so fucking tawdry and desperate. I don't want that to be my legacy."

"Then we need to accept reality and deal with the hand we've been dealt," said Ava.

"How do we do that?"

"We need to find out who sent the disk and who controls the original, and then we have to find them and make the video disappear."

"Is that possible?"

"Anything is possible," Ava said, with more confidence than she felt.

Fai nodded in a way that implied she wasn't so convinced. "Do you think it was Mo who sent it?"

"Given the timing, he seems to be the most likely candidate, but I don't think we should automatically leap to that conclusion," Ava said. "For one thing, if it is him, why is he asking for money instead of using the video to get us to back down on exposing his son?"

"I don't know."

"Neither do I, which is why we need to find out who actually sent you this video and what their real intentions are."

"Fuck," Fai said as she extracted herself from Ava's arms and rolled to the side of the bed.

"What don't you like about that as a plan?" Ava asked, surprised by her reaction.

"Earlier today, when we were walking on the wall, and tonight at dinner, I was so happy. I thought that with Mo and all that shit behind us, we would now be able to focus on each other and enjoy all the small things that make a relationship work. Then this happens…"

"We'll deal with it."

"But I have all this baggage, and I hate it. I hate the life I had that contributed to it."

"There's no point in berating yourself. We all have baggage."

"Except your baggage has no impact on us."

"Not yet, but it could, and then you can help me deal with my shit," Ava said. "Right now, let's forget about the past and focus on what we need to do to make this go away."

Fai shook her head. "If it is a blackmailer, and if money is all he wants, I might be able to come up with the five million."

"Don't worry about the money. I can cover it."

"No, no, no!" Fai shouted. "If you want to help me locate this guy and work out some kind of plan for dealing with him, I'm all for that. But I won't accept money from you, and I don't want you to mention it again."

"However you want to handle it is fine with me," Ava said.

"Good. Now how do we go about this?"

"Before we start, you should know that things could get ugly."

"It's ugly enough already. I think I can cope with whatever

happens," Fai said. She turned so that they were face to face, their breaths intertwined. "How do we start?"

"He left a phone number for you to call. Let's do it so he can confirm that you got the DVD and you understand what he wants," Ava said. "You'll tell him you'll pay, of course, but you need to do some negotiating."

"Negotiating?"

"Yes. At the outset I think you should tell him that five million is too much for you to raise, and that all you're prepared to pay is two million."

"What if he insists on five?"

"Insist right back and try to get him to compromise. If he won't, then you tell him that you might be able to raise two million in a week, but for five million it could take a month," Ava said. "This is all about buying the time we need to locate the son of a bitch, but doing it in a way that won't piss him off or make him think that you're playing games. You need to sound upset and a bit scared, but despite all that he needs to feel that you're being co-operative."

"I get it," Fai said.

"Then let's make the phone call."

"Ava, could we trace the phone number?"

"I'm quite sure it's a throwaway phone and that this is the last time he'll use it. If he wants us to call him again at the same number, then he's a fool and we will find a way to trace it."

Fai licked her lips. "My mouth is dry. I need a drink. I'll make the call from the kitchen."

Ava followed Fai down the stairs, noticing that she seemed steadier now. Her initial reaction hadn't been surprising, but she needed to be strong, to gain some control over her emotions, Ava thought. And she was going to have to show some resiliency, because this problem wasn't going to have an easy or efficient resolution. By its very nature it was messy and had the potential to get messier, but Ava wasn't about to say that. This wasn't the time to risk undermining whatever confidence Fai had.

When they reached the kitchen, Fai went to the fridge and took out a bottle of sparkling water.

"We need the phone number from the video," Ava said. "I'll get it and be right back."

She went into the living room and turned on the television and DVD player. The first part of the video featured a man wearing a balaclava, standing against a blank wall as he delivered his message in a muffled voice. Ava wrote down the phone number he recited and then returned to the kitchen.

Fai sat at the table with her phone and a glass of water in front of her. She looked more nervous than she had when she'd left the bedroom.

"I was thinking that you might tell the guy you have a girlfriend here with you," Ava said. "You don't have to tell him my name unless he asks, but it would give you a reason to put the call on speakerphone and give me an excuse to ask some questions."

"He might not like that."

"Then he'll tell us, and you can speak to him by yourself. If I want you to ask him something, I'll whisper."

"Okay."

"Good. Here's the number."

Fai lifted the glass to her mouth and drained half of it. Then she shrugged, put the phone on speaker mode, and called the number.

"Is this Pang Fai?" a man's distorted voice asked.

"It is."

"And the number you're calling from, can I reach you on it anytime I choose?"

"It's the only phone I have."

"The line doesn't sound right."

"I have it on speaker mode. I have a girlfriend with me. I need her for support, as I'm sure you can understand."

"Who is she?"

Fai looked at Ava, and Ava thought of several options before deciding that there was no value in telling a lie. "My name is Ava Lee, and can I say that your line doesn't sound right either. We can barely understand you."

"I have my reasons for disguising my voice," he said. "Where are the two of you right now?"

"Sitting in the kitchen of my home," Fai said.

The man became quiet, and Ava wondered if he could possibly be trying to confirm that. Then he said, "This is unfortunate."

"What is?" Ava asked.

"This entire event."

"Do you mean our conversation?"

"No, the situation in which we find ourselves," he said. "I want you to believe me when I say that I don't want to bring any harm to Pang Fai personally or to her career. I have nothing but admiration for her and her talents, but my personal circumstances force me to forget that."

"And by personal circumstances, you mean you need money?"

"I do."

"I can't pay you five million," Fai said quickly.

"You must have that much."

"I don't. I might be able to borrow it in bits and pieces from friends, but that would take time. All I can come up with on my own is about two million, and it's not readily at hand. I would have to sell some things."

"I want the five million. I can't settle for less."

"I can't guarantee I can raise it."

"You have to try."

"It will take time."

"How much time?"

"A few weeks."

"No," he said.

"I'm sorry," Fai said. "If you want five million, I can't do any better than that."

"Then we have a problem."

"You mean you have a problem," Ava said. "You need money and Pang Fai is prepared to give what she can, but you can't wait. Are things really that desperate?"

"My situation is no concern of yours. You should be worried about what this could mean for Pang Fai."

"Believe me, we are," Ava said. "But look at things from our side. Even if we pay you what you want, what guarantee do we have that the video won't be released or that you won't come back for more money?"

"You have my word."

"We don't even know who you are."

"Fai knows me," he said. "Why do you think I'm disguising my voice?"

"What!" Fai said.

"You worked with me."

"I've worked with a lot of people."

"And I'm one of them, but that's all I'm prepared to say."

"Since you want to characterize yourself as an acquaintance, even a colleague, can you find some room to compromise?" Ava said.

He paused and then said, "What do you have in mind?"

"Three million in two weeks."

"Not enough money and too much time."

"Three million in one week."

"That's better, but how about four million in five days?"

"It would be tough," Fai said.

"But not impossible?"

Fai looked at Ava, who nodded.

"We'll try," Fai said.

"You'll have to do better than try if you want this to end well," he said.

"I'll do everything I can."

"I don't want to hurt you and I know how devastating it would be if this video fell into the wrong hands. So please, for all our sakes, come through with the money," he said, then paused. "I'll be phoning you five days from now. Be prepared for my call." The line went dead.

Fai's head snapped towards Ava. "Well, I didn't expect that," she said.

"It was strange," Ava admitted.

"And a little encouraging."

"Do you mean the fact that he claims he doesn't want to hurt you?"

"Yes. And that he knows me and worked with me," Fai said. "So this isn't just some criminal with no sense of morality."

"Or else he's a very clever criminal who knows how to spin a tale."

"You weren't even a little encouraged?"

"Fai, we don't know who this person is and we don't know how he got his hands on the video. We also don't know how many copies he might have made and who has them, and we have no idea what he's actually going to do if we pay him the money in full and on time."

Fai's shoulders slumped and her head fell towards her chest. "I guess I'm looking for silver linings."

"I don't mean to sound negative. Something good did come from that call."

"What?"

"We now have five days to find him."

25

AVA LEFT FAI IN THE KITCHEN WHILE SHE WENT UP upstairs to get her Moleskine notebook. She didn't actually need it, but it gave her time to gather her thoughts. She had been more encouraged by the phone call than she let on, but her old work habits were still with her. During her years with Uncle, one of their most difficult jobs was managing the expectations of clients who assumed that because Uncle and Ava had taken on their problem, it was on its way to being solved. Uncle promised them nothing but their best efforts and kept expectations as close to zero as he could. It was a policy that had nothing but upsides. If they failed on a job, the clients weren't surprised and normally attached no blame. If they were successful, it was as if they'd wrought some miracle. It was a lesson Ava had learned so well that when she was in the field working on a job, she even practised it when she was communicating with Uncle. She knew it occasionally frustrated him, but it also made it possible for him to be honestly obtuse with the clients. Now she was operating in the same manner with Fai. The truth was, she couldn't bring herself to do it any other way.

Ava believed Fai had probably been correct in her assessment of the man they'd called. He'd been polite enough — the furthest thing from a foul-mouthed thug. But did that mean he'd told them the truth about having worked with Fai? The revelation hadn't been necessary, and she couldn't help but wonder if it was a deliberate plant, intended to mislead. But even if it wasn't, and even if his conversation with them had been reasonable — subject matter aside — did that make him potentially more or less dangerous?

"I've made tea," Fai said as Ava returned to the kitchen.

"I'll have it later," Ava said. "I want to talk to Mr. Fan. Which house is his?"

"Why do you want to talk to him?"

"I have some questions about the package and the man who delivered it."

Fai nodded. "He lives two doors to the left. Do you want me to come with you?"

"No, what I want you to do is find the name of the woman in the video, and once you've done that, find out how we can contact her. You may have to watch the DVD again to see if it jogs your memory."

"I don't want to watch that video again. And besides, I have a better idea," Fai said. "I have a rough notion of which year that happened. I have records of every film I've made, including cast lists, some of them with photos. I'll go over the ones from that time period. I'm sure if I see her name or get lucky and find a photo, I'll be able to make the link."

"We will still need to know where she is and how to get in touch with her."

"If she's still active in the business, I should be able to locate her online. If she isn't, I may have to call around."

"Be careful who you call and what you say. You'll need a reason for looking for her that sounds plausible."

"I'll come up with something."

"Anyway, I may be back here by the time you need to do that."

"Do you really think Fan can help any more than he has?"

"He probably saw more of the person who made the delivery than he realizes," Ava said. "Now I'd better get going before it's too late in the evening to be making house calls."

Fai walked with her to the door, opened it, and said, "His light is still on. It's the green door."

The rain had stopped but the air was damp and cold. Ava was beginning to wonder if Beijing ever had weather that encouraged people to go outdoors. She hurried to Fan's door and used the lion-shaped brass knocker that was fixed at eye level. She counted to ten and then rapped it hard twice more. The door opened a crack and she saw part of Fan's face. The door swung open.

"Ms. Lee. I didn't expect to see you again tonight."

"I'm sorry to bother you, but I have some questions about the package you delivered to Fai."

Fan took a step back into the house. "Come inside. It's cold out there."

"Thanks," she said as she entered.

The house was constructed identically to Fai's, and probably to every other house surrounding the courtyard, but it was so crammed with stuffed furniture and bookcases that it seemed smaller. Everywhere she looked there were books — in and on top of the bookcases, stacked on several coffee tables, and strewn across a sofa.

"Would you like some tea, or something stronger? I have beer."

"No, thanks. I don't think I'll be here that long."

"But at least you'll sit," he said, removing books from the sofa to create space for her.

She sat down, and he sat in an easy chair to her right. An ashtray on one of the chair's arms was full to overflowing with cigarette butts. That surprised her, since she couldn't remember seeing him smoking and had never detected any cigarette odour on his breath or clothes.

"Now, what can I do for you?" he asked.

"I'm curious about that package — actually, about who delivered it."

"Why?"

"As you know, not only wasn't there a name or address on the outside, there was nothing on the inside to indicate who sent it. Fai would like to contact whoever did, but right now that's impossible."

"I told you everything I know."

"Do you think you could search your memory again?"

"I don't think it would do much good."

"The thing is, the package was delivered during the day, so there was good light. Your house is very close to Fai's, and if you were at the window like you said, you must have had a very clear view of the man. You are a writer, and from what I've experienced talking to you, you seem to be observant."

"I told you, he was wearing jeans and a hoodie that was pulled over his head and covered most of his face."

"But you could see some of his face?"

"I saw part of the bottom half. He had a scrawny black beard. That's all I can say for certain."

"That's a start," Ava said with a slight smile. "Now, as you told us earlier, he obviously wasn't in a uniform, but are you sure there wasn't a name on the hoodie? I don't mean a business name, but how about a brand name?"

"None that I can remember."

"What colour was the hoodie?"

"A dark blue."'

"Like the jeans?"

"No, they were light brown."

Ava had brought her notebook with her. Now she opened it and made a note of Fan's description. She felt his eyes on her and knew he was wondering what he'd said that warranted being written down. "What was he wearing on his feet?" she asked.

"Shoes."

He was getting annoyed, Ava knew, but that wasn't necessarily a bad thing. "What kind of shoes? Dress, work, running?"

"White running shoes."

"Did you see what brand?"

"Nike."

"Your memory is improving. I thought it might if you made an effort," Ava said. "Now, how tall do you think he was?"

"Five eight or nine. Medium height, anyway."

"Was he skinny, fat?"

"Hard to tell under the hoodie, but I'd guess medium again."

Ava sat back on the sofa with the notebook open on her lap, all of her attention on Fan. "When the man came to Fai's door, did he knock on it, did he wait to see if anyone was home, or did he just leave the envelope by the door?"

"What are you, some kind of detective or police officer?"

"As I told you when we first met, I'm an accountant. It's a profession that values detail."

Fan shrugged. "I didn't see him knock. He just leaned the envelope against the door."

"Did you find that strange?"

"I didn't think about it."

"And after he placed the envelope at the door, did he hurry off? Was he looking around as if he was afraid someone would see him?"

"None of the above. He looked perfectly relaxed."

"How could you tell when you couldn't see his face?"

"He walked naturally enough."

"This is terrifically helpful, Mr. Fan," Ava said, looking down at her notebook. "Now there's just one more question I have for you. I hope it won't cause offence."

"I have found most of your approach offensive."

"Good. So this shouldn't be any worse," Ava said with a smile. "What I'm anxious to know is whether or not you switched envelopes."

"What the fuck are you talking about?" he said, starting to rise from his chair.

"Please sit. I don't want to have to insist," Ava said.

He stared at her, and she stared back. He was the first to break eye contact, and a few seconds later he fell back into his chair.

"The reason I ask is that it is highly unusual to get a package or envelope delivered with simply a name on it. In this case the name was written in some kind of black felt pen. You told us that you went to get the envelope because it was raining and you were afraid it would get wet. Well, there isn't any overhang at Fai's door. If it was already raining, the envelope would have gotten wet and the ink on the envelope would have run. The envelope you gave us looked as if it had just come out of a drawer."

He turned his eyes away from her and she watched him lick his lips.

"Please don't lie to me," she said. "This could be important."

"I didn't look at the disk," he said. "I don't have anything to play it on."

"Was there a note with the disk?"

"No."

"Where's the original envelope?"

"In my trash."

"Please get it."

He pushed himself up from the chair and, still not looking at her, went towards what she knew was the kitchen. She glanced around the room. There was no television, but that didn't mean he didn't have one upstairs or that he hadn't watched the disk on his computer.

"Here it is," he said, walking out of the kitchen with his hand extended.

The envelope was grey and about the same size as the brown one. Fai's name and address were smudged but still clearly visible. There was no information about the sender or anything that would indicate a delivery company had been used.

"It doesn't look like it really needed to be rescued," Ava said.

"The rain had just started. It got worse."

"And you're certain there was no note inside."

"There was only the disk."

"Which you didn't watch."

"Correct."

"And everything you've told me about the person who left the envelope at Fai's door is all you can remember?"

"I swear it is."

Ava slipped the envelope into the back of her notebook. "Mr. Fan, there are several crimes you could be charged with," she said slowly. "But I think that Fai will be prepared to maintain a good relationship with you as a neighbour if you agree not to do anything like this ever again."

"Never," he said quickly.

"And if you don't talk about this incident to anyone."

"Why would I?"

"One last thing. Can you tell me how to get in touch with Lau Lau?"

"What does he have to do with any of this?"

"I may need to talk to him. That's all you need to know."

"I'm not sure I —"

"Mr. Fan," Ava said, leaning in close. "When I met you in the tea room, you told me that you've seen Lau Lau from time to time. How did that happen? Did he call you? Did you call him? Did you meet by accident on the street?"

"He called me."

"Do you have a phone number for him?"

"I'm not sure it's still in service."

"Give it to me anyway. We'll take our chances with it."

"The book with those numbers is in my bedroom."

"Go and get it. I'll wait," Ava said. "But Mr. Fan, please don't try anything fancy. Please don't try to call Lau Lau or anyone else while you're upstairs. I may not look particularly fearsome, but I am adept at martial arts and I have no reservations about hitting a man of your age."

He raised himself slowly from the chair and then stared down at her. "What kind of woman has Pang Fai become entangled with?"

"One she needs."

26

AVA LEFT FAN'S HOUSE, WALKED A FEW METRES TO THE right, and opened the door to find Fai on her knees in the living room, surrounded by boxes.

"I didn't put dates on any of these — I feel so disorganized. But I think I've finally found the right time period," Fai said. "How did it go with Mr. Fan?"

"It went well enough. Among other things, I confirmed that he's a sneak and not to be trusted."

"Why do you say that?" Fai asked as she leafed through a stack of paper.

"He opened the original package that was delivered and put the DVD in a new envelope."

"How do you know?"

"He told me after I confronted him," Ava said, taking the envelope from her notebook. "There's no information on it that's of any use, and he swears there wasn't anything but the DVD inside."

"Did he watch the disk?" Fai asked, her voice rising.

"He says he didn't, and I didn't see anything he could watch it on inside the house."

"Is he involved in this?"

Ava lowered herself onto the floor next to Fai. "I don't think so. If he was, there would be no reason for him to switch envelopes. He's just a nosy old man."

Fai hesitated, nodded, and then opened a red binder and began to leaf through it. "This may be the one," she said suddenly.

Ava looked at a photo of a thin, long-faced young woman with large, luminous eyes.

"Her name is Mak Guang. She had a minor supporting role in this film. I feel so stupid now that I couldn't remember," Fai said.

"You said it was a difficult time."

"The film was called *Peasant Dreams*. It was the first one I made that wasn't directed by Lau Lau. So in addition to all the personal stuff we were going through, I was massively insecure about the prospect of working with a new director. I wanted to impress him and everyone else so badly; I wanted to prove that I was a real actress and not simply Lau Lau's creation."

Ava looked at Mak Guang again. "There is a definite similarity between her and the woman in the video," she said.

"Oh, it's her, I'm sure of it. It's all coming back to me now."

"So you went back to her place? It wasn't someone else's, or a hotel room?"

"She said it was her place, but how would I really know? She could have been sharing it or borrowing it."

"What did you know about her?"

"What do you mean?"

"Did she work full-time as an actress or did she have another job? Did she have a boyfriend or a girlfriend? Was she out?"

"Ava, I wanted sex. I didn't go with her for the conversation," Fai said. "I had hardly spoken to her until we hooked up that night, and I didn't see her or speak to her again after that. In fact, I think one of the reasons I went with her was that it was her last scheduled day of shooting, so I wouldn't have to deal with her on the set the next day."

"Okay," Ava said, not particularly surprised by Fai's admission. When she was younger, she herself had indulged in that kind of almost anonymous sex. "But now that you do know her name, can you locate her?"

"Let me see what I can find online. My phone is in the kitchen," Fai said, getting to her feet.

Ava thought about joining her but decided that looking over Fai's shoulder would be more intrusive than helpful. Instead she picked up the *Peasant Dreams* binder. In the front was a list of the cast and crew. Only the director, producer, cinematographer, and cast warranted photos. The bulk of the binder was the script. Fai — at least, Ava assumed it was Fai — had highlighted her lines in yellow marker and had written comments in the margin. Some of the comments were less than complimentary about the lines she was expected to speak, and Ava wondered how many of them had survived as written.

"I'm not finding very much," Fai shouted from the kitchen. "She seems to have packed it in not long after that film was made. It might be more productive to make some phone calls."

"Then let's do that."

"Check the cast list on that film, will you?" Fai said. "I think Jin Delun was part of it, and if he was, I'll call him. He makes a point of staying in touch with just about everyone he's ever worked with."

"He's there."

"Great. I have his number," Fai said.

Ava walked into the kitchen just as Fai was raising the phone to her ear. "Popo. It's me, Pang Fai."

Ava blinked. *Po po* was the slang term for "old lady" or "grandmother."

"I'm well, and it sounds like you are too," Fai said. "The reason I'm calling is that I need to contact Mak Guang. Do you remember her? She was tall and skinny, played one of my sisters in *Peasant Dreams*."

Ava watched Fai as she listened to Jin. After a few minutes a slight nod of Fai's head and a small, tight smile told her they were having some success.

"Well?" Ava said as Fai hung up.

"She lives somewhere in Tianjin," said Fai.

"Somewhere? Tianjin is a large city."

"He's texting me her phone number. Popo says her husband's name is Yao Bolin. He's the deputy mayor."

"She married well."

"That's one of the benefits of being an actress. The exposure expands your marriage pool."

"So Mak is bi?"

"Who knows? She could be like me. It could be a marriage of convenience. God knows there are enough of them."

"Did Jin ever marry?"

"No," Fai said. "He's so flamboyantly gay he couldn't fool a blind and deaf woman."

"Is that why you call him Popo?"

"That's what he calls himself. If I had asked for Jin Delun, he might not have recognized right away who I was talking about."

Ava looked at her watch. "Well, even if he's correct about her living in Tianjin, and especially if he's right about her being married to the deputy mayor, it's a bit late to call her tonight."

"Why is it too late?"

"We want her to be honest with us. Do you think she'll be forthright if we call her at home when her husband's there?"

"Why would she be honest if he isn't there?"

"Because you're not the only person in the video. She'll be as anxious as you are not to have it made public."

"Of course she will." Fai groaned. "I'm not thinking very clearly."

"You came up with her name, so your memory isn't that bad," Ava said. "How are things with Lau Lau?"

"Why do you mention him?"

"It's the video. I know it's crude, but he was capable of arranging it."

"Why would he do that?"

"Jealousy? Revenge? You said things were a mess between you at the time, and he knew about your fondness for women."

"He was never vindictive."

"Maybe he was confused, screwed up. Maybe he filmed it for kicks. Who knows what his rationale might have been? But he could have done it and then hung on to it, until things went bad financially and he decided he could use it to cash in."

"Do you really believe that?"

"I don't know what to believe, except that we can't discount anything, and that we shouldn't be surprised by anything Mak tells us tomorrow."

"You seem sure that she'll know who filmed us."

Ava hesitated, not sure how far to take her questions. "Fai, when you and Mak hooked up, who did the hooking? Who made the first move?"

"I can't remember."

"Think harder. If it was her and she took you back to the apartment, it could have been a setup. If it was you and her apartment was a convenience, then we're dealing with something far more complicated."

"You said earlier that you don't believe in coincidences," Fai said.

"And it doesn't seem believable that you'd accidently end up in an apartment that had a surveillance system of some sort, does it."

"No. If it wasn't an accident, it had to be someone close to me who had a hand in it."

"We don't know who did what yet. We need to keep completely open minds."

Fai shook her head. "My mind can't handle any more tonight."

"Then let's go to bed and put our minds on hold until tomorrow morning."

27

AVA WOKE IN AN EMPTY BED. SHE'D SLEPT THE ENTIRE night, foregoing her usual early-hours bathroom run, and had been so out of it that she hadn't heard Fai get up. She felt the sheets on Fai's side of the bed. They were cool; Ava wondered when she'd risen.

She slid from the bed, slipped on some underwear and a pair of black Adidas training pants, and then pulled a black Giordano T-shirt over her head. Before going to the bathroom, she went to the top of the stairs. "You down there?" she shouted.

"I'm making breakfast."

"I have to go to the bathroom. I'll see you when I'm done."

Five minutes later, washed and brushed, Ava was halfway down the stairs before the first hint of aroma tickled her nose. She guessed it was congee, but that confused her, because the rice porridge normally took hours of preparation; in most cases it would have been started the night before. Just how long had Fai been up?

When she walked into the kitchen, Fai was standing over the stove stirring a pot, her back turned. She was wearing only underwear and a T-shirt. On the table were plates of pickled tofu, salted duck eggs, and youtiao. "I know you bought the food on the table, but when did you find the time to make congee?" Ava asked.

"I bought that too," Fai said. "There's an old woman with a stall on the hutong that opens from six to ten in the morning to sell congee and all the things that go with it. She usually runs out of congee by eight. This is one of the few times I was early enough to get some."

"What time was that?"

"Before seven."

Ava glanced at the clock on the stove. It was almost nine. "And when did you get out of bed?"

"Around six, but I woke up about an hour before that."

"You should have let me know."

"Why? You were sleeping so soundly it would have been selfish to disturb you. Besides, when I woke up I had a bit of a panic attack. I couldn't stop thinking about the horrible things that might happen. So I eventually came downstairs, made some tea, and sat in the kitchen by myself with all the lights on. By the time the sun came up, things didn't seem quite so dire and I was famished. So I went to see the congee woman."

"I like congee. I used to eat it with Uncle. There was a shop in Kowloon near his apartment that we went to virtually every morning towards the end, when he was really ill. I haven't eaten it much since then."

"Were you afraid it would trigger bad memories?"

"I have no bad memories where Uncle is concerned. I think I just needed a break from congee."

"You don't have to eat any."

"Don't be silly. It smells wonderful, and I'm hungry — although I'll pass on the duck eggs."

"Then let's eat," Fai said.

Ava sat down while Fai spooned the white gruel into bowls that were so large she had to carry them to the table one at a time.

"I added some double-smoked ham and spring onions," Fai said. "It makes it less bland."

Ava sprinkled white pepper across the top, stirred it in slightly, and then took a stick of youtiao and dipped in the fried dough. "This is really good," she said after taking a bite. "I think I can even taste the smoked ham."

"Adding this and that is the extent of my cooking skill."

"I can't even do that much," Ava said.

The congee was hot, so they ate slowly, hardly saying a word. When the bowls were empty, Fai refilled them and they resumed what was becoming a long, drawn-out breakfast.

Ava glanced at Fai from time to time. Whenever she did, she saw that her friend's focus was on the congee. "Do you want to talk about your panic attack?" she finally asked.

"It came and it went."

"You're okay?"

"Maybe I'm just becoming fatalistic. You know, 'what will be, will be.' And if I'm really being objective, that might not be such a bad outcome."

"Are you up to phoning Mak Guang now?"

"Am I ever."

"Her husband will have gone to his office by now, so we can call anytime."

"Then let's get it over with," Fai said, picking up her bowl and carrying it to the sink. Her phone lay on the counter nearby.

"Do it the way we did with the blackmailer."

"Speakerphone?"

"Yes, and let Mak know that I'm on the line and I'm a friend who's helping."

Fai brought the phone back to the table, found the text from Popo, and punched in the number.

"Yao residence," a woman answered.

"Can I speak to Mak Guang, to Mrs. Yao?" Fai said.

"Who's calling?"

Fai drew a deep breath. "Pang Fai."

"Just a moment," the woman said hesitantly.

They waited for a minute that seemed like ten.

"Fai, is it really you?" another voice said. "My housekeeper thought someone was playing a joke on her."

"It is me."

"I'm flattered that you've called, but I can't imagine why you would."

"Are you alone? Are you free to talk?" Fai said.

"Yes, but why do you ask?"

"I should have told you before I asked that question that I have a friend, Ava Lee, with me here, and that we're on speakerphone."

"What difference does that make?"

"None, really, but I don't want you to think I'm trying to do anything underhanded," Fai said. "Ava is more than just a friend, actually, and she's helping me with a problem. She has some questions she wants to ask you."

"Why would I think you're being underhanded, and what kind of questions could she possibly have for me?"

Fai looked across the table at Ava.

"You and Fai both have a problem that you may not want anyone else to know about," Ava said. "The fact that I do know might make you uncomfortable."

"What problem?" Mak said.

"You can't imagine what it might be?"

"No."

"You slept together."

"As I remember," Mak said, "we didn't sleep."

"I'm glad you can make light of it, but it isn't such a trivial matter on Fai's side."

"Why? What does it matter?"

"She's being blackmailed because of it."

"What!"

"By your reaction I'm assuming that you haven't been contacted. You haven't been threatened?"

"Of course not."

"How fortunate for you. Fai hasn't been so lucky."

"She's being blackmailed because of our adventure together?"

"Yes."

"Are you suggesting that I somehow had something to do with this?"

"No, but why do you ask?"

"Because who else knows what happened that night? It was just Fai and me, just the two of us."

"That's not precisely true. Someone else was there — in person or by proxy. A video exists of what you refer to as your 'adventure.' A copy was sent to Fai on a DVD, along with a request for a substantial amount of money."

"That's impossible!" Mak blurted.

"What is? That a video exists or that someone is using it to blackmail Fai?"

"I'm telling you, there was no one else there."

"Which raises the question of exactly where 'there' was. Was it your apartment you were in?"

Mak paused, and Ava knew the answer before she gave it. "It belonged to a friend," she said.

"What kind of friend records your sexual exploits?"

Mak went quiet again. Then she said, "I find all this confusing, and quite disturbing."

"Who was the friend?" Ava pressed.

"Is Fai going to pay?"

"What does that have to do with my question?"

"Nothing. I'm just curious, because if she does pay, maybe it will go away."

"That's wishful thinking," Ava said. "The only chance for it to disappear is for us to find the person who has it. And even then there's no certainty we'll be successful."

"What do you want from me?"

"Help. You could start by telling us who lived in that apartment."

"I'm not sure I should be getting involved in this," Mak said carefully.

"You do understand how damaging the publicity could be to Fai?"

"Yes, but she's a star — a huge star — and I'm sure she'll be able to get past this after a while."

"How about you? Will you able to get past it?" Ava said. "We know your husband is the deputy mayor of Tianjin. How is he going to react when the video becomes public? What's the mayor going to say? What's the provincial Party secretary going to do? He's got instructions from Beijing to uphold — publicly, at least — the highest standards of morality. It would be a mess."

"No one would care about the other woman in that video. The spotlight would be completely on Fai."

"We'd make sure you got your fair share of the limelight, particularly with people who matter politically."

"Guang, how can you be so self-centred? How can you be so fucking dumb to think that you wouldn't be smeared as well?" Fai exclaimed.

Ava looked at her. Throughout the conversation with Mak she'd sat quietly, her face impassive, but now her lips were drawn tight and her jaw was clenched.

"We need your help if we are to have any chance of keeping this thing private for both your sakes," Ava said.

"I need to think," Mak said.

"About what?"

"How to help."

"Tell us the name of the friend who had the apartment. That's a good start."

"But then you'd want to talk to her, yes?"

"Of course."

"I'm uncomfortable about that for a number of reasons, one of which is that I don't believe she knew Fai and I were together in her apartment that night. I kept my little romances secret, even from friends, and I'm quite sure she thought I was with a man," Mak said. "Another reason is that I'm convinced she knew nothing about any recording system...but she might be able to point us in the direction of who did. In the end there could be multiple conversations. If you truly want to keep Fai's name out of this, you might be wise to let me have them."

"That actually makes some sense," Ava said.

"Assuming we can trust you," Fai added.

"As you said, I have almost as much to lose as you."

"I'm sorry I had to point that out the way I did," Ava said.

"No, you were right to do that. I have a tendency to hide from unpleasantness."

"So where does this leave us?" Ava said.

"I'll make some phone calls and get back to you as soon as I can."

"We have a deadline, and not much time to waste," Ava said.

"I'll start as soon as we hang up."

"Is Fai's number on your screen?"

"Yes."

"That's how you can reach us," Ava said. "I'd like to hear from you today. And please, don't make us chase you."

"You didn't have to say that."

"Sorry," Ava said, and ended the call.

"What do you think?" Fai asked. "Will she help?"

"Is she smart? Is she really self-centred?"

"Yes."

"Then she'll help."

28

THE CALL FROM MAK GUANG CAME IN LESS THAN AN hour. Ava and Fai were about to leave the house for a walk when Fai's phone rang. She answered, listened for a few seconds, and then said, "You'd better speak to Ava."

"This is far quicker than I expected," Ava said, after putting the phone on speaker.

"I had one person I needed to talk to, and I got hold of her right away," Mak said. "She's the friend who loaned me the apartment."

"What's her name?"

"Is it really necessary that you know?"

"Guang, we need to trust each other."

"Her name is Ren Lan. She was — and is — an actress. Fai knows her," Mak said. "But I promised her I'd keep her out of this. She doesn't want to create enemies."

"Did you tell her it was you and Fai in the video?"

"No, I just said I've been told there's a video of me in circulation that I'm sure was made at her place. I said the other party in it is someone important enough to have vengeful friends."

"Well, she doesn't have to worry if she had nothing to do with the recording."

"But she did, indirectly."

"Meaning she knew that whatever went on in that bedroom was being recorded?"

"There was a switch on the wall linked to the camera. She turned it off and on as she saw fit. It was always off when she was in the bed and it was on when she knew someone else would be using it."

"Why did she do it?"

"Money."

"Yes, of course it was money, but how did she make money by doing that?"

"She was being paid by the person who installed the camera."

"Did she see the recordings?"

"No, she let him know whenever there had been action in the bedroom, and he'd come by and pick them up."

"So she wasn't selling the videos herself?"

"No."

"What did she think was being done with them?"

"She thought they were being sold as porn films."

"They would have been unscripted, amateurish. Who would have any interest in them?"

"There wasn't much else available. Besides, maybe the people buying them liked the fact that they were natural rather than contrived."

"But if that was the case, why hasn't this one surfaced until now? Surely a video of Pang Fai with another woman would have attracted a lot of attention."

"I can't answer that question."

"Then answer these: who installed the camera and who was paying her?" Ava asked, bracing herself for a reply she didn't want to hear.

"Bai Lok."

"Who?"

"Fai will probably remember him. He was an AD."

"What's an AD?"

"An assistant director. He worked on a lot of films, and I'm sure she was in some of them."

"Did you talk to him?"

"I couldn't."

"You couldn't or you didn't try?"

"I said I couldn't. He died of cancer three years ago."

Ava sighed. "Great. So that means all we have is the word of this Ren Lan," Ava said. "That's convenient for her, isn't it."

"You're very cynical."

"My life experience has taught me that you can never be too cynical," Ava said. "Now tell me, how receptive was Ren Lan when you called her?"

"Not very at first, but I was insistent, and I think I scared her a little," Mak said. "She lives on the outskirts of Tianjin, so she knows my husband's position and knows that things can be made to happen."

"So you believe her?"

"I do."

"What else did she tell you?"

"Like what?"

"How long did this scheme go on?"

Mak hesitated and then said, "Ren claims it was for a year. It stopped when she gave up the apartment. She figured Bai must have had ten to fifteen recordings by then."

"Was there anyone else taped who might be worth blackmailing?"

"I did ask her that question, as much for my own peace of mind as anything. She said she'd never heard of anyone being blackmailed before, and that she couldn't remember everyone who used the room."

"When precisely did the recording end?"

"It would have been about seven years ago."

"And for seven years nothing happens. How strange is that?" Ava said.

"Stranger than I care to think about. It's several lifetimes ago for me. I have a husband and two kids now; the last thing I want is for this to become public," Mak said. "Why doesn't Fai just pay the money to make it go away? If she needs help, maybe I could chip in."

"That's generous of you," Fai said.

"Yes, thanks for the offer, but it isn't going to come to that, because paying won't make it go away. All it will do is encourage the scum who's blackmailing her to ask for money again at some point in the future. She — and you — can't have that hanging over your heads indefinitely," Ava said.

"What are you going to do?"

"Find the blackmailer and eliminate that possibility."

"To find him you're going to have to talk to a lot of people who knew Bai Lok. You aren't worried that that will draw attention to the situation, to Fai and to me?"

"I'll do everything I can to avoid that."

"That's not encouraging."

"It's the best I can promise."

"Fai, I don't know who this Ava Lee is, but it seems to me that she could land you in a heap of trouble," Mak said.

"Please reconsider paying the blackmailer. If you decide you're going to and you need help, give me a call."

"I'm following Ava's advice," Fai said. "If anyone can resolve this, it's her."

"Okay, but if things start to go sideways, could someone call me to let me know? The last thing I need is for my husband to hear about this from someone other than me. If I'm going to become collateral damage, at least I deserve a chance to minimize it."

"You'd get a call," Ava said. "And from our side, we want to hear from you if you can think of anyone or anything else that might help us. I know this has been sudden. As you think more about it, you may remember extra details."

"Well, let's hope for all our sakes that we never have to talk again," Mak said.

Ava turned off the speaker and ended the call. "That went reasonably well. After the initial shock, I think she realized she was at risk. Her co-operation seems genuine," she said. "It's too bad we have only one lead and he's dead, but he did leave a legacy — even if it's in the form of just one video — and there's bound to be a trail of some kind attached to it."

"I worked with him a couple of times," Fai said. "He was the AD on *Peasant Songs*, and before that he was the AD on one of Lau Lau's films."

"What was he like?"

"He was a little guy, maybe five three or four, but he had a thick moustache and a crazy, floppy head of hair that he was always running his fingers through," Fai said. "He was a yes man, an ass-kisser, and that made him a good AD, since his main job was to keep the director happy."

"Did Lau Lau know him well?"

"Not particularly. They only did the one film together that I know of, and I can't remember them socializing off set," Fai said. "Bai was one of those people on the fringes of the business who know they're never going to make it big, so he just tried to hang on. He did work on a lot of films, though, and he knew a lot of people."

"From our viewpoint, that's not necessarily a good thing."

"I can see that."

"Was he married? Did he have a partner of any kind?"

"I don't know."

"Who would?"

"I can look online. There are quite a few websites devoted to Chinese filmmaking, and many of them have bios, even of people like Bai Lok."

"See what you can find," Ava said. "Do you mind if I go outside for some fresh air while you look?"

"Not at all."

Ava left the kitchen, put on her Adidas jacket, and went outside. She was starting to walk across the courtyard when a thought came to her. She stopped, turned, and headed towards Fan's green door. She rapped the lion knocker. The door opened almost at once; she figured Fan had been watching from the window.

"Good morning," she said. "I was wondering if you could help with something. Did you know or did you ever work with a director named Bai Lok?"

"Does this have to do with the disk?"

"Only indirectly," she said.

"I can't help you."

"You don't know him?"

"I've never heard of him."

"How about the actress Ren Lan?"

"Her I've heard of, but we've never met."

"Thanks. And during the night, did you have any further thoughts about the man who delivered the envelope?"

"No, but I did think about you saying I might have broken a law," he said. "Since when does being a good neighbour deserve that kind of threat? You're not from here. You don't know us or how we support each other."

"You're quite correct. I apologize if you thought I was unnecessarily direct."

He took a step back, as if he'd been expecting a more aggressive reply.

"And while I'm staying at Fai's home, I'll try to be a better neighbour myself," Ava said. She smiled and headed towards the exit to the hutong.

She stayed in the hutong, travelling its length in both directions four times. The sky was overcast and the air was cold and damp, but there wasn't any wind and her jacket kept her warm enough. The lane was crowded with what looked like local shoppers, and the stalls and shops were full of the sound of people bargaining. Nothing, it seemed, had a set price. This was the most time Ava had spent in the hutong, and she noticed shops she hadn't seen before, including one that had interesting jewellery and another that had a small but good-looking selection of antique vases and sculptures. In a different time and given different circumstances, she might have looked for something for her mother and sister. But at that moment, all she could focus on was Pang Fai and the disk that could undo a career.

Despite her veneer of confidence, Ava wasn't kidding herself about the enormity of the problem they faced. But she couldn't afford to dwell on it, because she knew that overthinking often led to paralysis and inaction. When she worked with Uncle, she had taken pride in her businesslike approach to problems that were sometimes huge, sprawling messes involving any number and manner of people. But regardless of how messy it was, she attacked every problem in the same way: one small step at a time, going from A to B and resisting the temptation to leap ahead, not making assumptions that the facts on hand couldn't immediately support.

It could be boring, plodding work, but when she got things right and the outcome fell her way, the satisfaction was overpowering. When her friend Derek was still help- ing her in the field, he used to say that a day working with her was twenty-three hours and fifty-five minutes of tedium followed by five minutes of mayhem, terror, and adrenalin highs. She hoped that Fai's problem wouldn't need to be resolved that way, but in the back of her mind she began to prepare herself to come face to face with the blackmailer. If she did, it would be a last resort; it would mean that every- thing else she'd tried had failed. Ava didn't like last resorts; they implied desperation.

On her fourth circuit of the hutong, she checked her watch, saw she'd been gone for close to forty-five minutes, and ducked into Fai's courtyard when she reached it. Fan was standing outside his door talking to an elderly woman. She waved at him, and he acknowledged her with a nod of his head before resuming his chat. Ava assumed he was telling the woman what a vile thing Fai had living under her roof.

"I'm home," Ava said when she walked through the door.

"I'm still in the kitchen. Come and join me," said Fai.

"What did you find?"

"Not that much, but it's interesting," Fai said. "It doesn't appear that he was married or had a partner, or at least a partner with whom he had children. But he had a brother, Bai Jing. I worked with him on a couple of films. He's a set decorator. I found him on one of the websites where film people post job vacancies and their work experience and availability. According to his most recent status update, it seems he's still alive and living in Beijing."

"So he's the next of kin? The beneficiary of whatever Lok left behind?"

"That's what I was thinking."

"A good lead," Ava said.

"But there's more," Fai said, staring down at her tablet. "Lok's agent was Xia Jun."

"The name means nothing to me."

"Right now it's a toss-up between him and Chen for who is the most important agent in China."

"Why does that matter?"

"Xia worked for Chen before going out on his own. In fact, he handled a lot of the day-to-day details for clients."

"For you?"

"No, but certainly for someone like Bai Lok, and even Lau Lau."

"Would Bai Jing use him as an agent?"

Fai shook her head. "Jing isn't important enough to warrant having an agent."

"Was Xia's departure from Chen's organization collegial?"

"Xia walked out one day about three years ago, giving absolutely no notice. And he took as many of Chen's clients with him as he could."

"So that's a no."

"You would have a hard time finding two men in China who hate each other more."

"Well, we should probably avoid both of them for now. I think Bai Jing is the man we most need to talk to, and I'd like to do that in person."

"There's a phone number for him on that job-posting website."

Ava opened the window on Fai's phone. In addition to the number, there was a photo of Bai Jing. He was clean-shaven but had a mop of thick, unruly hair. She wondered if he shared any other genetic similarities with his brother. "What's the best way to arrange a meeting with him?"

"I could call him and say a film I've committed to is looking for a set decorator. I could say the producer asked me for recommendations and I mentioned his name. You'd be the producer, of course."

"That should work," Ava said. "But Fai, this is another time when I think I should meet him alone. I don't want you associated in his mind with the kind of discussion I might have to have with him. If he doesn't know anything, there's nothing to be gained and quite a bit that could be lost by having you there. I'm going to ask him about his brother's amateur porn business, and he might think it odd that you're with me. We don't want him fantasizing or trying to put two and two together."

"I understand."

"Good. So call him. I'd like to meet him today, anywhere he chooses."

"He should be coming to you, not you going to him. That's the way the system works. You set the time and place and it's up to him to find a way to get there. The only excuse he could have for not doing that is if he already has a job and can't get away from it."

"Okay, then tell him to meet me in the Kempi Deli at the Kempinski Hotel at three."

29

AVA ARRIVED AT THE KEMPINSKI AT A QUARTER TO three and went directly to the Kempi Deli. There had been no sign of Bai Jing outside the hotel or in the lobby, and he wasn't waiting for her in the café. Ava was desperate for a coffee and ordered a double espresso. There were many things she liked about staying at Fai's, but the lack of coffee wasn't one of them. Fai preferred tea and didn't have coffee in the house. Ava had thought about buying some but didn't want to appear too pushy or presumptive. Besides, she didn't mind tea, just not a constant flow of it.

She sat at a table by the window that gave her a view of the lobby. She gulped down the coffee and signalled to the server that she wanted another. While she waited, she took out her Moleskine notebook and reviewed the questions she had prepared for Bai. If he knew nothing, she suspected this was going to be a very short meeting. As she changed the sequence of some of the questions, her phone sounded. She couldn't remember if Fai had given Bai her number, and looked at the screen.

"Hi, Suki," she said.

"I'm with our lawyers. We've just finished going over the draft of the agreement and it looks good to go. Are you available tomorrow to sign off on it?"

"Well done, Suki. That's a great piece of work. I should be available. Where and when?"

"How about we meet at the Suns' offices at eleven? We can sign the contract and then go for a celebratory lunch."

"That sounds wonderful," Ava said, just as she saw Bai Jing walking across the lobby. "Unless you hear from me, I'll see you there at eleven."

Bai was short, like Fai's description of his brother. He couldn't be much more than a wiry five foot four, she figured, but unlike many of the short men she had known, he didn't look very assertive. In fact he looked rather nervous, and that suited her fine.

"Mr. Bai," Ava said, rising from her chair. "Thank you so much for coming at such short notice."

"Ms. Lee?"

"Yes. Can I get you a coffee or a piece of cake?"

"No, I'm okay, thank you," he said.

He had a folder with him. Ava assumed it contained his résumé and examples of his work. "Then please sit," she said.

He eased himself into the chair and placed the folder in front of him. His hair was more carefully coiffed than it had been in the photo. He had hardly any wrinkles and his teeth were sparkling white. His shirt was ironed and his brown chinos were sharply creased. Ava guessed he was in his forties, but the way he presented himself made him look younger.

"I have to say this is a rather strange introduction."

"In what sense?"

"I've only met Pang Fai a few times in my life, so it was almost surreal when she called me out of the blue and suggested that I meet with you."

"Mr. Bai, I have to be honest with you — Ms. Pang is a friend of a friend. She did this as favour to him. I have never met her."

"Oh," he said, his confusion obvious. "So...this film you want to make?"

"There is no film. I just wanted a chance to meet with you."

"Why?"

"I want to talk to you about your brother."

He looked around the deli as if he was expecting someone else to arrive, which set Ava on edge. "My brother has been dead for years," he said.

"I know. Were you his only sibling?"

"I was."

"Did he ever marry? Did he have a partner? Did he have children? Are your parents still alive?"

"Whoa, those are a lot of questions."

"And easy enough to answer."

"But why should I? And who are you to ask questions like that? Why am I here?"

"Those are a lot of questions as well," Ava said, sitting back in her chair and trying to appear as non-threatening as possible. "Is it sufficient for me to tell you that I have a client who became involved with your brother in a project that didn't work out so well for him? There aren't any hard feelings and there's nothing illegal or sinister attached to it, so we're not looking to cause you or the memory of your brother any harm. But my client wants to clear the record, so to speak. Our hope is that you can help us do that...for a fee, of course."

"A fee for what? What is it you think I can do?"

"Well, just for agreeing to meet with me and for the inconvenience it cost you, we're going to pay you ten thousand renminbi," Ava said. "If you continue to assist us and if you can help us clear that record, we'll pay you substantially more."

"How much more?"

"That depends on the level of your co-operation and the information you provide."

"What could I possibly know that could help your client? I mean, I have no idea what you're even talking about."

Ava sipped her espresso, her eyes locked on Bai. He looked nervous but not scared, and she sensed that the prospect of making more money had captured him.

"Before getting to that point, can I return to the questions I asked earlier?" Ava said. "The answers will help clarify how much help you might be."

"I guess so," Bai said, and then glanced towards the service counter. "I'd like a coffee now too, if that's not a problem."

"What do you want?"

"Espresso, like you."

Ava waved to the server and then said loudly, "Two double espressos, please."

"You asked me if my brother was married. Well, he wasn't," Bai said. "He also never had a live-in partner and there weren't any kids."

"Are you his only living relative?"

"No. We have an aunt who lives in Dalian, but it's been twenty years since I saw her, and I don't think Lok saw her either."

"I was told your brother died of cancer about three years ago."

"That's right."

"Were the two of you close?"

"We moved to Beijing together when we were young, and we lived together for a few years while we tried to get established in the business. After that we stayed in touch, but I wouldn't say we were close. He smoked, drank a lot, and fucked any woman who would have him. My lifestyle was quite different."

"Did you see him before he died?"

"He lived with me for about three or four months before it got too bad and he had to go into a hospital. I was with him when he died."

"It was good of you to look after him."

Bai shrugged. "What else could I do? He needed someone, and I was all he had."

"Did he leave an estate?"

"A what?"

"Property, money, any possessions of note?"

"He spent every renminbi he ever made. The only things he ever owned that had any value were his cameras, and he sold them one by one over the last six months of his life. Some of them he sold for peanuts, but he needed money so badly he didn't care. I used the little cash he had left to pay for his cremation and a small gathering for some colleagues."

The server arrived with the espressos. That gave Ava a chance to hide her disappointment at the way the discussion was going. She waited until Bai had dissolved a cube of brown sugar in his coffee and taken his first sip, before continuing. "So your brother left nothing at all behind, no possessions?"

"His clothes, which I threw out, and a couple boxes of stuff."

"Stuff?"

"A box of films, DVDs, and some CDs. I imagine they're copies of some of the films he made. And another box with more DVDs and a bunch of paper."

"Did you watch any of the films or disks?"

"No."

"Did you go through the paperwork?"

"Why would I do that?"

"Where are the boxes now?" Ava asked.

"In the back of my closet."

Ava took a deep breath, trying to stay calm. "I think my client might have an interest in looking at what's in those two boxes."

"Why?"

"It isn't something that I'm free to discuss, but we would pay you for the opportunity."

Bai hesitated and then said, "How much?"

"Another ten thousand."

"Just to look?" he said.

"Yes."

"How would we arrange that?"

"Well, you could take me to the boxes or bring the boxes to me."

"It might be easier for you to go to them rather than me lugging them around."

"I'm fine with that."

"When would you want to do it?"

"How about right now?"

He looked uncertain.

"How close is your place to the hotel?"

"Half an hour by taxi."

"I'll give you the first ten thousand before we leave here, and of course I'll pay for the cab."

"It's just that my place is a bit of a mess right now."

"All I care about is the boxes."

"Then I guess it should be okay," he said hesitantly.

Ava reached into her Louis Vuitton bag and extracted a wad of notes. They were strapped together in stacks of twenty-five. She handed four stacks to Bai.

He stared at the money. "I can't begin to imagine what your client did with my brother that's worth this kind of money — and ten thousand more."

"Nothing that's of interest to anyone but him," Ava said.

30

BAI JING LIVED IN TONGZHOU, A DISTRICT ON THE eastern perimeter of Beijing, about twenty kilometres from the Kempinski Hotel. The cab ride took close to an hour, and Ava passed the time by quizzing Bai about his brother's career and his own. He was reluctant to say much at first, but her soft-spoken, if feigned, interest eventually got to him and she learned more about the ins and outs of set decoration than she imagined was possible.

He was also candid about his brother. In his opinion, Bai Lok had squandered an enormous talent. Lok had started his career as an apprentice with a famous director. By the time he was in his mid-twenties, he was already acting as an assistant director and was a peer of, among others, Lau Lau. The problem, according to Jing, was that Lok had no self-discipline. He was easily distracted and couldn't resist the temptations of booze, drugs, and women. When he was younger, those vices had no impact on his ability to work, or on its quality. But as he got older it was harder for him to recover after a big night, and he developed a reputation for being unreliable. Work became harder to find, and no one trusted him to direct a film on his own.

"My understanding is that Lau Lau had the same weaknesses," Ava said.

"As a young man, Lau Lau was regarded as a prodigy and given every opportunity. My brother was never held in that same high regard," Bai said. "But eventually it all caught up to Lau Lau as well. He hasn't made a film in years, and I'd be shocked if he was ever given another chance. But back then he was still thought of as a genius, and people were willing to cut him all kinds of slack."

"You worked with Lau Lau?"

"Once, years ago, towards the end of his successful run. He was already starting to fray at the edges. You could see he was going to have problems if he didn't start looking after himself."

"And your brother worked with him?"

"He was AD on a film when they were both struggling. The film was shit."

"When was the last time your brother saw him?"

"A few months before he died."

"How do you know that?"

"Lok told me he'd met him."

"What brought them together?"

"I don't know. It could have been by chance; they did hang out in some of the same circles," Bai said, and then leaned forward and pointed. "My building is over there on the right," he said to the driver.

Ava looked out the window at streets lined with high-rises. The area reminded her of the worst of Hong Kong and Shanghai. It was like being in a concrete tunnel, except that overhead, somewhere behind a shroud of grey cloud, there was sky. Bai's building was about thirty storeys high and dotted with windows that weren't much bigger than portholes.

The taxi pulled up in front. Ava paid the fare and followed Bai inside. The lobby had a beige tile floor and green walls and was completely bare of furnishings. There were only two elevators to service the entire building, and a group of about ten people stood waiting for one.

"I'm on the sixth floor. It's usually faster to take the stairs," Bai said.

"Let's go," Ava said.

The stairwell was clean and smelled of disinfectant. Ava followed Bai, thinking as she went about the contrast between Fai's little house, the courtyard, and the hutong, and the monstrosities built by the Chinese government.

They exited the stairwell and Bai led her to the end of a hallway that had the same tile and green walls as the lobby. Most of the apartments had an extra metal gate fronting their door. It was something Ava was accustomed to seeing in Hong Kong; she knew that the brightly adorned gates were as much about expressing individuality as they were about security.

Bai didn't have a gate, but when he opened the door to his apartment, his individuality almost screamed at her. Photos and paintings of naked men covered every inch of wall, and a coffee table and two end tables supported various sculpted renditions of penises and complete male genitals. Ava now understood why Bai had been reluctant to have her visit his apartment.

"I'm gay," he said, his face turning slightly red.

"So am I," said Ava.

"Really?"

"Yes, and I've seen more explicit art than this, so don't think I'm shocked."

"Male art?"

"I was invited to the villa of Dominic Ventola in Italy — he owns VLG. Some of the artwork he has can only be described as raw. I think yours is in better taste."

"Thank you," Bai said. "Now let me get those boxes from the bedroom. You can take the art off the coffee table so I can put them there."

When he left, Ava gingerly picked up a sculpture of a large erect penis and laid it on the leather sofa. It was the first time she'd put her hand on a penis. Even in the abstract she found it unpleasant.

"Here is the box with the films and disks," Bai said, placing it on the table. "I'll get the other one."

The box top was folded shut. Ava opened it and saw a layer of DVDs covering what looked like at least ten reels of film. The DVDs were in plain boxes. Most of the reels had stickers with titles written across them.

Bai put the second box next to the first. This time the DVDs sat on top of a couple more reels that were without titles, plus several bundles of envelopes and paper held in place by rubber bands.

Ava read the titles aloud.

"Those are all movies he worked on," Bai said.

"What about the disks and reels with nothing to identify them?"

"I have no idea what they are."

"You never looked?"

"I told you I didn't."

"I'd like to see what's on them."

"Does this have to do with your client?"

"Possibly."

"There's a lot of material."

"Can I take it with me?" Ava said.

"All of it?"

"Yes, to be safe. Those titles might not match what's on the reels."

"I'm not sure I want you to do that."

"These boxes have been sitting on the floor of your closet for three years."

"But they're all I have left of my brother."

Ava reached into her bag and took out money. "Here's the ten thousand I promised," she said. "And here is another twenty thousand. Keep the twenty as a deposit. When I bring back the boxes, you can keep ten and return the rest to me."

"What if you keep the boxes?"

"Then you can keep the whole twenty thousand."

"I have a feeling that they could be worth a lot more than that."

"If I decide to keep the boxes, we'll have a separate discussion about their value," Ava said. "I'll give you my phone number and my office address in Hong Kong. You'll be able to find me if you have to — but you won't, because I don't do business that way."

"Are you always this persuasive?"

"I've found that nothing persuades better than money, and if this works out properly, you could make a lot more."

He put the thirty thousand on top of the coffee table. "Let me help you carry the boxes downstairs," he said.

31

AVA CALLED FAI AS SOON AS THE TAXI HAD PULLED
away from Bai Jing's apartment building. "I'm in Tongzhou.
It took me an hour to get here from the hotel, but now I'm
headed into rush hour, so I don't know when I'll get home."

"What are you doing there? I thought you were meeting
at the Kempinski."

"I did, and then we came here to his apartment. I'm leaving with two boxes of films, disks, and paperwork that we
need to go through," Ava said. "They were left to Jing by Lok,
and if I believe everything I've been told, they represent his
entire estate and legacy."

"Good god. How did you manage to persuade him to give
them to you?"

"I used my considerable charm and then sweetened it with
money."

"How much? I want to pay you back."

"Never mind about that right now. What we need to focus
on is the contents of these boxes."

"Is my video in one?"

"I don't know what's on any of the films or disks. That's

why we need to look at them all," Ava said. "The disks aren't labelled, so god knows what they contain. Most of the reels are marked, and it seems they might be legitimate films he was involved in. Do you have any equipment that would allow us to play the films?"

"Are they on reels?"

"Yes."

"I don't have anything."

"So, what can we do?"

"Once I see what we're dealing with, I'll find a film editor. They all have systems at home or have access to one."

"Okay. In the meantime, plan on spending the evening at the house."

"What do you want to do about dinner?"

"We'll eat in. Is there any congee left?"

"Yes."

"Considering that what we'll be watching might turn our stomachs, congee seems perfect."

"I'll start heating it," Fai said, and then paused. "Ava, I know you don't like to make assumptions, but getting those boxes has to be a good thing, yes?"

"It has that potential," Ava said, not wanting to speculate on the usefulness of what they might find, despite knowing that Fai wanted to hear something more positive. "Look, I'll call you when I get near the hutong. I can't carry both boxes myself, so you should meet me at the entrance."

"Yes, boss," Fai said, laughing.

Ava smiled as she ended the call. Whatever pressure Fai was under, she wasn't letting it affect their personal relationship. Ava wasn't sure she herself could handle that amount of strain and maintain a positive perspective. Thinking of perspective, she looked out the cab window and saw darkness settling. Then, as if to accentuate how dreary it was outside, it began to rain. The Beijing winter was starting to wear on her. It was so cold, so wet, so gloomy, and the air was so foul that even the coldest, snowiest day in Toronto seemed more appealing. *What's the weather like at home now?* she thought. She picked up her phone to check and then saw an incoming call from a familiar number.

"Xu, how are you?" she said.

"I'm well enough, and you? Are things still settled on the Pang Fai front?"

"All is quiet with Mo, but another problem has raised its ugly head."

"Do you need help with it?"

"There's not much anyone can do at the moment, but if I need help, I'll call."

"And this problem is in Beijing?"

"Yes. Why do you ask me that?"

"I was hoping you'd be available to go to Hong Kong."

"What's going on there?" Ava asked, surprised at the request.

"Lop is still feeling a bit paranoid about Sammy Wing. He's found out that while he was in Beijing with you, Sammy was in Sha Tin. He has a nephew there who just took over one of the gangs, and Lop's convinced that Sammy is conspiring with him."

"To do what?"

"Take back control of Wanchai."

"Do you really take that idea seriously?"

"No, but Lop is like a dog with a big soup bone — he can't stop chewing. My fear is that he might create a problem where there isn't one."

"Can't you intervene?"

"I can't tell Lop to stop worrying. I can't tell Sammy not to talk to his nephew. And, as chairman of the Triad Societies, I can't step in between Wanchai and Sha Tin when there's no cause, and when we're still pretending that Sammy runs Wanchai."

"What did you want me to do in Hong Kong?"

"You have no official standing with any of the parties, but you know your way around the city and you've got some great contacts in men like Sonny, Andy, and Carlo. You also know Sammy better than most of us, and he has tremendous respect for you."

"Xu, he tried to have me killed — twice."

"But he failed, and you made him pay for it. He's a man who respects strength."

"Even so, I'm hardly in a position to browbeat Sammy."

"That's not something I'd ask you to do," Xu said. "I thought you could put out some feelers and try to ascertain whether Lop's concerns have any basis. You'd be able to get a better reading if you were in Hong Kong, and I thought if you invited Sammy to dinner it wouldn't seem threatening or strange."

"Is there real urgency to this?"

"Not really, except the sooner I can calm Lop, the better I'll feel."

"I was planning to go to Hong Kong after I finish here," Ava said. "The problem is that I have no timetable. I could be here another four or five days. Can you wait that long?"

"I guess so," Xu said.

Ava felt a touch of disappointment at his response and reacted to it. "What I can do right now is ask Sonny to poke around. I'll leave it to him if he wants to involve anyone else. I'll tell him only what he needs to know — although it doesn't matter how much I tell him, because no one is more loyal and discreet."

"I have no worries about Sonny."

"Then that's the plan," she said. "I'll get to Hong Kong as soon as I can. In the meantime we'll have Sonny gathering information."

"Thanks. I'm quite sure it will amount to nothing, but why take the chance."

"Exactly, and spending a bit of time in Hong Kong isn't a sacrifice. I'll get to see Amanda and some of my family, and May Ling will probably fly in from Wuhan."

"Will you take Pang Fai with you?"

"Yes, if she'll come."

"I wish I could join you, but there's too much going on here."

"Well, we'll find a time and place to get together before too long," Ava said, and then was thrown forward as the taxi came to a sudden sliding stop before starting to move again. "That's assuming I survive this taxi ride."

"Make sure you do," Xu said. "Now I'd better go. Call me if Sonny unearths anything."

Ava ended the call. "How close are we to my hutong?" she asked the driver.

"Ten minutes or so."

Ava called Fai and, when she answered, said, "I'm ten minutes away. It's raining, so I think you should bring an umbrella with you."

"See you in ten," Fai said. "The congee is on the stove."

The taxi slowed, but Ava could see some familiar

landmarks and knew his ten-minute estimate wasn't far off. She thought about calling Sonny but her mind was drawn back to the boxes. There wasn't much he could do that night anyway, and Hong Kong would still be there in the morning.

32

THEY SAT IN THE KITCHEN OVER BOWLS OF CONGEE. FAI had opened a bottle of Chardonnay; as incongruous as the wine seemed as a partner for rice porridge, the mood made it seem perfect.

The boxes were waiting in the living room and weighing on their minds. "I think it would be more efficient if we divided the work," Ava said finally.

"How?"

"Why don't you work your way through the disks while I look at Bai's paperwork."

"What am I looking for on the disks?"

"We need to know exactly what's on them. When you've got one figured out, make a note of it and mark the disk and the box so we have a record," Ava said. "I imagine you might see more displays of private sex, but what's most important is the participants. Try to identify as many of them as you can."

"Why is that important?"

"You may not be the only person being blackmailed. If other people have the same problem, we could find some new leads."

"Do you really think they're blackmailing more than one person?"

"Maybe not at this exact moment, but who knows what went on in the past. These disks have been around for years."

"What do you expect to find in Bai's papers?" Fai asked, clearing the bowls from the table.

"I have no idea. I took a quick look inside the box when I was with Jing, but truthfully it looked like a jumble of this and that."

Fai shook her head. "Well then, let's get started. But I'm going to need more wine to get through this."

"Take the bottle with you," Ava said as she stood up.

They walked into the living room, where the boxes sat on the floor near the television. Ava opened them both and took out several bundles of papers that weren't organized in any discernible way. Fai took a black marker and a sheet of paper from a table drawer and then turned on the television and the DVD player.

"I'm not looking forward to this," Fai said. "And I hope you'll understand when I say I hope I don't recognize anyone."

"It's something you'll only have to do once."

"Do I have to watch them till the end?"

"I think its best," Ava said. "There could be multiple scenes on each disk. We need to be sure of what we have."

"This is going to take hours — but that isn't a complaint. I'm grateful that we have something to work with," Fai said, picking a disk from a box.

"And who knows what we'll find," Ava said, taking more bundles of paper and sticking them under her arm.

"Where are you going with those?"

"I'm going to use the kitchen table," Ava said, leaving the living room.

The table was bare, and Ava piled the paper at the point farthest from her seat. She took the bundle on top and quickly leafed through it. It was a hodgepodge of bills, receipts, bank statements, letters, contracts, and random pieces of paper. She checked the dates on those that had them. Most were five or six years old. *What the hell*, she thought, and decided to sort them by type. Five minutes later she had six neater stacks in front of her, and then she reached for another bundle. It took her an hour to finish sorting, but she knew she still couldn't make sense of any of it the way it was so randomly piled. She picked up the stack of receipts and organized them by date from the oldest to the most recent — which was just over three years ago, only weeks or maybe months before he'd died. Then she repeated the process until all six stacks were in chronological order.

"Ava," Fai said from the kitchen entrance.

"What is it?" Ava said, startled as her concentration was broken.

"I've watched five of the disks."

"Already?"

"I think he edited them. All the foreplay and anything romantic or tender has been taken out. They're all about graphic sex in as many forms as you can imagine. They're short, but certainly to the point."

"Have you recognized anyone?"

"I just did, which is why I'm standing here," Fai said. "It's Lau Lau with a young man, maybe even a boy. What's strange is that it's just a snippet, just ten or twenty seconds tacked onto the end of a disk that featured another man with a woman."

"But there's enough that you're certain it's him?"

"It's him."

"You look upset."

"It's kind of silly. I mean, obviously I knew he'd been with men, but that video is so impersonal, so dirty, that it almost removes the human element from what they were doing."

"Are you up to watching more?"

"Yes. I just want to get it over with."

"Before you go back, can you remember when you made *Peasant Dreams*?"

"Just over seven years ago."

"Mak Guang told us that Bai stopped taping around the same time, after doing it for about a year."

"We must have been two of his last performers."

"Are there any dates or credits on the disks you've watched? Are there any clues to when they might have been made, or who's in them?"

"Nothing."

"I'm surprised there aren't more movie people in them."

"There might be. I just haven't recognized them if they are. Besides, Ren Lan was as much a party girl as an actress. She had a wide circle of acquaintances outside the business," Fai said, and then pointed at the paper. "How are you doing with all of that?"

"I've just finished getting it organized. Now I have to start going through it in some detail."

"What are you hoping to find?"

"I won't know until I see it," Ava said, and then realized that might have sounded condescending. "I'm going to start eight years ago, which is when the taping began, and then work forward until Bak died, three years ago. That's five years of paperwork. I'll begin with his bank statements and see if I can figure out who was paying him and who he was paying. Some of the statements have cancelled cheques attached, which is a very good thing. When I say I won't know what I'll find until I see it, what I mean is that there could be a name or a company or some weird payment that triggers questions. You can tell a lot about a person from their bank statements, and from the other pieces of paper — such as receipts — that they choose to keep."

"Sounds complicated."

"It's like doing a jigsaw puzzle, except you're working with numbers and not images."

"I'm not much good with jigsaw puzzles either," Fai said. "Now I'd better get back to those disks if I want to finish them tonight."

Ava waited until Fai left before taking out her notebook. She turned to the section she'd designated for Pang Fai and wrote *Lau Lau ten seconds?* Regardless of what she found in Bai's paperwork, Lau Lau was now at the top of her list of people to question. But she pushed that thought aside as she turned her focus back to the paperwork, starting with the bank statements. That eighth year was crucial. It was the year that all the taping was supposedly done, and if she was going find out who Bai Lok was doing business with, it should appear in those statements, unless he was operating on a strictly cash basis. Her assumption was that Bai was simply doing the recording and then selling the product, an assumption based partly on necessity and partly on wishful thinking, although there was nothing in his past to indicate that he had the ability or the willingness to get into mass production and distribution.

As she scanned the bank statements, Ava realized he

hadn't kept them all. Four months were missing from that year, but as she read the ones he'd hung on to, she wondered if that would make a difference. *Could it be this easy?* she thought as she noticed the name "Tiger Paw Video" on virtually every statement. Over eight months, Tiger Paw had sent ten wire transfers to Bai Lok, each transfer for thirty thousand renminbi. She turned to the statements for year number seven. One transfer had been made in January and there were none after that. She looked at year six and found no mention of Tiger Paw. Years five and four were equally barren.

She reached for her phone, brought up a search engine, and entered "Tiger Paw Video." There was no result. She grabbed the bills and receipts from year eight to see if any paper had been exchanged between Bai and Tiger Paw. She couldn't find any.

She went into the living room to talk to Fai, arriving just in time to see a large man penetrate a woman with a vibrator.

"Gross," she said.

Fai turned towards her. "There's worse, but the good news is I haven't recognized anyone else."

"What about the disk that was sent to you?"

"I haven't seen it yet."

"Good. Now, could you turn that off for a minute, please?"

Fai hit the remote. "What's going on?"

"I've found something worth pursuing. Have you ever heard of Tiger Paw Video?"

"No."

"Could you search for it on those websites you use?"

"Do you want me to do it right now?"

"Please. I'm going to phone Bai Jing."

Ava went back to the kitchen and stood at the window while she called. It was still raining, and the brick courtyard looked slick and dangerous under the glare of lights from the neighbours' homes.

"Bai Jing," he answered.

"It's Ava Lee. I hope I'm not disturbing you."

"Actually, I've been disturbed all evening. I've been having second thoughts about letting you take those boxes. I feel a bit guilty, like maybe I've betrayed the trust my brother placed in me to look after them."

"If it makes you feel better, you'll get them back," Ava said, wondering what had spurred Bai's feelings.

"Are you finished with them?"

"Not yet."

"Have you found anything useful?"

"We might have, and truthfully there are some disks we might want to keep. We'll buy them from you, of course," she said, seeing no point in mentioning the bank statements, since she doubted he even knew they existed.

"What price are you prepared to pay?"

Ava smiled. Bai's concern about his brother's trust had passed quickly enough the second that money entered their conversation. "Let's wait and see how many we want. But that isn't the reason I'm calling," Ava said. "Have you ever heard of a company called Tiger Paw Video?"

"It doesn't ring a bell."

"Your brother might have done some work for them seven or eight years ago. Did he ever mention them?"

"It's possible, I guess, but I can't remember hearing that name. What is it he was supposed to have done?"

"If you don't know them, it doesn't matter. But there's

something else I'd like to know," Ava said. "You mentioned that your brother met with Lau Lau shortly before he died. Do you know how that meeting came about?"

"What do you mean?"

"Did Lau Lau contact him or did your brother reach out? Or did they simply bump into each other somewhere?"

"Don't hold me to this, but I think my brother called Lau Lau," Bai Jing said slowly. "He called a lot of people after he found out he was going to die. He needed to say his goodbyes, and there were some people he needed to ask for forgiveness."

"Forgiveness for what?"

"He hurt a lot of people."

"Could Lau Lau have been one of them?"

"I wouldn't think that was possible. The two of them were equally insensitive to other people's feelings."

"So why did he reach out to him?"

"I don't know."

"They worked together. Did that create a bond?"

"I doubt it, but even if there was one, my brother never mentioned it."

"One more thing," Ava said. "After your brother met with Lau Lau, did his financial position change?"

"Change?"

"Did he have more money?"

"I don't know, although I do have a vague memory from around that time of Lok saying he had the money to look after his funeral. But I don't know if that had anything to do with Lau Lau or if he had just sold more cameras," Bai said. "If I have to guess, I'd say he sold cameras. Lau Lau doesn't have a reputation for being generous, even where sick and dying former colleagues are concerned."

"You obviously don't like him very much."

"I've never made a secret of my sexuality. Given the job I was doing, it didn't matter much, and most people were respectful. But not Lau Lau," Bai said. "When I worked on one of his films, he mocked me, he treated me with contempt. The thing is, there were lots of rumours going around about his own sexuality, and later I heard stuff from people I trust that made it clear he's at least bisexual."

"You didn't say or do anything?"

"On a film set, directors are gods. I would have been fired on the spot, or maybe even worse. I mean, I imagine he was lashing out at me as a way of coping with his own self-loathing. I hate to think what he would have done if I had suggested that."

"I might have to meet with him," Ava said. "You don't make it sound like something I'd enjoy."

"Maybe hard times have mellowed him?"

"Yes, let's hope so … And now, about your boxes," she said. "I'll call you when I've finished going through them and then we can finalize our accounts."

"There's no rush. You know where I am."

Ava ended the call. She was still standing at the window looking out onto the courtyard, but her mind was occupied by things other than the rain. She turned and walked into the living room. Fai was sitting on the sofa with her tablet on her lap.

"I found Tiger Paw Video," she said, looking up.

"Where?"

"They used to operate in Beijing."

"Used to?"

"They've been out of business for at least two years."

"What did they do?"

"Make and distribute adult films," Fai said. "Are you thinking that Bai Lok sold his recordings to them?"

"I'm almost certain of it."

"Oh shit."

"Why do you sound so surprised?"

"I'm not surprised. I'm disappointed."

"Why?"

"One of the names associated with Tiger Paw is Ding Fa. I've known him for years and I think of him as a friend. He's one of the film editors I would have called tomorrow about viewing the films that are on reels."

"Now you have even more reason to call him," Ava said.

(33)

THEY LAY FACE TO FACE, THEIR ARMS WRAPPED AROUND
each other, Fai's breath hot on Ava's neck. The sun was up
and they'd been awake for a while, but neither of them felt
impelled to move. It had been a late night as Fai viewed the
rest of the disks and Ava finished going through Bai Lok's
papers. The disks didn't reveal anyone else Fai knew, and a
disk with her and Mak Guang wasn't in either box. There
were also no further sightings of Lau Lau. Ava's paper chase
was equally unproductive, but at least when they went to bed,
they did it knowing they'd done everything they could with
the box's contents.

"We need to get up," Ava said finally. "We've a busy day
ahead of us."

"What are you planning?"

"I have to call Hong Kong. Xu thinks he might have a
problem there that he's asked me to look into. I need to talk
to Sonny and get him started on it," Ava said. "Then Suki
and I have an appointment with Mr. and Mrs. Sun at eleven
to sign the purchase agreement for their business. They want
to have lunch afterwards. I really don't want to go, but I can't

be rude to them and Suki. That will keep me occupied until at least one."

"What do you want me to do?"

"Call Ding Fa and arrange for him to meet with us later this afternoon."

"What excuse do I use for wanting to see him?"

"Tell him the truth, or at least part of the truth — that someone sent you some film reels and we want to confirm what's on them. You said Ding is a friend. Will he need more of a reason than that?"

"No, that should do."

Ava swung her legs over the side of the bed. "I need to start getting organized. Do you mind if I shower first?"

"Go ahead. I'll phone Ding while you do."

Ava came out of the bathroom twenty minutes later. She went to the bedroom and quickly put on a white button-down shirt and black slacks. She grabbed her phone, note-book, and bag and headed downstairs.

Fai sat at the kitchen table with a pot of tea in front of her. Ava sat in the chair across from her and poured a cup.

"Ding will see us whenever we can get there, early or late," Fai said. "Our timing was good. He's supposed to start edit-ing a film the day after tomorrow and won't be seeing anyone until he's finished, which could take weeks."

"Did he ask many questions?"

"No, he took my excuse at face value."

"How well do you really know him?"

"I've worked on four or five films with him. We socialized a bit off the set with the rest of the crew, but nothing too personal. He's a really good editor, and he always makes my performance look better than it was. After I saw the final cut of the first film with me in it that he edited, I sent him a very expensive pen as a thank-you gift. He appreciated it, so I made a habit of doing that after every film."

"Clever you. Let's hope that Ding still values your gratitude."

"When we talk to him, are we going to be direct?"

"Do you mean are we going to ask him if he knows that you and Lau Lau appear in two of the nasty little videos Bai Lok made and sold to Tiger Paw?"

"Yes."

"I think we have to play it by ear, but it's a hard subject to slide around, given that our objective is to get clear answers. Would it bother you if I was direct?" Ava said.

"Not with him."

"That's good to know."

Fai stood, walked around the table, and kissed Ava gently on the lips. "I'd better start getting ready myself," she said.

"Where does Ding live?"

"In a hutong about ten streets west of here."

"Then I'll come back here after my meeting and we can go there together."

Ava waited until Fai left the kitchen before picking up her phone to call Sonny in Hong Kong. Of all the men in her life, no one was more absolutely and unquestioningly loyal. She'd first met him when she went to work with Uncle. Sonny was his driver and bodyguard. Uncle had recruited him from his gang in Fanling, in the New Territories, where Sonny had cut a violent — and sometimes out-of-control — swath. Uncle had calmed him down and taught him how to control and focus his ferocity.

He was large man, about six foot four, and over the years

Ava had known him, his weight had varied between 250 and 300 pounds. Despite having a body that looked bulky and soft, he moved with incredible speed and could unleash bone-breaking power. He was one of the few men Ava had met whom she doubted she could best in hand-to-hand combat.

Sonny had no friends that Ava was aware of. Women came and went, but none lasted long. He had some male acquaintances, nearly all Triads, whom he'd meet occasionally for dinner and drinks or a night at Happy Valley Racetrack. When Uncle was alive, Sonny's sole purpose on earth was to serve and protect him, a commitment that was extended to Ava when the bond between her and Uncle became clear. And when Uncle died, among the bequests he left to Ava was Sonny. "If Sonny is left to his own devices, if he has no purpose, if he has no boss he respects, he is going to get into trouble, and the kind of trouble he can get into is beyond most imaginations," Uncle had told Ava. "You need to keep him. You need to employ him. He has to know he has a home with you."

The problem was, of course, that Ava lived in Toronto while Sonny lived in Hong Kong and wasn't suited to living anywhere else. The arrangement they came to was simple enough. When Ava was in Hong Kong, she had one hundred percent of Sonny's time and attention. When she was in Toronto, he drove for Amanda, Ava's brother Michael, and her father, Marcus, with the understanding that if Ava needed something done in Hong Kong — or anywhere else in Asia — that would take immediate priority.

It turned out that Ava had needed Sonny often, and he had shown her the same kind of dedication he'd shown

Uncle. He was well known and respected within the Triad community, and Ava didn't doubt he could have held a senior position in any number of gangs. But she knew he'd never voluntarily leave her, and she would never as much as hint that he work for anyone else. They were joined; Uncle had seen to that, and Ava didn't doubt his wisdom.

"Sonny, it's Ava," she said when he answered the phone with a brisk "*Wei.*"

"Hey, boss."

"I'm in Beijing, but I have a job for you in Hong Kong. How's your schedule?"

"I was supposed to drive your father to a meeting in Tai Wai New Village later this morning, but I can cancel."

"No, this isn't that urgent. Drive my father, but don't take on anything else for the next day or two."

"What's the job?"

"Xu is worried about Lop."

"Lop is a rock."

"I know, but Sammy Wing may not be," she said. "Lop seems to think Sammy is going behind his back with a gang in Sha Tin."

"Sammy's nephew just took over that gang."

"So I've been told by Xu, and that's Lop's concern. He thinks Sammy and the nephew are trying to find a way to reclaim Wanchai."

"That fat old fuck never knows when to quit."

"You've heard something?"

"No. I just hate the guy."

"Sonny, you have to forget the history between me and Sammy. You can't make this personal. What Xu and I want to know is if there's any truth at all to Lop's suspicions," Ava said. "Can you pay some visits and make some calls?"

"Quiet, right?"

"Very. We don't want Lop to know we're asking questions."

"I can keep it tight."

"And Sonny, this has nothing to do with not trusting Lop," Ava said. "You know Xu has complete faith in him. It's just that sometimes Lop gets a bit suspicious. Xu doesn't want him doing anything that isn't warranted and could get him into trouble. He wants some objective eyes looking at the situation."

"I'll be careful."

"Thank you. Phone me when you have some sense of what's going on — or not going on."

"Will I be seeing you on this trip?"

"Yes, but I don't know when yet. Once the schedule is set, you'll be the first to know."

"Okay. Do you want me to say hello to your father for you?"

"That would be wonderful, but don't mention that I might be coming to Hong Kong. I love to see him when I'm there, but if he knows ahead of time that I'm coming, he'll try to program me."

"I won't. I'll be in touch."

Ava ended that call and then immediately phoned Xu. Four rings later she was in his voicemail. "I've spoken to Sonny. He'll start working on the Hong Kong project this afternoon."

She checked the time and saw that it was getting tight in terms of getting to the Suns' office by eleven. She hated being late for anything. Her mother had preached that being late was rude and disrespectful, and though Ava often rolled her eyes when her mother said it, the message had stuck.

She could hear the shower running upstairs and knew she was going to have to leave before Fai finished in the bathroom. She tore a page from her notebook and wrote: *I had to leave. I should be back here around 1:30. Love, Me.*

The overnight rain had stopped but Ava took an umbrella from the entrance anyway. She had developed a mistrust of Beijing weather that was verging on a fixation, and she was almost surprised when she made it across the courtyard, down the hutong, and into a taxi without getting wet. As the cab pulled away from the stand, her phone rang.

"Good morning, Suki. I'm on my way," she said.

"I hope you haven't gone too far, because our meeting has been postponed."

"Why?"

"It isn't anything that will affect the deal," Suki said. "The Suns' lawyer is ill. He was supposed to meet with them last night to finalize some of the arrangements with their banks, but he had to call it off. They thought they'd see him early this morning, but he's still under the weather. They want to reschedule for tomorrow. Same time, same place."

"And you're sure there is no other problem?"

"Completely."

"Okay, then tomorrow it is. I'll see you then," Ava said, and then leaned towards the cab driver. "Take me back to the hutong please."

Five minutes later she exited the cab at the exact spot where she'd gotten in and then retraced her steps to Fai's. She expected that Fai would still be upstairs, but when she entered the house she saw her standing in the living room staring at the television. Bai Lok's video of Fai with Mak Guang was playing.

Fai turned towards her with tears in her eyes. "I know that anyone who sees this will recognize me, but when I look at that woman, I don't know who she is."

34

THEY LEFT FAI'S HOUSE JUST PAST NOON. THEY COULD have walked to Ding Fa's if they hadn't been carrying the box of film reels. As it was, a two-minute cab ride followed by a big tip left them at the entrance of a hutong that was almost identical to Fai's.

Ava hadn't bothered to change her clothes. Walking next to Fai, who was wearing jeans and a thick sweater, she felt a bit overdressed. When she mentioned this, Fai said, "You look professional, and believe me, so will Ding. He dresses formally every day."

"Are we going to his home?" Ava asked.

"His office."

"Is it in his home?"

"No, it's right over there," Fai said after they'd walked no more than twenty metres.

Ava looked at a storefront whose front window was completely black except for the words DING FA, FILM EDITOR painted in white.

"It was a herbalist's store. He bought it and converted it."

Ava paused. "Do you still think there's any point in fooling around with the story about the films?" she said, reactivating the conversation they'd had before leaving the house.

"Ding is a very structured and precise man. He may not react well if we jump right into the Tiger Paw business. Let him view a few reels and then we'll find a way to ease into it."

"Easing in is not my style."

"I know Ding. It's the best way."

"Then that's how we'll do it," Ava said.

Fai knocked lightly on a solid black door and then tried the handle. The door was locked. She knocked with more force. The door opened onto a wall of bright light.

"So good to see you," Ding Fa said, smiling at Fai.

"Thanks for this," Fai said, moving to one side so Ava was clearly visible. "I brought my friend Ava Lee with me. I hope that's okay."

"Why not?" Ding said. "Come in."

Ava guessed he was in his late forties or early fifties. He was of medium height, rather thin, and bald with a hint of fashionable stubble on his head and face. Ding was immaculately dressed in grey wool slacks, a light blue dress shirt, and a red Hermès tie. He squinted slightly when he looked at her.

She half expected to see some remnants of the space's former life when she stepped inside. Instead she was engulfed by equipment and films. The space wasn't that large — maybe ten by fifteen metres — and every wall was covered from floor to ceiling with racks filled with film cans, each of them carefully labelled. Two workstations were set up side by side, with projectors and other equipment she couldn't identify sitting on them. The only bit of wall without racks contained a door that Ava assumed led to a washroom and maybe a small kitchen.

Fai held out the box. "These are the reels I mentioned."

Ding opened it. "I recognize some of these titles. In fact, I edited a couple of them."

"I just want to confirm they are what they claim to be."

"How did you come by them?"

"I've started collecting Chinese films. My agent, Chen, sent me this lot. I'd like to know if they're worth keeping."

"Then let's take a look, shall we?" Ding said. "Why don't you two ladies sit over there at that workstation? We can look through the viewfinder or, if you want, I can project the film onto the window."

"It would be clearer if you project it," Fai said. "But all we have to watch is enough to make sure they're real films."

"If you want to watch more, that's not a problem. I've blocked off the entire afternoon for you, Fai."

"That's very kind."

"It's the least I can do for someone who's been so kind to me."

Ava saw Fai flinch ever so slightly, and wondered if she was feeling a touch of guilt for lying to Ding.

He took out the first reel, loaded it into a projector, and then dimmed the lights. Five minutes later he loaded another and then did the same four more times. When the last film in the series moved past its credits and into the first scene, Ding said, "Do you know what all of these films have in common?"

"No," Fai said.

"Bai Lok was the assistant director on all of them. They must come from his collection. He died, you know, about three years ago."

"Yes, we do know," Ava said. "Actually, we know a lot more about him and his work than we've let on."

Ding glanced at Fai, who looked uncomfortable but nodded. "We're here because of him. It's good to know he worked on these films, but there are others we're more interested in. If you don't mind, I'd like Ava to explain it to you."

"All this mystery," Ding said calmly.

"We're here because of Tiger Paw Video and the movies they distributed. Our understanding is that Bai Lok contributed a large number to their catalogue," Ava said.

"Ahh."

"We tried to find Tiger Paw but it appears to have gone out of business. When we looked at who was involved, yours was the only name that Fai recognized. So here we are."

"Yes. So here you are."

"Did Bai Lok sell tapes, films, or whatever you want to call them to Tiger Paw?"

"Why on earth do you want to know that?" Ding said, his tone hardening.

Fai reached for his hand and took it in hers. "I'm being blackmailed," she said. "Someone sent me a DVD that had been copied from a tape we think Bai Lok made. It's a sex tape. I'm in it with a partner."

"I don't believe that," Ding said, shaking his head. "Or maybe I should say I don't get it."

"You don't get what?"

"I've never seen a video with you in it."

"It's real enough," Ava said.

Ding shrugged. "In this day and age, who isn't in a sex tape? If I were you I'd tell the blackmailer to fuck off and take my chances that the public won't care."

"The movie syndicate wouldn't be so blasé," Ava said.

"Ding, the partner in the tape is another woman," Fai said.

He closed his eyes for a few seconds, blew some air through his lips, and shook his head again. "That does make a bit of a difference."

"Yes, I know it does," Fai said.

"Can we back up for a second before we explore the possible consequences?" Ava said. "Are you being truthful about never seeing a tape with Fai in it?"

"Absolutely, and I edited all the tapes that Bai sold to Tiger Paw."

"So he did sell them?" Ava said.

"He did."

"And you edited them?" Fai said.

"Don't look so startled," Ding said to her. "I'm an editor. I don't get paid unless I'm editing. Movie work, as you know, can be sporadic. Tiger Paw provided a regular stream of income."

"But it's such crap," Fai said.

"That opinion is not shared by everyone. Tiger Paw had a large customer base and was doing very nicely until the two major shareholders and executive officers got caught importing drugs and were shot," Ding said. "And although my finished product wasn't to everyone's taste, it was raw and natural and action-packed. And, I have to say, a massive improvement over the hours of footage that Lok supplied."

"What happened to the original tapes?"

"After I finished editing them and made a digital transfer, they were destroyed."

"And how many of Lok's tapes did you edit?"

"I'd have to check my records."

"Could you, please?"

"Give me ten minutes," he said, standing up. He looked

down at Fai and Ava. "There's a coffee shop a couple of doors down from here. Why don't you two ladies get me a latte and a scone while I'm looking."

"You're not going to lock the door on us while we're gone, are you?" Ava asked.

"I've told you, I set the afternoon aside for Fai. That hasn't changed."

The two women stood up and walked towards the door. As they reached it, Ding called out. "One more thing," he said. "I've been in love with Fai for so long that if I'd seen a tape with her in it, it would have been burned into my memory. So don't believe it's possible that I could have over-looked one."

"What do you think?" Fai said as they walked out into the hutong.

"I think he's being honest, but you know him better than I do."

"I think he's being honest too."

"The only problem with that is it doesn't get us any closer to the origin of the DVD," Ava said as they reached the cof-fee shop, which was actually a stall with two tables. One had urns of coffee on it, the other several platters of baked goods covered with plastic lids.

"What do you want?" Ava asked Fai.

"I'll have a latte and a scone as well."

Ava ordered three lattes from the elderly woman sitting on a chair between the tables, who turned and yelled the order to someone behind a curtain. "And three scones," Ava said.

The woman nodded at the platters. Ava looked for some-thing she could use to pick up the scones. There wasn't even a paper napkin in sight. "Oh well, we'll have to use our fingers," she said.

They carried the large paper cups of coffee back to Ding's. Ava hesitated at the door, afraid he might have had a change of heart. But it opened and they took their seats at the workstation. Ava figured they'd been gone ten minutes, and another ten passed before Ding emerged carrying an accounting ledger. He sat at the other workstation, took a bite of the scone, had a couple of sips of coffee, and then said, "It looks like I edited twelve tapes in one year, plus one more early in the following year."

"How many did you watch?" Ava asked Fai.

"Fourteen."

"You have that many? How in hell did you get your hands on them?" Ding asked.

"I paid Lok's brother for them and the film copies we just watched. They were in a box in his closet. They were all Lok left behind," Ava said.

"And you actually watched them?"

"I did. It was painful," Fai said.

"Ding, if you edited thirteen, one is missing," Ava said. "And Fai, are you counting the one that you were in?"

"No."

"Then two are missing," Ava said to Ding.

"My records are accurate."

"I don't doubt you, but we do have an inconsistency here," Ava said. "Is there any way we can correlate what we have on disks and what you know you edited?"

Ding turned around the ledger and passed it to Ava. "I've marked all the tapes I did for Tiger Paw in yellow. Those descriptions are all I have to go on. My memory isn't good enough to remember anything in detail."

Ava scanned the ledger. "These are descriptions of sex acts, with the scantiest of information about the participants. They all read about the same."

"Sorry. I was making notes as I went, as a way of recording what I was owed. I didn't realize that one day you'd want to catalogue them."

"Is it possible there were more than thirteen?"

"I edited every one that Tiger Paw bought. That was the deal, and despite the nature of their business, they were honourable enough when it came to keeping an agreement."

"Is it possible that Bai Lok made two that he didn't sell to Tiger Paw?"

"Sure."

"Was he capable of doing his own editing?"

"He knew enough that he could probably give it a go."

"Fai, I know this is a strange question, but did you notice any difference in editing quality between the disk you're on and the others?"

"It wasn't exactly something I was comparing."

"Maybe we should."

Fai nodded but didn't look particularly pleased with the idea.

"One last thing," Ava said to Ding Fa. "Was there anyone at all on those tapes whom you recognized?"

"I told you, I didn't see Fai, or anyone else I knew."

"How about Lau Lau?"

"Is that a joke?"

"No."

"I most definitely did not see Lau Lau on any of those tapes."

Ava turned to Fai. "If you don't have any more questions, I think we're done here."

Fai stood up and went over to Ding Fa, who stood to meet her. She wrapped her arms around him and hugged. "I can't thank you enough for your friendship and support," she said.

"Friends are hard to come by. Whenever I've found one, I've tried to hang on to them," Ding said, and then looked at Ava. "You don't have to worry about what was said here today. No one else will ever hear about it."

"Thank you," Ava said.

"Are you going to take your box with you?" Ding asked.

"I guess we should," Ava said.

It took a few minutes to pack it and then another for Ava and Fai to make their way to the doorway. As soon as they reached the lane and the door had closed behind them, Ava said, "We need to talk to Lau Lau."

"What does he have to do with this?"

"Something. Exactly what, I don't know. But I have a feeling he's in the middle of whatever is going on."

35

THEY SAT IN THE WARMTH OF THE HAI WAN CANTEEN
with a large bowl of hot and sour soup in the centre of the
table and the box of films sitting on the floor. The short cab
ride from Ding Fa's had been quiet as each of them filtered
thoughts about what they'd been told and what it might
mean. Fai had seemed shaken when Ava mentioned Lau Lau,
but it was a subject that Ava couldn't let go. She knew, sooner
rather than later, they would have to talk to him.

The soup had no duck meat and it didn't pack as much of
a kick as the one they'd had two days before. But it did have
more pearl-sized scallops, the vinegar flavor was slightly
tarter, and Ava thought it was equally as good. She'd begun
on her second bowl before she said, "I think I need something to drink. How about you?"

"What are you going to have?"

"I want something strong, and all they have is cognac."

"I'll order two," Fai said.

When the drinks arrived, Ava raised her glass.
"Friendship."

"And love," Fai added.

Ava sipped her cognac and felt its warm glow. "I was thinking when we were in the taxi that I really don't know much about Lau Lau," she said. "I know you've talked about him a bit, and I know him by reputation, but could you tell me more?"

"What do you want to know?"

"Well, how did he get into the film business, and what was it that inspired him to make those great early films? I read somewhere that the story of Lau Lau is the story of modern Chinese film — both the best and the worst of it."

"His friends and most movie critics like to remember the best, but he's obsessed by the worst. This country, this system, wore him down and turned him into something he didn't want to be but was too weak to fight."

"Where was he born?"

"In Wuxi."

"Where's that?"

"It's a small city about halfway between Shanghai and Nanjing. His father, who was some kind of Party official, died when he was young, and he was raised by his mother. She loved Chinese opera and movies of any kind, so she saturated him with them. He was always quick to identify her as the person who had the greatest impact on his life. When one critic asked how, he said that living with her was like being engulfed in drama on a daily basis. And then he went on to say that his favourite art form was Chinese opera, because it took drama and raised it to the heavens."

"His mother was a drama queen?"

"So he claimed, but I never met her. She died towards the end of the Cultural Revolution. And, of course, that was something else he maintained shaped him."

"It provided the fodder for his best films."

"Yes, and for his later decay."

Ava finished her cognac and noticed that Fai had done the same. "Two more?" she asked.

"Why not?" Fai said. She waved at the server and pointed to their glasses.

"*The Air We Breathe* is one of the best films I've ever seen," Ava said.

"It was the peak of his career and the start of mine. It seems like a long time ago."

"How did he ever manage to get it made?"

"He was more politically sensitive then, more astute," Fai said. "Remember, he was in his early teens when the Cultural Revolution started, so he was old enough to observe it but young enough to be protected from its excesses. His mother aligned herself with the revolutionary movement, which elevated the family's status. Lau Lau met some of the right people and learned the language of the Revolution. He stayed in touch with the people and used that language as a way of convincing them he was one of them. He could condemn revisionists and the bourgeoisie for hours on end without meaning a word of it. Later in his life he used to do it at parties to entertain people, except some of the wrong people were listening and didn't think it was funny."

"But *The Air We Breathe* is tremendously political."

"The authorities only realized that after it was made," Fai said as the fresh cognacs arrived. "But if they'd been paying attention, they would have seen that all his earlier films were political as well. He just set them in earlier time periods, filmed them as allegories, and described them in ways that made it seem like he was skewering the bourgeoisie. What he was actually doing was condemning anyone who wielded power over another human being."

"They banned the film in China, right?"

"Yes. At first Lau Lau treated that as a badge of honour, especially after all those foreign awards from Venice and France and the U.S. were heaped on it. He began to act as if he didn't need the system here, as if he was somehow above it. But he was a Chinese director making Chinese films about Chinese subjects, and he quickly found there was nowhere else for him to go. He made a couple of small-budget films with private financing, but they were as politically unacceptable as *The Air We Breathe* and were banned as well."

"I remember them. They also won all kinds of foreign awards and accolades. And you were in them all."

"Yes, I was in them. And I worked for peanuts, like everyone else associated with them. The films may have won awards, but they didn't make much money, and that began to have an effect. A lot of the crew who'd been with Lau Lau since the start left to find work that paid better. He became more and more isolated and marginalized, and when that happened, the drinking and drugs really took hold."

"But he made some big-budget films later."

"Yes, he got tired of the struggle and crawled back to the Syndicate. They gave him the money he needed and controlled every aspect of what he made, and what he made were those shitty kung-fu and Chinese warrior–myth movies. Whatever self-respect he had left had disappeared."

"When was the last time you saw him?"

"I can't remember."

Ava wasn't sure she believed that but wasn't going to press the issue. "It doesn't really matter," she said. "I'm just pleased you've shared this with me. I wanted to understand him better."

Fai looked pensive. "I wish you didn't feel you have to talk to him."

"There are two disks that Ding Fa didn't edit. There's the one with you on it — that's the obvious one. Ding said he didn't see Lau Lau on any of the tapes, but you saw him, however briefly, at the end of a disk. I'm quite sure that's the missing disk," Ava said. "If it is, there's a chance that Lau Lau has been blackmailed as well. Or, if we're very lucky, he'll know some of the people behind this."

"I understand your logic, but it's still going to be difficult."

"You don't have to be there."

"Yes, I do. This is something I wouldn't want you to do alone."

"Then let's try to set up a meeting."

"I don't know how to contact him anymore."

"I have a phone number that our friend Mr. Fan gave me."

"I'll make the call," Fai said.

Ava took out her phone, found the number, and sent it to Fai. "You should have it now."

Fai nodded. "I'm not sure he'll want to talk to me, but here goes." A minute later she said, "He didn't answer and he doesn't have voicemail. I'll send a text."

"Who would know where he is?"

"Xia Jun might."

"The agent?"

"The last I heard he was still representing Lau Lau."

"Could you call him?"

"Only as a last resort. It would be a bit awkward, given that I'm represented by Chen. Are there are any other options?"

"I could press Fan."

"We both can."

Ten minutes later they left the canteen and walked into a light drizzle. "Goddamn weather," Ava said.

They took turns carrying the box back to the hutong. It was still daylight, but it was so overcast that most of the houses had their lights on, including Fan's. They dropped off the box at the house, towel-dried their hair, and headed back outside.

Ava knocked on Fan's door, and then knocked again. There was no answer. Fai moved to the right, peered through the window, and rapped on it. "He's coming now," she said.

"Another visit. What do you want this time?" he said.

"For starters, we'd like to come in from the rain," Ava said.

Fan stepped to one side. They walked into the living room, pushed some books aside, and sat down.

"This doesn't look like a social call," Fan said as he joined them.

"We have to find Lau Lau," Ava said.

"I gave you a phone number."

"I tried it. He didn't answer and there's no voicemail," Fai said.

"What else do you expect me to do?"

"Be more helpful," Ava said.

"How? I've told you all I know."

"I doubt that. You said you've met him from time to time. Where? Here in the hutong?"

"Please, it really is quite important that you help us if you can," Fai said.

Fan glanced at Fai, and Ava saw his attitude immediately

soften. "Do you know the Fengsheng District very well?" he asked.

"Some of it."

"Towards the north end, just west of Xisi Street, there are four or five warehouses. Most of them are obviously commercial and in use, but one looks abandoned. It's not. It's been taken over by a group of artists. The last time I saw Lau Lau, he told me that's where he was staying. Whether he's still there or not, I don't know."

"How long ago was this?" Ava asked.

"A few months, maybe a bit longer than that."

"Do you have any idea where those warehouses are?" Ava asked Fai.

"I think I do."

"Then in that case, thank you, Mr. Fan," Ava said.

"But don't come back here and blame me if you can't find him," Fan said.

"You do know how to ruin appreciation," Ava said.

THEY PUT ON JACKETS, GRABBED UMBRELLAS, AND SET out almost as soon as they got back from Fan's. There was still daylight and Ava didn't want to lose it, but they still had the problem of not knowing exactly where they were going. Fai tried to explain to the cab driver where she thought the warehouses were, but he acted as if he didn't even know where Beijing was.

"Just turn right on Picai Hutong and then left on Xidan," Fai said. "Xidan turns into Xisi Street. I'll tell you where to turn after that, when I see the street."

"Has Lau Lau answered your text?" Ava asked.

Fai looked at her phone. "Not yet. I hope he's still where Fan thinks he was."

"If he isn't, we'll ask around. Someone should know where he's gone."

Rush hour had started and the traffic was crawling. Ava felt herself becoming impatient and told herself to calm down; Fai didn't need to see her out of control.

They'd been driving for twenty minutes when suddenly Fai perked up. "I recognize this area. I think the warehouses are another street or two north of here, on the right."

The warehouses were actually three streets to the north and within easy walking distance of where Xisi intersected with the street they were on. There were five of them, of identical design and size. They filled a large tract of land in a reverse U shape, two running down each side and the one farthest from the street completing the U. They were four storeys high and probably double that in breadth.

As they approached, Ava could see a plethora of commercial signs affixed to every building and figured that the warehouses were servicing small to medium-sized businesses. There weren't as many signs on the farthest building, and those looked weather-beaten and ratty. Above the main entrance someone had painted THE BEIJING ARTISTS' WAREHOUSE CO-OPERATIVE.

"That looks like the place."

"I remember it now," Fai said. "I've been here once before. I came with an actress who was dating a sculptor who worked and lived here. The ground floor has really high ceilings; it's occupied mainly by sculptors and artists who specialize in large installations. The other floors have a mixture of painters, potters, and people who work with all kinds of textiles."

"How many of them live here?"

"I think most of them do."

"Where?"

"The entire top floor has been converted into one-room apartments, and there are large communal bathrooms and a kitchen."

"Is Lau Lau that broke?"

"Probably. I don't think he'd be here otherwise. He was always a man who liked his comforts."

"Did you notice that all the other warehouses have trucks and cars filling every parking space in front of them?" Ava said. "The Co-operative has three cars and about twenty bicycles."

"I'm sure bicycles are all most of them can afford."

They climbed eight wide stone steps to the large double-door entrance. Fai pushed a door open and they walked into an empty, high-ceilinged space that lacked even a building directory. There were doors leading in all directions from it, and straight ahead was a wide circular staircase. There was no sign of an elevator.

"We'll have to ask around, but we'll find him. I'm sure he's their most famous resident."

As they stood near the entrance they saw a steady stream of people going back and forth and up and down the stairs. Ava walked towards the stairs, Fai trailing, and stopped a young woman who was on her way down.

"Excuse me, but we're looking for Lau Lau, the film director," Ava said.

The woman looked annoyed at the question and seemed to be on the verge of an abrupt reply when she noticed Pang Fai. She blinked and her hand flew to her mouth. "Are you really who I think you are? Pang Fai?"

"Yes."

"Oh my god, I can hardly believe it."

"We're here to see Lau Lau. Do you know where we can find him?" Ava repeated.

"He could be working in the film lab on the third floor, or maybe the fourth," the woman said. "I'll take you."

"But you were just coming down," Ava said.

"It's not a problem, believe me," the woman said.

They followed her up the stairs, a process that was slow because the young woman kept turning to stare at Fai. A few people on the way down appeared to recognize her as well, coming to a complete stop as they passed.

When they reached the third floor, the woman ran ahead to open a door, stood to one side as they walked through, and then slipped in front of them again.

If there was a film lab, Ava couldn't see it. In one corner of the floor the walls were covered with film posters, including one for *The Air We Breathe*, a screen was set up, and there was a projector on a table. But there were no people.

"He must be upstairs. I'm sure he'll be really pleased to see you," she said to Fai.

"Yes," Fai said, her face blank and her tone neutral.

They followed the woman up the last flight of stairs and walked into a communal living space. Off to their immediate left and right were bathrooms. There weren't any signs to indicate that, but neither facility had doors and Ava could see people inside going about their business. This floor wasn't as open as the others they'd seen. A corridor that ran from the bathrooms opened onto a cluster of tables and chairs at the far end. Ava assumed that's where the kitchen was, and that the corridor was flanked by the one-room apartments.

"His room is near the end," the woman said. "Come with me."

Many of the doors they passed were open, and most of the rooms were empty of people. It seemed to be, thought Ava, an open and trusting environment.

The door the woman stopped in front of, though, was closed. She raised her fist as if about to knock and then stopped. "It might be better if you did this," she said to Fai.

Fai rapped on the door.

"Who's there?" a voice rasped.

"Lau Lau, it's me, Fai."

There was silence — a long, prolonged silence. The young woman looked at Fai and then said, her discomfort obvious, "I'd better head back downstairs. It was such a thrill to meet you."

Fai waited until she left before saying, "Lau Lau, open the door, please. I need to talk to you."

"About what?"

"Whatever it is, I won't do it through a closed door. And I'm prepared to wait until you come out."

"What the hell are you doing here?"

"I came to talk to you."

"How did you find me?"

"You're too famous to be invisible."

"You're a bitch, Fai."

"I know, but I'm the only one you ever had who meant anything."

There was another silence, and then he said. "Wait a minute."

"He'll come out," Fai said softly.

A moment later the door opened. Ava found herself looking at a man who bore only a vague resemblance to the picture she had in her mind of Lau Lau.

He looked at Fai and then at Ava. "Who's she?" he said.

"Her name is Ava Lee. She's my friend."

"What kind of friend?"

"My girlfriend. My lover."

"Just like that? You say it just like that?"

"Why not? It's the truth."

"This is a new Pang Fai," he said, and then looked again at Ava. "You must be a very special kind of woman."

"Not particularly."

"I don't believe that. But then I really don't care either way," he said.

"We need to talk to you," Ava said.

"About what?"

"Do you want to do it here or shall we find someplace a bit more private?"

"What's better?"

"Private, for everyone's sake," Ava said.

He nodded. "We'll talk in the dining room."

As Ava followed him and Fai towards an empty table in the corner of the dining area, she thought about the Lau Lau she'd just met. He was about five foot nine and lean, like the man she'd seen in photos, but the cropped black hair that had once been receding was now grey and shaved up the sides, so all that was left looked like a small grey skull-cap. The high, well-defined cheekbones were still there but clouded by large discoloured bags under his eyes, and the square, defiant chin that had once highlighted a sculpted face now hung almost around his neck.

The tables were long and narrow, more North American cafeteria style than Chinese. Lau Lau sat at the far end of one and they sat across from him. He stared at them, and Ava saw that his eyes were bloodshot and watery. She felt a wave of sympathy.

"What is it you want?" he asked.

"It's a bit complicated to explain," Ava said. "I hope you'll be patient."

He smiled and waved a hand in the air. "What else do I

have to do tonight? I have all the time in the world for you as long as your story is interesting enough. If it isn't, then you two can fuck off and I'll go back to my room and talk to myself."

Ava leaned forward, her eyes focused on his. "Our story concerns a tape that was made of a famous film director having sex in bed with another man, and the steps the director took to destroy that visual record."

His smile was forced. When Ava saw his eyes flicker to above her head and his hands clench, she knew she'd found part of the truth.

"That's an interesting start," he said. "I'm just not sure I want to hear the rest."

"We're searching for the rest," Ava said. "We're here because we need your help to find it."

"Why would I help?"

"Because the visual record the director thought was destroyed wasn't. A part remains, and we have it."

37

THERE WAS ALWAYS A MOMENT DURING A NEGOTIATION when the outcome became clear to Ava. It could come early or late, it could be positive or negative, but the signs were there to read if one took the time to pay attention to them.

Lau Lau's first reaction to Ava's news about the tape was an attempt at defiance. He said, "Fuck off," and almost rose from his seat. Then he sat down and stared across the table. As his eyes wandered away from her and Fai, Ava knew he was going to co-operate.

"How did Bai Lok approach you?" she asked.

"What do I have to do with that guy?"

"We know he met with you shortly before he died."

"So what?"

"And we were told he sold you something. We think the tape was transferred to a disk and you were sold a copy of the same disk we have, although I'm quite sure he told you it was the only one that existed."

"How do I know you have what you claim to have?" he shot back, not quite conceding yet.

"We bought several boxes of films and disks from Bai Jing,

Lok's brother, that Lok had left to him. You and a partner are on one of the disks."

"How do I know that's true?"

"We'll show it to you if that's necessary, but I would think the fact that we know it exists should be proof enough."

"Why would you buy anything from Jing?"

"I'm being blackmailed," Fai said, her voice steady. "We traced the source of the material they're using to Bai Lok. I assume you can guess what kind of material I'm referring to."

"That little prick."

"Did he try to blackmail you too?" Ava asked.

Lau Lau reached into his jeans pocket and took out a pack of Zhonghua cigarettes. Ava was surprised that he was smoking such an expensive brand. Then, as she looked around the room at the non-smoking signs hung on every wall, she was surprised that he would smoke at all. He lit a cigarette, inhaled deeply, and blew the smoke across the table at them.

"Did he try to blackmail you?" she pressed.

"Not directly. He was smoother than that. He called me to say he had cancer and not long to live. He said he needed money and he was selling off some of his possessions. He said he had some things I might be interested in. I told him I doubted that, but he kept pushing and finally I agreed to meet him for a drink."

"Did you take money with you? Did he bring the disk?"

"I didn't know anything about a disk, and I didn't take any money," Lau Lau said. "I agreed to meet him for a drink, and that's all. I didn't expect to get leaned on."

"So he did lean on you?" Ava asked.

"Eventually, but only in the most roundabout and convoluted way imaginable. He spent the first ten minutes telling me how terrific I am and how my films had inspired him. He said my focus on ordinary people, the way my movies recorded their resilience in the face of hardship and adversity, was the model that future generations of Chinese filmmakers would be measured against. It was excessive."

"But still more true than not, and well earned," Ava said. "You have set the standard."

"Thank you," he said, searching Ava's face for any signs of cynicism.

"When did your meeting with him move from praise to pitch?"

"We had a couple of drinks and gossiped about the industry. Then he asked me about my plans," Lau Lau said. "I told him I was trying to get back into serious contemporary filmmaking, that I couldn't handle another bullshit historical war drama. At that point he reminded me that I'd been removed from my last film because of 'health issues.' That's how he referred to the fact that I was drunk or on drugs nearly every day I was on set, because that was the only way I could cope with the crap I was expected to film. I told him that I was working hard at rehabilitation. He didn't point out that we were sitting in a bar drinking. Then he said—he was a bit sly about it—that it would be tragic if I resolved all my 'health issues' and then had my reputation sullied in some other way that would make me unemployable."

"That was clever," Ava said.

"And of course, without a second thought, I asked him what he meant."

"Who wouldn't?"

"At which point he became even slyer," Lau Lau said. "He told me that four or five years before he'd been hired by a company to make some sex films. He said they were unscripted, that the objective was to make them as real and natural as possible. So he made an arrangement with a friend to set up a secret taping operation in her apartment. He told me that I'd paid a visit to that apartment, and that he had it on tape. That's all he said, and then he sat back and waited for my reaction. Truthfully, I didn't handle it very well."

"Did you hit him?"

"No, the opposite. I kind of fell apart. It was a fragile time for me and I thought I was on the mend. I guess I wasn't."

"How did he react?"

"He couldn't have been kinder. At least, on the surface it was kindness," Lau Lau said. "He told me he'd never shown the tape to anyone, not even the people who'd hired him. He'd edited it himself and transferred it to a disk that he'd kept locked away for years. He said the disk was the only record that remained. He wanted me to have it. He didn't want to die and have it fall into the wrong hands. He said he hadn't shown it to anyone because he wanted to protect me and my reputation, and that he still wanted to."

"Then why didn't he get rid of it himself? Why did he even tell you about it?"

"I wasn't thinking that clearly. And besides, we both knew, just like you do, that it wasn't about a tape or a disk. It was about money."

"How much did he want?"

"He didn't say at first. He said he was worried about paying for living expenses during his last months, and that he wanted a respectable funeral. I told him I'd be pleased to help and offered him ten thousand renminbi. He said that wouldn't even look after the funeral, and asked if I could find fifty thousand to help him. We settled on thirty; that's about all I had."

"Five thousand U.S. dollars. That's a lot less than Fai's blackmailer wants."

"She's still a star. I'm not even on the radar anymore."

"What did you get for your thirty thousand?"

"The disk."

"What if there were others?"

"It had been four or five years since it was made. I figured if there were others, they would have surfaced by then. Besides, I didn't have a lot of choice."

"So you paid him the money and you got the disk."

"Yes," he said, throwing the cigarette on the floor and grinding the butt with the heel of his shoe.

"And you never heard from him again?"

"No."

"And no one else contacted you about the video?"

"Not until now. I'm sure you understand that I'm not happy it still exists."

Ava saw Fai tense and suspected she was about to tell him that all they had was a snippet. She reached out and touched her arm. Fai nodded and said nothing.

"We have no reason to do anything with the one we have," Ava said.

"Then give it to me."

"Eventually, I imagine, that's what we'll do," Ava said. "For now it's the only motivation you have for speaking to us, so we're not going to do anything with it until we know exactly how things stand for Fai."

"I've told you everything I know."

"So you say, but it would be foolish of us to take the risk that you might have forgotten something."

"Like what?"

"Like, what did Bai Lok tell you about Fai?"

"He never mentioned her."

"I have trouble believing that."

"That's the way it was."

"Even before I met Fai, I was never involved in any discussion about Chinese film where your two names weren't linked. If someone spoke about what a great director Lau Lau was, someone else would mention Fai's contribution to your success. And vice versa, of course," Ava said. "It's hard to believe that someone in the movie business in China, someone who knew you both, wouldn't make some kind of passing reference to her."

"He might have asked me if I'd seen her."

"That's a mention."

"I thought you meant something more serious."

"What do you mean by 'serious'?"

"Nothing," he said, taking another cigarette from his packet.

"Did he tell you he had a video of Fai with a partner that she might not want people to know about?"

"No."

"You are absolutely sure about that? He didn't even hint or suggest it in some sly way, like he did with you?"

"Why would he? Everyone knew that Fai and I were done. Why would I care about what he had on her?"

"But if he had something on her, why didn't he use it?" Ava asked. "Until a few days ago she didn't know the tape had been made. Then, out of the blue, it's dropped on her with a huge blackmail price tag attached to it. If Bai Lok needed money so badly, why didn't he go to Fai at the same time he approached you? He had to know that she had more money than you."

"Don't ask me to explain why a dying man did what he did. I wasn't inside his head. All I wanted to do was resolve the problem I had."

Ava turned to Fai. "I'm just about done. Is there anything you want to ask him?"

Fai shook her head but then leaned forward abruptly. "Are you happy here?" she asked Lau Lau.

He shrugged. "I have somewhere to live. I have admirers — and you know how much I love attention. I'm surrounded by young, creative, energetic people that I can feed off. But I can't help thinking of the co-operative as a halfway house, as a place where I can recharge my batteries. Because all I really want is the chance to make films again," he said.

"I pray you get that chance."

38

IT WAS DARK WHEN THEY LEFT THE WAREHOUSE TO walk back to Xisi Street. On one level Ava thought the meeting had gone well, since they now knew what had gone down between Bai Lok and Lau Lau. On another level it had been very disappointing; it shed no light on the source of Fai's disk, other than that she was now absolutely sure it had originated with Bai Lok. But what had he done with it? Had he sold it the way he had sold Lau Lau's? If so, to whom? And why had it taken so many years to surface?

"What did you think of him?" Ava asked as they left the complex.

"He's a shell of the man I knew."

"It's sad. I'd be surprised if there's a road back to film-making for him," Ava said. "But what I really want to know is whether you believed him."

"I did."

"Me too, I think he told us the truth. The question is, did he tell us everything he knows?"

"Do you doubt that?"

"Yes, but I have nothing to base that on except my

instincts," Ava said. "I had this feeling when he was talking to us that he was holding something back."

"He was always a bit secretive. It's second nature to him. I wouldn't put too much emphasis on it."

"Still—" Ava said as her phone sounded. She looked at the screen and hit the answer button. "Sonny."

"Ava, is this a good time to talk?"

"Not really. I'm on my way to catch a cab. Is this urgent or can I call you back in twenty minutes?"

"Call me when you get settled."

"Will do," she said, pleased that there wasn't any urgency.

"There's a cab now," Fai said, rushing to the sidewalk and flagging it down. "Where do you want to go?" she asked Ava as they climbed in.

"Let's go home."

Fai gave the driver directions to the hutong and then turned to Ava. "So what do we do now about that disk?"

"We still have some mysteries to resolve. Who has it? How did they get it? And why did they take so long before contacting you? We should take some time to think about our day, about what Ding and Lau Lau have told us. Maybe something will pop into our heads that will be useful or that we can follow up on. I also want to talk to Bai Jing again."

Fai took Ava's hand. "We only have a few days left. I'm starting to think that we're not going to resolve this before we have to pay that creep."

"Pay him or not, the problem won't go away, so I don't believe paying him is a realistic option."

"Maybe not, but it might be the only option we have."

"You say that so calmly."

"Well, as weird as it seems, given everything at stake,

I don't feel any sense of panic. I'm concerned, of course, and I have moments when I feel really afraid, but I think I've come to grips with the reality of it," Fai said. "*Que sera, sera.*"

"I don't buy into that *que sera* shit," Ava said. "The future is what we make it, not what we let be imposed on us."

"I wasn't suggesting we give up," Fai said. "I think the fact that we've been working to find a solution is the reason I'm so calm, and I don't want to stop until we reach the deadline. I'm just saying, regardless of how this ends, I'll know we've done all we can."

"I didn't mean to sound dismissive," Ava said.

"I didn't take it that way."

"It's just that I hate losing. I hate losing at anything, and this is important to me. I don't want anyone taking away your power to make decisions about your life and career."

"I know, and I feel the same," Fai said. "But if I have to pay, I will, and then hope that we can find a way to do it that will force the creep to honour his word."

It began to rain again and the wind seemed to have picked up. "When this is over, I want us to go somewhere warm — where it's not raining," Ava said.

Ten minutes later they arrived at the hutong entrance, got out of the cab, opened their umbrellas, and made a dash for Fai's. As they stood inside the door shaking off the rain, Ava said, "I should phone Sonny in Hong Kong."

"If you're ready for dinner, I have some of my mother's dumplings left."

"I'm ready, and that sounds perfect."

Ava went into the living room, stepping around the boxes of films and disks, and sat on the couch to call Sonny. He answered instantly.

"Hey, boss."

"How was your day?" she asked.

"I spent most of it in Tai Wai New Village waiting for your father, but when he was in his meetings I had the chance to make some calls about that thing we discussed," Sonny said. "I spoke to some old friends in Sha Tin who're retired but keep their ears to the ground, and I talked to a guy in Tai Po that I trust. He referred me to another guy, in Kwai Chung. Tai Po and Kwai Chung border on Sha Tin, so I figured they were close enough to hear things."

"And have they heard anything?"

"There are some rumblings. Nothing specific, but there's definitely some noise."

"What kind of noise?"

"The kind that would be easy to ignore if you weren't look-ing for it. A lot of complaining mainly, but it seems to have picked up since Carter Wing took over Sha Tin."

"Carter is Sammy's nephew?"

"Yeah, and according to my guys he's really aggressive and ambitious."

"That's not unusual for a Mountain Master."

"But he's been running things there for only a few months. Normally there's a period of settling in. He's not showing that kind of patience."

"What are the complaints about?"

"There's a lot of talk about Lop. You know, about him not being local, about whether he's really Triad," Sonny said. "It's all based on jealousy. They hate the fact that he controls distribution of all the knock-off software and devices that Xu makes."

"They're still bitching about that? That's why Xu and Sammy went to war in the first place. I thought that was resolved."

"As long as Sammy is still in Wanchai, I can't see it going away."

"Lop runs Wanchai. Xu let Sammy stay there as a figure-head, out of respect and as a way of keeping peace. If he starts causing trouble, Xu will remove him entirely."

"Leaving him in place even as a figurehead may have been a miscalculation," Sonny said. "Uncle used to say that when you humiliate a strong man, all he ever thinks about is revenge. You should never expect him to be loyal."

"How would Uncle have handled Sammy?"

"Sammy would be dead."

"I don't think —" she began to say, and then stopped. There was no point in arguing with him about something hypothetical. "Sonny, these rumblings you're hearing, is it possible it's just talk?"

"Well, there's still a lot of resentment that a Shanghai-based gang runs Wanchai, and then there's the grumbling about the software and devices. And Lop isn't the easiest guy to get along with," Sonny said, and then paused. "But even with all that in play, I think it probably is just talk, just bitch-ing. It goes on all the time. Even when Uncle was running Fanling, there were guys who did nothing but complain."

"I think you're probably correct, but I'd still appreciate it if you could dig a little deeper," Ava said. "Lop seems to think that the Carter-Sammy connection is strong and that there's some plotting going on. I'd like to be able to tell him and Xu otherwise."

"I'll make some more calls and I'll take a few guys out for drinks."

"Do that, but keep it low-key."

"I know the ropes. I watched you and Uncle for long enough."

"Uncle was the best."

"He used to say you were."

"That's a lovely thing to say."

"*Momentai*, boss," Sonny said, sounding embarrassed.

"Call me tomorrow night with an update."

Ending the call, Ava felt uncomfortable. She hadn't expected the report Sonny had given her; it had caught her off guard. Was it possible that Lop's paranoia was justified? It was still difficult to believe. She suspected that Sonny's explanation would prove to be correct.

"The dumplings are ready whenever you are," Fai said, appearing in the kitchen doorway. "And I've opened a bottle of wine."

Ava joined her and they managed to eat and drink their way through half an hour without discussing the disk.

"What do you want to do tonight?" Fai asked when they had finished the dumplings.

"I should phone Bai Jing."

"No, please don't," Fai said. "My head needs a break from all this stuff. Besides, if we leave it alone for a while, maybe we'll create room for some fresh ideas."

"That's not a bad thought," Ava said. "What would you prefer we do?"

"I was thinking about doing something you might find strange."

"How strange?"

"I'd like to watch *The Air We Breathe.* I have the DVD, and it's been years and years since I last saw it."

"That's not what I expected. I remember you telling me that you don't particularly like revisiting your performances."

"This will be different. I don't think of the film as mine — it's entirely Lau Lau's creation. I knew so little and he guided me the whole way through it. At least, that's how I remember it," Fai said. "Seeing him today made me so sad. I'd like to think of him in a different light, at a different time, and nothing could do that better than watching all three hours of his masterpiece."

Ava thought about how dark and gloomy the film was, right down to its depressing ending, but there was no argument that it was a masterpiece. "Then that's what we'll do," she said.

39

THE RINGTONE WASN'T FAMILIAR, AND WHEN AVA FIRST heard it, she thought she was dreaming. Then Fai's sleep-filled voice said, "Who is this, and why are you calling so late?"

Ava knew she wasn't dreaming and was instantly awake. She picked up her own phone and looked at the time. It was five past two.

"I'm going to put this on speaker. You can tell her yourself," Fai said.

Ava moved closer to Fai's phone. "Are you there?" a man's voice said.

"I am."

"Come outside. We need to talk to you."

"Come outside where?"

"We're in the courtyard."

Ava slipped from the bed and walked to the window. She pulled back the curtain ever so slightly at one edge and peered outside. She didn't have the best of angles and there wasn't a lot of light, so all she could see clearly was the middle of an empty, rain-spattered courtyard. If someone was there, he had to be lurking on the perimeter.

"I don't think coming outside is a good idea," Ava said.

"You're not listening well. I wasn't making a request. I'm telling you what you have to do."

"Both of us?"

"Just you."

"Why?"

"You're still not listening well. We need to talk to you."

"Whatever you have to say, you can say over the phone."

The line went quiet, and Ava wondered if he was talking to someone else.

"Here's the deal," a different man's voice said. Ava thought it sounded familiar. "You either come outside now or the contents of that disk will be public by noon tomorrow."

"That's not our arrangement," Ava said, now recognizing the muffled voice of the blackmailer, the man on the DVD. "And why would you do that? You'll lose the money that Pang Fai has agreed to pay."

"We have other people who are willing to pay as much. We came to her first out of respect."

Ava looked at Fai, who in turn was staring at her, shaking her head. *Don't go*, she mouthed.

"I'll need a few minutes to get dressed," Ava said. "Where are you when you say 'outside'? In the courtyard? On the hutong?"

"Just come outside. You'll find us."

"In a few minutes," Ava said, ending the call.

"You can't go," Fai said.

"I don't think it's wise to call his bluff about releasing the disk, and I think it would be foolish to think we can avoid them indefinitely. They're outside now and they might not go away until I come out," Ava said. "Besides, I'm interested to hear what they have to say. It might get us that much closer to knowing and understanding who's behind this."

"It could be dangerous."

"The way I look at it, it's as dangerous to stay in here as it is to go out," Ava said, pulling the curtain open a little but still not seeing anyone. "It's raining like hell. I'll put on my running gear and my baseball cap."

Fai slid from the bed. "I'll go with you."

"No, you won't. He was quite specific about me being alone," Ava said. "What you can do is come to the front door and keep an eye on what happens. Who knows, you might be able to identify one of them."

Fai nodded and reached for her housecoat. Ava went to the closet where her jacket and training pants were hanging. She put them on over underwear and a black Giordano T-shirt, then jammed the cap on her head, tucking her hair in at the back. "Let's go," she said to Fai. "My running shoes are at the front door."

They went down the stairs in the dark. When they reached the ground floor, Ava turned on all the hallway and entrance lights. She kneeled to put on her running shoes. "Turn off all the lights after I go outside, and don't stand near the door until you do. I don't want them to see you, and it will be easier for you to see them."

"Okay," Fai said, reaching for Ava.

As they hugged, Ava realized that Fai was trembling. "Don't worry. I'm sure they just want to talk," she said, gently disengaging and reaching for the door handle.

Cold rain was the first thing she noticed as she stepped into the courtyard. The wind was stronger than it had looked from the bedroom window, and the rain hitting her face stung like tiny ice pellets. She looked left and right and saw no one. *What the hell*? she thought. Then the main door that led from the hutong into the courtyard opened. Three men came through it and started to walk towards her.

Only one was of any meaningful size, while the other two were about the same medium height and weight. They walked in a cluster, the largest lagging slightly behind, his head constantly turning as if he was looking for someone else. As they drew near, Ava saw that one of the smaller men was wearing brown jeans and a dark blue hoodie, which fitted Fan's description of the man who'd delivered the package. The large man also wore a hoodie, and they both had the hoods pulled tightly around their faces. The third man wore a black balaclava like the one she'd seen on the disk.

Ava walked slowly towards them, away from the front door.

"You can stop right there," the one in the balaclava said when they were about five metres apart.

"Is this really necessary?" Ava asked. "We could have done this over the phone without getting wet."

The large man shifted a few steps to the left and moved slightly closer to Ava.

"You've become a pain in the ass," the man in the balaclava said. "We had a deal, and all you've done since we made it is to go behind our backs and try to undo it."

"How did I do that?"

"We know who you've been talking to. We know what kind of questions you've been asking. You should have left things alone. You shouldn't have interfered."

"It was a natural enough thing for us to do, wasn't it. Why wouldn't we want to know who was blackmailing Fai?"

"Stop saying 'we.' This has nothing to do with her. If you weren't here, if you hadn't stuck your nose where it doesn't belong, there would be nothing to discuss. We wouldn't have to visit you in the middle of the night."

"But I am here. I am involved."

"You need to get uninvolved. Without you, there's no problem. Without you, Fai will do the right thing and be able to get on with her life."

"And if I choose not to?"

He turned his head to the left and nodded. "Then we'll make sure you don't have any choice," he said. "We didn't want it to come to this, but we expected it would. And truthfully, we almost hoped that it would. You don't have any friends in our circle."

"This was your intention all along, wasn't it."

"I've said enough."

The large man took two steps towards her as the one in the blue hoodie moved to the right and then started forward. It wasn't hard to gauge which of them on the surface presented the most danger, so Ava pivoted to face the larger man while trying to keep the other one in her line of vision. The footing wasn't the best, and Ava's running shoes slipped on the wet bricks. She swore and then steadied herself.

"Get her," the man in the balaclava said.

The big man grunted and lunged, his right hand reaching for her hair. She stepped back and the hand clawed at air. She moved to the right, her hand forming the phoenix-eye fist. Her target was his ear, but as she gathered the power to strike, she slipped again and found herself face to face with him. He threw a punch that was aimed at her nose. She ducked and his fist scraped the top of her cap. It was her turn to lunge.

She went at him head-on, the phoenix eye driving into his upper belly at the exact point where his ribs met, where the tangle of nerves was most sensitive. He groaned and fell back a couple of steps, but he stayed on his feet and didn't buckle over as she'd expected.

He raised his head and he stared at her with as much anger as she'd seen in any man. He reached into his back pocket and pulled out a knife. He pressed a button and the blade hissed into sight. "Get your knife out," he said to the man in the blue hoodie.

Ava knew time was short. The longer she waited, the greater their advantage. Her choices were to attack or to run. As the word "run" crossed her mind, her body reacted. She leapt at the big man and, as she got to him, extended her right leg and propelled the heel of her shoe into his groin. This time he did buckle, if only slightly, but it was enough to give her a clear shot at his head. She rammed the base of her palm into his forehead, and as his head rocketed back, she moved closer still and drove her fist into his throat. He collapsed onto the wet bricks, both hands clutching at his neck.

Ava saw the man in the balaclava moving away from them, back towards the entrance. As he did, his eyes flickered to the left. Ava swivelled in time to see the other man coming at her with a switchblade in his right hand.

"You don't want to do this," she said.

"You fucking bitch!" he said. "I'm going to cut you open and watch you bleed."

As he measured Ava for an attack, she was measuring him. He was right-handed and his body was turned slightly to the left, another indication that he favoured his right side. His steps were deliberate and he didn't appear to be particularly agile. Ava knew that if she could avoid his first swipe, it was unlikely he'd be able to gather himself quickly enough for a second.

"Come and get me," she said, shaking her hips and then sliding her feet back and forth to either side. He took a couple of slow, careful steps forward and then jumped at her, the knife sweeping from right to left, aimed at her midsection. He was faster than he looked. As the knife slashed across the front of her jacket, for a second Ava thought she had miscalculated. But even if he had found flesh, it wouldn't have stopped her from grabbing his wrist with one hand as it moved by and then gripping his lower forearm with the other. She took a step back, straightened his arm, and then snapped. She didn't know if she'd broken both his ulna and radius, but it really didn't matter. She'd done enough damage to make his arm completely useless and to cause him to scream in agony.

At that moment the courtyard suddenly became better lit. Ava turned and saw Fai, Fan, and an elderly couple in their doorways. Fai started to run across the courtyard.

"Let's get out of here," the man in the balaclava shouted.

Blue Hoodie tried to gather himself. He stumbled towards the man on the ground and nudged him with his toe. "Let's go," he said.

The big man was still gasping for air as he struggled to his feet. Ava thought about knocking him down again, but Fai had almost reached her. The last thing Ava wanted was for the men, injured or not, to turn on her friend.

Ava looked up to see the man in the balaclava leaving the courtyard. The other two followed him, not looking back.

40

THEY GATHERED IN FAI'S LIVING ROOM — FAN, AVA, FAI, and the elderly couple. Ava wanted to be alone with Fai, but it was difficult to be rude to the old couple, and they couldn't let them in without admitting Fan.

The couple wanted to call the police. Ava talked them out of it by arguing that she knew nothing about her attackers, and that as a visitor to China, the last thing she wanted was to get involved in a police investigation. Her last point made a bigger impact than the first, which didn't surprise Ava; she'd never met anyone in China who trusted the police to do anything but uphold the status quo and look after their own interests. The couple understood that if the attackers had any kind of link to the police, it could be Ava who was charged with assault and not them.

Still, even after that was settled, Ava and Fai couldn't get anyone to leave. A lot of concern was expressed about the knife that had cut Ava's jacket, until she took it off and showed them that her skin was untouched.

Then the old woman asked the question that Ava knew was coming, because she'd heard it so many times before.

"How did you do that?" It was asked in a solicitous manner, but there were undertones of both fear and excitement, which Ava had also heard before.

The truth was that she couldn't even think about how she'd done it. She'd reacted as she had since she was a teenager first learning martial arts. They attacked, she defended. Or, more properly, they attacked and she counterattacked. The impulse was so natural to her that it was like breathing. There was virtually no thought process attached to it, and certainly no emotion. No fear, no anger, no elation. Simply, they attacked and she counterattacked.

The hardest thing to learn had been technique. That hadn't been challenging until she met Grandmaster Tang and was introduced to bak mei. Even then she progressed faster than any student he'd ever taught, because she so readily embraced the demands he made on her in terms of focus and precision.

One day he said to her, "How fast am I?"

"What do you mean?"

"When I attack you, what do you see?"

"I see you. I see a fist, a foot."

"Do you sense them or do you actually see them? Are they a blur or are they real?"

"I see them, and sometimes it's like they're in slow motion."

"I thought so," the Grandmaster said. "Do you ever think I'm going to defeat you?"

"No. I don't think about whether you will or you won't. I don't think at all. I just see and I react."

But Ava couldn't say that to the old woman, so she said, "I was terrified. Luckily I had some martial arts training when I was young, and some of it came back to me."

After a few pots of tea the couple finally left. Fan lingered, which gave Ava a chance to ask him if he knew any of the men who'd been in the courtyard.

"No," he said.

"But one of them was wearing brown jeans and a blue hoodie, like the one you told us delivered the package."

"Oh, him. Well, of course I recognized him, but I don't know who he is. Those are two different things."

"Don't mess with me," Ava said abruptly. "I'm losing my patience with you. I think you know more than you're telling us."

"How could you say that?"

"I just did, and let me repeat, I'm losing my patience with you. If I find out that you've been playing games, I'll make your life miserable."

Fan turned to Fai. "How can you let her say things like that?"

"She can say what she wants," Fai said. "I'm with her."

Fan lowered his head. "I think I should be going."

"A great idea," Ava said.

Fan pushed himself to his feet and started towards the door, with Fai following him. Ava leaned back on the sofa as the door closed behind him. Fai joined her and started to speak, but instead she just slumped against Ava. "I was so frightened," she said finally.

"You didn't look frightened when I saw you running across the courtyard."

"I was frightened and angry at the same time."

Ava stroked Fai's hair. "Well, I thought it was very brave of you. I just wish it hadn't been necessary."

"Who were those men?"

"Didn't you get a good look at them?"

"No. I was more concerned about you," Fai said.

"One of them wore a balaclava. He's the guy from the disk, the one who issued the blackmail threat. I recognized his voice when they called," Ava said. "The other two are thugs. I don't think they're anything more than that, just hired muscle, and not very good at that."

"Why did they come here?"

"To warn us off. The guy in the balaclava said they know we've been trying to find out who's behind the blackmail. They want us to stop asking questions, and I think it's fair to assume that they want me gone."

"What happens now?"

"I don't know," Ava said. "You heard what he said on the phone about releasing the video at noon today if I didn't go out into the courtyard. Well, if he meant it, we may have just pissed him off even more."

"I see."

"But I'm not sure he meant it. I'm not even sure he's got any real role in this, beyond being the guy someone else chose to communicate with you," Ava added quickly.

"Why do you think that?"

"It was so amateurish — the phone call, the guys in the courtyard. A professional wouldn't have bothered phoning. He would have used surprise as an element and then bluntly delivered the message instead of pretending to have a conversation," Ava said. "But even if the thugs aren't amateurs and just not very good at their job, why would the person who's supposedly blackmailing you come to the courtyard in person? Why risk exposing himself? It doesn't make sense."

"So who was the guy in the balaclava?"

"Someone hired to do a job, but an amateur, which is why I think he did it badly," Ava said. "I think it's possible that our poking around did get back to whoever is behind this, and they told this guy to put a stop to it. Phoning us in the middle of the night and meeting me in the courtyard with two thugs is what he came up with as a solution. The instructions may not have come from the blackmailer. At least, that's what we should hope."

"It sounds kind of logical."

Ava sighed. "Yeah, 'kind of logical' is the right description. If I'm wrong, then by noon today the video could be all over the Internet. If I'm right, we're still stuck with the challenge of finding out who's behind this and putting a stop to it."

"Or finding the money to pay them."

"Let's not talk about money," Ava said. "What I'd like to know is who you think would have told the blackmailer that we're asking questions. Because someone we spoke to did. That's the only positive thing I got out of my courtyard conversation."

"Well, who did we talk to? Mak Guang. Mr. Fan. Lau Lau. Ding Fa."

"I spoke to Bai Jing."

"And Guang talked to Ren Lan."

"And anyone we've mentioned could have spoken to who knows how many other people. It could have been an innocent exchange with no malice intended. It could have been just passing along gossip."

"What are we going to do?"

"I don't think we should start phoning people to ask them who they've spoken to. We need to sit down face to face, and my first two priorities are Lau Lau and Bai Jing."

"That makes sense. Mak Guang won't want the video released any more than we do, and I truly believe that Ding is a friend. And, despite the fact that you don't like him and he can be sneaky, I can't believe Mr. Fan knows anything," Fai said. "When do you want to meet with the other two?"

"Normally I'd say tomorrow morning, but that could be pointless if they release the video before noon," Ava said. "And I have a meeting scheduled for eleven o'clock with the Suns and Suki. I could cancel it, I guess, but it wouldn't be wise from a business or relationship viewpoint."

"I think you should go. Don't cancel," Fai said. "You're right that there isn't much point in meeting with anyone if they release the disk. And like you said, we're not going to know until noon."

"How will you stay on top of that?"

"I don't imagine there's much I'll have to do," Fai said. "I'm quite certain that if it appears I'll hear from Chen about a minute later. He's got a young woman in the office who obsessively tracks every reference and comment made about the talent."

"It's going to make for a long morning," Ava said.

"After a long night."

Ava looked at the time and groaned. "I'm going to leave here by ten, which means I have to be up by nine. And I'm not sure I'm going to be able to get any more sleep."

Fai put her hand around Ava's waist and pressed closer. "We can stay here like this for a little while."

"Sure we can," Ava said, closing her eyes.

41

SHE DREAMED ABOUT UNCLE. BEFORE UNCLE'S DEATH,
her father had dominated her dreams, in endless futile chases
through hotels with shifting floors and rooms, in airports
with gates she could never find, on taxi rides that never quite
reached their destination. She was always searching and never
finding. Glimpses of her father far in the distance was the
closest she could ever get to him. But when Uncle died, all
that changed. He was the one who visited her at night, taking
the time to sit and talk, to explain, to calm, and to advise. It
seemed to her that he was always there at times of crisis, but
oddly, he dealt with the future as well as the present.

On this night they were sitting in a noodle shop that she
knew was in Hong Kong, because it was his favourite. He was
eating noodles with beef and XO sauce. The place was empty
except for them, with no sign of the old man who was the cook
and owner or his wife, who served the tables. Ava had a bowl
of soup with noodles and shrimp dumplings; for some reason
the dumplings kept slipping from her chopsticks, which made
Uncle laugh. This upset her, and she said, *I'm not quite myself.
I'm worried about Pang Fai. I think I've brought her bad luck.*

She made her own luck long before she met you, said Uncle. *She has had a complicated life and now some of it is catching up to her. But I would not worry so much. She is resilient.*

What if things go badly? Can I trust her?

With what?

My love.

The answer to that question is as complicated as her life.

Please don't speak in riddles.

He shook his head. *I am only reflecting on the breadth of your question. Do you mean can you trust her now or do you mean can you trust her with your love over many more years?*

Both.

I believe you can trust her now. She understands everything, including the worst of consequences, and she will not disappoint you. The future is more difficult to predict, because when two people with complex pasts try to make a life together, who really understands what ghosts will return?

Uncle, you aren't helping me very much with this.

I am sorry, but I have some worries of my own tonight.

Such as? she asked, feeling panic.

Xu is going to have a problem.

He called me about Wanchai, about Lop and Sammy Wing. I have Sonny working on it.

This has nothing to do with Wanchai, he said as he disappeared.

"Ava."

She opened her eyes and saw Fai standing over her. She was still on the couch, wrapped in a blanket, and the sun was streaming in the window. "What?"

"Your phone has been ringing for the last hour. I didn't want to answer it but I finally had to. There's a woman calling who says she's Auntie Grace."

Ava took the phone from Fai. "Auntie, what's going on?"

"Xu is ill."

"What?"

"He's ill."

"I heard you Auntie, but I don't know what you mean," she said as she sat up.

"It started late yesterday afternoon. He had a headache and started to develop a fever," she said, her voice catching. "I gave him a herbal potion and he went to bed. Then I heard him in the middle of the night, wandering around the kitchen. He was confused about where he was and started to complain again about headache and a stiff neck."

"Did you call a doctor?"

"He doesn't have one. He's never needed one."

"Where is he now?"

"In his room."

"Auntie, do you have regular painkillers in the house? By that I mean something like Tylenol or Advil or even plain Aspirin."

"I've always given him natural remedies. I don't believe in pills."

"In this case I want you to. It sounds like he has some sort of flu. The pills will help."

"Okay. I'll go and buy some."

"Thank you. Call me later and let me know how he's doing. I'll keep my phone on."

"Is everything okay?" Fai said.

"I think it should be. Xu's having headaches and his

housekeeper is worried. She's been with him since he was a baby, and from time to time she still treats him like one."

"I was going to wake you anyway. It's almost nine-fifteen."

"And I spent the night here on the couch?"

"You slept very well. Me, not so much. I was out early enough to get some congee," Fai said. "I also bought you some coffee, since I know you prefer that over tea."

"I have to pee," Ava said as she got up, her head still a jumble of Uncle and Auntie Grace.

"Everything is in the kitchen when you're finished," Fai said.

Five minutes later Ava came downstairs and sat at the kitchen table.

"You look upset," Fai said.

"I had dreams, and then the phone call from Auntie, and now I'm thinking about our day."

"Our half-day, because until we get to twelve o'clock, we won't know what the rest of it will be like."

Ava sat back in her seat and stared across the table. "You seem to be resigned to whatever the day brings."

"I can't control it but I can accept it."

"I'm not so good at accepting things I can't control."

"Which is why I'm depending on you."

"Are we going in circles?"

"What I'm trying to say is that I can live with whatever the outcome is, as long as you and I are together."

"Why wouldn't we be?"

"Not everyone wants to be associated with a soon-to-be washed-up middle-aged lesbian actress who can't speak English well enough to act anywhere outside China."

"I do," Ava said. "And fuck anyone who doesn't."

"If enough people feel that way, maybe I can salvage part of my career."

Ava stared across the table at Fai and wondered if she was simply putting on a brave front. There were times when she had to remind herself that Fai was an actress, even though she'd never felt she was being played. Ava sipped her coffee from the cup Fai had placed on the table. It was lukewarm, but she wasn't going to complain. The congee, on the other hand, was hot and needed only a dash of white pepper.

Ava dug in. "Aren't you going to eat?" she asked Fai.

"I've had two bowls already."

Ava ate slowly, her mind returning to the problem she faced and her last conversation with Fai the night before. She remembered that they'd talked about the candidates most likely to have spoken to someone else and had decided on Lau Lau and Bai Jing. A decent sleep later, removed from the emotions of the incident in the courtyard, she still felt they were the two. Part of her wished she didn't have the meeting scheduled with the Suns and Suki and that she could go after them right away, but she knew the decision they'd made the night before — to wait until noon — was the most rational one. At least the meeting would provide a distraction.

"Do you want more?" Fai asked.

Ava looked down at her empty bowl. "No, thanks. I have to shower and get ready for my meeting."

"Will you have your phone on all morning?"

"Yes, and you have to call me the instant you hear anything at all."

"You can count on that," Fai said.

Half an hour later, Ava came down the stairs dressed for business. She wore a black pencil skirt, a light blue Brooks

Brothers shirt with French cuffs, and black pumps. There was a touch of mascara on her lashes and her lips were glossy red. The shirt cuffs were held closed with her green jade links, the Tank Française watch adorned her left wrist, and her hair was pulled back and held in place by the ivory chignon pin. She carried her Vuitton bag, in which she had her phone, cash, wallet, and the Moleskine notebook that contained the data on the Sun business purchase and her notes on Fai's dilemma. She hoped that during this day she would only have to turn to the front pages.

Fai came out of the kitchen and smiled when she saw her. "The power woman," she said.

"What?"

"That's what the girls in London called you when they saw you dressed like this. They meant it as a compliment," Fai said. "They liked the way you looked — professional and ready to do business, but still attractive as hell."

"Then I'll take that as a compliment," Ava said, opening the front door and looking outside. "It isn't raining, but I'll take an umbrella with me just in case."

"I'll walk with you to the end of the hutong," Fai said.

"You don't have to."

"I know, but I want to. It's becoming a habit," Fai said. "And I like the fact that we're developing habits. It makes me feel that our being together isn't so casual."

42

THE BEIJING TRAFFIC WAS, AS USUAL, HORRENDOUS, and Ava was glad she had allotted extra time for the trip. She phoned Suki to let her know she was on her way. Suki was already at the Suns' office and told Ava not to fret if she was a bit late. Everyone understood the traffic situation.

Ava took out her notebook, turned to the front, and began to review the numbers involved in the deal. They didn't favour Three Sisters to any degree, but they were fair, and if Suki applied the same kind of discipline she had to the other Beijing business they'd bought the year before, Ava was confident they would swing to their advantage.

She closed the book, then frowned and turned to the back. She read the list of names that had somehow attached themselves to Pang Fai's problem. Who did she want to talk to first? It was still a toss-up between Lau Lau and Bai Jing, assuming that the video wasn't distributed and the question made irrelevant. Emotions aside, she couldn't believe that after going to all that trouble, the blackmailers would release it in reaction to the events of the night before. They would still want to get paid, she assured herself. The only danger she could anticipate was that they'd be so angry with her they'd release the disk out of revenge. But then again, that assumed the petty thugs who'd come to the courtyard actually had anything to do with the blackmail attempt. Ava wasn't convinced they did, not even the guy in the balaclava.

She underlined Lau Lau's name. He would be the starting point. He was the one who'd cut the deal with Bai Lok. He was the one who'd confirmed that Lok hadn't turned over all his tapes to Ding Fa for editing. But had Ding received the tapes directly from Lok or had they come through Tiger Paw? She turned to her notes from the meeting with Ding. He claimed to have received the tapes from Tiger Paw. Could Tiger Paw have withheld one? If they did, why did Lok have it? Maybe he'd made copies. And Ding said the guys who'd run Tiger Paw were dead. Even if they were, they could have left something behind.

I'll start with Lau, she thought. *But if he can't help, I may go back to Ding Fa before Bai Jing.*

Her phone rang. Ava looked at it with a touch of panic, but instead of Fai's Beijing number she saw a familiar Shanghai one. She answered with a sense of relief. "Is that you, Auntie Grace?"

"It's Xu."

"How are you feeling?"

"That's why I'm calling. I know Auntie Grace called you a little while ago, and I didn't want her to alarm you. She's too overprotective, although there's not much I can do to prevent that," he said. "I have a touch of the flu or something. She's just came back from the store with some extra-strength Tylenol. It should do the trick, and thanks for suggesting it to her. She listens to you. If she hadn't talked to you I'd be drinking some concoction made from twigs and grass that looked like mud and tasted worse."

"You're lucky to have someone who cares so much about you."

"I know, and I'm not really complaining. I've taken a couple of pills and now I'm going to lie down. I should be fine by later today or tomorrow."

"Have you heard any more from Lop about his Sammy Wing concerns?" she asked.

"No, but with him you never know if that's a good thing or bad."

"I've talked to Sonny. He made some discreet enquiries and didn't find anything that should be a cause for concern. He said there's some grumbling and complaining at the ground level in Sha Tin and, I think, Tai Po, but that it isn't anything out of the ordinary."

"Grumbling about what?"

"The fact that someone who isn't from Hong Kong is running a Hong Kong–based gang."

"That was to be expected for the first year or so. It will eventually stop, as long as they're all making money."

"And there were complaints about the way some of the software and electronic devices are being distributed."

"We have a formula that we haven't deviated from. Everyone is treated fairly."

"You don't have to convince me," Ava said. "I'm sure it's all like Sonny said — nothing out of the ordinary. But just in case, I've asked him to keep looking. He's sharp enough to pick up any negative vibes that could be more than just the usual grumbling."

"Keep me posted."

"You go and rest. I won't bother you unless it's something major."

Ava ended the call and then double-checked to make sure she hadn't missed one from Fai. *Lop isn't the only person with a touch of paranoia*, she thought.

The taxi finally reached the Suns' offices at ten after eleven. They came to the entrance to greet her and then led her to the boardroom. Suki was there, with two middle-aged men and two younger-looking women. Ava recognized one of the men as the lawyer they'd used for their previous Beijing deal. She nodded at him and he introduced one of the women as his assistant. The other couple were lawyers representing the Suns.

Half of the boardroom table was covered with neatly arranged rows of paper. "These are for signing, initialling, and chops," said Suki. "I reviewed them again this morning and everything seems to be in order, but you might want to read through them yourself."

"You and our lawyers are satisfied?" Ava asked.

"We are," Suki said.

"Then there's no need for me to do it. Where do I sign?"

"You can work from left to right along the table," their lawyer said. "The red tabs are for the Suns, yellow is for you and Suki, and blue is for you alone."

"Mr. and Mrs. Sun, why don't you start and we'll follow," Ava suggested.

And so began a slow and laborious process. After thirty minutes Ava had lost track of how many pieces of paper she'd signed. It wasn't that there were so many; it was that

Mr. and Mrs. Sun took forever to sign each one. As the time drew close to twelve o'clock, Ava's impatience began to show. She knew part of it was the anxiety she was feeling as she waited to hear from Fai, but that wasn't something she could explain to the others in the room. Anyway, the Suns were oblivious. It was Suki who caught on to it and who, almost exactly at noon, tapped Ava on the hand and motioned for her to join her at the far end of the table.

"I know they're being very slow," Suki said. "But we need to remember that they're signing over their entire life's work to us. It isn't just another deal for them. They want to make an occasion of it, a ceremony. We have to let them take as much time as they need."

"Sorry. I'm waiting for a really important phone call."

"Just step outside when you get it. No one will object."

"And Suki, if this goes on much longer, I might have to skip lunch."

"Lunch isn't a big thing. The dinner the other night was, and Pang Fai made it completely memorable. Anything else will be anticlimactic."

"Okay, let's go back to signing," Ava said.

At twelve-twenty the last document was signed and the company chops were affixed. There was a round of hand-shaking and then Mr. Sun went to the door and yelled to someone in the hallway. A few minutes later one of the assistants arrived with a tray holding seven cognac snifters, and behind him another man carried a bottle.

"Do you remember this cognac?" Mr. Sun asked Suki.

"No."

"It is Louis XIII by Rémy Martin. I bought it in Shanghai four years ago, when we came to visit you and your husband.

It cost three thousand U.S. dollars. He joked with me and asked what occasion in my life would justify drinking something so expensive. Well, this is it."

The entire room smiled, and Ava felt a touch of guilt at having wanted to rush them through the signing. Mr. Sun opened the bottle, poured a tiny amount into one of the glasses, swirled the golden liquid, and then put his nose into the glass and sniffed. "If it tastes as good as it smells, that was money well spent," he said.

Seven glasses received a moderate portion of cognac. Seven heads dipped noses into the glasses and made appreciative noises.

"To a deal very well done," Mr. Sun said, raising his glass. "We're especially pleased that you've decided to keep the company name as it is. You can be sure that we'll follow your growth and success with as much interest and pride as if we still owned it ourselves."

Ava took a sip, fully expecting the cognac to burn her throat. There was no sensation, until a few seconds later a warm glow rose from her stomach. She was about to compliment Mr. Sun on his selection when her phone rang. It was Fai. "Excuse me, but I have to take this call," Ava said.

She stepped out of the boardroom and into the hallway, closing the door behind her. "What have you heard?" she asked.

"The blackmailer just called," Fai said. "They didn't release the video, but now they want ten million renminbi within the same deadline."

"That's good news," Ava said.

"How is ten million good news?"

"Right now, time is a lot more important to us than money."

43

UNDER NORMAL CIRCUMSTANCES AVA WOULDN'T HAVE
bothered to change her clothes, but the way she was dressed
couldn't have been less appropriate for the artist's co-operative. Her running shoes, training pants, and jacket — especially with the front slashed — were better suited to making
her look like she belonged.

When she'd gotten back to the hutong, Fai met her at the
door, and five minutes later they were walking to the taxi
stand carrying umbrellas and holding hands.

"What made you decide to see Lau Lau first?" Fai asked.

"If we can believe Ding Fa, and given what we found in
Bai Lok's boxes, there are only two videos that Tiger Paw
didn't buy. Lau Lau is the only definite connection we have
to either of them. I have to assume that if Bai Lok told him
about one, he also told him about the other. I know that isn't
necessarily true, but it does make rough sense, and we don't
have much else to go on."

This time their driver knew where they wanted to go and
dropped them off directly in front of the warehouse complex.
They crossed the parking lot to the co-operative and walked

through the front door into a lobby that was quieter than the day before.

They climbed the stairs to the fourth floor, encountering few people as they went. When they reached the fourth, things changed. The hallway was crowded, and both bathrooms had lines waiting outside. Inside, Ava saw more lines of people waiting for sinks and toilets. At the far end, the dining room didn't have many empty seats.

"People tend to start their day a bit later here," Fai said.

No one gave them a second glance as they walked to Lau Lau's room. Ava knocked. A few seconds later a groggy voice said, "Fuck off."

"This is Ava Lee. Fai is with me. We need to talk to you again."

"Oh, for god's sake, go away."

"We can't."

"I don't want to see you."

"Do we have to go through this nonsense again? You know you don't have any choice, because we're not leaving until you come out and talk to us," Ava said, and then pressed her ear against the door. "I hear more than one voice," she said to Fai. "I think he's with someone."

"And he sounds different. He's probably on something," Fai said. "This could be difficult."

"You try talking to him," Ava said.

"Lau Lau, please don't make this so hard," Fai said. "Do you know what we did last night? We went home and watched *The Air We Breathe*. Please show us even a little bit of the dignity and courage of the man who made that film."

"Go away."

"Let's make this easier on all of us," Ava said. "I'll pay

for your time. Give us fifteen minutes and I'll give you ten thousand renminbi."

"My time isn't worth that much."

"It is to us."

"I have nothing to say that could be of any value to you."

"Then it will be an easy ten thousand."

Ava heard what sounded like someone approaching the door, and stepped back. The door opened and a young man dressed in boxer shorts and a white T-shirt walked past them. She looked inside and saw Lau Lau sitting on a single bed, wearing only a pair of jeans.

"The two of you are psychotic," he said.

"The dining room is jammed. It might be best if we talked in here," Ava said.

"Be my guest, but there's only one chair."

"I'll stand," Ava said.

"And I want my money before you come in."

Ava reached into her bag and took out a stack of notes. "Please put on a shirt," she said.

Lau Lau reached under the bed and pulled out a black T-shirt. He slipped it over his head with a grunt and then held out his hand.

Ava stared at him. His eyes were glassy and not really focusing. His hand trembled. *Fai was right about him being high,* she thought, as she gave him the money.

"What can't I tell you?" he said with a smile.

"There isn't anything funny about this," Ava said.

"That's because you're not sitting where I am."

"Do you really care so little about what happens to Fai?"

He shrugged and reached for his pack of cigarettes.

"Is that why you phoned your contact when we left here

yesterday?" she said. "You should know they sent some thugs to Fai's house last night to threaten and intimidate us."

"I have no idea what you're talking about," he said, lighting a cigarette. "And by the looks of you two, it couldn't have been much of a threat."

Ava took several steps into the room. "My past is littered with the bones of men who thought they could step on me. If our conversation keeps going like this, you're going to be one more."

"Fuck off, woman," he said, waving at her as if shooing away a fly.

"Who did you call?" she said, moving closer to him.

He shook his head. "You don't know shit."

Ava sat on the bed, her leg touching his. He recoiled.

"Lau Lau, they've doubled their blackmail demand, and I don't have that kind of money," Fai said.

"And you seem to be forgetting that we still have the video of you with a boyfriend," Ava said. "You seemed to care about that yesterday."

"I thought about that last night. I decided that I won't believe you have it until you show it to me," he said. "Bai Lok wouldn't have had the nerve to bullshit me."

"But you now think he might have been bullshitting you when he told you he had only one copy of Fai's video as well?"

His head snapped towards Ava. He was about to say something when he stopped. His eyes dropped away from her, and in that second she knew he was lying about Bai Lok.

She placed her hand on his knee. "You need to understand that I don't care that you bought the video of Fai from him. I can believe you did it with the best of intentions. But what I really need to know is who you gave it to."

He lifted a shaking hand to his mouth and took a deep drag on his cigarette. His eyes blinked rapidly, and Ava knew the after-effects of whatever drug he'd been taking were kicking in. "Who did you give it to?" she repeated.

He glanced at Fai and then at Ava's bag, which sat next to her on the bed.

"I'll give you another ten thousand," Ava said.

He lowered his head. "Fifty."

"I don't have that much with me. I can give you twenty now and the rest later."

"How do I know I can trust you?"

"Really? You're really asking that question of us?" Ava said. "Tell me what we need to know and you'll get your money tomorrow. And you'll get our copy of your video. I'll gift-wrap them for you."

He put his cigarette butt into a half-glass of water on the bedside table and then lit a fresh one. Smoke was starting to fill the small room, but if smoking helped him talk, Ava was willing to put up with a lot more of it.

"Where's the twenty?" he said.

She reached into her bag. "There," she said, throwing two stacks of bills onto his lap.

He stared down at the money but didn't touch it. Ava wondered if he actually cared about the transaction.

"All you want is a name, right?" he said.

"Yes, but before we get to that, I'd like to clear up a few things," Ava said. "For example, Bai Lok sold you two videos. Is that correct?"

"Yeah."

"One with you in it, and the other with Fai?"

"You know that already."

"Lau Lau, I want to hear you say it. There can't be any confusion about this."

"Yeah, I bought two videos from Lok — one with me in it and the other with Fai."

"Did you watch the one with Fai or did you just take Lok's word for it?"

"I watched it, or as much as I could stomach."

"Did you recognize the other woman in the video?"

"She looked a little familiar. I can't remember now."

"Try harder."

"She was an actress, maybe, a bit player, no one important. Her name might have been Mak something or other."

Ava nodded, pleased with that confirmation. "Yesterday you told me that you paid Lok thirty thousand renminbi for your video. What did you pay him for Fai's?"

"The same."

"You also told me that you only had about thirty thousand. How did you manage to pay him sixty?"

"I wanted to protect her," he said, seeming distracted.

"We're sure you did, and that's why you cut the deal with Lok," Ava said. "But how did you come up with the other thirty thousand?"

"I sold the video with Fai in it."

"For how much?"

"Two hundred thousand."

"To whom?"

He looked at the money in his lap and then at Fai and Ava. "I didn't phone anyone," he blurted. "After you left yesterday I didn't talk to anyone, except for the guy who just left here."

"That wasn't my question."

"But I want you to know that I didn't. It would be crazy of

me to piss you off, knowing that you might have that video of me. I didn't do it."

"Okay, we believe you didn't phone anyone," Ava said. "Now, who did you sell the video to?"

"Xia Jun."

44

AT FIRST MENTION, THE NAME XIA JUN DIDN'T REGISTER with Ava. Fai must have seen her confusion, because she quickly said, "He's an agent. He's Chen's competitor. I mentioned him to you before."

"Why in hell would you sell the video to him?" Ava said to Lau Lau. "Fai had no connection to him."

"He was my agent at the time," he said.

"Yes, but what possible interest could he have had in that video, beyond some kind of kinky or morbid curiosity?" Ava asked.

"There's nothing kinky about Xia," Lau Lau said. "He's one of the most conservative guys I've ever met. That's one of the reasons we split. He couldn't handle my issues."

"Was he still working with Chen then?" Fai asked.

Lau Lau looked slightly confused.

"I think Xia might have been connected with Chen's agency when Lau Lau sold him the video," Fai said to Ava. "He went out on his own just over three years ago, which was right around the time Bai Lok met with Lau Lau."

"Didn't someone tell us that Xia was Lok's agent as well?"

"Yes."

"So how does this make sense? Why would Lok go to Lau Lau and not directly to Xia?"

"Maybe Lok and Xia weren't connected any more. Maybe Lok thought Lau Lau was more likely to buy the video."

Lau Lau was slumped to one side, and Ava could see that his energy and interest were waning. She grabbed his arm and turned him to face her. "When you mentioned the video with Fai in it to Xia, how did he react?"

"What do you mean? He bought it."

"Yes, we know he bought it, but did you have to convince him to, or was he eager to get his hands on it? Or was his reaction something in between?"

"Once I told him what it was, he was interested right away. He wanted to see it, though, before buying it. After he watched five minutes of it, he asked what price I wanted and I told him. He agreed to it without any argument," Lau Lau said. "I probably could have gotten double the price."

"So he was anxious to buy it?"

"I guess."

"Why?"

Lau Lau looked at Fai and then nodded. "I think Fai's right that Xia was still working for Chen then. She was the agency's biggest client and money-maker, so it made sense they'd do anything to protect her. That was my reasoning, at least as best as I can recall."

"Why didn't you go directly to Chen?"

"He and I had stopped talking. He'd handed me off to Xia, so all my day-to-day business was with Xia."

Ava turned to Fai. "Is it likely that Lau Lau was managed by Xia? Is that the way it worked within Chen's agency?"

"Yes, that's exactly how it worked, and still works. Chen only has time for the A-list clients. The others are handled by juniors. It's a flexible arrangement, because you can move from the A list to the B list to the C list to out the door in a matter of months. You can also move up, of course, but that's rarer," Fai said. "Lau Lau was in the middle of a very rough patch around that time. If he says Xia was his agency contact, I believe him. Chen wouldn't have wanted much to do with him."

"Assuming that's true, and assuming that we believe everything Lau Lau has told us, that leaves us with some large questions to answer," Ava said. "Did Xia pass the video to Chen or did he keep it and not tell Chen he had it? Or is it possible that he sold it to someone else?"

"Chen would have told me if something like that had been given to him," Fai said. "It's also hard to believe that he would have sold it to someone else and it's just surfacing now."

"I agree with you that it's unlikely some unknown third party was involved, but are you certain about Chen? Maybe he didn't want to worry you. Maybe he thought he could look after it better on his own."

"He would have told me," Fai insisted.

"If that's true, then we have to believe that Xia kept the video," Ava said. "But if he did keep it, why did he hold on to it for so long? I remember you telling me that Chen and Xia hate each other. Why wouldn't Xia have used the video ages ago, to damage you as a way of damaging Chen and his business?"

Fai shook her head. "I can't answer those questions. In fact, I can hardly keep up with them."

"We're going to have to talk to Xia. Where does he work?"

"Beijing. His office is a stone's throw from the Syndicate's offices."

"That's convenient."

"It's practical. The Syndicate generates about sixty or seventy per cent of his agency's income, one way or another. Why not be as close as you can to them. Chen's office is in a building only a few hundred metres farther away from the Syndicate's."

"Well, we need to talk to Mr. Xia."

"That won't be easy to arrange. His schedule is likely to be booked solid."

"You'll have to make the call. You need to get him to agree to meet with us today. We're running out of time and I don't want to wait until a more professional group of thugs pays us a home visit or we have to start collecting ten million renminbi," Ava said. "We finally have a solid lead. We can't afford to sit on it."

"What if he won't take my call?"

"I can't imagine any agent would reject a call from the country's biggest movie star."

"What if we do talk but he won't give us a meeting as fast as you want?"

"Then we'll go to his office or we'll go to his home or we'll crash whatever party or dinner he's at tonight," Ava said. "But getting an appointment is our best option by far."

"What can I use as an excuse for a meeting?"

"Tell him you're tired of working with Chen. Tell him you're prepared to switch agencies."

"Ava, he's plugged in at the Syndicate. He may have heard that I have issues with them. He might not think I'm that attractive an acquisition right now."

Ava sighed. "Tell him whatever you think he might want to hear most."

"I could say that I've got some big offers from the U.S. I'll tell him I'm finally ready to make that jump but I want new management to negotiate and close the deal. I'll say I've lost confidence in Chen's ability to take on something that important."

"I like the way that sounds," Ava said.

"Okay, that's what I'll dangle."

"Do you have his number?"

"No, but it's easy enough to get."

"Do you want to call him from here or outside in the hallway?"

"I'll go outside," Fai said, looking at Lau Lau, who seemed to have mentally wandered off again.

Ava waited until Fai had left the room before she grabbed Lau Lau's knee and dug her fingers into nerves along the sides. He jumped, pain registering across his face. She didn't let go but eased up on the pressure. "I want you to look at me. I want to be sure that you're hearing me and that you understand what I'm saying."

"I hear you."

"Good. I'm going to leave this twenty thousand with you. Tomorrow, if your story checks out, I'll have the other thirty thousand and our copy of the DVD delivered to you here."

"You didn't set any conditions for the other thirty thousand," he protested.

"Be serious," she said. "You can't expect me to give you the money if you lied to me, can you?"

"No, I guess not."

She smiled encouragingly at him. He seemed to be having a moment of lucidity, which made her more confident that he hadn't lied to her. "But let me change the subject. I watched *The Air We Breathe* with Fai last night. It's a fantastic movie, on so many levels. Do you have any ideas for another film that isn't kung-fu crap?"

"I think about films all the time. I see them in my head and I make them there. I've got three or four of them shot. All I need is a camera and a crew and I could shoot any of them in less than a month."

"Would those films in your head ever be shown in China?"

He smiled. "Not this China. They'd be banned for sure, and that's why I'll never get the chance to make them."

"What if someone gave you the money and said they didn't care about the Chinese market? What if they told you to go ahead and make the film you want and they'd worry about the marketing and distribution? Could you still make a film that would break hearts, make people cry, make them think?"

"Don't mess with me."

"I'm not."

"I couldn't make a film to suit Western tastes. I'm Chinese to my soul. The films I dream about making are about the people I know and this insane fucking system they're forced to live in. I hate the system, but I understand it and I can't bring myself to escape it."

"What if someone made it possible for you to make the kind of films you want to make? No restrictions. Are you still capable of doing that? Could you actually finish?"

"I don't know," he said, staring at her as if seeing her for the first time. "I have problems. Everyone knows what they are."

"What if we could find someone to help you with those problems?"

"You are messing with me."

The door to the room opened and a smiling Fai stood there. "We have an appointment with Xia at five o'clock — in two hours," she said.

"Great work," Ava said, and turned back to Lau Lau. "We have a deal. Don't break it, please. No phone calls, no texts. Stay here nice and quiet, and with any luck, by this time tomorrow you'll have another thirty thousand and the DVD."

"I'm not stupid," he said.

Ava stood and walked to the door. She looked at her training paints and her ripped jacket. "Do I have time to change? I don't want to meet Xia dressed like this."

"We have time, as long as traffic isn't a nightmare," Fai said, and then gestured in the direction of Lau Lau. "What were you two discussing so intently?"

"We were talking about resurrecting his career."

"Is that a joke?"

"No."

45

TRAFFIC WAS BAD BUT NOT A NIGHTMARE, AND THEY managed to get back to the house, change, and arrive in front of the building that housed Xia's agency at ten minutes to five. The building was like most of those that crowded the Chaoyang central business district — about forty storeys of glass and steel without any real character or any attempt at architectural originality.

Ava and Fai had been chatting constantly from the time they left Lau Lau until the taxi pulled up at Xia's office tower. Fai did most of the actual talking as Ava asked question after question about Xia Jun, his relationship with Chen, and the structure of their business.

Several things surprised Ava about the conversation. First, the two men seemed to be polar opposites. Chen, as Ava knew from meeting him and Fai's various comments about him, was a bit of a dandy, slippery in the way he operated, and a man who talked a lot about trust but rarely extended it — and didn't warrant getting it. Fai's description of Xia couldn't have been more different. He was, as Lau Lau had said, very conservative, in both dress and manner. In a business filled with ego and narcissism, he was low-key and understated, and in people used to hyperbole, this attitude generated a level of trust that was hard to justify rationally.

"Justify rationally?" Ava said when Fai made that remark. "What do you mean by that?"

"Just because he doesn't blow smoke up people's asses and doesn't exaggerate and under-promises, that doesn't make him a saint," Fai said. "He's been in this business his whole adult life, and he worked for Chen for more than ten years. He has survived — no, make that thrived — in a business that is cutthroat, and you don't accomplish that by being Mr. Nice Guy all the time."

Fai was making that remark as they exited the taxi, and then she pointed to the right. "Chen's office is over there, a ten-minute walk away. The Syndicate is a five-minute walk. Everyone is close — nice and cozy."

"I'll keep that in mind," Ava said, Fai's words reminding her that she was an interloper trying to operate in someone else's world. There were unspoken rules and unwritten codes that she wasn't privy to, and she was certain there were also understandings and alliances that were tightly held.

"You look very professional," Fai said as they walked to the entrance. "It's a look that should appeal to Xia."

"Why, thank you. And I have to say that you look absolutely glamorous."

"It's amazing what a little makeup, some jewellery, high heels, and a tight dress can do," Fai said. "It's all part of the show, you know. You can't disappoint your public."

The building lobby was busy and they had to circumvent a throng of people, all of them in a hurry, to reach the security desk. Just before they got there, a voice said, "Ms. Pang," and an elegantly dressed young woman came towards them.

"My name is Zeng Chun. Mr. Xia asked me to escort you to his office," she said in a deferential voice, her head lowered.

"That's very kind of you," Fai said.

"It's a tremendous honour," Zeng said, and turned and motioned towards a bank of elevators.

Ava and Fai followed her and then stood and waited for an elevator to arrive. It was a strange experience for Ava. She had grown accustomed to being with a casually dressed Fai in places like the hutong, where no one made a fuss. Now, as they waited for the elevator, it seemed that everyone recognized her. No one spoke to or approached Fai, but Ava could feel that every eye was on them, and she could see people whispering and pointing.

When an elevator arrived, Fai got in first and pressed into a back corner. Ava stood to one side and a bit in front of her. Zeng took the other side. They rode to the eighth floor, and when the elevator stopped and Zeng said, "Excuse us, but we need to get off here," the crowd evacuated almost completely so that Fai could leave without being troubled or jostled.

Zeng led them down a carpeted hallway to a set of wooden doors. The name XIA was on one door in gold metal, and on the other was a carved metal depiction of a red monkey. Ava assumed that the monkey was Xia's zodiac sign, and tried to remember the sign's characteristics. Until Ava was in her late teens, her mother Jennie had bought the massively detailed annual zodiac guides that were published for Chinese New Year, and she would read aloud from them at breakfast. The monkey, Ava recalled, was smart, wily, and vigilant. Its sign was the start of the metal cycle, which might explain Xia's name being painted gold. Gold was supposed to accrue to the red monkey, but it was also attached to water, which implied wisdom.

When they got to the double doors, Zeng turned right and walked about ten metres to an unmarked single door. She knocked, the door opened, and another elegant young woman stood before them. She bowed to Fai. "It is such a privilege to meet you," she said. "Mr. Xia is waiting."

The door led into a small outer office that contained a desk, two padded chairs, and several credenzas, all in rosewood. The wooden floor was covered by a thick pale blue carpet. The walls were decorated with paintings, prints, and lithographs that depicted the red monkey in various forms. The woman led them to yet another door, knocked, and stepped back to let them enter first.

From Fai's description, Ava had a picture of Xia in her mind. The man who stood in front of her fitted it quite well. He was close to six feet and slim, with a full head of black hair that was combed straight back and fell slightly over the top of his ears. He was immaculately dressed in a grey suit, white shirt, and dark blue Ferragamo tie. The suit was light wool and looked tailored. She glanced at his feet and saw black Oxfords that could have been handmade.

"It has been far too long, Fai," he said. When he leaned forward to offer her a cleanly shaven cheek, Ava caught a whiff of cologne.

"It's nice to see you again, Jun," Fai said.

"And who is this young woman?" he said, looking at Ava.

"Her name is Ava Lee. As I told you on the phone, she's a friend who's doubling as a personal assistant."

"Great to meet you, Ms. Lee," Xia said.

Ava knew he was somewhere in his late thirties or early

forties — not that much older than her — so she wasn't sure how to take his comment about being pleased to meet "this young woman." She gave him the benefit of the doubt. "The pleasure is all mine," she said.

"Come in, come in," he said, standing to one side. "Take a seat."

The office was three or four times larger than the outer one, but more spartan. There was nothing on the walls, the wooden floor wasn't carpeted, and all the furniture was plainer. Ava looked at the round glass boardroom table surrounded by six leather director's chairs, and at a black leather sofa and two matching seats. "Where do you want us to sit?" she said.

"The sofa," he said. "And before we settle down, can we get you something to drink? We have just about everything imaginable."

"I'm fine," Fai said.

"Me too," said Ava.

Xia nodded and then said to his assistant, "No phone calls."

Ava and Fai sat side by side on the sofa. Xia sat directly across from them, separated by a bare glass coffee table. The sofa was firm and quite high. When Ava sat back in it, her feet didn't touch the ground. She leaned forward until they did.

"Thanks for seeing us at such short notice," Fai said.

"I was understandably surprised to hear from you, but pleased, definitely pleased," he said. "And it is gratifying to hear about the foreign opportunities. It's about time that the markets outside China and Asia began to give you the recognition you deserve."

Fai turned away from Xia to glance at Ava, and then stared at him. "This is awkward," she said.

"I naturally assume that Chen doesn't know you've contacted me," he said. "But does he know about the foreign offers?"

"No."

"And what is your contractual status with him?"

"I haven't looked at my contract in years."

"Fai, that has to be clarified. We don't want to create a situation that could see either of us involved in a lawsuit with Chen."

"The situation we're involved in goes well beyond the potential for a lawsuit," Ava interrupted.

"Pardon?" Xia said.

"I'm sorry to butt in, and I apologize on behalf of Fai and myself for having asked for this meeting under false pretenses."

Xia looked at Fai and then at Ava. All she could see on his face was confusion. *He has nothing to do with this*, she thought.

"Fai, what's going on?" he asked.

"I'm being blackmailed," she said.

He sat back in the seat, his hands pressed together in front of his face, his fingers covering his eyes. "Why? How?"

"There's a video of me in bed...with another woman."

His eyes closed and he shook his head. "Oh."

"Oh what?" Ava said.

"I had almost completely forgotten about that."

"Well, someone hasn't, because they have a copy of it and they're asking for ten million renminbi to make it disappear," Ava said. "However, I don't believe there's any amount of money that will make that happen."

"You don't sound much like a personal assistant," Xia said, looking at Ava.

"I have some experience with this kind of extortion and the people who perpetrate it. Fai asked me to help out."

"Now it's my turn to say this is awkward, and by that I don't mean your involvement."

"I imagine the video's existence is enough to make things awkward for everyone, but we still have to talk about it."

"Have you discussed it with Chen?"

"Not yet."

"Why not?"

"Things haven't been very good between us," Fai said. "We thought we'd be better off trying to handle this ourselves."

"But why come and see me?"

"Because you have a role in this, and if we're going to end it, we need your help," Ava said.

"How can I possibly help?"

"You were the one who bought the video."

"Yes, I did," he said without hesitation, and then stared at Fai. "I bought it to protect you. I was told there was only one copy, and I was assured that it had been destroyed."

"You bought it from Lau Lau?"

"How do you know that?"

"He told us."

"You and he are friends again?" Xia said to Fai.

"Friendly enough."

"Yes, I bought it from him," he said after a slight hesitation.

"Then what did you do with it?" Ava said.

"I gave it to Chen."

Fai gasped. It was the answer Ava had anticipated, and she

realized she should have forewarned Fai. "And who assured you that it had been destroyed?"

"Chen."

"Fuck," said Fai.

"I'm sorry."

"Could Chen have given it to anyone else or made copies?" Ava asked.

"Why on earth would he do that? Fai was — and is — his most valuable asset. He'd never put her at risk, and that video, as we all know, would have done more than that."

"But he could have kept it, not destroyed it?"

"Of course he could have, but even if he did, what makes you believe he might be involved, directly or indirectly, in anything like this? It doesn't make any sense. And I'm saying that as someone who detests Chen and would love to see him crash and burn," Xia said to Ava. "Look, I'm still sitting here talking to you because I adore Fai. If I didn't, I would have asked you to leave the second you mentioned blackmail. She's the best film actress I've ever seen, in any language. She's also one of the nicest people I've met in this business. I don't want to see any harm come to her. But as much as I hate Chen, I still have trouble believing that he'd be involved in blackmailing his own client."

"But you gave the video to him and to no one else?" Ava said.

"Yes."

"So how does that fact bring us to this point without Chen being implicated in one way or another?"

"I have no idea," he said, looking uncomfortable. "And don't ask me to speculate."

Ava leaned closer towards Xia. "Fai is having issues with the Syndicate and with Mo. Have you heard?"

"There are rumours, gossip. Nothing of any substance."

"Well, it's true, there are issues. She's told him the days of sexual favours are over. Mo hasn't reacted well, and as a result I think Chen is afraid of losing even more of his business than what Fai represents."

Xia turned his attention away from Ava. "Fai, as much as I want to be helpful, I won't get into a personal discussion about Mo or the Syndicate, with you or your friend."

"Are you that afraid of him?" Ava pressed.

"I prefer to use the word 'cautious' when it comes to describing our dealings."

"And Chen, of course, is equally cautious?" Ava asked.

"I imagine he would be."

"He would be or he is?"

Xia nodded. "Chen is very sensitive to any mood swings within the Syndicate."

"If Mo decided to put either of you out of business, could he do it?"

"I repeat, I will not discuss Mo on any level."

"Okay. But if your agency for some reason fell out of favour with the Syndicate, whether he's there or not, how serious would the repercussions be?"

"It could certainly damage our business, but I like to think I'd find a way to compensate."

"Is Chen as flexible as you?"

Xia shrugged. "He's much older than me. He's accustomed to doing business a certain way, and I don't think he likes change anymore."

"So the answer is no?"

"On balance, I guess it is, but it's an opinion and nothing more."

"Given those circumstances, how do you think Chen would react if the Syndicate decided it wanted nothing more to do with Fai?"

"I can't imagine them taking that position, so your question is hypothetical."

"I think he'd drop her in a heartbeat," Ava said.

"If he ever did," Xia said, extending a hand towards Fai, "I'd take her on a second later."

"Even if that video were made public?"

"That would complicate things, especially here in China and other parts of Asia," he said, now squeezing Fai's hand. "But I'm sure I could make it work, somehow, somewhere."

"Thanks, Jun. You're very kind," said Fai.

"Truthfully, I'm also very disappointed. When you called and told me about foreign offers, I starting making plans for us in my head," Xia said. "This meeting isn't quite what I expected."

"Maybe we'll still get a chance to work together," Fai said.

"I can only hope that's the case." Xia stood up. "Now, I don't think I have anything else to contribute, so you'll have to excuse me. I bumped several meetings to accommodate you, and I have people waiting."

"You've been very helpful," Ava said. "We'll let you know how this plays out."

"You don't have to do that. If something of any importance happens, you can be certain I'll hear about it ten seconds later."

46

FAI WAITED UNTIL THEY WERE OUTSIDE XIA'S OFFICE building before she grabbed Ava by the arm and said, "Do you really believe Chen is involved in this?"

"Did you believe what Xia had to say?"

"Yes."

"I did too, and that can lead us in only one direction."

"But, like Xia said, why would he do it?"

"Maybe he didn't. Maybe he just made it possible, even inadvertently, for someone else to do it. Either way, we need to talk to him. Which building is his office in?"

"That one," Fai said, and pointed.

"Let's go."

It was the end of the day for many office workers, who now began to empty out of the towers and crowd the sidewalks. Fai took a cap and an oversized pink cashmere cardigan from a tote bag and put them on. She jammed on the cap so hard that the tops of her ears bent downwards, and she pulled the cardigan up to her mouth.

"I'm cold," she said. "And I don't want to be recognized in this crowd."

Their anticipated ten-minute walk took closer to half an hour. As Ava and Fai shuffled along, they didn't talk, and they wouldn't have heard much if they'd tried to amid the rush-hour noise. When they reached the building — another forty-storey generic tower — Fai removed the cap and cardigan.

"What do we do if he's not in?" Fai asked as they walked through the lobby.

"Will his assistant or secretary know where he is?'

"Most likely."

"Then we'll go to wherever that is."

"I could phone him now."

"No. I'd like to surprise him, if at all possible."

"He's on the sixth floor," Fai said, walking past a security desk.

The elevators arriving in the lobby were full, but empty going back up. Fai pushed the sixth-floor button and muttered something.

"What are thinking?" Ava said.

"I don't want to believe Chen is behind this."

Chen's offices were, like Xia's, behind double doors, except these were grey metal with the initials CCA embossed in gold on both doors.

"CCA?" Ava said.

"Chen Creative Artists."

Fai opened a door and led Ava into a surprisingly plain office. On their left was a small reception desk with a middle-aged woman sitting behind it, and on their right a floral sofa, a couple of padded chairs, and a wooden coffee table. Directly ahead of them were ten or twelve desks scattered around an open floor, and beyond those desks were six offices, all of them with their doors closed. Through their glass walls Ava could see that four of them were occupied. There was no sign of Chen.

The woman behind the desk looked up at them impatiently and then recognized Fai. She leapt to her feet. "Ms. Pang. Was Mr. Chen expecting you?"

"No, we were in the vicinity and decided to pay a surprise visit."

"He's not here," the woman stammered.

"Where is he?" Fai said.

"I think maybe you should talk to Ms. Yi, his assistant. That would be more appropriate."

"Then get Ms. Yi."

The woman hit an extension button. Ava, watching the offices, saw a young woman pick up the phone and then look through her glass wall at them. She smiled in their direction and then hurried from her office.

"Ms. Pang, it's so good to see you. What brings you here?" Ms. Yi said, lowering her head and smiling as she approached.

"Nothing in particular. My friend Ava had a meeting nearby, and we just decided to drop in and say hello."

"Mr. Chen will be sorry to have missed you. You don't come to our office very often. In fact, I have trouble remembering the last time."

"Maybe a year ago." Fai smiled. "Where is Mr. Chen? Is there an event in the city?"

"He's in Shanghai," she said, looking at her watch. "He's in meetings until at least seven, and then there's a dinner. He's planning on catching a late flight back to Beijing."

"When did he go?"

"This morning."

"Was it a last-minute thing?" Ava asked, as innocuously as she could.

"It's been planned for months."

"Can you reach him?"

"He never has his phone on during meetings, and it's a business dinner, so he'll probably have it off for that as well," she said, turning from Ava to Fai. "I do expect him to call in for messages at some point, though. Is there anything, Ms. Pang, that you'd like me to tell him?"

"Just ask him to call me whenever he can."

"Is there something urgent you need to discuss? Maybe I can interrupt his meeting."

Fai glanced at Ava, who gave a slight shake of her head. "It isn't that important," Fai said. "I have some worries about *Mao's Daughter* that I want to discuss with him."

"That is such a wonderful film," Ms. Yi said. "I'm sure it will be a great success. It reminds me in some ways of the early films you made with Lau Lau."

"I still want to talk to him about it."

"I'll tell him, and I'm sure he'll call you as soon as he can."

"Thanks. Sorry to have dropped in like this."

"Oh my god, Ms. Pang, you're welcome anytime. We're always thrilled to see you."

Ava left the office with less energy than she'd had walking in. During the walk she'd been getting psyched up for a showdown with Chen, and now felt the letdown.

"What do you want to do?" Fai asked as they made their way to the elevator.

"We need to talk to Chen. Until then, I'm not sure what else there is for us to do."

"We can have dinner," Fai said. "I'm starving."

"I ate with Lop in a restaurant near here called Da Dong, which specializes in duck."

"I don't want to be that public. Dressed like this I'm sure to be noticed, and I'm not going to wear that cap and sweater during dinner," Fai said. "I'd be more comfortable at the canteen. And I do have a yearning for zhajiang noodles and those jiaozi with scrambled eggs and chives."

They caught a taxi and began the hour-long trip back to Xicheng. What made it seem even longer was that any conversation they might have had was inhibited because the driver seemed to recognize Fai and kept staring at her through his rear-view mirror. They were both relieved when they reached the entrance to the Hai Wan Canteen's hutong.

As Ava was paying the driver, Fai fidgeted. "It's going to rain," she said. "Let's hurry."

The rain didn't start until they were safely seated inside the canteen. "That was good timing," Ava said as she watched rain pelt against the windows. "But we don't have umbrellas to get from here to the house."

"We'll take our time over dinner," Fai said. "If it's still raining I'm sure I can get someone to lend us an umbrella."

"How do you handle this weather? I find it rather depressing," Ava said.

"There's nothing I can do about it, so I just ignore it."

The waitress had made a bit of a fuss when they arrived, insisting that they sit at the best table and bringing the owner and cook from the kitchen to greet them.

"You're being so regular again," the owner said. "We worry when we don't see you. I'd like to get you some drinks on the house."

"That's not necessary."

"You can't say no," he said. "Beer for you as usual? And what does your friend want?"

"I'll have a cognac," Ava said.

Fai ordered their food, including hot and sour soup. "I'm boring when it comes to food. If I like something I can eat it day after day and not get tired of it."

"I'm like that as well, at least to some extent."

Fai took her phone from her bag and looked at it.

"Did you miss a call or text?"

"No. I was just making sure it's on," Fai said, laying it on the table.

Ava did the same with hers. "We'll see if Chen calls."

"I can't imagine that he won't."

"If he does, I want you to talk to him, but keep it low-key. We don't want to panic him over the phone. It's important that he agree to meet us face to face."

"That could be difficult to arrange tonight if he arrives late."

"Then try to schedule something for first thing tomorrow morning."

"Where?"

"His office will be fine, I think. It will make it harder for him to run out on us, and I can't imagine he'll do anything as drastic as calling security to escort the great Pang Fai from the building."

"Do you always think in those terms?"

"It's a habit. I was in a business that chewed up careless people, so I learned very quickly to be cautious. And part of that is preparing, mentally even more than physically, for all possible eventualities."

"I'm so lucky to have you," Fai said suddenly, her voice breaking. "I was sitting in that meeting with Xia and thinking that I would never have had the nerve to ask for a meeting, let alone go to one, if you weren't by my side. In fact, I could never have handled any of this. I would be curled up in a ball at the house, waiting for fate to do what it chose."

"I don't believe that. You're much stronger than you think, and I'm impressed with the way you're handling things. We make a good team."

Fai smiled and was starting to speak when the owner arrived with their drinks on a tray. He had brought two beers and a water glass more than half filled with cognac. As he put the drinks on the table, Ava's phone rang. She saw Sonny's number. "Fai, do you mind if I take this call? It's my man Sonny in Hong Kong."

"Go ahead."

Ava picked up the phone. "Sonny, what's going on?"

"Hey, boss, I'm in the car. I've just left the Kowloon Tong MTR. I had dinner with Andy at his noodle restaurant."

Andy had worked for Uncle, usually in partnership with another Triad named Carlo. Ava knew Andy well; she trusted him enough to have used him on several sensitive and dangerous jobs. He'd never let her down. "How is he?" she asked.

"He's good, and he sends his regards."

"Why did you see him?"

"He stopped working full-time at the restaurant about six months ago. He said being with his wife twenty-four hours a day was ruining his marriage, but I think he just missed the excitement on the street. Anyway, he started doing some part-time work for the gang in Tai Po, and that brought him into contact with some of the guys from Sha Tin. Ava, he thinks something is going on."

"Like what?"

"He's not sure. It's a feeling he has more than anything. But you know Andy — he's always sensitive to his surroundings and how people are treating him and reacting to him. He says that the Sha Tin guys were friendly enough, but then things changed almost overnight. They know he worked for Uncle and that he's done work for you, and that you're still close. None of that seemed to matter until about a month ago, when one of the Sha Tin guys asked him if he knew you're tight with Xu and Lop. He said sure he did, and then he made a remark about how well they're running things. No one has wanted to talk to him since."

"Sonny, with respect, that hardly constitutes evidence that anyone is planning to move against Lop."

"I know, but then the Tai Po guys started cutting Andy out of stuff as well. He went to one of them he thought he was close to and asked what the hell was going on. The guy told him that no one trusted him anymore because of his ties to you, and your ties to Xu and Lop. Andy said he was loyal to whoever he worked for. The guy pulled Andy aside and told him to be careful. He said that when they took back Wanchai, there was going to be a lot of payback."

"'When they took back Wanchai.' He actually said that?"

"According to Andy he did, and when I challenged him on it, he didn't back down or change his story in any way."

"This isn't good," Ava said. "Even if it doesn't come to fruition, it isn't healthy to have gang members talking like that."

"That's what I thought too," Sonny said. "You want me to keep digging?"

"A bit more, but again, be cautious."

"*Momentai.*"

"And Sonny, don't say anything to Lop," she said. "I'm going to give Xu a heads-up, and he can make the decision about when and what to tell him."

"I would never have talked to Lop."

"No, of course you wouldn't," Ava said, realizing immediately that she might have insulted Sonny. "I'm tired and I'm not thinking very straight."

"Look after yourself, boss. You're the one person none of us can afford to lose."

"Thank you, Sonny."

"And Ava, you will let me know if Xu decides to do something?"

"Of course I will, but don't expect to hear back from me tonight. He isn't feeling that well and I'm going to let him get some rest and peace of mind. I'll call him in the morning."

Ava put down her phone as the large bowl of hot and sour soup arrived at the table.

"Sounds as if you have another problem," Fai said.

"There could be a problem, but if there is, it isn't mine. It belongs to Xu and Lop," Ava said, dipping into the soup.

They ate quietly, Fai constantly looking at her phone. Ava didn't want to add any additional stress by appearing anxious, so she focused on the food. Her comments were restricted to how good it was and how bad the weather outside remained.

Chen still hadn't called by the time they'd finished dinner. "He's avoiding us," Fai said.

"Possibly."

"The son of a bitch."

"He can't do it forever. Eventually he'll have to talk to you," Ava said, and then looked at the rain-streaked window. "In the meantime, we have to worry about getting home without getting soaked."

Five minutes later they stepped out of the restaurant holding a gigantic Callaway Golf umbrella over their heads. The umbrella belonged to the owner, who laughed when Ava asked him if he actually played golf.

They hurried along the sparsely populated streets, and as they turned right into the hutong, there wasn't a person in sight. When they reached the entrance to Fai's compound, Ava held the umbrella while Fai opened the door. They went inside and had taken no more than four or five steps when a voice said, "Don't go any farther."

Ava turned and saw four men standing in the dark with their backs pressed against the wall. "Not again," she said.

"You just won't listen, will you," the now familiar man in the balaclava said.

"Go to the house," Ava said to Fai. "Alert the neighbours. Get some help. Hurry."

Fai took several steps backwards and then spun and headed for the house. One of the men started to move in her direction, but Ava went to the right and stood in his path.

Ava stared at the men. She recognized only the one in the balaclava. The others formed another motley crew, two in hoodies and the third in a frayed denim jacket and base-ball cap. They fanned out and moved towards her. That part of the courtyard was dimly lit, and Ava started retreating towards where there was more light. As she backed up, they followed, not rushing, and looking purposeful.

It was still raining hard. Ava didn't care that she was getting wet, but she was worried about the rain getting into her eyes and clouding her vision. *These guys are more professional*, she thought. It was one thing to take on two overconfident thugs, but another to fight three guys who knew what they were doing and knew what she was capable of.

"Why do you keep doing this?" she shouted at Balaclava, who was hanging back. "You're going to get your money."

He said nothing, and Ava saw that the men were now uncomfortably close. She thought about turning and running to the house, but she was wearing pumps and didn't know how fast she could move. She also knew that if they caught her from behind, she would be essentially defenceless. *Come on, Fai*, she whispered, and then tried to think how she could buy more time.

The men couldn't have known what was on her mind, but they weren't waiting anyway. They came at her in unison. She reacted instinctively, her right fist driving the phoenix eye into the face of the man on her right while her left foot found the groin of the one in front of her. That left the man on her left free. As he swung at her, she saw in the courtyard light the glimmer of metal. The cleaver struck her upper left arm. She staggered back, trying to find a better position from which she could defend. He took two steps forward and raised the cleaver again, but before it could descend, a gunshot rang out.

"Drop that weapon or I promise I'll kill you," a man's voice said. "I'm an ex-cop. I know what I'm doing with this gun. I won't miss."

Ava glanced behind her. Fai was standing with Fan and the elderly couple from the night before. In front of them, a man was pointing a gun at the attackers.

The man with the cleaver stared at Ava and then shook

his head. "Let's get the fuck out of here," he said to his colleagues as he threw his weapon on the ground.

Ava saw them start to run towards the exit, but her interest in them began to wane as her vision blurred and she felt a searing pain in her arm. She looked at it. Her shirt sleeve had a six-inch rip over the upper arm, exposing her flesh. The gash was several inches long, but Ava was more concerned about how deep it was. *It looks deep enough*, she thought as blood ran down the length of her arm and trickled over the back of her hand.

"This young woman needs to go to a hospital," said the man with the gun.

47

THE MAN WITH THE GUN WAS NAMED LAM. HE WAS A former policeman, five years retired, and he had lived in the house on the other side of the elderly couple for more than twenty years. He hadn't been at home when Ava was attacked the previous night; otherwise, he said, she would have met him then. She and Fai tried to express their gratitude for his coming to her rescue, but after a few words he cut them off.

"We're like a family here," he said.

He went back with them to Fai's house and joined them in the bathroom. He tore the sleeve of her shirt until the wound was fully exposed. "You'll need stitches — probably a lot of them. You might need blood as well, because you've already lost quite a bit," he said. "We should wrap that arm as tightly as we can before we head for the hospital."

"I don't have anything to wrap it with," Fai said.

"I have bandages at my place. I'll go get them," he said. "In the meantime, you help her off with that shirt and then, as gently as you can, wipe off as much blood as possible. She should be wearing a T-shirt or something short-sleeved."

Fai didn't start crying until they heard the front door close. "This is too much," she said through her tears.

"I agree with you, but it's also ridiculous, and we have to end it. If Chen doesn't contact you tonight, we'll find him tomorrow."

"How?"

"We'll figure that out later."

Fai stared at the gaping wound. "Does it hurt badly?"

"My adrenalin is still pumping. It will hurt more in an hour or two."

"I can't begin to imagine what that feels like."

Ava was sitting on the toilet seat, and now she slumped forward. "I'm feeling a bit weak."

Fai kneeled and wrapped her arms around Ava's waist. "I'll stay quiet," she said.

It was only a few minutes, but seemed longer, before Lam returned. He ran up the stairs and stopped at the bathroom door. "You didn't change her shirt," he said.

"Sorry," Fai said.

"It's okay, but you need to move away from her if I'm to put on a bandage."

Fai stood and retreated a couple of steps. Lam went to Ava's side, gripped the shirt sleeve, and ripped it wide open. "Do you have a clean sponge?" he asked Fai.

She took one from the bathroom cupboard and handed it to him. He gently patted the area around the cut until it was clearly visible, then he squeezed ointment onto the wound and began to wrap layers of white gauze around it. "I was told you didn't call the police last night," he said.

"We had no idea who those guys were," Ava said. "The same is true for tonight."

"And you don't know why they seem to have targeted you?"

"No."

"That's hard to believe." He shook his head as he kept wrapping. "Are you going to be able to walk to the corner so we can get a taxi?"

"I think so."

"I understand you're not from Beijing."

"That's true."

"So I assume you don't know our local hospitals. Fai, which one do you prefer?"

"I've always gone to the United Family Hospital in Chaoyang."

"Well, get your friend a coat and we'll head there."

Ava stayed seated until Fai returned with her Adidas jacket. When she stood to put it on, she felt a bit woozy and leaned against Lam. He was tall, at least six feet, and sturdily built, so he could easily support her.

"Could you wait one more minute?" Fai asked. "I want to change. I don't want to go to the hospital dressed like this."

"I'll take your friend downstairs. We'll meet you there."

Lam walked ahead of Ava, her right hand resting on his shoulder, as they descended. When they reached the front door, she stood with her back against it as they waited for Fai.

"How deep did the cut look?" Ava asked.

"It's more of a slash than a cut. He didn't hit bone — which isn't to minimize it, or the pain you must be feeling."

"Thanks for the help."

"I'd feel better if you let me contact some of the local police."

"No, there's no point to it. We don't know who they are," Ava said. "But do you think it's possible they could be hanging around outside, waiting for a second chance?"

"I still have my gun with me," he said. "If they try again, I won't be firing warning shots."

"I'm ready," Fai said from the top of the stairs, and then came bounding down in jeans and a bulky blue sweater with a shawl collar. She grabbed a cap from the stack by the door, put it on Ava's head, and took one for herself.

"I'll need my wallet, Fai. It's in my bag on the other side of the door."

Fai removed the wallet, put it into her bag, and then grabbed the Callaway umbrella.

When they stepped outside, they found the rain had let up, but Fai opened the umbrella anyway and held it over Ava.

"Put your good arm around my waist," Lam said.

Ava did, and felt the gun tucked into the back of his trousers. "Let's go."

It was a slow but uneventful walk to the end of the hutong, where they all got into a taxi. Lam gave the driver the hospital address and then told him exactly what streets he wanted him to take to get there.

"Have you checked your phone recently?" Ava asked Fai when they were en route.

"I did as I was changing. No calls."

Ava laid her head on Fai's shoulder. "If he doesn't phone in the next hour, start calling him."

"I will."

The drive from the hutong to Chaoyang was far quicker than it had been earlier in the day. In less than thirty minutes the taxi stopped in front of the emergency services entrance of the United Family Hospital. Lam paid the driver, despite objections from Fai, helped Ava from the car, and led her inside. The waiting room wasn't full, but Ava estimated there had to be about twenty people there.

"We have to register before a doctor will see you," Fai said.

They went to the registration desk, where Ava and Fai took seats facing a woman who wore what Ava assumed was a nurse's uniform. The woman was working on her computer and ignored them for several minutes. Finally she looked up and said, "What seems to be the problem?"

"My name is Lam, and I'm an officer with the Municipal Public Security Bureau," he said, standing behind Ava and Fai. "This young woman is a visitor to our city. She was attacked in public by a mugger who had a meat cleaver. He struck her on the arm and there's a large wound that needs immediate treatment."

The woman looked up at Lam, and as she did, he thrust a badge in her face. "I want you to give her priority."

"Yes, officer. We'll see that she's looked after right away," the woman said. "But can I see her identification so she can be properly registered?"

Fai reached into her bag, took out Ava's wallet, and passed it to her. Ava handed over her Canadian driver's licence and health card.

"No passport?" the woman said.

"I forgot it."

"Don't bother her with that right now," Lam said. "I'll get it later if you need it."

"I still need a local address."

Fai rattled off hers.

The woman looked displeased, but Lam was a looming official presence and she wasn't going to argue with him. A few moments later she pushed a button on the side of her desk. Double automatic doors with the sign EMERGENCY PATIENTS ONLY above them swung open. "You can go through now," she said to Ava.

"Can I join her?" Fai asked.

"No visitors are allowed until the doctor has seen her and decided on a course of action," the woman said, looking at Lam. "That's the policy and it's firm."

"I'll wait for you here," Fai said.

Ava walked through the doors and was met by the woman. She handed Ava a card with a number on it and pointed to a line of cubicles beyond a nursing station.

"You're in cubicle C. Take a seat or lie down. The doctor will be with you soon."

Ava had an aversion to hospitals. She couldn't remember how it had started, but from an early age she felt afraid every time she stepped inside one. She didn't like the smells. She didn't like being surrounded by sick people. And she couldn't stop thinking about death. She knew rationally that hospitals were where people went to be cured, but she couldn't stop thinking about how many wouldn't be.

When Uncle was dying of cancer, she had stayed in Hong Kong for several months and visited him every day. Even though she knew for certain that he was dying, she was able to handle it emotionally while he was still living at home. But as soon as he moved into the hospital, she started to fall apart. The hospital represented finality, and even when someone wasn't desperately ill, being admitted to hospital felt like the beginning of a path that led to finality. Or so she thought as she sat on the bed in cubicle C with the curtains drawn, listening to a man in the next cubicle moan in pain.

After a few minutes her curtains were opened and she found herself looking at a handsome young man with a nurse standing behind him.

"I'm Doctor Chew," he said. "And you're Ms. Ava Lee?"

"I am."

"I see from the chart that you're from Canada."

"Toronto."

"I went to medical school at McGill University in Montreal."

"Great school."

"It certainly is, from my experience," he said, and looked at the chart. "It says here that you were attacked by a mugger who had a meat cleaver. That's odd, even for Beijing."

"I wouldn't know."

"And he struck you on the upper arm?"

"Yes."

"Well, let's take a look at it," he said and nodded to the nurse.

She was a short, stout, middle-aged woman who had a nice smile, warm eyes, and gentle hands. She helped Ava take off her jacket and then said, "We have to remove these bandages. It will be easier if you're not wearing the shirt."

"Sure," Ava said.

Dr. Chew left the cubicle while the nurse removed Ava's shirt and replaced it with a short-sleeved hospital gown. In spite of the nurse's gentle hands, the nerve endings in Ava's arm burned as the shirt passed over them. The pain started to ramp up even more as the bandages were unwound. Ava winced, her eyes watered, and she felt a slight sense of alarm when she saw the blood-soaked gauze.

Dr. Chew stepped back into the cubicle and examined the wound. "You can move the arm?"

"Yes."

"Good. Then the bone is probably intact. But it's still a very nasty cut. It will have to be cleaned and sewn up, and I believe you'll need an anaesthetic," he said. "Unless you have an incredible threshold for pain, I don't recommend you be awake while we do it."

"You'll do the procedure?"

"No, a colleague will. He's very good."

"When?"

He looked at his watch. "Sometime during the next hour. You've been given high-level priority," he said, and then looked at the chart again. "Can I ask you, how is it that a superintendent from the Municipal Public Security Bureau brought you here in person?"

"I guess I was just fortunate that he was nearby when I was attacked," Ava said. "And Doctor, I'm here with a friend. Can she come in and see me?"

"No visitors are allowed in here. She can see you in the recovery room after you've woken from the procedure."

"Will someone tell her what's going on?"

"Sure, I'll ask the registration desk to inform her. What's her name?"

Ava hesitated and then said, "Pang Fai."

"Please don't joke with me."

"I'm not."

He smiled. "You were brought here by a superintendent from the Security Bureau and the actress Pang Fai?"

"That's right."

"What is it you do in life, Ms. Lee?"

"At present I'm simply a Canadian tourist trying to enjoy Beijing — and not doing a very good job of it."

48

THE FIRST THING SHE WAS AWARE OF WAS PAIN. IT WAS indistinct, almost detached from her. But then she turned to her left and her body lit up. Ava groaned and opened her eyes to see a white ceiling and bright overhead lights. She heard someone else groan and looked to her right. She was in a room with four other patients, all of them hooked up to IV drips. She looked down and saw she had an IV as well.

I'm in a hospital in Beijing and I've had surgery to repair my left arm, she thought. A thick wad of bandage stuck out below the sleeve of her gown. "Hello?" she said.

"Ah, you're awake," a nurse said, approaching the bed. "How do you feel?"

"A bit rough."

"The doctor will prescribe painkillers. They'll take the edge off."

"What time is it?"

"Ten past eleven."

"When can I leave?"

"You'll have to stay until the doctor examines you, but

if you're fine then, there's really no reason you can't leave tonight."

"Can you let him know I'm awake?"

"I will."

"And I have a friend waiting for me. I was told she could see me in here."

"She's with someone else — a man — in our administration offices. Once we knew who she was, we were reluctant to leave her in the general waiting room. It would have caused a ruckus if she'd been recognized."

"Thank you for doing that."

"It isn't often we have celebrities here."

"Could you ask her to come and see me?"

"Sure, that won't be a problem. The doctor is occupied with another patient, so you won't see him for another half-hour at least."

Ava closed her eyes and pressed her head back into the pillow. She imagined she'd now have another scar, and unlike the one on her hip and the smaller ones on her lower back, this one would make it more difficult to wear dresses. Then she thought, *That's vain*, and then as quickly, *What's wrong with caring how I look? I am my father and mother's daughter.*

She looked at her arm and grimaced as it struck her that she'd been sloppy in the way she had handled almost everything and everyone connected to this blackmail. She had spent too much time running around and not enough time thinking. She had made a lot of assumptions, including the belief that the blackmailers wouldn't try to assault them again. But really, how wrong had she been to think that? What kind of blackmailers resorted to physical violence before getting paid? None that she had ever encountered.

And this time there had been no warning phone call or follow-up demands that she knew of. Was the blackmail just bullshit? Was it a smokescreen to disguise another purpose? They had targeted her twice and left Fai alone. Maybe they thought getting rid of her would make Fai more compliant to their demands. But how did they even know who she was?

"Ava," Fai said from the entrance to the recovery room.

Ava turned to look and saw that Fai wasn't alone. Except the man with her wasn't Lam. Walking a few paces behind her was the short, round, well-dressed and coiffed figure of her agent, Chen.

"What the hell is he doing here?" Ava exclaimed.

"I'm so sorry to see you in this condition," said Chen.

"It's a bit late for being sorry, isn't it?"

Fai reached the bedside, leaned down, and kissed Ava gently on the lips. "He phoned me just over an hour ago from the airport. He'd just landed. I couldn't hold back when I heard his voice, so I unloaded on him. I told him about the video and Bai Lok, and Lau Lau."

"I got here as quickly as I could," he said.

"He did," Fai said.

"I never wanted anything like this to happen," Chen said. "I know you and I have had our disagreements, but I also know that we both love and want what's best for Fai. It's true that I've been maybe a little jealous that you're taking up some of my space and influence, and you must understand how afraid I've been for her future."

"That's no reason to act the way you did."

"I apologize as sincerely as I can for the way I behaved at the premiere, and for the way I spoke to you on the phone."

"That's not what I mean."

"But that's all I can apologize for."

"Chen insists he's had absolutely nothing to do with the video, the blackmail, or the attacks," Fai said.

"I swear to you on my mother's memory that I know nothing about any of it."

Ava looked at him and then at Fai. Her face said she believed him, and his seemed desperate to be believed. "Are you telling me that you don't have the video of Fai?"

"I destroyed it the same day I got it. Xia brought me the DVD and I broke it into little pieces in front of him and Ms. Yi."

"Are you sure it was the DVD with Fai?"

"Ms. Yi and I watched enough of it to confirm what Xia was telling us. You can call her now if you want to ask her what we saw and what we did with it."

"There must be another copy," said Fai.

Ava nodded. "I guess that's possible. Bai Lok could have kept one. Except if he did, I think it would have been in the boxes we got from his brother. Ding Fa may have lied to us about never having seen a tape with you on it —"

"He wouldn't have lied about that," Fai said.

"How many copies did Xia bring you?" Ava asked Chen. "One."

"He could have made another and kept it," Ava said.

"Why would he have done that?" Fai asked.

Ava looked at Chen. "At the time this happened, how was the relationship between you and him?"

"It was rocky. He was champing at the bit to start his own business. It was obvious to me that I was going to lose him, and maybe I was a bit harder on him, a bit more demanding than I should have been."

"But he didn't just pick up and leave, did he? He would have had a plan."

"When he gave me his notice, he had more than that. He had a plan, an office, staff, and the beginning of a roster of clients."

"And none of those things happened overnight," Ava said. "So when he got possession of the DVD, he was already making plans. He knew you were going to become rivals."

"So he made a copy of the DVD and put it away as insurance," Chen said. "It was something he could always use for leverage against me, or to strongarm Fai into changing agents."

"Then why didn't he do either of those things?" Ava said.

Chen shrugged. "Probably because he didn't have to. He was successful from the first day he opened his business. I wasn't any danger to him and he didn't need to hurt Fai."

"So why has the video appeared now?"

"I have no idea," Chen said.

Fai sat on the edge of the bed and placed a hand on top of Ava's. "Ava, I think we should tell Chen the truth about Mo."

"What do you mean?" Chen asked.

Ava looked at him, searching his face and body language for any sign of insincerity. He seemed to be genuinely confused. "Fai didn't actually meet with Mo. I did, with an associate."

"I know. That's why I phoned and yelled at you."

"You yelled at me after our first meeting with him. There was a second meeting. My associate and I went to the Hotel Kempinski in place of Fai. When Mo got to the room, we were waiting."

"That's when Ava convinced him to drop his objections to

the distribution of *Mao's Daughter* and got him to promise to continue to support me," Fai said.

"Why didn't you tell me this?" Chen said to Fai, his voice sharper.

"You weren't being particularly supportive and you didn't seem to care what I had to do to make amends with Mo. I simply let you believe what you thought might be true," Fai said. "Besides, what Ava did probably wasn't legal. Why involve you in that?"

"What in hell did you do?" Chen said to Ava.

"Mo's son is gay. I have pictures of him with his black boyfriend in some compromising circumstances. I told Mo I was prepared to make those photos and information public."

"He's crazy about that boy," Chen said.

"So I was told, and so it appeared when I put the proposition to him, because he quite readily agreed to what I wanted."

"Lay off Fai and release *Mao's Daughter*?"

"Exactly."

"I wish I could have been there for that," Chen said with a slight smile, which quickly disappeared. "But it's odd. When I spoke with Mo later that day, after Fai told me she had met with him, he was calm, even friendly. This is a man who loses control of his anger over the tiniest of slights. He yells, he screams, he insults, he threatens, and then he carries the grudge forever. I've never known anyone more vengeful."

"What are you saying?"

"I have trouble believing that he could have kept control over his emotions when he was talking to me so soon after meeting with you and your friend," Chen said. "Even if he didn't want me to know what had transpired, I would have expected him to be, at best, terse, tight-lipped, and in a foul mood. Instead I got Mr. Friendly."

"Knowing him, and knowing now what we did to him, why do you think he was so friendly?" Ava asked. "Could it have been an act?"

"How so?"

"He could have wanted you to think that he and Fai were back on good terms and that there were no lingering hard feelings. He knew that was an impression you'd pass on to Fai, which you did, and he'd assume that Fai would tell me the same thing."

"Why would he do that?" Fai asked.

"He could have decided to come after us but wanted to make it difficult for us to connect him to it, because of the threat I posed with his son's photos. The blackmail attempt could have been a diversion, a smokescreen."

"The man in the balaclava?" Fai said.

"He could have been hired to do the job."

"And what about the demands for money and the deadlines he set?"

"Part of the diversion. I'm sure if we'd been stupid enough to pay, they'd have taken the money, but I'm convinced that the video was going to be released whether we paid or not. It was always about the video."

"And the attacks?" Fai asked.

"They were directed squarely at me and could have been intended as payback. If he's as vengeful and as angry a man as Chen says, he might not have been able to resist the temptation to hurt me."

"And he does all this without worrying about repercussions, about his son?" Fai said.

"He has deniability, or so he believes. He's told Chen that he adores you again and that all the issues with *Mao's Daughter* have been resolved. He believes there's nothing to connect him to the video and we have nothing to connect him with the blackmail or the attacks — those were simply random events."

"But how did he get the video?" Fai asked.

"Xia," Ava and Chen said, virtually as one.

49

THEY LEFT THE HOSPITAL AT TWELVE-THIRTY. AVA WORE
what was left of her blue shirt and took with her a couple of
painkillers and a prescription for more. They drove back to
the hutong in Chen's car. He sat in front with the driver but
spent the entire trip facing the back seat as he talked with
Ava and Fai.

Ava's antipathy towards him had begun to recede in
the hospital. As he continued to analyze the situation and
talk about the people involved, she found herself starting
to respect his intelligence and his perception. That respect
really started to kick in when he said, "I know we've both
voiced the opinion that Xia gave the video to Mo, but I'm
thinking it's possible Mo doesn't know the video exists. He
may not know anything about the blackmail or the attacks.
So, in terms of deniability, it could be real."

"Are you suggesting he's not involved?" Ava said.

"No, but I am suggesting that he may not be aware of the
details, or at least all of them."

"Explain that to me."

"Mo doesn't always operate in a straightforward manner.

His language can have double meanings; he spins stories that you're supposed to interpret and he has code words he likes to use. I eventually caught on, and I'm sure Xia did as well," Chen said. "It's possible that Mo could have reached out to Xia and insinuated that Fai had insulted him or degraded him in some way. He might have hinted that it was time she was taught a lesson, maybe even brought down, and there would have been the unspoken suggestion that it was a job he wanted Xia to take on."

"Without mentioning his real motivation?" Ava asked.

"He wouldn't have mentioned his son at all, let alone that you have photos that could embarrass him. Anyway, Xia is cold-blooded enough not to need real justification. The fact that Mo was angling for a favour would have been enough for him. He wouldn't have cared that Mo wanted to hurt Fai. And my business being part of the collateral damage would have appealed to him."

"So you're saying Mo didn't know about the video when he reached out to Xia?"

"It is at least possible. And I'm not even sure, if he did, that it would have come up in his conversation with Xia," Chen said. "It is conceivable that Xia simply said he knew how the lesson could be taught and Mo trusted him enough to give him free rein."

"Conceivable or likely?"

"More likely conceivable, because Mo is a stickler for detail," Chen said, pleased with his play on words. "I presume that Xia would have given him some idea of what he had, and the impact it would have on Fai."

"So who came up with the idea for a phony blackmail scheme?"

"After thinking about it a bit more, my guess is that it was Xia."

"And what about attacking me? Whose idea was that?"

"That would have been an afterthought, a sort of 'by the way.' Mo is known for finishing meetings like that. Anyone who has dealt with him up close understands the importance of those afterthoughts. He would have said, 'By the way, there's this woman named Ava Lee who is a friend of Pang Fai. I never want to see her or talk to her again, and I'd like someone to make sure that isn't possible, and I don't care how it's done.'"

"Lovely."

"I know I'm presenting Xia and Mo in their worst possible light, but I'm not exaggerating."

"So what do we do now?"

The question came from Fai as the car approached the entrance to the hutong.

"I need to sleep on this," Ava said.

"Me too. It's one thing to spin a conspiracy theory, but it's something else to prove it and figure out how to deal with it," Chen said.

"We don't have a lot of time. Whatever we do, we have to do it tomorrow," Ava said.

"Will you need me?" Chen asked.

"Possibly, so be available."

Chen turned to Fai. "Is she always so bossy?"

"She can be, but I don't mind it, and neither should you."

"I wasn't complaining."

The car stopped at the hutong. Fai climbed out with the Callaway umbrella and went around to Ava's door. Chen joined them on the sidewalk.

"There's one thing I need to ask," he said to Ava. "Were

you prepared to release the photos of Mo's son if he hadn't agreed to co-operate with you?"

"It would have been a really difficult decision for any number of reasons, and it's something I would have hated to do."

"But you would have done it?"

"At that point it would have been a choice between preserving Fai's future or his son's," Ava said. "So yes, absolutely, I would have done it."

"And if he tries to fuck us over tomorrow or the day after?"

"The photos will be released."

"Regardless of what happens to Fai?"

"If I release the photos, it will mean that Fai's video is already out there."

"I hope it doesn't come to that."

"Me neither. But if it does, I won't hesitate," Ava said. "Meanwhile, there are more important things for you to think about."

"Like what?"

"Who should we meet with tomorrow? How will it be arranged? And what will we say when we have the opportunity?"

"I'll sleep on those questions," Chen said. "When should we talk?"

"Call Fai at nine," Ava said, and began to walk down the hutong.

Fai caught up with her after a few strides. The rain had started again. "It's either rain or smog," Fai said. "If I didn't love my house so much, I'd move back to Yantai, where you can breathe and stay dry."

"Tell me," Ava said, "did you believe everything Chen told us?"

"You didn't?"

"I don't know him as well as you."

Fai didn't say anything at first. She kept walking, holding the umbrella over their heads. When they reached the door to the compound, she hesitated before opening it. "Chen is an agent, and like any agent, including Xia, he tells you what he thinks you want to hear and then convinces himself he's being truthful. The difference is that Xia always sounds sincere, while Chen's bullshit is so blatant it's laughable. Tonight there was no bullshit."

"Thank you."

They entered the courtyard, Ava glancing left and right to make sure no one was lurking. As they started to walk to the house, Mr. Lam's door opened and he came out to meet them.

"How's the arm?" he asked.

"No bone damage," Ava said.

"That's good."

"Thank you for everything you did for me."

"As I said, we're family here."

He walked them to the door and waited until they got inside.

"I need to take one of these painkillers and get to bed," Ava said.

"Do you need help undressing?" Fai asked.

"I don't think so," Ava said, and then paused. "I should check my messages. I left my phone here when I went to the hospital."

Fai reached for Ava's bag and handed it to her. Ava turned on the phone. She'd missed three calls. May Ling had called to congratulate her on closing the Sun deal and asked her to call back anytime. The other two were from Xu's Shanghai number, and one was a message. She accessed it and heard Auntie Grace say simply, "Call me, please." She hit the number.

"Ava, thank goodness you called," Auntie said.

"What's going on? You sound upset."

"Suen took Xu to the hospital a few hours ago." Suen was Xu's Red Pole, his enforcer, and his de facto second in command in Shanghai.

"Why?"

"The pills and rest didn't help. I went to see him in his room around eight o'clock and he was still feverish, aching all over — especially in the neck. He had a headache and said he felt nauseous. What really scared me was that he was confused about where he was. I tried to call you, and when I couldn't reach you, I called Suen. He drove him to the hospital."

"Have you heard from Suen since?"

"No."

"Give me his phone number. I'll call him."

"Then you'll call me back?"

"Of course."

Ava ended that call and immediately made the next. Suen's phone rang five times. She was prepared for the voicemail prompt when he finally answered. "Suen," he said quietly.

"It's Ava."

"I know. I'm not supposed to be using my phone in here. I've got the ringtone silenced, but I saw your number."

"I just spoke to Auntie Grace. She told me you took Xu to a hospital."

"We're still here, and by the sounds of things he's not getting out tonight or tomorrow."

"She said she thought he might have a bad flu."

"It isn't flu," Suen said. "They think its meningitis. They're still running tests, and the big fear is that he has the bacterial strain rather than the viral one."

"What's the difference?"

"The viral is curable and the bacterial can kill you. But if he has that, they've probably caught it early enough."

Ava caught her breath and felt a cold wave descend over her like a shroud. "Suen, are they even sure it is meningitis?"

"They said it's unusual but not unknown for someone his age, but he has most of the symptoms, and the doctor I spoke to didn't seem to have any doubts."

"But they don't have the test results yet?"

"They have some, not all."

"When will you have the rest?"

"By late morning or early afternoon."

"Call me the instant you know anything."

"I will... And Ava, what do I do about Auntie Grace?"

"I'll talk to her."

"Thanks. I think it's better that way."

Ava ended the call and turned to Fai. "There's a problem in Shanghai. Xu is ill. I have to call Auntie Grace again. While I'm doing that, could you do me a favour? Go online and look up meningitis and its symptoms."

"Sure," Fai said.

Oh, fuck, Ava thought as she phoned Auntie Grace. *Don't let anything happen to Xu.*

"Ava," Auntie Grace said.

"I spoke with Suen. The doctors think that Xu has a form of meningitis. They're still running tests, but he seems to be in good hands. Suen is at the hospital and won't leave. He'll call me as soon as they know anything definitively."

"What's meningitis?"

"Just a second," Ava said, and walked across to Fai, who was hunched over her laptop. She looked over Fai's shoulder and read what was on the screen. "It's caused when bacteria enter the brain or spinal cord. The symptoms are a lot of what you described—headaches, neckaches, nausea, fever, and disorientation and confusion. It can be treated with antibiotics, but I can't see anything about how long it takes for them to kick in."

"How do you get something like that?"

"It can be spread by a sinus or ear infection. Did he have either of those?"

"He's been sniffling and blowing his nose a lot."

"That probably explains it."

Auntie Grace became quiet and then said, "I'm so scared. Given the life he leads, you'd think I would be used to the idea of him dying young, but I can't imagine my world without him."

"He's in good hands," Ava said, tears welling in her eyes in response to Auntie Grace's emotional honesty.

"Ava, I know Suen is capable, but is there any way you can come to Shanghai? Xu mentioned that you're in Beijing. That's not so far."

"Yes, but I can't do it tomorrow, or maybe even the day after. I'm involved in something here that is very serious, and I can't leave until it is resolved. As soon as it is, I promise you I'll fly to Shanghai. In the meantime, I'll stay in touch with Suen and with you, and you can call me anytime you wish."

"Okay, my dear."

"And Auntie, when I do come, I may bring a friend with me, if that's all right with you."

"A woman?"

"Yes."

"Pang Fai?"

"Yes."

"Xu mentioned that you and she are friends. He was very happy for you. I'm happy too, and I'll be thrilled to have her under my roof — although not as much as having you here."

Ava ended the call and slumped onto the couch next to Fai. "I didn't mean to make any commitments for you," she said. "You don't have to join me in Shanghai if you don't want to."

"I'd love to go to Shanghai with you. But do you think we'll be able to wrap things up here as quickly as you told the Auntie?"

"We can't let them drag this out, or make our decisions for us," Ava said. "One of the few Western films Uncle ever saw was *Doctor Zhivago*, and the thing he always remembered about it was how Zhivago's indecision changed his life."

"I'm not sure what he was referring to."

"In the film, Zhivago is married to Tonya and in love with Lara, and he keeps going back and forth between them, not able to decide which woman he should be with. One day, as he's riding a horse from one house to another and still dithering, a Red Army partisan unit swoops out from behind the trees and forces him to join them as their battlefield doctor. Uncle said it served Zhivago right. Whenever you put off making a hard decision between A and B, don't be surprised if you end up with C — something you didn't expect and don't want."

"How does that apply to our situation?"

"I want us to act first. We need to force the issue towards resolution."

"With Mo or Xia or both of them?"

"I don't know yet. I'd like Chen's input before we make a final decision."

"So you trust him a bit more now?"

"I trust his analysis. Do you?"

"It makes too much sense not to be true."

"That's another good thing about being aggressive," said Ava. "We'll get to the truth that much faster."

50

AVA DIDN'T SLEEP WELL. HER ARM ACHED AND SHE FELT dehydrated, twice getting up to drink large glasses of water. But her biggest problem was her mind. It was on fire as it leapt from thinking about how to approach Mo and Xia to worrying about Xu and Auntie Grace.

She finally got out of bed at seven, went to the bathroom, drank more water, and took a painkiller. When she came out, Fai was making her way downstairs dressed in jeans and a sweater. Ava joined her in the kitchen.

"I was thinking of going out to get congee and coffee," Fai said.

"That sounds great. I'll make some phone calls while you're gone. What time does Chen start his day?"

"Early. Do you want his number?"

"I already have it on my phone."

Ava walked Fai to the door and then reached for her phone as soon as it closed. She called Suen first.

"Ava?"

"Yes. Where are you?"

"I'm in my car, heading back to the hospital. I went home for a change of clothes."

"How is he?"

"Sedated. He slept most of the night."

"Any word on the test results?"

"Now they don't expect them to be completed until some-time this afternoon."

"Is he still feverish and achy?"

"I haven't spoken to him since very early this morning, and he wasn't exactly communicative."

"Being at loose ends mentally is one of the symptoms."

"I know. They told me."

"I talked to Auntie Grace again last night," Ava said. "I told her I'm going to come to Shanghai. The problem is, I don't know when. I'll try for tonight, but tomorrow is more likely."

"I'm glad you're coming. I'm not very good at handling these kinds of things."

"I'll keep you informed about my schedule, and you call me as soon as you hear the results of those tests."

"Okay. And Ava," he said, "have you heard from Sonny about Wanchai?"

"What do you mean?"

"Xu told me he asked you and Sonny to poke around a bit."

"Sonny hasn't uncovered anything that should be of any immediate concern."

"Good, because with the boss indisposed like this, we don't want that to flare up again. Those sons of bitches would use any weakness as an excuse to cause trouble."

"How many people know the boss is ill?" she asked, Suen's point hitting home.

"Auntie, me, you, and a couple of the men who guard the house."

"Make sure it stays that way. We don't need this being broadcast."

"I agree, but a lot of people call him every day. If he's not available, some of them are going to call me, and questions will be asked."

"Tell them he's gone to Thailand with a girlfriend for a few days and doesn't want to be bothered unless it's really urgent."

"That's not something he'd do."

"What do you suggest?"

"It has to be business-related."

"How about he's gone to Vietnam to meet with a gang that wants to formally join the society?"

"Better."

"Then use it. I'll tell Auntie Grace to pass along the same story to anyone who calls her."

Ava called Auntie next, and the old woman answered before the first ring ended. "How is he?" she asked.

"They're waiting for some final test results that will be in this afternoon. In the meantime, he's resting and seems better. Suen will stay at the hospital with him and I'm planning to fly to Shanghai no later than tomorrow."

"Thank you."

"One more thing. If anyone calls the house looking for him, I want you to say that Xu is in Vietnam on business. If they want to know more than that, tell them to call Suen."

"I've already had two calls this morning."

"So early? From whom?"

"I don't know, but one of them spoke Cantonese."

"What did you tell them?"

"I said Xu wasn't available, that he was indisposed," she said. "That's what he normally tells me to say when he has a girl with him or he's having dinner and doesn't want to be disturbed."

"I'm sure that was exactly the right thing to say," Ava said. "Now, I don't want you to worry about anything. Suen won't leave the hospital until I get there, and I'll stay in touch."

Xu being ill in Shanghai was the last thing she needed, she thought, as she ended that call and searched for Chen's number.

"*Wei*," he answered.

"I hope I'm not calling too early."

"I've been up half the night."

"We have that in common."

"I was thinking about our entire conversation, and in particular your last comment about who we should meet with and what we should say."

"Do you have an opinion?"

"Yes, but I have a feeling you're going to do whatever you want, regardless of what I think."

"That's not entirely true," Ava said. "Chen, you're sounding nervous. Have you had a change of heart about working with us?"

"I am nervous, I won't deny it. The more I thought about it, the more I realized I could be signing my own death warrant — figuratively, not literally."

"If you want to back out, no one is going to stop you."

"I said I'm nervous, not that I'm pulling back."

"And I wasn't suggesting that you were. You are a practical man, and the practical thing to do is stand on the sidelines and let whatever happens, happen."

"But I don't want to do that."

"What do you want to do?"

"I thought at first we should go after Xia, but then I realized that was because I didn't want to risk going after Mo. It was a selfish idea and, more important, it was an ineffectual one. Mo is the only person who can call off this vendetta against Fai and you. Xia could just tell us to go fuck ourselves and then release Fai's video, without realizing there would be consequences for Mo."

"You're that sure that Mo didn't tell him about the photos we have of his son?"

"One hundred percent. He'd never tell Xia anything so personal," Chen said. "Mo is a closed book to all of us. Besides, as I said last night, he wouldn't have to give Xia a reason to go after Fai. He'd just have to make it known that he wanted it done."

"So you want us to confront Mo?"

"Sooner or later, that's what has to happen. Let's make it sooner."

"I like your approach," Ava said.

"I suspect that's because it's what you've already decided to do."

"I was leaning that way," Ava said with a smile. "You just pushed me over the edge."

"I had another thought, though it might sound silly," Chen said. "What if it transpires that Mo had nothing to do with this and it was all Xia?"

"Do you really think that's possible?"

"Possible, yes. Probable, no."

"A very clever agent convinced me last night that Mo has to be behind what's happened. Maybe Mo didn't plan it all out, but he planted the seed that made it possible. I see no reason to change my mind."

"So, when do you want to meet him?"

"As soon as you can arrange it."

"He's usually unreachable until about nine. Where do you want to meet him?"

"Anywhere he chooses. My message won't change."

"And what is that message?"

"I'm still working on it."

"I doubt that, but I've never minded surprises."

"Good, because I haven't decided yet how harsh I want to be."

"That sparks another silly question. What if he refuses to meet?"

"If that happens, you can tell him that Ava Lee, the bitch he met at the Kempinski Hotel, has told you she'll make public at noon today the pictures she showed him at the hotel."

"Would you really do that?"

"I would."

"That does define 'harsh.'"

"Well, it's where we're headed. There's no point in playing nice anymore."

51

AVA PHONED MAY LING WHILE FAI REHEATED THE CONGEE.
She got the voicemail on May's cellphone and then on her
office phone. She left the same message on both: "I'm going
to be tied up most of the day. I'll call again when I can." She
thought about mentioning Xu but didn't. There were hints
of sexual tension between Xu and May that Ava found disturbing. The last thing she wanted was for them to begin
a relationship, so she found herself avoiding any personal
comments when she discussed one with the other.

Fai served the congee. They ate slowly, Fai drinking tea
and Ava drinking coffee. It was all about killing time.

At eight Ava said. "Even if Chen can arrange a meeting,
you don't have to be there."

"I wouldn't miss it."

At eight-thirty Ava went into the courtyard and began to
walk its perimeter. The sky was overcast; she could barely
find the sun through a haze that was a mix of cloud and
smog. She was tired of Beijing, she decided, fed up with rain
and smog and traffic. *Well, I'll be out of here soon enough*,
she thought.

"Can I join you?" a voice said from behind as she started another lap.

She turned and saw Mr. Lam.

"I'd be pleased if you did."

"How's your arm this morning?" he asked, coming to her side.

"Sore."

"That's a nasty weapon he was using. You were lucky he hit just that part of the arm."

"I guess that's one way to define luck," she said, and smiled.

"Two attacks in two nights. And according to Fan, the three who attacked you the night before had knives."

"That's right."

"Someone doesn't like you very much."

"My hope is that we'll deal with that today. It won't happen again."

"I still think you should go to the police."

"No," Ava said, and glanced at Lam. "I hope you don't take this the wrong way, but my experience with police forces in China — and in places like the Philippines, Indonesia, and Vietnam — is that they tend not to be overly concerned about the welfare of foreign visitors. It's as if they figure we'll be leaving their country in a few days or weeks, so why bother doing work that will probably amount to nothing. And — again I hope you're not offended — that attitude is even stronger where women are concerned. In your career, for example, how many charges do you know of that were brought against local men who'd raped or molested a foreign female visitor to Beijing?"

"In cases like those, there was always the problem of the witness leaving China," he said.

"That's a poor excuse."

"Yes it is, and you make a very good point. But I'm curious. When you mentioned those other countries it struck me that this kind of thing may have happened to you before."

"It has a few times. I was in the debt-collection business — large debts, nasty people."

"Ahh. That might also explain your martial arts expertise. It's impressive, by the way."

"Thank you. My mother made sure her two daughters are able to look after themselves."

They continued to walk, the conversation lagging, until they came to the courtyard entrance for a second time.

"Pardon me for asking this, but do you think you're going to be a regular visitor to the hutong?" Lam asked.

"I think so. I hope so."

"The reason I ask is that we try to look out for each other. It could be interpreted as us being nosy, and maybe it is a bit, but I guarantee that not many people went to bed last night until they saw you and Fai safely entering her house."

"Your intervention last night was the furthest thing from being nosy. And in case I didn't thank you appropriately, let me say that I'm immensely grateful."

"I like to think that you'd do the same for me."

They were near Fai's and Ava stopped walking. "Mr. Lam, I can promise you that I most certainly would, although I can't guarantee the same rate of success."

"Ava," Fai said from the doorway.

"Yes?"

"Chen is sending his car to pick us up at ten."

"I'll be right there," Ava said, and then turned to Lam. "We're going to a meeting to resolve the differences that led to the adventures of the past two nights. If we're not around tomorrow, that means it went well. If we are, you should keep your eyes open and your gun handy."

"Well, then, here's hoping that I don't see you again for quite some time."

Ava entered the house to find Fai waiting at the bottom of the stairs. "Our meeting with Mo is at eleven. Chen is completely stressed out."

"Where is it?"

"The Syndicate offices."

"Did he say how he convinced Mo to meet with us?"

"He said the three of us had to see him, and Mo agreed without asking him why. He thought that was really strange."

"Or really obvious."

"That would make it easier," Fai said with a big sigh. "We should be getting ready. I have to shower, but I was thinking that if you need any help in the bathroom, you should go first."

"I didn't read all the directions the hospital gave me about looking after the wound and the bandages, but I can't imagine that standing under a hot shower will be allowed for at least a few days. When it comes to washing and fixing my hair, I have limited flexibility and mobility with this arm, so I might need some help with those things."

"I played a nurse in a movie once, and a woman who looked after her elderly mother in another."

"You sound superbly qualified. Let's go and get ourselves cleaned up for Mr. Mo."

52

THEY LEFT THE HOUSE AT TEN MINUTES TO TEN. AVA wore black slacks and a white shirt topped with a navy blue cardigan. Fai seemed to have deliberately dressed down. She had on a baggy black dress that had a high neckline and fell to just below her knees. Ava was in high heels and Fai in flats. It was as close as they could come to being the same height, but Fai was still a few inches taller. Fai put on a raincoat at the door and grabbed one of the smaller umbrellas.

"After talking to Mr. Lam this morning, I can't help but feel that everyone who lives here knows our every move," Ava said to Fai as they started to walk across the courtyard.

"That's not always a bad thing."

"Unless someone was passing along our comings and goings."

"Do you think that's possible?"

"Why not?"

"I don't want to think of my neighbours like that," Fai said. "I'll be so glad when this is over."

They left the compound and turned right onto the hutong.

"Fai, I hope you're prepared for the eventuality that Mo may not be co-operative this morning."

"I am," Fai said rather loudly. "I thought about it last night in bed and again this morning, after Chen called. I think we're in a better place than we were a few days ago, but I understand there is no guarantee that things will go our way. I'll cope with whatever the outcome is."

"That's good to hear. But I wasn't being pessimistic when I said that. I expect the best, not the worst result."

Fai squeezed Ava's right arm. Then she said with a laugh, "Look! My god, Chen brought the Bentley."

The night before, he'd driven them home in a grey Mercedes, but it was a black Bentley that was now parked at the entrance to the hutong. Ava recognized it from the night of the premiere of *Mao's Daughter*.

"Why did you bring this car?" Fai asked as they approached Chen, who was standing next to it.

"I thought a grand entrance would be appropriate. Mo won't see the car, but I'll feel very good arriving in it."

They exchanged hugs, Chen being careful with Ava, and then they all climbed into the car. "How's the arm?" he asked.

"It's fine as long as the painkillers are working and I don't have to hit anyone."

The car pulled away from the curb and eased into heavy traffic. Ava had been in a Bentley before and had noticed that it made the drivers around it cautious. That wasn't the case in Beijing. The other cars crowded it as if it were a cheap Fiat.

"The drive will be slow, but I took that into account," Chen said.

"Fai told me that Mo agreed to the meeting without asking why you wanted it," Ava said. "How did that strike you?"

"As odd — but then, so was his entire manner. He seemed cautious when we started speaking, and even more so when I asked for a meeting. Then when I told him that you and Fai would be with me, he became calm, almost icy."

"Which leads me to assume he knows why we want to see him."

"I'll be shocked if it's otherwise."

"And how does that make you feel?"

"Far less apprehensive than I felt last night and before I called him this morning, but not overly confident."

"Why? What do you expect him to say or do?"

"I don't know. With him, you never know. He's clever and he's devious."

"There are some realities that even being clever can't help you avoid," Ava said.

Chen started to respond and then fell into silence. Ava wondered if he was having second thoughts about the meeting. She could see that Fai was showing signs of stress as well. "Would you mind if I switched subjects?" she said, knowing that talking about something else would diffuse some of the tension.

"To what?" he said.

"Lau Lau."

"What about him?"

"When we met with him, he told me he has all kinds of ideas for films in his head. Do you think that could be true?"

"It could be, but who'd trust him to take those ideas and turn them into anything resembling a movie?"

"What do you mean by 'trust'?"

"I don't even know where to start. He's unreliable in so many ways."

"Let's say someone did have an interest in giving him another chance. What would be the starting point?"

"A screenplay," Chen said, casting a questioning eye at Fai, who shrugged.

"Who wrote the screenplays for his earlier films?"

"He did."

"Do you think he's still capable of writing one?"

"I don't know."

"If someone wanted to commission him to write a screenplay, how much would it cost?"

"You're joking, right? You wouldn't do that, would you?" he said.

"If you were his agent, how much —"

"I'm not his agent, and I don't know of anyone who's representing him."

"But if you were, how much would you ask for an original screenplay written by Lau Lau?" she said. "I'm curious, that's all, so don't be completely dismissive of the idea."

"At the peak of his game he could get anywhere from half a million to a million renminbi," Chen said. "These days, who could possibly put a number on it?"

The car was now moving at a steady pace. Ava guessed they were going to reach Chaoyang early. "At some point in time I might ask you to do that," she said.

"Don't get sucked in by Lau Lau," Chen advised. "Many people have thought they could resurrect him, and none of them came close to succeeding."

Ava looked out the window and saw the China Movie Syndicate building in the distance. "We're well ahead of time. I don't know if that's a good or a bad omen," she said, changing subjects again.

"Well, either way, I'm not going to sit in the car," Chen said. "We'll go in. If we have to wait in the lobby it's no big deal."

It was ten-forty when they walked into the building. Ava was prepared to go through the sign-in and nametag ritual, but the middle-aged woman who had greeted her and Lop on their previous visit was waiting in front of the security desk. She almost raced towards them.

"Mr. Chen, you and your group should come with me. We can go right up," she said, and then nodded respectfully to Fai.

"This is unusual," Chen said softly to Ava.

They rode the elevator to the forty-fifth floor, exited, and were led immediately into the boardroom.

"You can sit wherever you wish, and there's coffee and tea on the table over there. Can I get a cup for anyone?" the woman asked.

The three of them shook their heads.

"Excellent. Then excuse me while I tell Mr. Mo that you're here. He wanted to be informed the moment you arrived."

"This is the royal treatment we're receiving," Chen said to Ava when the woman had left. "What do you think is going on?"

"I have no idea, but we'll know soon enough."

Fai looked around the boardroom and through its open door into the maze of offices that surrounded it. "I've never been here before."

"Never?" Ava said.

"Not even once. Chen took care of all the business with these people. I had no need to meet with them," Fai said. "I'm surprised at how ordinary it all looks. I had imagined something grander."

"Given how glamorous the industry appears to outsiders, this is probably a bit of reverse psychology," Ava said.

"Here's Mo," Chen said suddenly.

Ava looked through the boardroom door and saw Mo approaching. "He's not alone," she said. "I recognize the woman. I met her when I was here. She's his personal assistant, but I can't remember her name. I've never seen the other man."

"That's Fong. He's the deputy chairman. The woman is Hua. The only person who knows more than them about what goes on inside these walls is Mo himself."

Ava, Chen, and Fai had taken black leather chairs along the side of the table that faced the office, with the windows behind them. Fong and Hua stood to one side to let Mo enter the room ahead of them. He walked directly over to Chen, who rose to his feet. Mo offered his hand, Chen took it, and they shook.

"Thanks for coming. I was pleased when you called, because it saved me from making the same kind of call to you," Mo said. Then he turned to Ava and Fai, who remained seated. "It's nice to see you again, Ms. Lee, and it is always a genuine pleasure to see you, Fai."

While those pleasantries ensued, Fong and Hua slipped into the room and took seats directly across from Ava and the others. Fong was thin and about five foot six. Ava guessed he was in his fifties, maybe even sixties. He wore a blue suit, white shirt, and red tie. The clothes looked expensive but were either ill-fitted or Fong had lost a lot of weight since he'd bought them; there was a large gap between the shirt collar and his neck, and the suit jacket looked several sizes too large.

"Were you offered tea or coffee?" Hua asked.

"Yes, and we declined," Ava said.

"Oh," Hua said.

Ava thought her tone seemed almost mournful, and took a closer look at her. The time they had previously met, Hua had been wearing a lot of makeup. Now her lips were pale, and around her eyes there was only the slightest trace of mascara — a small streak along one side. *She looks like she's been crying*, Ava thought. She saw Hua bite her lower lip and rub her right eye with her index finger. When she moved the finger away, Ava saw that the eye was slightly bloodshot and the skin beneath was puffy.

Mo left Chen and sat in his red leather chair at the head of the table. "Ms. Lee, you've met Ms. Hua, but you don't know Fong. He's my second-in-command at the Syndicate."

Fong nodded at her and then gathered his fingertips in front of his mouth.

"Thank you for seeing us," Chen said.

"No thanks are needed," Mo said quickly. "It's probably more appropriate for our side to offer an apology for the fact that this meeting was necessary in the first place."

"If I heard correctly, you just told Chen that you would have called him to arrange a meeting if he hadn't called you," Ava said.

"That's correct."

"Why?"

"Pardon me for a moment," Fong said, leaning towards them. "I'm a lawyer as well as an administrator, and the Syndicate's legal department reports to me. I met with a few of our lawyers this morning and explained to them — in the most general terms, of course, avoiding any specifics about either side at this table — the situation in which I thought we might find ourselves. Their advice to me was to make it clear that whatever we discuss here and now is to be treated as confidential and without prejudice. I talked this over with Mr. Mo and he's agreed that's the position our side will take. Can I have a similar undertaking from yours?"

Chen looked at Ava.

"Sure."

"Chen?" Fong said.

"Ava speaks for us."

"Then we can proceed," Fong said. "And if you don't mind, I'll ask Mr. Mo to begin."

Mo closed his eyes and leaned back in the chair, gathering himself. "My understanding is that some events have transpired over the past several days that may have caused Ms. Lee and Fai emotional distress and even physical pain," he said, slowly putting his hands on the table and looking at Chen, Fai, and Ava in turn. "I want you to know that the Syndicate had nothing to do with the commission of those events, and had no knowledge of them."

"I'm slightly confused," Ava said. "If you had no knowledge of them, why are we here and why are you discussing them?"

"That's a bit complicated to explain, but it starts with understanding that any involvement the Syndicate might have had in what happened would not have had any legitimacy without the specific approval of Mr. Fong or me. We approved none of it. And given the illegality of what we've been told has happened, neither of us would ever have approved it."

"What do you think happened?" Ava asked.

"I've been told that there has been an attempt to blackmail Fai, and that attempts were made to physically intimidate her and you."

"When were you told this?"

"Late last night. That's why I was prepared to call Chen this morning, before he called me."

"And who told you?" Ava asked.

"I don't think that matters as much as the fact that I was told."

"We did agree to confidentiality, but to my mind that implied you would be more forthcoming with us. If you can't be, then I'm already starting to doubt what I'm hearing."

Mo glanced at Fong, who blinked and then nodded.

"We were informed by Ms. Hua," Mo said.

"How did Ms. Hua know these things?" Ava said, looking across the table at the young woman, whose head was turned away from them and who couldn't have looked more uncomfortable.

"Ms. Hua is loyal and devoted and a valuable member of our Syndicate team," Mo said. "Unfortunately, this is a circumstance where her devotion seems to have crossed the lines that separate official action from unofficial, and personal from business."

"Are you trying to tell me that Ms. Hua instigated the blackmail and the attacks?" Ava said. "If you are, it's hardly believable."

"She did not initiate anything directly. What she did was express to a third party some concerns that I had voiced to her within the confines of my office. At the time, I admit, I spoke with some frustration and maybe even a little anger. But my comments were general in nature, made almost in passing, and should have been treated as nothing more than a complaint stated in confidence to a trusted assistant."

"What was the nature of your complaint?"

"I was frustrated and not pleased by the pressure you brought to bear on the subject of *Mao's Daughter*," he said. "I agree that it's a good film, but it isn't suitable for viewing in this political climate. I believe the film has artistic value, but authorizing its release would have brought unwanted attention to the Syndicate, and to me, from people with more power than I have. Second, I did not like the way you approached me, or indeed that you approached me at all. You don't know this business, and any concerns Fai had about the film should have been channelled through Chen. Instead, you and that man Lop came here to my office under false pretenses and then tried to use what you thought was leverage against the Syndicate. Is that honest enough for you?"

"As far as it goes," Ava said, knowing he wouldn't go any further.

"Later that day, Ms. Hua had a conversation with a third party during which she repeated — and probably enhanced — Mr. Mo's remarks," Fong said. "In fact, from what I've been able to piece together, I think it is highly likely she implied that Pang Fai and you, Ms. Lee, were irritants who represented an obstacle to the Syndicate, and that anything that could be done to remove that irritation would be appreciated."

"She was obviously indiscreet, violated the confidentiality of my office and her position in it, and displayed terrible judgment," Mo said. "But I don't believe there was any malice in what she did. She's exceedingly devoted to me and the organization, and I think she made those comments out of concern. Were her concerns misplaced? No, I don't think they were. But she should have kept them to herself."

"Ms. Hua," Ava said, staring at her, trying to capture even a sliver of her attention, "they're talking about you as if you're not in the room. Is there anything you want to say?"

The woman glanced at Mo and then lowered her head. "I made a mistake. I'm sorry," she said. "But I didn't think he would go that far. I never asked him or expected him to be so cruel."

"Who is 'he'?"

"Xia Jun," Fong said.

"Of course it would be Xia Jun," said Ava.

"What do you mean by that?" Mo asked.

"It's too obvious for it to be anyone else."

"I think the point we need to re-stress here is that the Syndicate had zero involvement in initiating or approving what Xia Jun chose to do," Fong said. "A trusted assistant was a little too talkative, that's all. There's nothing more to be made of it."

"What's going to happen to the assistant?"

"She's been reprimanded," Fong said.

"But keeps her job?"

"She's been reprimanded. Beyond that I'm not going to discuss internal human resource issues."

"What's going to happen to Xia?"

"I'm not quite sure I understand the nature of that question," Mo said.

"What are you going to do about Xia?"

"Why would we do anything?" Mo said. "As far as we're concerned, this is a private matter between the three of you and Xia. If he's broken the law — and it seems obvious to all of us that he has — then you should either go to the Security

Bureau and report him or hire a lawyer and take action against him in a civil court."

"We have no first-hand knowledge of what he's done or hasn't done," Fong interjected. "He's an important man in our industry and, as much as we might like to, we can't just unilaterally take action against him. We have to be neutral. We can't take sides."

"Besides, he has a large number of clients — directors and actors — who are colleagues and friends of Fai. Hurting Xia would only end up punishing them as well. I'm sure Fai wouldn't want that to happen," Mo said.

"This is all so neat and tidy," Ava said, and smiled at Mo. "Very well done."

"The truth is usually simple. It's lies that get complicated," Mo said.

"So you're telling us that you just mumbled something or other to Ms. Hua, and she decorated it a little and said something or other to Xia, and he did absolutely everything else by himself?"

"There is bad blood between Xia and Chen. Perhaps he saw it as an opportunity to strike at an enemy while mistakenly thinking it would ingratiate him with us."

"It is a rationale, although it seems a bit far-fetched, given the lengths he went to," Ava said, and then turned back to the woman. "Ms. Hua, when did Xia Jun last contact you?"

"Last night, around the middle of the evening."

"What did he say that alarmed you enough to call Mr. Mo?"

"You have to understand that, after my initial conversation with him about Mr. Mo's concerns, I didn't talk to him again until last night. I had no idea what he had done or was thinking of doing."

"What did he say?" Ava pressed.

Hua took a deep breath and looked at Fong.

"Go ahead," he said.

"Well, he told me that our project had run into some problems. He said that you and Pang Fai had gone to his office and that you were closing in on who was blackmailing her. He said that if he had been able to put you out of circulation, Ms. Pang would crumble, but that the men he'd used had turned out to be useless. He told me to expect you to contact Mr. Mo. When he said that, I panicked. I told him I didn't know what he was talking about. He then claimed that I'd asked him, on Mr. Mo's behalf, to discredit Ms. Pang any way he could. I told him I hadn't. At that point he said he'd speak to Mr. Mo directly."

"Which prompted you to call Mr. Mo yourself?"

"Yes."

"Did Xia call you?" Ava asked Mo.

"No."

"And if he does, what will you tell him?"

"I'll tell him I've been told that he's been doing things I find personally disturbing, and that I strongly recommend he stop," Mo said. "But I will also stress that I can't involve myself or the Syndicate in a private vendetta."

"Do you understand our position?" Fong said.

"It's clear enough."

"So, is there anything else we need to discuss?"

"There are a couple of things. First, if we decide to pursue legal action against Xia, I would like you to guarantee the co-operation of Ms. Hua. I would never ask her to lie on our behalf, but I would expect her to reiterate everything she's told us today."

"That's up to Ms. Hua," Fong said.

"No, it isn't," Ava said. "It's up to you and Mr. Mo. If you give her the order, I have no doubt she'll obey. Anyway, that's how I read it. If she doesn't co-operate, I'll blame it on you and act accordingly."

"I guarantee her co-operation," Mo said quickly.

"Thank you."

"Is there anything else?" Fong said.

"Yes, I'd like everyone but Mr. Mo to leave the room. He and I need to have a personal discussion."

53

WHILE EVERYONE FILED OUT OF THE BOARDROOM, AVA went to the side table and poured herself a cup of coffee. When the door closed, she returned to the table and took the seat next to Mo. He didn't recoil, but he did ease his chair back a few feet.

"That was a terrific performance," she said.

His face impassive, he stared at her through hooded eyes. "I've found out some things about you since our last meeting," he said. "A wealthy young woman, smart, tough, difficult if not impossible to scare, and very well connected — in fact, even better connected than your man Lop."

"Is there a point to this?"

"I don't want to fight with you and those powerful friends of yours. I don't want to end up like the Tsai family in Nanjing, although you might find me harder to put down. But I don't see any reason to take the chance. I want to put our misunderstanding behind us."

"When did you reach that conclusion? After you knew I'd met with Xia or after the man with the meat cleaver failed?"

"Those are silly questions. You've been given an

explanation for what happened. There won't be any other."

"Tell me, do Fong or Hua know about Xia's video of Fai?"

"What video?"

"Mr. Mo, if this is going to end well, if we're going to put our misunderstanding behind us, there has to be a measure of honesty. I understand that I won't get a confession, but there are some things I need to know."

His stare intensified, and Ava felt the strength in the man. "They don't know," he said.

"Have you seen it?"

"Yes."

"And if it was made public?"

"We'd never again be able to finance or distribute any film she was in. It would completely ruin her."

"So, let's agree that it won't be made public."

"That's not under my control."

"If it isn't, you have to take the necessary steps to ensure that it is."

"What about those photos of my son?"

Ava heard the anger in his voice. "What about them?"

"Do Fai and Chen know they exist?"

"No," Ava lied. "The only people who know are Lop and three friends who don't live anywhere near Beijing and have no connection to this industry or Fai or Chen or anyone but me. And my understanding with them hasn't changed. They won't release the photos unless something unfortunate happens to me or Lop. That's something that should have been considered before Xia sent those men after me. If they'd succeeded, the photos would be on every website in China that my friends could access, and sent the old-fashioned way to a large number of people in power."

"I knew nothing about the attacks, and if I had I would have stopped them. It was stupid."

"Yes, it was. It forced me to reconsider the agreement we made at the Kempinski."

"Why? I'll still do everything I can to get *Mao's Daughter* released. I'll support Fai."

"That's fine, but I also need you to add Chen and Fai to my 'no harm, no foul' list."

"You don't need a list. But if it makes you more comfortable, I can promise you I'll do nothing to hurt either of them in any way."

"Including not releasing that video."

"I told you, I don't control it."

"Just to be clear — since you like clarity so much — if Fai's video is made public, I won't care how, when, or where it happened or who was directly responsible for doing so. I'm holding you accountable, completely and personally accountable. And your son will pay the price for your inability to stop it happening."

"How can I possibly know how many copies there are and who has them?"

"I am reasonably confident that the only copies in existence — at least, as of a few days ago — are the one that was sent to Fai and the one in Xia's possession. Fai will destroy her copy. You have to persuade Xia to do the same."

"If there are more copies?"

"Then they originated with Xia. Get him to retrieve them," Ava said. "Mr. Mo, you need to motivate Xia to make every effort to do what's right. I'm sure you have all the leverage you need to make it happen."

"I'll talk to him."

"I'm sure you will."

"But if there's a problem —"

"Then it's your problem, not mine. I don't want to hear about it."

"Even if it involves Fai's video?"

"Especially if it does." She leaned towards him. "Mr. Mo, you may be listening to me, but you're not hearing very well. *That video is no longer my problem.* I have no way of knowing or controlling who has it and what they choose to do with it. You *do* have that ability, and I expect you to exercise it. When I leave this room, I'm not going to think about it again, and I'm going to tell Fai that she has no worries where it is concerned. If it pops up in a week, a month, or even a year from now, then I'll figure that you didn't care enough to stop it."

"I understand."

"Good."

"And you'll understand that I'll find a way to reciprocate in kind if the photos you have make an unwelcome appearance."

"Absolutely. I wouldn't expect anything less."

"Then we seem to have reached an agreement. I won't say that it makes either of us particularly happy, but on the surface it seems workable."

"One last thing. I'd like you to tell your friend Xia that if he or any of those incompetent thugs he hired come anywhere near me or Fai again, I'll take his fucking head off."

"You wouldn't have to. I'd do it myself."

54

THE MIDDLE-AGED WOMAN ESCORTED THEM TO THE
elevator and rode with them down to the lobby. The Bentley
was waiting for them at the curb in a no-parking zone. It
seemed that even in the capital of a Communist country a
Bentley had special privileges.

"What did you and Mo talk about?" Chen asked as soon
as they had settled into the car.

"I congratulated him on a fine performance."

"Performance?"

"What went on in that boardroom was mostly bullshit.
He knew about Xia and Fai's video, and I've no doubt that
he signalled what he wanted Xia to do just as you described.
He might have gone through the assistant, but she wouldn't
have done it without his permission."

"Then why did she take the blame, and why did she look
so miserable?"

"She failed. She let down the mighty Mo."

"He admitted all that?"

"Not precisely, but close enough that I don't doubt it's true."

"Has he seen the video?" Fai asked.

"Yes, and he claims that Fong and Hua haven't. I don't believe him. But then I told him you and Chen don't know about his kid's photos. So we traded a few lies."

"How did you leave it?" Fai asked.

"We're at a stand-off. If anyone releases the video, we release the photos. If anyone releases the photos, he'll release the video. It isn't actually a bad deal. Self-interest has a way of prevailing."

"What about Xia?" Chen said.

"He'll be told to cease and desist. We'll have to assume that he only did what he thought would please Mo. I can't imagine he'll be punished for it."

"So, back to the status quo?"

"Probably."

"That's crap."

"You're right. But Chen, it's crap you're going to have to live with, because we have a deal. Don't do anything to disrupt it."

He shook his head. "So now what? What do we do?"

"You should make sure that *Mao's Daughter* is released and properly promoted."

"What about you and Fai?"

"I'm going to Shanghai to see a friend, and I've asked Fai to come with me."

"I am going with her," Fai said.

"You're both deserting me."

"There's something called a cellphone, with which you can call and text. Use it if you need us," Ava said.

"That's not funny. When will you leave?"

"We should be able to get out of here today."

"I was just starting to appreciate you."

"With any luck, you'll have many more opportunities," Ava said.

He started to respond, but Ava's phone rang and she saw Sonny's number. "Sonny," she answered.

"Where are you?"

"I'm still in Beijing," she said, surprised by his abruptness and the sense of urgency in his voice.

"Have you heard from Xu?"

Ava couldn't remember if she'd told Sonny that Xu was seriously ill. She decided that if she hadn't, there was no reason to do it now. "No, but I'm planning on flying to Shanghai later today. I'll see him tonight," she said. "Sonny, what in hell is going on?"

"Lop's just been shot."

"What!"

"I'm told he isn't dead, but it isn't good. They're rushing him to Dr. Lui's private clinic in Kowloon, the one where Xu was."

"Good god, what's next?"

"I'm told that what's next has already been decided," Sonny said. "There's going to be a war in Wanchai, and I'd guess it's going to spill over into other parts of the city and the Territories."

"Sammy Wing?"

"Sammy and his nephew want Wanchai back, and if that means taking on Xu, they'll do it. The other local gangs are sitting on the sidelines for now, but they're going to have to take sides sooner or later. The only good thing about that is they'll wait as long as possible. They'll want to be as certain as they can be about who's going to win."

"That fucking Sammy Wing, he can't leave well enough alone. He can't leave Xu or me alone," Ava said.

"Will you call Xu?" Sonny said.

"Does Suen know about this?" she said, not too subtly sidestepping his question.

"He might not."

"You should tell him."

Sonny hesitated, and Ava knew he was confused by her request. She also knew he wouldn't ask why she had made it.

"Okay, boss, I'll call him right now."

"When you talk to him, tell him I'll be in Shanghai tonight. I'm staying at Xu's house. And you call me as soon as you know more about Lop," Ava said, ending the call and slumping back into her seat.

"Is there a problem?" Fai asked.

Ava nodded.

"In Shanghai?"

"Hong Kong."

"Will you have to go there?"

"I hope not," Ava said. "But there's a man in Hong Kong who tried to kill me twice and tried to kill Xu, and now he's shot our friend Lop. He may not be giving me a choice."

COMING SOON
From House of Anansi Press
in July 2019

Read on for a preview of the next thrilling
Ava Lee novel, *The Mountain Master of Sha Tin*.

AVA LEE LOOKED OUT OF THE WINDOW OF THE FIRST-
class cabin as the China Eastern Airways jet began its descent into Shanghai. It was a city she normally loved to visit, but on this occasion she was filled with apprehension.

"Are you okay?"

Ava turned towards Pang Fai, her friend and lover. "I'm worried sick about Xu. If he has bacterial meningitis, we have to hope they caught it in time."

Fai squeezed Ava's hand. "At least he's in a hospital. I'm sure he's receiving the best care. You'll see him soon and then you can relax."

Xu was Ava's closest male friend. He was also, significantly, the head of the Triads in Shanghai, chairman of the Triad Society in Asia, and a silent partner in the investment business that Ava co-owned with May Ling Wong and Amanda Yee. "I keep telling myself the same thing, but as soon as I manage to convince myself that he's going to recover, I find myself thinking about Lop and the mess that might create," Ava said. Lop was one of Xu's key lieutenants, and he had been shot in Hong Kong the day before.

"You told me Hong Kong isn't your problem," said Fai.

"I said I don't *want* it to be my problem. If Xu is incapacitated, it could create a situation that I may not be able to avoid."

"Why?"

"It's complicated," Ava said. Then, realizing that she might have sounded condescending, she quickly added, "By that I mean I played a role in Xu's takeover of the Wanchai Triads. I am at least partially responsible for deposing — in fact, if not officially — Sammy Wing as Mountain Master, and for the appointment of Lop as the de facto boss. So, whether I like it or not, I have ties to Wanchai that some people will not forget."

"What will happen if Xu's health improves?"

"He could still find it difficult dealing with a problem that's twelve hundred kilometres from his hospital bed in Shanghai. And I can guarantee that the last thing he'll want anyone to know is that he's unwell. His rivals — and for Triad gang leaders, everyone is a potential rival — would be quick to pounce."

"What if he's not in the hospital and is well enough to travel?"

"That's very optimistic. But if he can travel, he's the best person to restore equilibrium in Hong Kong. Although there would still be the question of what to do about Sammy Wing, and the fact that Lop has been shot can't be easily ignored. If Lop dies, it's going to be almost impossible for Xu to turn the other cheek without appearing weak," Ava said.

"Who is this Sammy Wing?"

"He's a lifelong Triad, now in his seventies or maybe even eighties. He ran the Wanchai gang for years. I first encountered him about five or six years ago, when he took out a contract on me for a conman I'd pissed off—"

"A contract?"

"Yes, Sammy was hired to kill me. Not personally, of course. He sent a couple of his men to do the dirty work. Later, thanks to Uncle's intervention, he cancelled the contract, but not until his men had tried to do me in," Ava said. "Then, about a year ago, trouble flared again when Wing took exception to Xu's growing influence. He decided to kill Xu, and I got caught in the crossfire. Obviously he wasn't successful. In the aftermath, Xu took control of Wanchai and put Lop in charge. There are people who think Xu made a mistake when he kept Wing on as a figurehead; they think he should have killed him. If Lop's shooting is connected to Sammy, it will look like they were right and Xu was wrong."

"Do you think there's a connection?"

"There are rumours that Sammy's nephew, Carter Wing, who has just taken over the Sha Tin gang in the New Territories, wants to help his uncle reclaim his turf," Ava said. "If that's true, a lot of blood could be spilled."

Ava saw Fai flinch, decided she'd said enough — maybe even too much — and turned towards the window again. Their two-hour flight had originated in Beijing and would be landing at Hongqiao Airport rather than Pudong International, where Ava felt more comfortable. "We'll be on the ground in about ten minutes. I think I've arrived at Hongqiao only once before."

"Pudong is on the eastern edge of Shanghai. Hongqiao is in the western part and is only ten kilometres from the centre of the city," Fai said, sounding relieved by the change of subject.

"Suen will be waiting for us with the car. The plan is to go directly to the hospital to see Xu," Ava said. "You've met Suen before, right?"

"I don't know if 'met' is the right word. I've seen him, but he was always lurking in the background; he's so large that he's impossible to miss. I thought he was just a bodyguard until Tsai told me he has another role...although I don't remember exactly what that is."

"He is Xu's Red Pole, which means he's the gang's enforcer and runs all the muscle on the ground. When things are going well, the job is more preventive than proactive."

"And in this case?"

"I won't know until I talk to Xu."

Fai looked awkwardly at Ava. "It is going to be uncomfortable for me to meet some of these people. They've only seen me with Tsai, when I was basically his whore. It might be difficult for someone like Suen to understand why I did that, and how I finally came to terms with my sexuality at this point in my life."

Ava shook her head. Pang Fai, although perhaps China's greatest film actress, wasn't well paid by Western standards, and she was not financially self-sufficient. In the past she had augmented her income by dating and sometimes sleeping with wealthy men. Tsai Men, the son of the governor of Jiangsu province, had been one of those men. Ava had first met Fai at a dinner with Tsai and Xu. "Fai, pay no attention to what others think or say. I can't imagine that anyone associated with me or Xu would ever be disrespectful. All that matters is that you're happy and at peace with yourself."

"Which I am, but I still need reminding now and then that it's okay for me to feel that way." Ava and Fai had been a couple for a year, but because of Ava's business demands and Fai's film commitments, they had spent only about two months of that time together. The reason they were flying from Beijing to Shanghai was that they had spent the previous week in the Chinese capital sorting out a problem Fai was having with the China Film Syndicate. Their intention had been that when those issues were resolved — which they now were — Ava would travel with Fai to Yantai to meet her parents. Xu's illness had changed those plans, and now the troubles in Hong Kong were threatening to change them again.

The plane's descent quickened and the pilot announced that they were making their final approach to Hongqiao. Ava closed her eyes and said a short prayer to Saint Jude, the patron saint of lost causes. She had given up most of her Roman Catholic faith in reaction to the Church's position on homosexuality, but she still turned to Saint Jude whenever she felt as if events in her life were spinning out of control. She didn't know what she would find when she landed in Shanghai, so her prayer simply asked for things to be as normal as possible.

Hongqiao, like most of the newer airports in Asia, had been built for efficiency. Within fifteen minutes of landing, Ava and Fai were walking through the doors of the arrivals hall into a horde of people waiting for travellers.

"Ava!" a man's voice called out.

Ava looked to the right and saw Suen. Even in a throng he was impossible to miss. At six feet four and with his 240 pounds of muscle accentuated by a tight-fitting polo shirt, he was an imposing figure. She and Fai walked towards him.

He reached for Ava's bags. "I'm very happy to see you," he said.

"Do you remember Fai?" Ava asked.

"Sure," he said, nodding at her. "Good to see you too."

"How's Xu?" Ava asked. "Have they finally settled on a diagnosis?"

"They are now quite definite that it's bacterial meningitis," Suen said.

"I was hoping it would be something else."

"Don't panic. They've shot him full of antibiotics, and the doctor told me he's sure they caught the disease in time."

"Is Xu alert? Is he responsive?"

"Sometimes he's lucid and sometimes his mind wanders and he starts talking nonsense. And he's still physically weak."

"Have you told Auntie Grace about the diagnosis?" Ava said, referring to Xu's lifelong housekeeper.

"I thought I'd leave that to you. She'll trust whatever you tell her, whereas with me she always has a hundred questions that I can't answer," Suen said. "I assume you'll be staying with her?"

"We will."

"And I assume you'll want to see Xu first?"

"Of course."

Suen looked at the gold Rolex on his wrist. "Then we'd better get going. It's already quarter to eight and visiting hours end at nine. He's in the Shanghai East International Medical Centre in Pudong, which is a thirty-minute drive from here. Wen is waiting for us with the car."

Ava and Fai followed in Suen's wake as he barrelled

through the crowd. He stopped to let them pass when he reached the arrival hall's exit doors. When Ava stepped onto the sidewalk, she saw Wen directly in front of her, standing next to Xu's silver S-Class Mercedes-Benz.

Wen bowed his head when he saw her. "*Xaio lao ban*," he said.

Ava smiled. Wen had been the first person to call her *xaio lao ban* — "little boss" — to her face, although he had been quick to add that most of Xu's men, even Xu himself, often referred to her that way when she wasn't around.

"Good to see you, Wen, although I wish the circumstances were different," she said.

"The boss will be okay," he said with determination.

Wen was a small, wiry man, but his size was no indication of his grit. Ava had seen his bravery first-hand the year before, when a special unit attached to the People's Armed Police had come to Xu's house — where she was alone with Auntie Grace — to arrest her. Wen had organized the resistance and had been prepared to exchange fire with the police. Thankfully it hadn't come to that, but Ava didn't doubt for a second that Wen had been ready to do whatever it took to protect her.

"Yes, I'm sure he will be okay," Ava said.

As Wen loaded their bags into the trunk of the car, Ava and Fai slid onto the back seat and Suen sat in the front. "You haven't mentioned Lop," she said. "How is he?"

Suen turned to face her. "He's still alive."

"And what's happening in Hong Kong?"

"The last time I heard, it was quiet. Nothing out of the ordinary."

"Except for Lop getting shot."

"I'm hoping that was an aberration, a mistake of some sort."

"Do you really believe that?" she asked.

"No. I said I hope that's the case, not that I believe it is."

"Does Xu know about Lop?"

"Not yet. Telling him now doesn't seem to be the right thing, given his state of mind."

Ava shook her head. "He needs to know. Not telling him is usurping his authority. I know your intentions are good, but they could be misconstrued."

"If we do tell him, it might be better coming from you," Suen said. "You're the one he told about his concerns there, and it's your man Sonny who's been poking around."

"Speaking of Sonny, have you heard from him?"

"He called me a couple of hours ago. He wanted you to call him when you landed," Suen said. "I'm sorry, I should have told you earlier."

"No need to apologize. I know you've got a lot on your plate," Ava said, reaching for her phone.

Sonny Kwok was as large as Suen, and probably more vicious. He had been a member of Uncle's Triad gang in Fanling before becoming his fanatically loyal bodyguard and driver. When Uncle became ill and knew he was going to die, he'd asked Ava to employ Sonny, saying, "A Sonny with nothing to do and no ties will eventually get into trouble, and it is the kind of trouble that you cannot begin to imagine." So Ava had hired him. The fact that she lived in Toronto and Sonny wouldn't fit in anywhere but Hong Kong was a challenge, but they agreed that whenever she was in Asia, she had first call on his services. The rest of the time, Sonny drove for Ava's father, Marcus, her brother Michael, and Amanda

Yee, who in addition to being Ava's business partner was married to Michael. They all lived in Hong Kong and the arrangement had worked well so far. Ava knew that Sonny was as loyal to her as he had ever been to Uncle.

"*Wei*," he answered.

"It's Ava."

"How is Xu?" he asked.

"I'll know soon; I'm on my way to the hospital. Suen tells me he has bacterial meningitis but it's treatable. I'll call you after I see him," Ava said. "How are things on your end? How is Lop? Any noise from Sammy Wing?"

"Lop is at Dr. Lui's clinic in Kowloon. Lui thinks he should be moved to a regular hospital, but I talked it over with Ko, Lop's right-hand man, and we decided to leave him where he is. If he goes to a hospital the cops will get involved, and there will be a lot of questions that no one wants to answer."

"But if Lop's life is at risk…"

"Lui is a really good doctor and he has all the equipment you'd find at most hospitals," Sonny said. "He's just nervous about having someone like Lop at the clinic."

"Then why did he agree to take him in?"

"He didn't, really. We showed up on his doorstep with Lop in tow. He couldn't turn us away."

"Lui is your girlfriend's brother, right?"

"Ex-girlfriend's brother. That might also be why he's reluctant to help."

"So you think Lop is going to live?"

Sonny paused. "I don't know. He caught three bullets, one in his gut and two in the upper chest. Lui got them out but Lop lost a lot of blood, and Lui isn't sure how much damage was done internally."

"Lop is incredibly fit."

"Bullets do their damage whether you're fit or not."

"How about Ko? Is he strong enough to take over, even temporarily?"

"He's a good number two, but that's what he is — a number two. I can't see him running a gang on his own. Besides, he's a Shanghai man, and that's not the best of references around here right now."

"Shit."

"The good news is that nothing else has happened since Lop was shot," said Sonny. "If Sammy and Carter were going to make a play for Wanchai, they would have followed up more aggressively."

"Maybe they're waiting to see how Xu reacts. The last time Sammy tried to take him on, Sammy and his gang were taken apart in less than twenty-four hours."

"But that was with Lop in charge of the troops on the ground."

"Even so, the Wings have reason to be cautious."

"The other reason might be that the shooting doesn't have anything to do with Wanchai. Maybe someone just has a hate on for Lop."

"Do you believe that?" Ava asked.

"Not really. I trust Andy's information. If he heard that Sammy and Carter's Sha Tin gang are going to make a play for Wanchai, then I believe it," Sonny said. Andy was an old Triad colleague of Sonny and Ava's who was loosely connected to the Sha Tin gang.

"What do you know about Carter?"

"He's young, tough, ambitious, and aggressive. He's only been heading that gang for a couple of months, but already he's making a lot of his neighbours nervous," Sonny said. "One more thing you should know: Carter's father died when he was young and Sammy has always looked out for him, so they're close. Now that Carter's got some power, he might be trying to use it to repay his uncle."

"But you haven't heard anything definite?"

"No, just rumours."

"Well, until something else happens, we'll have to assume that's what we're dealing with," Ava said. She saw that Suen was listening to her end of the conversation. She didn't blame him. With Xu in hospital and Lop in the Kowloon clinic, it might fall to him and the rest of the Shanghai executive to decide on a course of action if the rumours materialized into something more sinister. "Sonny, I have to go. I'll call you after I see Xu. In the meantime, stay on top of things there. Let's try to avoid any more surprises."

"How is Lop?" Suen asked as soon as Ava ended the call.

"He's not dead, but he's in no condition to run anything, let alone a war."

"This couldn't happen at a worse time."

"How close are we to the hospital?" Ava asked, in no mood to respond to something so obvious.

"Ten minutes," Wen said.

"Then let's have some quiet time. I need to gather myself. Being in two hospitals in as many days is a lot for my system to deal with."

ACKNOWLEDGEMENTS

The Goddess of Yantai is the twelfth book in the Ava Lee series, and I have to confess they don't get any easier to write. One reason is the growing expectations from my readers. I am loath to disappoint them and when I send the first draft to my first readers, the next weeks are hell as I await their (always) honest verdicts. Fortunately, *Goddess* did not disappoint, so big thanks to Kristine Wookey, Robin Spano, Farah Mohammed, Catherine Roseburgh, and my wife, Lorraine, for giving me their time and support.

I can't think of the word "support" and not think of my agents Bruce Westwood and Carolyn Forde. I know there are times when I try their patience, but they do persevere and help me get through the ups and downs that plague many writers. I trust their judgment — which is no small thing — and that hasn't steered me wrong.

I have enjoyed and appreciated Chinese films — whether mainland or Hong Kong-based — for many years, and that formed part of the core of this book, and will form as large a part in several books to come. But my appreciation was rather insular until I met Karen Walton — the brilliant Waltz.

She expanded what I knew, and I can only hope that she's onside with where I want to take Pang Fai, Ava, and Lau Lau in future books.

This is my first book with my new editor Doug Richmond after eleven books with Janie Yoon. A big thank you to Doug for his efforts, and for leaving me feeling that I'm still in good hands.

IAN HAMILTON is the author of twelve novels in the Ava Lee series. His books have been shortlisted for numerous prizes, including the Arthur Ellis Award, the Barry Award, and the Lambda Literary Prize, and are national bestsellers. BBC Culture named Hamilton one of the ten mystery/crime writers from the last thirty years that should be on your bookshelf. The Ava Lee series is being adapted for television.

NOW AVAILABLE
From House of Anansi Press
The Ava Lee series.

Prequel and Book 1

Book 2

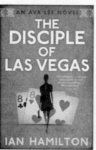

Book 3

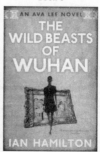

Book 4

Book 5

Book 6

Book 7

Book 8

Book 9

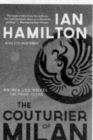

Book 10

www.houseofanansi.com • www.facebook.com/avaleenovels
www.ianhamiltonbooks.com • www.twitter.com/avaleebooks